Praise for *The Dog of the North*

'Stretton skillfully chronicles court intrigue in rival city-states in this unique fantasy tale...adeptly uses courtly, carefully structured discourse and Italianate names and places to evoke an almost Shakespearean atmosphere...full of intelligent dialogue, enthralling characters, and dramatic world-building that will hold readers' attention to the last page'

Publishers' Weekly

'Combining a hint of Renaissance Italy with a Shakespearean gravity leavened with touches of humor, the author of Dragonchaser and The Zael Inheritance has created a vividly detailed world that should appeal to fans of David Drake, Midori Snyder, and George R.R. Martin'

Library Journal

'I couldn't get the female characters out of my head... rounded, convincing, engaging'

Helen McCarthy, Deathray

THE
LAST FREE CITY

Also by Tim Stretton

The Zael Inheritance
Dragonchaser
The Dog of the North

THE LAST FREE CITY

Tim Stretton

::*Acquired* Taste Books
timstretton.blogspot.com

First edition 2011

Copyright © Tim Stretton 2011

The author asserts the moral right to be identified as the author of this work

Set in Palatino Linotype

ISBN 978-1-257-03682-0

This novel is entirely a work of fiction. The names, characters and incidents portrayed in it are the work of the author's imagination. Any resemblance to actual persons, living or dead, events or localities is entirely coincidental.

All rights reserved. No part of this publication may be reproduced, stored in a retrieval system, or transmitted, in any form, or by any means, electronic or otherwise, without the prior permission of the author.

for Sue and Danielle

I am grateful for the support of my readers in producing this novel. Particular thanks are owed to those who read and commented on earlier drafts: Patrick Dusoulier, Aliya Whiteley and Steve Sherman.

All writers are indebted to greater or lesser extent to the artists they admire. *The Last Free City* draws especially on the works of William Shakespeare, whose sonnets are grossly abused to provide Todarko's verse to Linnalitha, and Jack Vance, who gave permission for the use of 'Evulsifer' in Chapter 57.

LIST OF PRINCIPAL CHARACTERS

Aladar	Head of House Tantestro, leader of the pro-Emmen p
Bartielko	Head of House Oreste, leader of the pro-Gammerling
Bodazar	Intimate of Todarko
Crostadan	Head of House Umbinzia, father of Dravadan and M
Dravadan	Ally of Aladar, latterly Head of House Umbinzia
Glastarko	Younger brother of Raguslan
Iselin	Emmen ambassador
Kropiselko	Head of House Zamilio
Linnalitha	Wife of Dravadan
Malvazan	Younger son of Crostadan
Monichoë	Daughter of Kropiselko
Nelanka	Wife of Zanijel
Oricien	Emmen Lord Ambassador to Taratanallos
Palankijo	Steward to Dravadan
Raguslan	Head of House Vaggio
Ribauldequin	Emmen ambassador
Rodizel	Rival of Malvazan; latterly fencing-master
Sanoutë	Childhood sweetheart of Malvazan
Sulinka	Mother of Raguslan and Glastarko
Todarko	Poet
Zanijel	Son and heir of Raguslan

BOOK ONE

FLOOD TIDE

CHAPTER ONE

Hendos Wood, Taratanallos

Ahead of them, between the close-flushed leaves of the manzipar trees, Todarko could see lights flickering. The path led to the illuminated glade known as Fangardo's Clearing and Rodizel stepped out briskly.

"Hurry along, gentlemen. We do not want to be late."

"Is this worth taking us from the tavern for?" Todarko asked. "The Hour of Noble Pleasures is nearly over."

Rodizel gave a tight smile. "And the Hour of Secret Deeds nearly here."

"Hmmph," said Bodazar, panting slightly. "We have paid for a fencing lesson, Rodizel, not a walk in the woods."

"And a fencing lesson you shall have, believe me," said Rodizel, pulling aside the branches as they reached the trees.

In the gap Rodizel had created between the branches, Todarko could see a circle of lanterns around the edge of the clearing, a dozen or so men ranging the perimeter and a couple more groups nearer the centre.

The three of them ducked under the branches and stood somewhat apart from the group: Rodizel, short and wiry with greying hair and graceful hands; Todarko, dark hair disarranged to give an air of languid negligence; Bodazar, thin-lipped and sturdy.

"Zanijel is here," said Todarko tonelessly, indicating one of the men on the far side of the circle.

Rodizel nodded. "I confess I am surprised you did not know about this evening's event, given your connections," he said.

Todarko grimaced. "I take no interest in my cousin's affairs, nor my uncle's. Their political ambitions bore me."

Bodazar grinned. "Wenches and wine are sufficient to maintain Todarko's attention. A reasonable enough programme, if you ask me."

Rodizel raised an arm to attract the attention of a nearby man wearing a grey cloak and a saturnine expression. "Kupitar! Twenty florins on Dravadan," he said.

Kupitar's dour face flickered with a hint of a smile. "You know better than that, Rodizel. No-one in Taratanallos will match that bet."

"You will not give me a price?"

"Not on Dravadan: a bookmaker does not thrive by giving money away. Come, I'll give you a good price on Godaijkin."

"Godaijkin is a dead man."

"Such is the consensus."

Todarko looked into the circle, where two men in loose white shirts and flared black pantaloons limbered up, flexing their muscles and their rapiers. He knew both Dravadan and Godaijkin by sight, and, if as it seemed, they must fight, he could see why no-one wished to back Godaijkin, obviously pale even in the torchlight.

"If you want to back Dravadan," said Kupitar, "let us try this: put your twenty florins on him to win in a shortglass. That bet I will take."

Rodizel raised an eyebrow. "You think he'll take longer?"

"I'll back your wager to prove it."

Rodizel shrugged. "If you must." He handed Kupitar a purse. "Dravadan will take him in minutes."

"We shall see," said Kupitar with a smile, and walked away.

"This is our fencing lesson?" asked Bodazar. The breeze-blown lanterns cast long shadows, the images of the fencers dancing like grotesque puppets on the ground.

"You'll learn more from watching Dravadan in the two minutes it takes him to kill Godaijkin than in the hour I would have had you sparring."

Todarko stiffened as Zanijel sauntered over to them. "It is too late to be making friends with Dravadan now, cousin," said Zanijel, burly and broad-shouldered with an ease of manner which was indistinguishable from arrogance.

"Nothing was further from my mind."

Zanijel jerked his head back to indicate where Dravadan was limbering up. Next to him was a still figure in a rich scarlet robe. "You will see that Aladar is here with us tonight. These are great days for House Vaggio."

Bodazar said: "What if Godaijkin kills Dravadan tonight? What of your schemes then?"

Zanijel peered at him. "Why, it's the runt of House Belario! You may dream of Dravadan's death: it will not be tonight. If you will excuse me, I must be on hand if Dravadan requires me." He stalked off without further comment.

"I apologise for my cousin," said Todarko. "A charmless fellow: you see why we are not intimate."

Rodizel shrugged. "He has an eye for his own advantage. You cannot deny that Aladar's faction is the strongest on the Masavory: and now

Aladar's right hand is Dravadan; and your uncle is Dravadan's intimate. Such is the way of the world."

Bodazar shook his ruefully. "Are you certain Godaijkin will not kill Dravadan?"

A flicker from the lantern briefly illuminated Rodizel's face. "Utterly certain."

Bodazar replied only with a gloomy nod.

Todarko's attention returned to the circle. Dravadan's steward Palankijo handed him a goblet and proffered a selection of foils, while Aladar stood listening to Zanijel's animated points. Todarko did not recognise Godaijkin's companions, but they radiated no more confidence than their principal.

A figure in the black and white robes of a Viator stepped into the centre of the circle and held up his arms for attention. Rodizel's mouth gave a sardonic twitch. "This should be amusing."

"Noble citizens!" cried the Viator. "I am on hand, as I must be when two men approach Harmony with such purpose. Godaijkin, you have challenged Dravadan to a blood duel under the Quietus Est, and one or the other of you will meet eternity tonight. Is this Harmony? I cannot say. Godaijkin, are you firm in your purpose? Can there be no other settlement?"

Godaijkin sheathed his sword and stepped deliberately into the centre of the circle. He licked lips which had barely more colour than his face. "Dravadan characterised my wife with slights as untrue as they were infamous. Unless he wishes to withdraw his remarks, and apologise for his intemperance, I must chastise him tonight."

Dravadan paused from the wooden-sword drill he was running through with Palankijo. "I believe I described Radocasta as the greatest whore of Taratanallos, a statement I can support with evidence if necessary. In denying it Godaijkin calls me liar; even if he withdrew his own challenge, I would therefore be forced to challenge him. This duel is regrettable, but it must proceed. If there is a lesson, Viator Bismaijo, it is that a man must choose his wife with care if he does not wish to be embarrassed by her antics. Now, I am ready to proceed."

Todarko watched the two men conclude their preparations. Dravadan, tall and slender, his dark hair dusted with grey at the temples, moved with unhurried ease through his drills. Godaijkin, by contrast, skipped with a nervous intensity as he worked up a sweat.

Bodazar leaned across to Rodizel. "Godaijkin must be ten years younger," he said. "Surely that must count for something."

Rodizel raised an eyebrow. "Nothing at all. I am twenty years older than you, and I could kill you with my left hand."

"Well—"

"Your enthusiasm to see Dravadan defeated is understandable," said Rodizel. "If you truly believe it, Kupitar will be happy to take your money. Otherwise, simply watch the lesson I have brought you learn."

"Choose your wife with care?" asked Todarko with a smirk.

"It is good advice, but you do not need Dravadan to teach it you."

They fell silent as Viator Bismaijo clapped his hands. "Gentlemen, proceed."

As the two duellists eyed each other, Kupitar turned over the shortglass which would determine the success of Rodizel's wager.

Dravadan and Godaijkin circled each other, neither seeming willing to make the first move. Occasionally a twig underfoot cracked, booming like thunder in the tense silence. Attracted by the light, gnats buzzed around the combatants' heads, but in the intensity of their concentration neither man noticed.

Godaijkin, one arm akimbo on his hip, took a brisk step forward, probed at Dravadan's defences, withdrew as the older man parried. Dravadan leaned to one side, watched Godaijkin track the move, lunged at the other side. Godaijkin turned the blow, his blade sliding down Dravadan's until it caught the hilt. Dravadan stepped back and they were as before.

Rodizel nodded in appreciation. "Godaijkin is better than I expected."

"How can you tell?" asked Todarko.

"He is not committing himself. He watches and waits. It will not be enough, of course."

Now Dravadan pressed forward, and Godaijkin used his feet nimbly to keep his opponent away. His face had a ruddy flush now, his nerves dissipated in the exertion of the moment. All around the circle were rapt faces, Zanijel's jaw slightly ajar, Aladar's eyes narrowed with the intensity of his regard. Todarko could not suppress a quick smile. *You cannot afford to see your ally killed.*

Godaijkin counter-attacked, rushing forward and seeming for a moment to have driven Dravadan back; but at the last second he stumbled, and Dravadan sprang forward. Godaijkin jerked aside, breathing heavily.

"Good recovery," nodded Rodizel.

"Dravadan is sorely pressed, I think," said Bodazar.

Rodizel looked at him with a scornful expression. "He is not even sweating; he has not yet moved above walking-pace."

Bodazar shrugged, and as he did so Dravadan made a movement so swift Todarko could barely follow it. A soft curse from Godaijkin and a sudden blotch of red on his shirt. There were a couple of gasps, some muted applause, from around the circle.

Godaijkin put a hand to his side and looked in seeming disbelief at the blood on his hand. He charged forward, launched a huge unsubtle thrust. In one movement, Dravadan turned the blow and flicked his own blade into Godaijkin's face. Godaijkin reeled back, barely retaining his balance

"My eye!" he cried.

Todarko winced. In the dark it was hard to be sure, but Dravadan looked to have put his opponent's eye out, whether by accident or design.

Rodizel seemed unperturbed, simply nodding his approval at the stroke. "Now he finishes it."

Dravadan moved in, stepping with a grace incongruous to the situation. Godaijkin tracked the movement with his good eye but he seemed transfixed, unable to respond. Todarko half turned away, not sure he could watch the bloody conclusion to the duel.

Dravadan's arm shot out again—but it was not to spit Godaijkin's heart, as everyone in the circle seemed to expect. There was another cry from Godaijkin, at least one cry of horror from the circle: Dravadan had stabbed at his other eye. Blood ran down both of Godaijkin's cheeks.

"Animaxia help me!" he cried.

Dravadan stood back and watched. Noiselessly he glided round behind Godaijkin, kicked at the back of his knee to send him sprawling forward.

"I am over here, Godaijkin," he said in a level voice. "You seem to be facing in the wrong direction."

Godaijkin scrambled to his feet, turned to the sound of the voice—but Dravadan was already gone. "Too slow!"

Godaijkin stood, the point of his sword on the ground, his other arm at his side. The lower half of his face was a mass of blood. Dravadan sheathed his sword, took out his dagger instead.

"For Hissen's sake, finish it, Dravadan!" called a voice from the crowd. Aladar's face was expressionless, as was the steward Palankijo: Zanijel looked on with a rapt avidity.

Dravadan nodded. "Very well." He stepped crisply forward, slashed his dagger in an upward motion into Godaijkin's groin. Godaijkin gave a squeal of pain and terror. The cut had sliced a rent in the front of his breeches and blood gushed forth. Godaijkin dropped his sword as he fell to his knees, his hands pressed to his crotch.

"Mercy!" he gasped.

"A little late for that, my friend," said Dravadan in a conversational tone. "You will bleed to death in twenty minutes."

Godaijkin reached out a bloody hand to where the voice was coming from. "Kill me, then, Dravadan. I do not fear death."

Dravadan stepped back fastidiously to avoid the red touch. "Do you not?" he said. "Then I have not done my work well enough. Let us see how you feel in five minutes or so."

Godaijkin fell forward onto his front, a pool of blood already leaking from under his body.

Viator Bismaijo stepped into the circle. "Dravadan, this is not Harmony!"

"It is my Harmony, old man. Do not interfere. I am fighting within the Quietus Est."

Godaijkin rolled over onto his back. His white shirt was soaked through with blood. "Dravadan," he said in a barely audible voice.

Dravadan grimaced. He walked forward, kicked Godaijkin's sword away and flicked his dagger out of its scabbard. With his other hand he pulled Godaijkin aloft by his bloody shirt.

"A man should die on his feet." Godaijkin swayed. "Even if he cannot stand on them."

Dravadan swung Godaijkin's dagger in a long slow arc, which ended with the knife buried hilt-deep in Godaijkin's eye. He released his grip and Godaijkin slumped to the ground.

Dravadan turned to Viator Bismaijo. "Now, Your Salience—is that not Harmony? He is slain with his own dagger."

Bismaijo gave him a steady gaze but said nothing. Dravadan took his sword of its scabbard, wiped the blade with a handkerchief before throwing it back to Palankijo. "I believe that concludes tonight's business." He gave a brisk nod to Aladar and stepped noiselessly from the circle. "Wine, Palankijo: I am somewhat thirsty."

Bodazar fixed Rodizel with a glare. "I am unclear what you wish us to learn from that."

Rodizel shook his head. "Neither am I. Neither am I."

"At least you won the bet," said Todarko in a shaky voice.

"Not even that. Dravadan took so long carving his man up that the glass turned. There is only one winner tonight."

Bodazar said: "Not even that. There can be no-one here who thinks Dravadan a greater man tonight."

"I was not referring to Dravadan," said Rodizel. "The only man who never loses is the bookmaker."

He turned slowly on his heel and walked from the clearing, leaving Todarko and Bodazar to follow at their own pace.

CHAPTER TWO

Two months earlier
Emmen

On the upper floor of the Summer Palace at Emmen, far above the baking heat of the plain, was an open terrace overlooking Lake Dravante and surrounded on the other three sides by snow-capped mountains. The terrace was a spot favoured by King Enguerran both for relaxation and for the transaction of occasional private business.

One morning in the early days of spring, the King finished his modest breakfast and summoned the three men who had waited inside while he ate. All three dropped to one knee as they approached the royal presence: Lord Oricien, calm and sober in a black doublet and white shirt; Lord Iselin, clad in a supple umber velvet; and Lord Ribauldequin, dashing in a black jacket slashed to reveal the scarlet lining.

"Gentlemen, stand," said the King, rising from his table and leaning on the stone railing overlooking the lake. "I wish to discuss a most important matter of state. Sit, if you wish."

Iselin rose and bowed. "We are of course at your disposal, Puissance."

King Enguerran looked back over his shoulder and pursed his lips, dark against his pale face. He returned to the table and sat at one end, facing his visitors. "I spent much of yesterday outlining to my Council my intentions with regard to Gammerling and the irksome ambitions of King Ingomer. It is no secret that Lord Graiaume takes a view of events I can only consider contrary."

The lords remained silent, each hanging on the King's words.

"It has been necessary to dissemble my plans from the Council, given my Chancellor's opposition to my programmes."

"You are the King, sir," said Ribauldequin, the youngest of the lords, flicking his fringe from his eyes. "You need only dismiss him."

Iselin drew in his breath. King Enguerran gave a chilly smile.

"Matters are not quite so simple," he said. "For now, it is more practical to conciliate the Duke than destroy him. Indeed, I made a gracious acquiescence to his views, and abandoned for the nonce my plans to take the throne of Gammerling."

"Puissance—"

King Enguerran raised a hand. "Peace, Lord Iselin. I do not need the Council to achieve my goals—particularly when I have such devoted servants as yourselves on hand."

Oricien's calm grey eyes flicked around the group, as if he sought to read the meaning behind the words.

Iselin said: "You need only speak, Puissance."

"You leave—tonight, and in secret—for Taratanallos. Oricien, you are as of this moment my ambassador to the city. Iselin and Ribauldequin will advise and support you."

He reached into his gold-embroidered doublet and brought forth a package. "These are your orders, and a letter of credit. Your task is a simple one: to secure the submission of Taratanallos to my rule, or failing that, to bind the city to us in a treaty of perpetual amity."

"But—" said Oricien. "I am hardly fitted for such a task. I know nothing of affairs in Taratanallos."

"Lord Iselin has wisdom enough for us all," said the King. "He has been working assiduously to bring about my aims. With his guidance all will be well."

"Might Lord Iselin not then make a more suitable ambassador, Your Puissance? I am not hungry for glory."

King Enguerran frowned. "Lord Iselin is the grandson of a candlemaker, as we all know." Iselin flushed behind his neat red beard. "I overlook his low birth in view of his merits and the services he renders this kingdom: I cannot expect the Masavory of Taratanallos to do the same. You, Lord Oricien, are head of the House of Croad: the only men of better pedigree in the kingdom, I would not trust out of my sight."

Oricien gave a curt nod. "Your encomium is less than whole-hearted, Your Puissance. I beg your leave to return to Croad: my sister has been regent too long in my absence."

King Enguerran rose from his seat. "I considered you a loyal subject, Lord Oricien, a man ready to put this service of his king before himself. Was I mistaken?"

"No, my lord."

"I thought not. Should you complete this mission to my satisfaction, you will return to Croad with my blessing, although the honours available to you at court may make you change your mind."

"I am at your command, my lord."

"Good. I have business to carry out in the council chamber. The three of you may wish to remain here and discuss your plans; make any arrangements you need and be gone by nightfall." King Enguerran strode from the room without a backward glance.

Oricien sagged back in his chair, not meeting the gaze of either of his companions. He had known all along that Enguerran had summoned him to court for a purpose; and suspected that the purpose would be one he would not enjoy. The King might not have stripped him of his rank for allowing Croad to fall to the brigand Beauceron, but there was always going to be a price to be paid.

From the corner of his eye he looked at Iselin, still seething from the king's dismissal of his origins. Iselin had never displayed much amity towards Oricien, and having to defer to him in matters of a policy Iselin himself had devised was unlikely to make their relationship any more cordial.

At least Ribauldequin was accompanying them: young, handsome, well-born. From what Oricien had heard, Ribauldequin's name was linked with a scandal involving more than one of Princess Melissena's attendants and some unwise thaumaturgical divinations. No doubt he was travelling to Taratanallos to keep him out of the way, but he was good company and should be an ally against Iselin if one were needed.

Lord Iselin interrupted his reverie. "Well, my Lord Ambassador: do you have any instructions on how we should proceed? As the head of our enterprise, naturally I will defer to your judgement."

Oricien poured himself a goblet of wine. "Iselin, I understand how difficult this situation must be for you. Clearly you have advised the King on his schemes to subdue Taratanallos, and now you must cede precedence." He poured another goblet and passed it to Iselin.

"I very much doubt that you understand my present feelings."

Oricien shrugged. "I have been given an assignment by His Puissance, not once I have sought. Nonetheless I will carry it out as best I can. If events are not to your suiting, then you too must accommodate yourself to circumstances. I would prefer to have your enthusiastic support, but in its absence I will be content with unhesitating obedience."

Iselin narrowed his eyes.

"Be assured, Iselin, that I have been given command of this embassy, and command it I shall. I care nothing for your birth, so long as you comply. If you do not like it, you may petition the King."

Iselin gave a cold smile. "I hear and obey, Lord Ambassador."

Lord Ribauldequin reached for the wine pitcher. "I do so love the comradeship of a travelling party," he said.

Oricien sat up straight in his chair. "For now, Lord Iselin, you may outline the plans you have formed with the King so that we may determine our next steps."

"My folios are elsewhere," said Iselin. "We will have to repair to my chambers."

Some ten minutes later Oricien found himself in a bright airy room towards the top of the palace, a view of the mountains stretching away beyond the window. Lord Iselin's chambers were furnished with quiet good taste, the simplicity of the deep mahogany cabinets and the marble basin at first disguising the excellence of the materials. In spite of himself, Oricien was impressed: his previous experience of Iselin's self-aggrandising performances in Enguerran's Council bespoke a vulgarity of perception which was not in evidence here. Perhaps it was insecurity, rather than vulgarity, he thought. The Chancellor Graiaume was not the only one to mock his origins behind his back—or even to his face on occasion. Iselin was a prickly, difficult man, but he certainly had reason. Oricien set himself to be conciliatory: having lost a city himself, he understood the substratum of mockery which could be hidden beneath seemingly innocuous remarks at court.

"I admire your chambers, Iselin," he said.

Iselin's eyes narrowed. "The approbation of such a noble lord flatters me," he said. "I find the rooms tranquil after the cares of office. Others may prefer a more ostentatious style." His gaze moved smoothly to Ribauldequin.

"As long as the bed is not too hard I am content," said Ribauldequin. "One wishes for a certain amount of yield, but not too much—if you take my meaning."

Iselin inclined his head gravely. It occurred to Oricien for the first time that Iselin and Ribauldequin might generate a degree of friction if pent together for too long.

"Come, Iselin, there is much we would learn," said Oricien with a smile. "If I am to please the King I will need all you know."

Iselin gave a measured nod. "The essentials of the matter are straightforward," he said. "If you will sit, I will outline the situation."

Oricien and Ribauldequin each took a seat; Iselin sat some distance away and steepled his fingers. "You will understand, of course, that Taratanallos is a city of some strategic significance: the best natural harbour south of Vasi Vasar, a city secure from all but the most determined assault. It is the most sizeable city in Mondia to rule its own affairs without reference to a King, and to control it would be a valuable prize both for our side and Gammerling in the event of war."

Ribauldequin made an impatient gesture as he leaned back in his seat and placed his leather-clad boots on the table. "Even I know this," he said.

Iselin frowned. "Patience. I have been working for the past three years to secure a majority among the Specchio—the rulers of the city—in favour of making submission to King Enguerran."

"Why should they do so?" asked Oricien. "Taratanallos takes pride in being 'the last free city'."

Iselin nodded. "If there is a war, Taratanallos will be sucked in, regardless of its inclinations. The choice which faces the Masavory, the ruling council of the Specchio, is with whom they choose to ally. There are three main factions: I am attempting to buttress the ones who support an Emmen alliance, naturally. They are opposed to those who wish to make submission to King Ingomer, and become subjects of Gammerling; the final group wishes to ally with Lothar, the Duke of Aylissia. This faction thinks itself the cleverest: they know that Ingomer and Lothar hate each other as only brothers can, and look to play them off against each other."

Ribauldequin asked: "Do none argue to maintain independence?"

Iselin smiled briefly. "They have little influence."

"So, Iselin," said Oricien, "which faction has the ascendancy?"

"At long last," said Iselin, "and largely through my own diplomacy, the Emmen faction is the strongest—although not yet guaranteed of victory. Our embassy must address the Specchio, once our position is secure, and seal the alliance."

"Why do I think it is not that simple?" said Ribauldequin.

"We are dealing with personalities," said Iselin. "Proud, brittle men, jostling for advantage, always seeking to be on the winning side. Sometimes it is hard to convince them where their advantage lies."

"This has been your 'diplomacy'?" said Oricien.

"The Emmen faction has grown in power. Its leader, Aladar, is one of the city's most respected men, from House Tantestro, a prestigious family. He appeals to the older, more sedate wing of the Specchio. He is supported by the rather more flamboyant Dravadan, the head of House Umbinzia. He is a younger, ambitious man, ruthless and a feared duellist. He has made two highly advantageous marriages, and is popular with the younger Specchio.

Each acts as a brake on the other's power, and between them they command many followers. When we add in the support of other major houses—Vaggio, for instance—we have a mighty coalition."

Oricien nodded. "An impressive display. How do we retain their loyalty?"

Iselin shrugged. "The old-fashioned way."

"Gold?" asked Ribauldequin.

"The most effective weapon of all," said Iselin.

"No doubt you keep records," said Oricien.

Iselin gave him an unblinking stare. "Naturally."

"As Lord Ambassador I will need to see them."

"That is not necessary."

"On the contrary, Iselin, I must insist."

Iselin snapped erect and strode over to a cabinet, brought forth a slim leather wallet. "This is a record of my expenses."

Oricien flipped open the wallet, extracted the paper on the top. He ran a finger down the totals. "These payments are astronomical. Aladar in particular appears to command greater revenues than most lords of the Emmenrule."

"The power of the Specchio arises from the trade monopolies they grant themselves. The value of these monopolies has fallen in recent years, since Ingomer has built his Great Northern Road. Trade in the city is reduced: many of the Masavory have been bankrupted. We would not want the same to happen to our allies."

"King Enguerran appears to have given you a free hand with his treasury."

Iselin gave a half-smile. "I have his complete confidence."

Oricien rose and made to leave. "Let us hope you soon earn mine also."

CHAPTER THREE

The ancient city of Taratanallos, secure in the largest natural harbour in Mondia, was the home of many elevated inns and establishments; although by few reckonings was the Northern Star among the most salubrious. Its ramshackle exterior, downwind of the tannery, promised little in the way of comfort and luxury, so those who crossed the threshold had no-one to blame but themselves if conditions were not to their liking. Neither was its location in the West Chale district a commendation.

Nonetheless the Northern Star retained a loyal if sparse clientele, which covered all strata of society. Florijko, the landlord, chose not to enquire into the motives of those such as Todarko and Bodazar, sons of good family who could have afforded to patronise the Paladrian Club or the Thrice-Blessed Argosy if the mood took them. There was always a market for cheap ale, gaming tables and women willing to overlook the occasional indelicacy of conduct.

"Florijko, two more beers if you please!" called Bodazar, sliding past two squat fishermen to lean on the bar. He moved with an easy fluency as the crowd in front of him melted aside.

Todarko drained the dregs of his mug and shook his head. "My uncle requires my presence at the Masavory tonight," he said, his mouth twitching into a wry grimace. "Emissaries are arriving from the Emmenrule and I must be on hand."

Bodazar raised an eyebrow. "You are not normally so keen to dance to Raguslan's tune," he said.

Todarko shrugged and moved towards the door. "He threatens once more to curtail my allowance. 'The time for play is past'", he said in an exaggeratedly reedy voice. "'Now you must learn the responsibilities of the Specchio. One day I will tell him my views on the topic."

Bodazar followed Todarko out onto the street. "I am sure your uncle is all too familiar with your views," he said. "That is why he presses you so hard."

Todarko kicked the rotting corpse of a cat as he walked past, to raise a whiff of sickly-sweet charnel. "His high-handed behaviour is intolerable. He thinks because he is the head of the house he can decide what I should do. One day he will learn otherwise!"

Bodazar shook his head. "So you say, on every occasion. Nonetheless, you always come to heel when called."

Todarko's face clouded. "I am not his lapdog."

Bodazar shrugged. "Maybe not. But he controls your allowance. Without him you would be in a sorry shape. You might be forced to seek employment or residence at Grandille."

Todarko laughed. "We are some way from that, I hope! I could not endure to be cooped up with my grandmother."

"So in the meanwhile, you rail against him with no prospect of remedy."

"So it is," said Todarko with an air of resignation. "And who knows, the Emmen delegates may prove interesting. They may even have sisters…"

"Whom they will have left at home, if they have any sense."

"We can but hope."

As they walked towards the docks where the Emmen vessel was expected, the road was blocked by a series of rattlejacks athwart Slavetakers' Lane. Patricians' wives hidden under Hood and Veil stood in clusters awaiting an explanation.

"Stand aside there!" called Todarko to the nearest carter. "The merchants will not thank you for blocking their way. You are on the doorstep of the Dignified Jadinko, who'll whip your arses off the street if he finds you there."

The carter sniffed and despatched a globule of phlegm just far enough from Todarko to avoid direct insult. "It's Jadinko we're here for—or his goods, to be more precise."

Bodazar walked over to the carter. "What do you mean?"

"Can't pay his bills, can he? All his money was tied up in an argosy to the north—when Ion Issio plundered it he was ruined. Marelko has called in the debt."

Todarko clambered aboard the rattlejack. "You cannot remove these goods. Jadinko is on the Masavory! He is a byword for solvency!" He reached out for a richly-embroidered robe lying on the floor of the cart.

"Get off with you, man!" growled the carter. "I have a warrant for distraint of goods. My men are stripping the property as we speak. Whoever you are, bugger off before I call the constables. A man has to pay his debts, Dignity or no."

Todarko climbed down the cart's wheel. "Where will it end?" he asked Bodazar. "That is three Dignities bankrupt this year. Is there no respect for place?"

From the adjacent house came a wail as a middle-aged woman rushed out behind one of the carter's men. Todarko was shocked to see her unveiled face. Her hood hung slack at her neck to reveal her grey-blonde hair. "Not my jewels!" she cried. "My grandmother bestowed them on my wedding day. They are an heirloom!"

The bailiff shook off her arm. "You are improperly dressed, madam. Your husband should have considered his position before entrusting his security to the seas. It is too late now to regret his imprudence."

"Jadinko!" called the woman with a plangent howl. "Do not allow this!"

From inside the house came a corpulent man of late maturity, his long white hair dishevelled. "Desist! I am the Dignified Jadinko! Leave off my goods!" He waved a stick with a silver head in the bailiff's direction.

The bailiff stepped under the blow and wrested the cane from Jadinko's hand. "This is a valuable item!" he exclaimed. "You must yield it up."

Jadinko struck at the bailiff with a doughy fist. "You cannot treat me this way! I am a man of refinement!"

The bailiff stood back. "I will ignore your assault upon my person," he said, "other than to note it hardly betokens 'refinement'. Kindly stand aside while I distrain your goods. Your house is of course forfeit also."

Jadinko let out a howl. His wife clung to his arm. As Jadinko cast frantically around, his eye alighted on a potential rescuer.

"Todarko!" he called. "There is dreadful misunderstanding! Call your uncle—no, call Aladar or Dravadan. Surely they will intercede for me."

"I am sorry for your plight, Jadinko," said Todarko. "I am sure my uncle will be equally distressed."

Bodazar said quietly to Todarko: "Distressed he may be, but he will not lift a finger to help him—and most certainly Dravadan will not."

Todarko shrugged. "Probably not. But the prospect has calmed Jadinko, at least." Easing through the crowd, he and Bodazar left Jadinko to his woes.

By the time they arrived at the Kinezad Docks, where shipping which wished to avoid the throng of commerce docked, it was apparent that Todarko and Bodazar were late. Bodazar slipped into the crowd of waiting dignitaries while Todarko sidled up to his uncle Raguslan. Moored on the dockside was a cog with a richly-dyed cerulean sail, showing the battlecat emblem of the Emmenrule. On the bow was painted the bold legend: Noble Renown.

"My apologies, uncle," he said softly.

Raguslan, sweating in his robes in the late afternoon sun, mopped his forehead distractedly. "I cannot rely on you for anything," he said. "No doubt you have drunk and wenched the afternoon away."

"I was detained in Slavetakers' Lane," said Todarko with a smile. "The bailiffs were picking Jadinko's bones."

Raguslan peered into Todarko's face. "This is not an ill-conceived jest?"

"My pranks are normally more direct," he said. "Ion Issio plundered his argosy. He is ruined."

Raguslan squinted as the sun on the water shone into his eyes. "The Masavory must act. These Garganet pirates demand abatement!"

Todarko shrugged. "You are on the Masavory: perhaps you can initiate action."

"I am one man. What can I do?"

"Jadinko suggested you might wish to intercede on his behalf."

Raguslan's eyes widened. "To what purpose? The man is lost. I do not wish to draw the attention of his creditors upon myself."

Todarko took a quick step forward. "Do you have something to fear from your creditors? Since you control my inheritance, the matter is of some interest to me."

Raguslan raised a placating hand. "No-one wishes to remind his creditors that he exists. I meant no more than that. Although times are hard on the Masavory, and no mistaking it. Ion Issio on the seas, tolls on the Dimonetto Road... I am glad the gentlemen of Emmen are here to lend their counsel."

"I care nothing for the gentlemen of Emmen," said Todarko. "The evening stretches ahead, and I wish to compose a sonnet for Nelanka's birthday. Instead it seems I will have to listen to Aladar's speeches."

Raguslan's face darkened. "Nelanka needs no sonnets from you, Todarko. No woman is safe from you, even your cousin's wife."

Todarko grinned. "I thank you for the compliment, nuncle; but Nelanka need not fear my advances. I esteem her too highly to seduce her, whatever I may think of your son."

"I wish you and Zanijel could be reconciled. It causes me inconvenience and embarrassment."

"His buffoonery embarrasses and inconveniences me," said Todarko with a shrug. "His infantile malice is the goading of a gnat."

"I warn you, Todarko: do not make advances to Nelanka. You will have cause to regret it."

"You demean her virtue by implying she might respond."

Raguslan pursed his lips. "How have I nurtured such a viper?" he hissed. "If I had not taken you in, you would be nothing! Some gratitude would be seemly."

Todarko raised an eyebrow. "I view matters rather differently. You were under an obligation, and my grandmother demanded you comply."

"What a disappointment you would have been to your mother. It is fortunate she never lived to see the wastrel and popinjay you have become. You have all your father's vices and none of his virtues."

"Did you summon me from my pleasures simply to revile me? Your observations could have waited until tomorrow."

"You are here, in case you have forgotten, to welcome Lord Oricien from Emmen."

"I doubt that my presence is of material interest to him."

"Enough! You are the most contentious stripling alive—and Aladar is about to speak."

CHAPTER FOUR

Taratanallos
25 years earlier

By the time the first rays of dawn insinuated their way through the window, Malvazan was already awake. Few boys of fifteen rose with the sun, but Malvazan took a pride in his asceticism: his brother Dravadan would normally be abed for at least another two hours, although this morning no doubt the entire family would be awake early. Malvazan scowled as he rose from his bed: he was ill-disposed for company so early, and regarded the sunrise hour as his own personal domain.

There was little chance of any solitude this morning, though. Every family of birth would be out on the Archgate today to be introduced to Gundovald, the King of Gammerling, and his Queen, as they passed through the city on their way to Paladria. House Umbinzia might not be the most elevated among the Specchio, but they would still cut a dash. His father would no doubt have to cede precedence to Jirno of House Vaggio and Aladar of House Tantestro, but as long as the hateful House Granguigi did not attempt to usurp them, the situation would be tolerable.

Malvazan had selected his outfit with care the previous night; scurrying around in the dawn gloom to find appropriate attire might suit Dravadan but such haphazardness was not the way to success. He performed a brisk ablution in the ewer by his bed—fortunately he needed to shave only a couple of times a week—and ten minutes later made his way down the stairs into the dining room where the table was laid for an early breakfast.

To his surprise and contempt, his parents and brother were already at the table.

"Ah, the sluggard!" cried Dravadan, his dark fringe hanging into his eyes. "The boy who lies abed till noon!" He spread some honey on a slice of bread and conveyed it to his mouth with more enthusiasm than delicacy. "You would think—"

"Dravadan!" said his mother Flinteska sharply. "If you must bait your brother, at least do not speak with your mouth full."

Dravadan rammed the rest of the slice into his mouth and, for the moment at least, devoted his full attention to subduing it.

Malvazan's father Crostadan, head of House Umbinzia, raised his hands in a mollificatory gesture. "Can we not have peace at the breakfast table on a day like today?" he asked. "Malvazan, there is some minor amusement in such a habitually early riser being last among us. It would do you no harm to display a little levity."

Malvazan sat heavily as far from the rest of the family as the table allowed and reached for a slice of bread. "I am glad to be such a source of amusement," he said. "It is good to know that a second son has some purpose."

Dravadan let out a belch which escaped explicit reproof, accompanied by a smirk towards Malvazan.

Flinteska slapped her napkin down on the table. "Enough, both of you. Dravadan, as the eldest son you should show greater decorum; Malvazan, your invincible surliness oppresses us all. Today we meet the King and Queen of Gammerling: a pleasant demeanour is required."

"Ha!" said Dravadan. "Who is the King of Gammerling to me? We are not his subjects."

Crostadan set down his cup of apple tea. "Indeed we are not," he said. "Nonetheless, Gammerling is a powerful neighbour, and worthy of our friendship and conciliation. More to the point, all the great houses of the Specchio will be on hand, and all will wish to shine to advantage—even you, Dravadan. Malvazan, whatever are you wearing!"

Malvazan flushed. "Is it not obvious? I have selected my best outfit: there were no complaints when I wore it to the reception at Roblegast."

Malvazan felt that he cut a fine figure, his doublet and breeches of deep purple complemented nicely by the lilac of his shirt.

"Do you really think it appropriate," said Crostadan wearily, "to wear purple for an audience with a king? It is the colour of royalty. Only Gundovald and his family will sport purple today. Go and get changed!"

"But—"

"Malvazan," said Flinteska, "do as your father tells you. I gave you credit for more sense. You are fifteen years old. Do I still have to dress you?"

Malvazan pushed his chair back from the table with such force that it clattered backwards to the ground. As he strode from the room he heard Dravadan's laughter braying behind him.

So it was that some three hours later, at the Hour of Fiscal Scrutiny, House Umbinzia stood in its place of due precedence waiting to be presented to the King of Gammerling. The formal gardens of the Masavory had today been given over to the reception. Crostadan wore a rich doublet of golden cloth, Flinteska a robe of emerald and silver. Dravadan's proud scarlet doublet was set off by a matching scapegrace hat with snooting-bird plume. Malvazan was attired all in black, his arms folded in attitude of defiance. If he was not allowed to wear purple, he would wear no colour at all. This way, at least, he might catch the King's attention.

Clouds sat heavy over the city, threatening to dampen spirits with a summer storm. Malvazan chuckled at the thought of rain: no one had thought to erect awnings, and many expensive costumes would be ruined. The wreckage might even extend to Dravadan's hat...

The Masavory had decreed, for this day only, a relaxation in the rules of Hood and Veil. The women of the Specchio therefore exposed their faces in the street for the first time in Malvazan's recollection. This caused him to revise his opinions in several ways: he had long admired the trim sway of Marsinkija's walk and the slim grace of her figure; it was disappointing, therefore, to find her face plain at best, and an undeniable hint of a moustache on her lip. On the other hand, the ironic smile sported by Blastanka of House Zeciola was rather more alluring than he had imagined would be the case: a shame that she was nearly thirty and married.

After some preliminary jostling the houses of the Specchio were arranged in some broad order of precedence awaiting introduction to the royal party. This year the President of the Masavory was Lustenaijo of House Franchino, and to him fell the honour of escorting the royal party.

Despite his enthusiasm to meet King Gundovald, Malvazan could not help but find the introductory speeches tedious. Lustenaijo was not the most eminent member of the Masavory, either in birth or accomplishment, and his droning voice grated on Malvazan's ear. He contented himself instead with inspecting the King and his family as they sat on a raised platform to listen to Lustenaijo's fulsome compliments.

King Gundovald, a man seemingly as broad as he was tall, sat with a negligent ease; if he was bored by the speeches he gave no sign of it. His outfit, Malvazan could not help but notice, bore considerable similarities with the one he had intended to wear himself. Queen Ledica was rather younger than her husband, her copious blonde hair piled high on her head. She would have been attractive were it not for an air of peevishness arising from her narrow mouth. The two young princes, Ingomer and Lothar, sat with as much composure as they could muster, but Lothar, in particular, looked around and twitched his feet. Malvazan could not help but feel some sympathy with the boy; like himself, a second son, destined by an accident of birth never to enjoy the advantages of his older brother—although it was unlikely that Prince Lothar would ever be banished to spend his days on a country estate with no occupation beyond the hunting of bindlespith.

Lustenaijo raised his voice a touch and Malvazan understood that his speech was reaching a conclusion.

"Naturally, Your Puissance, we recognise the great press of affairs which prevents you from tarrying in the Last Free City: the tides are an inflexible master and your ship awaits. Nonetheless, such a visit is a rare honour for the people of Taratanallos, and we are most grateful for the opportunity to pay our respects to you in person. You will see below you in the gardens the flower of the Specchio, the nobility of our city. Please allow me to introduce you to these noble citizens."

King Gundovald rose with a grace belying his girth and bowed to Lustenaijo.

"I thank you for your kind words of welcome, sir. The fair city of Taratanallos has long been a friend to my kingdom and it is all too rare for me to sample your sea air. Would that we could tarry a little longer: I am sure both Queen Ledica and my sons would enjoy a sojourn among you. I would be honoured, in the time available to us, for the chance to mingle among the Specchio, if you would be kind enough to make the introductions."

To King Gundovald's eye, the small groups clustered around the garden might have appeared random, a pleasing touch of informality. Nothing could have been further from the truth. Those nearest the stage were drawn exclusively from the 'Prime Houses', the most influential among the Specchio. The main role of Lustenaijo was not to make the introductions, but to ensure that they occurred in the correct order. The mortification of Bartielko, the young head of House Oreste and holder of the Monopoly of both wool and tin, were he to be introduced after Mandizel of House Carmaggio, would know no bounds.

House Umbinzia was not in one of the groups nearest the stage. By no reckoning could it be considered a Prime House, and Malvazan had to watch from afar as Queen Ledica gave a well-bred laugh at some jest from Jirno of House Vaggio, or King Gundovald slapped Aladar of House Tantestro on the back.

Malvazan's mood was a mixture of boredom and anticipation. The day was unseasonably chilly and the slarinto whipped in off the sea, pushing heavy black clouds before it. The King and Queen made their way by indirect stages towards his group, but Malvazan had time to grin and wave at Sanouté, the pretty daughter of House Zamilio.

The royal party grew in size as it moved around. Aladar and Jirno, having been introduced at the outset, made themselves part of the entourage, Aladar in particular seeming to monopolise the King's conversation. Malvazan tightened his lips: the man was only ten years older than himself, and already the head of one of the greatest houses of the Specchio—an elevation that owed nothing to merit and everything to birth.

Crostadan smoothed down his doublet as the King approached. This was the moment they had all been waiting for. Malvazan removed the scowl from his face and tried to catch Queen Ledica' eye. At exactly that moment, however, a rumble of thunder accompanied a cloudburst and a sudden drenching rain fell from the sky.

"Oh!" cried Queen Ledica. "My dress! It will be ruined."

"Noble lady…" murmured Lustenaijo. "I—"

"We must find shelter immediately!"

"Of course. Let me…"

Jirno, the grey-haired head of House Vaggio, briskly removed his cloak and held it above the Queen's head. "Forgive my proximity, madam. This may keep you dry for a few moments."

Lustenaijo looked around the garden to see a small gazebo some thirty yards away. "Your Puissance, madam: this way!"

With more haste than dignity the party dashed over to take shelter from the increasingly heavy rain. Malvazan, the rain coursing under his collar and down his back, stared on open-mouthed. The last he saw of King Gundovald was his broad back as he scurried to the gazebo.

That evening Malvazan's mood was as black as his clothes. "It is not fair," he said to Crostadan. "All the Prime Houses received their introduction and we had nothing."

Crostadan, warming his feet before the fire, merely shrugged. "It would have been an honour to meet the King," he said, "but it does not do to repine at such things. You could hardly expect Queen Ledica to stand there in the rain. Her gown probably cost ten thousand florins."

"Yet the Prime Houses consorted with them for hours while we stood on and watched. Is House Zano really so much better than us?"

Malvazan jerked his head away as Flinteska ruffled his hair. "We are among the greatest citizens of Taratanallos," she said. "Your father is the head of a great house and one day will be President of the Masavory. The workers in the Chale must certainly envy us."

"That is not the point," said Malvazan. "I know I am the equal of Aladar and Jirno and all the men of the Prime Houses: why should I not be accorded equal respect?"

Flinteska looked into his eyes. "You are my son, and I love you dearly; but you should attend the Viatory more often. We all have our places and our own roads to Harmony," she said. "We cannot all be leaders of the city. We have much to thank Hissen and Animaxia for: birth, wealth, two fine monopolies."

Malvazan sniffed. "Father, is this your view?"

Crostadan raised an eyebrow. "Your mother's points are unarguable. I do not know how many thousand citizens live in Taratanallos: the only ones who enjoy precedence over me are the seven heads of the Prime Houses, and perhaps their heirs. It is not such a bad position. We must learn to be happy with what we have in life."

Dravadan scratched his crotch. "Some of us can enjoy being the heir of a great house," he said. "Others must make do with less."

Crostadan pursed his lips. "That is unnecessary, Dravadan. When you are head of House Umbinzia you will have great cause to rely on your brother. You should not antagonise him now."

"It is not antagonisation, father," said Malvazan, "it is the truth. One day Dravadan will be head of the house and I will be nothing."

There was a gleam of sympathy in Crostadan's eye. "You will always be entitled to live in this house, Malvazan, or you may choose to live at Folinette. My will ensures that a proportion of the income from our monopolies will be settled on you. You need not fear poverty."

Malvazan jumped to his feet. "None of you understand! It is not wealth I want, it is consequence! Today our house was slighted by the Queen of Gammerling and none of you seem to feel it. You seem content to be nobodies and you want me to be nobody too. I will not. You may care nothing for the honour of our house, but I do."

He turned on his heel and stalked from the room, an effect only marginally compromised when he became entangled with the curtain screening the doorway.

"Malvazan!" called Flinteska. "Come back!"

"Leave him," said Crostadan. "He is young, and the position of a second son is never easy."

"I cannot believe how meekly they take it," said Malvazan, sitting on the loggia at Splanatia, the manse of House Zamilio. Next to him was Sanoutë, the daughter of the house and, if all went according to plan, his betrothed in the next couple of years.

"We did not get to meet the King either," she said, pushing her soft blonde hair back from her eyes.

"Naturally not," said Malvazan. "Zamilio is no more prestigious than Umbinzia. I understand why it happens thus, but I cannot understand why they do not rage. Surely your father was angry?"

"Thrinko takes events as they come," she said. "I would have liked to be introduced to Queen Ledica and see her dress, but no-one else seemed too concerned. My father says we should never bow the knee to kings in Taratanallos."

Malvazan shook his head and sipped at his cup of watered wine. "They have all become fat and complacent," he said. Looking out of the corner of his eye, he could see Sanoutë's rapt expression. "They think that the Prime Houses enjoy all the good things by right. My father is more interested in keeping House Granguigi below us than in thrusting upward."

Sanoutë's eyes were wide in the twilight.

"I will never accept second-best," said Malvazan. "You are my witness. I will be a great man in this city. No foreign prince will ever visit Taratanallos and think to overlook Malvazan of House Umbinzia. Do you hear me, Sanoutë?"

"Yes, Malvazan."

"Do you believe me?"

Sanoutë's lips were parted to reveal her even white teeth. "Yes—but I don't know how. You are a second son."

Malvazan's eyes flashed. "And is not a second son with accomplishments a better man than an heir with none?"

"Of course."

He leaned forward, an inch from Sanoutë's face. She closed her eyes, sighed in anticipation. With a brisk shake of his head, Malvazan stood up. "I have no time for dalliance tonight," he said. "I have many plans to make."

CHAPTER FIVE

To reach Taratanallos from Emmen, the traveller must journey down from the mountains and head west to the old port of Lynnoc. Three men on robust gallumphers have little to fear on the well-maintained roads, a visible testament to the good use to which the King of Emmen puts his subjects' taxes.

The next phase of the journey requires a more intrepid constitution. The wise traveller will pay a premium to embark upon a sturdy and well-managed vessel such as the Noble Renown, and even then his fingers will be crossed against the mishap which can befall any sea venture. No escort will be necessary on this leg of the expedition, since the ship is a self-contained world, and the perils arise from the storms which may condense in an instant, or the privateers who may suddenly appear over an empty horizon.

The voyage south, through the Marthambles Canals at Garganet and across the open sea, will tax both the constitution and patience of the hardiest traveller, and all will wish to enjoy sojourn for a few days at the ramshackle market town of Gyerling, even if this means breaking their journey. In any event, the Noble Renown will have incurred at best superficial damage, and will need to replenish its stores, so the opportunity to explore Gyerling will be all but mandatory.

Once at Gyerling, the traveller falls under the sovereignty of Ingomer, the King of Gammerling, and the visitor from the Emmenrule, particularly a noble one, will be wise to walk with a soft step and softer voice. Having been so eager to make landfall only a couple of days previously, such a traveller will look nervously over his shoulder as he waits on the dock for the captain to signal that he is ready to depart.

Nonetheless the most dangerous part of the journey still lies ahead. Winds howling in from the west snarl and bicker in their enthusiasm to dash the ship against the coastline of the Peninsula of Taratanallos. The lookouts posted day and night will be alert not just for storm clouds, but also the low shapes of swift galleys on the water—for this is the domain of the rogue Garganet pirates such as the notorious Ion Issio. Many a rich prize has fallen to such ruthless and desperate men, but the Noble Renown is fortunate both in its relatively small size and its tall sides, which indicate a modest cargo accessible only at high risk. After another wearing voyage, then, the Noble Renown will perform a spiral loop around the base of the peninsula, out of the driving wind, to find itself at last approaching

Taratanallos from the south. The duration of the entire journey will depend upon variable factors such as wind direction and the level of repairs necessary at Gyerling; but what is certain is that passengers making the journey for the first time will vow to both Hissen and Animaxia that they will never repeat it.

The sun was just beyond its zenith when Captain Durolio made a wry aside to Oricien that the city of Taratanallos was at last in view. In the distance the grey-white city walls seemed to rise sheer from the rich deep blue of the ocean. Ribauldequin, who had been sick throughout the voyage, might have been expected to express the most delight at the prospect, but so wretchedly green did he remain that the significance of his deliverance seemed lost on him.

A cog of some sixty feet in length and less than a quarter of that in width provided few opportunities for the avoidance of vexatious companions. As the city grew ever larger, the sun giving a warm lustre to the red roofs of the houses and sparkling off the domes of the public buildings, Oricien found himself screening out the ceaseless commentary of Lord Iselin. "—of course I now know my way well around the city—" "—you would be wise to allow me to take the lead in matters of protocol—" "—we are fortunate that Aladar looks upon me favourably—" "—at the very least a state banquet—" "—may even be back in Emmen for the Midwinter Revels—".

Indeed, if it were not for Iselin, Oricien would almost be looking forward to his mission. Even from this distance Taratanallos looked a place teeming with energy, the docks packed with ships from all corners of Mondia. The King had entrusted him with this vital task. He had spent many years on campaign in the north, and the chance to visit this famous southern city was one to be embraced. It would clearly be necessary at some point to bring home to Iselin who was the Lord Ambassador and who the advisor, but this could wait a few days until negotiations began in earnest.

As they approached the shelter of the docks, a large square buff building ahead of them, Oricien wondered where they would moor, so tightly packed were the ships on the jetties. But with the blue and green colours of the Emmenrule flying from the mast, the Noble Renown bore off to the right and towards an inlet empty of shipping. On the shore stood a bank of seating before an ornate stone dais on which could be discerned two standing figures. There were no cheering crowds, and the mood of the seated ranks of spectators seemed to be one of restrained, if attentive, curiosity. From the dockside a small troupe struck up a lively fanfarillo, which to the charitable ear had something of an Emmen flavour to the measure.

The Noble Renown was moored with some deliberation by Durolio's crew and a gangplank placed into position, a purple carpet unfurled to cover its naked wood. Oricien walked over to the captain, shook his hand and thanked him for his professionalism in bringing them safely to their destination, while Ribauldequin essayed a sickly smile.

To his annoyance, Oricien saw that Iselin had not waited to convey his own thanks to the captain, and now was striding down the gangplank before any of the others: a serious breach of etiquette. It was not practical to call him back now, in front of the grandees of the Specchio, but it would be necessary to check his over-mighty advisor rather sooner than he had intended. He jerked his head at Ribauldequin and set off down the gangplank behind Lord Iselin.

Eight men in crisp black uniforms, tall pikes at their side and black three-cornered hats on their heads, stood at the bottom of the gangplank forming a guard of honour. Iselin was first on the scene and gave them a smart bow, while Oricien hurried to catch up.

"My lords," said one of the guards, "will you do me the honour of allowing me to introduce you to the Dignified Aladar." He led them towards the dais and up the steps. "My lords, the Dignified Aladar and the Dignified Dravadan."

Iselin strode over and clasped Aladar's hand with both of his own. Aladar, tall and grave, responded with a measured smile. "Iselin! I am happy to see you once more. You must introduce your companions."

The sea breeze whipped in from the harbour and flicked at Aladar's grey hair laboriously combed over a bald scalp, but even this could not disturb his dignity.

"This is Lord Oricien, King Enguerran's Lord Ambassador to Taratanallos. He speaks with the King's voice and happily will ratify our schemes. Next to him you see Lord Ribauldequin, a young man of excellent birth, and a great swordsman to boot."

Dravadan raised an eyebrow. "You are most welcome; some are kind enough to style me a swordsman, Lord Ribauldequin. Perhaps in due course we might fence a hit or two."

Ribauldequin gave an unsteady bow. "Once I have recovered from Animaxia's vengeance on the mariner," he said, "I should be delighted to spar awhile."

Oricien could sense the situation slipping away from him. Iselin clearly intended to use his acquaintance with the city's lords to appear the leader of the expedition, with Oricien nothing more than a figurehead. Even if he were prepared to defer to a candlemaker's grandson, he remained to be convinced that Iselin's arrogance was necessarily what the situation required.

Aladar addressed the group in a mellow voice. "You will be lodged at the Castle of Crostestini during your time as our guests," he said, "but I would be delighted were you join me at the Masavory tonight: I have booked the Exchequer Hall in your honour. The Hour of Evening Repast will soon be upon us, and you would honour me by accepting my hospitality."

Iselin beamed and bowed low. "Dignity, you do us too much honour. I should be—"

Oricien held up a peremptory hand and Iselin reflexively fell silent.

"I thank you, Dignity. I am sensible of the honour you do us. As Lord Ambassador, I should be delighted to attend. Lord Iselin's role is essentially administrative, and since we will wish to discuss matters of high policy after dinner, his attendance will not be required. Lord Ribauldequin is indisposed from his voyage, and I am sure will wish to rest."

Iselin opened his mouth but no sound emerged. Aladar said smoothly: "Lord Iselin is an old friend to Taratanallos. Surely there would be no impropriety in his attendance."

"I require Lord Iselin to draft a despatch to King Enguerran outlining our safe arrival. Sadly he will not be at leisure to join us. We will all have ample time to enjoy his wisdom in the days to come."

"Very well," said Aladar.

"You are most thoughtful, Dignity," said Oricien. "Iselin, is there something you wish to say?"

Iselin narrowed his eyes. "No, Lord Ambassador."

Dravadan stepped forward and said: "My lords, the cariolo awaits to convey you to the Castle of Crostestini after a brief circuit of the city walls. If you will allow me to call upon you in a long-glass, I will have the honour to escort you to the Masavory."

Aladar proceeded down the steps of the dais to where an open cariolo, drawn by four strong grey striders, awaited. Oricien was at his side. Behind them Dravadan had taken out his rapier to show Ribauldequin, and Iselin brought up a surly last place.

"This is my own cariolo," said Aladar. "Will you sit on the top seat next to me, Lord Oricien?"

"I should be honoured," said Oricien, conscious of the eyes of the assembled Specchio upon him as he vaulted nimbly into the cariolo.

Aladar's coachman clicked his tongue and the striders pulled off, moving gently up the hill towards the top of the city. At the side of the roads men and women stood aside to let the cariolo past.

"I notice that all the women's faces are covered," said Oricien. The noise of the wheels on the cobbles made their conversation all but private, even though Dravadan and Ribauldequin were animatedly comparing the hilts of their rapiers only a few feet away.

Aladar nodded. "This is the Archgate, one of the best addresses in the city," he said. "A woman of good birth would not be seen in public without Hood and Veil. Only women of low birth show their faces on the street, and our journey does not take us to the Chale. In the Wrill, of course, where the foreigners bide, anything goes."

"I had heard that the women of Taratanallos are uncommonly beautiful," said Oricien. "I am sorry that I shall not have the chance to verify the claim."

"Oh, but you shall," said Aladar with a smile. "In a woman's own home, before her family and guests, she remains unveiled. Even now I prepare my manse Roblegast that I might invite you and your party. You shall judge the beauty of Taratanallos for yourself! My own wife Benada, while no longer youthful, is certainly a handsome woman; Dravadan's wife Linnalitha is a delight by any standards."

"A shame, Dignity, to cover such pulchritude."

"Ha! It is because they are so comely that they must be concealed. What man would want his wife or daughter leered at in the street by boors and rogues? Do matters go differently in the Emmenrule?"

Oricien gave a wry smile. "Perhaps our women are more wilful, and would not consent to having their charms hidden away. I cannot allow that our women are so unappealing that none would wish to molest them: I myself was once betrothed to a woman of extraordinary beauty, and no power under the Consorts could have made her cover her face."

Aladar scratched his chin. "It sounds as if she did not become your wife."

Oricien gave his head a thoughtful shake. "It was not to be," he said. "I remain a bachelor to this day."

"Our poets would delight in such constancy of heart," said Aladar. "I pride myself that no city boasts such bards as ours."

Oricien broke the silence with a chuckle. "Lord Ribauldequin is less ascetic," he said. "He is a man who appreciates that Animaxia created women to be admired and enjoyed."

"The view is widely held in Taratanallos," said Aladar. "Why else would we have Hood and Veil? I look forward to making Lord Ribauldequin's better acquaintance; although I am sorry that Iselin will not be with us tonight."

The cariolo made its way up towards the top of the Archgate. On both sides of the street stood houses in soft yellow stone, three or four storeys high. Despite the similarity of design, each had somehow a quirky individuality: this was where the grandees of the city lived.

"Lord Iselin has been most valuable in implementing King Enguerran's policies," said Oricien. "His friendship for your city is well-known. Nonetheless, his antecedents lack true nobility, and His Puissance would not wish to insult the best society of Taratanallos by presenting such a man as his representative. He knows what is due to the Specchio."

Aladar frowned. "Lord Iselin had hinted of expectations that he might become King Enguerran's Chancellor."

"One cannot fault him for ambition. Of course, a successful conclusion to our negotiations will benefit us all—including, I am sure, those among the Specchio who advance it."

A half-smile crept across Aladar's lips. "I feel I will enjoy our acquaintance, Lord Ambassador."

CHAPTER SIX

There were several fencing schools dotted around Taratanallos. A quarrelsome aristocracy given to settling arguments via the blade meant that all but the most timid of the Specchio were well-advised to acquire a degree of proficiency with a sword. The Garland of the Foils, a fencing competition for young men of good birth aged twenty, was a rite of passage for many.

The most expensive of the schools was Odurazan's, just off the Archgate, but among the cognoscenti the best master was reckoned to be Farlankas, a cantankerous and eccentric exile from Paladria, who saw more through his one eye than most managed with two.

Malvazan had been taking lessons with Odurazan for several years but, one morning a few weeks after King Gundovald's visit, he presented himself at the run-down premises in the Chale owned by Farlankas.

As luck would have it, Farlankas himself was disengaged: his two pupils that morning, Raguslan and Glastarko of House Vaggio, were resting after a series of drills.

Farlankas eschewed an eye-patch, and Malvazan was disconcertingly aware of the gaping socket.

"What do you want, boy?" said Farlankas in a low voice. "I need no new pupils."

"I am no 'boy'," said Malvazan. "I am fifteen and the son of Crostadan. I'll thank you to treat me with some respect."

Farlankas looked down into Malvazan's face with a blue-eyed glare. "Respect is earned at my school, boy. Your Tarat titles mean nothing to me. Have you come to learn the noble art, boy?"

One of Raguslan or Glastarko, sprawled on the couch, sniggered and Malvazan felt his colour rising.

"Call me 'boy' again and I'll break your nose."

Farlankas gave what passed for a smile. "If I was so easily cowed I wouldn't have much to teach you now, would I? Tell me your name and I'll use it: the respect may have to wait a little longer."

Malvazan pondered a moment. Farlankas had a reputation; there was little to be gained by sparring with him further.

"My name is Malvazan. I'm the best swordsman of my age in the city and I intend to win the Garland. You will teach me."

Farlankas laughed aloud. "Will I, by Hissen? You are a certain one, and no mistake. Who says you are the best swordsman?"

"There is only one opinion I value, and that is my own. Odurazan believes my brother Dravadan has more talent, but I disagree."

Glastarko called out: "Farlankas chooses his pupils. You do not walk in off the street."

Malvazan turned to face Glastarko. "He took you, did he not?"

Glastarko laughed. Raguslan said: "My brother reached the semi-finals of the Garland this year. He has the skill of the blade."

"He might have won the competition," said Malvazan, "if he had been stronger in defending the ley quadrant."

Farlankas' eyebrows rose—a curious sight above the empty socket. "You are a student, then? I doubt Odurazan taught you that much."

"It is an obvious weakness," said Malvazan. "Indeed I wonder that you did not coach it out of him."

There was a moment of silence. Then Glastarko laughed. "Yes, Farlankas, you are to blame for my defeat. Why did you not coach me better?"

Farlankas turned his back and walked over to the wall where a series of practice blades hung. "You have an arrogant disposition, young Malvazan. I do not greatly care for you. That is neither here nor there. If you can back up your bravado with bladecraft, well and good; if not, you are a fool and one day soon someone will slit your gizzard. Since you know Glastarko's style, let me see you spar with him."

He threw one blade to Glastarko, the other to Malvazan. As the blade flew through the air Malvazan caught it with his left hand.

"Ah!" cried Raguslan. "A snark-blade."

Farlankas nodded. "A good start: a left-handed fighter is always an awkward opponent. Come, let me see you fight."

Malvazan took the blade, circled slowly as he watched Glastarko opposite him. Glastarko, a handsome man with a deceptively languid manner, was five years older, with a longer reach, and plenty of experience. Weakness in the ley quadrant or no, a man did not reach the semi-finals of the Garland by luck. Malvazan watched and waited.

"Come on, then," said Glastarko, feinting towards Malvazan.

Malvazan said nothing, covered the feint without committing himself. *He will expect me to attack the ley, since I know it to be a weakness.* Malvazan skipped into an attack, pressing the ley quadrant before flicking his wrist upwards towards the exposed petty-pectis quadrant. Glastarko responded quickly, chopped down and parried the stroke. Malvazan skipped back out of range, then used the advantage of his left-handed angle to probe at the grand-pectis. Glastarko sensed the move, stepped around it and tapped Malvazan in the middle of the chest with his blade. "Well fought, sir," he said.

Malvazan's head sank to his chest. To be outwitted so easily was galling. He held out his right hand for Glastarko to shake: Glastarko smiled and took it.

Farlankas nodded. "Enough," he said.

Malvazan's mouth drooped. Somewhere behind his eyes tears were massing.

"I am sorry to have wasted your time," he said. "I will return to Odurazan."

Farlankas shook his head. "You are in. Glastarko is the best swordsman in my school, and if I am not mistaken your attack troubled him."

"Correct," said Glastarko. "You are patient, you conceal well and you do not take the obvious choice. A snark-blade too—I'm sure Farlankas can do something with you."

"You have all the raw materials," said Farlankas. "Odurazan teaches next to nothing. A year under my tuition and we will add some guile to your reflexes. Come back at the Hour of Petitions tomorrow and we will begin."

CHAPTER SEVEN

After quitting Lord Oricien's dockside reception, Todarko stepped briskly back to his apartments in Tappinetto, the manse of House Vaggio and the seat of his uncle Raguslan. He kicked off his boots and lay back on his bed, looking out from his window to the sea and the horizon beyond. Hissen take Raguslan and his requirements! It now seemed that he was required to attend a tedious soiree. When would he learn that Todarko had no interest in the Masavory and the foolish intrigues of the Specchio? Having wasted the afternoon awaiting the arrival of the Emmen dignitaries, the prospect of spending the evening at a reception in the Masavory was not appealing. Lord Oricien and his cronies had seemed stiff and unyielding, not men to set arid protocol aside. True, Nelanka would be in attendance, but the presence of the cloddish and hostile Zanijel would take much of the savour from her company. If he pleaded indisposition, he could at least spend the evening working on his sonnet and polishing the final quatrain of that troublesome villanelle. It might also provide an opportunity to clarify matters with Ivanka before they grew out of hand.

He slid over to his desk and scratched two brief notes, which he despatched via the house-slave Luzio. No doubt there would be a reckoning tomorrow, but time enough to worry about that later. For now, Nelanka's sonnet awaited.

Just before midnight Todarko set down his pen. The wind coming through his window had freshened into a slarinto and the lantern cast a jerky shadow on the ochre-washed wall at his back. There would be no more writing done tonight: the sonnet was serviceable, if no better, and the villanelle marginally improved. It was a passable evening's effort, if not completely satisfactory. Too late now for more; if he delayed longer he would miss his rendezvous.

He slipped a dark cloak over his white shirt and, after a brief deliberation, strapped on his rapier. It was not inconceivable that trouble could ensue later. He stepped onto the smoothly-fitted cobbles of the Archgate and strode through the darkness towards the Chale, the area of the city inhabited mainly by artisans. The chances of meeting anyone who would recognise him were slim, since most of those would still be at the reception.

He made his way down streets that became darker, narrower and more indirect. Suspicious faces peered at him as he walked and occasional arguments or imprecations could be heard from within the close-packed houses. Eventually he came to the familiar covered passageway before him. "Ivanka!" he called in a quiet penetrating tone. "Are you there?"

From the shadow came a rustle of movement, arms thrown around his neck, the pressure of lips at once warm and cool. "Where have you been? I thought you had forgotten me!"

Todarko extricated himself from the embrace and looked into Ivanka's face. Her veil hung awry, her hood thrown back, and the moonlight exaggerated the shadows of her cheekbones to give a gleam of intensity to her dark eyes. Trembling slightly in the chill of the evening, she was undeniably an appealing picture.

"I have been busy with affairs of state," said Todarko, conscious even as the lie fell from his lips that it was not even superficially plausible. "My uncle has left me with little time for pleasures."

Ivanka put her hands on her hips. "Do not take me for a fool, Todarko. Your indifference has been increasingly apparent in recent weeks. I am sure you have another paramour!"

Todarko rubbed his chin. "You malign me unjustly. I have been constant in my attentions and my affections."

Ivanka turned her back on him. "You speak the dry language of a merchant, not a lover! Where are your yearnings of the spring? Where are the beautiful sonnets you once brought me?" He could hear the catch of tears in her voice.

Todarko took her by the shoulders and turned her to face him. "You are overwrought to no purpose. Whatever the strength of my feelings, tears will not water them to growth."

"You do not deny your indifference?"

Todarko grimaced. "'Indifference' is a cruel term—"

"It is a cruel fate!"

"Ivanka, you are undeniably the most charming and beautiful woman alive; but we both know that neither of our families will countenance our marriage. House Vaggio follows the Emmen party and House Klemenza follows Gammerling. It is best if we face reality."

"Reality! What of the reality in my belly!"

Todarko's arms fell to his sides. "You cannot mean…"

"Todarko, I am with child!"

Todarko felt his jaw slacken. This complicated matters even beyond their already twisted warp.

"Well? Have you nothing to say?"

Todarko paused. "It is conceivable, surely, that the child is not mine?"

A ringing in his ears accompanied Ivanka's slap. "No, it is not 'conceivable'", she cried. "What kind of slut do you take me for? You are the most callous man in Taratanallos! Who will marry me now?"

"You have always vaunted your high birth," said Todarko. "Your prospects are not as blighted as you suggest."

Ivanka gasped. "You are trying to palm me off already? Do you have no care at all for me?"

Todarko ran a hand through his hair. "In an abstract sense, I have every sympathy for your predicament. I even feel a degree of guilt for having been the agency of it. That falls some way short of being prepared to marry you, even if my uncle agreed."

Ivanka's face was so white the glare seemed to sting Todarko's eyes. He was conscious that he was not appearing to advantage; nonetheless, there was no practical remedy he could provide. House Klemenza would no doubt hush the matter up, and she would be back on the marriage market in less than a year. Seen from a certain perspective, he had even done her a service: she would certainly not yield her favours so readily in future. Her reaction was clearly exaggerated, and it was as well he had been alerted to her volatile nature before it was too late.

"Come, I will see you home," he said gently. "The night is chill."

Ivanka looked at him in mute astonishment. Collecting herself, she said: "That will be not be necessary. Such assistance as I require from you is not forthcoming. You will not see me again."

Before Todarko could reply, she dashed off into the darkness. At this time of night, he thought, the streets were all but empty, and her Hood and Veil marked her out as a woman of status. She would come to no real harm. In years to come no doubt she would look back on the affair with misty-eyed nostalgia for the excesses of her youth.

CHAPTER EIGHT

Tappinetto occupied a pleasant aspect near the north-eastern walls of the city. This district, known as the Aspergantia, was where the Specchio lived, and Raguslan's neighbours included Dravadan of House Umbinzia and the leader of their political faction, Aladar of House Tantestro.

To the artisans who lived and worked in the cheek-by-jowl bustle of the Chale, the lives and houses of the Specchio were of scarcely imaginable grandeur. The everyday rivalry and machinations, the lobbying for office and favour, which took up so much of a noble family's time, were disregarded by those who envied their wealth and leisure. The carpenter working all the daylight hours in a workshop on Pennyhouse Lane would neither appreciate nor understand the concerns of a man like Raguslan.

On the morning after the arrival of the Emmen ambassadors, Raguslan was basking in a small triumph. That evening, Aladar, perhaps the most powerful man on the Masavory, had invited Raguslan and his family to a soiree at his manse Roblegast. This represented a clear advance for Raguslan, who was not one of more influential patricians. Although House Vaggio was one of the most elevated among the Specchio, in recent years its influence had declined. He knew that this invitation owed nothing to his own merits, but instead arose from his connections with Dravadan — one of the coming men of the Masavory.

He read the invitation again. The phrase "warmest esteem" was clear; in the etiquette of the Specchio, it required the attendance not just of Raguslan but his entire household. With a frown his thoughts turned to Todarko: it would be an insult to Aladar to leave him at home; but potentially an insult of a different kind were he to attend. There was nothing for it: Todarko would have to be enjoined to sober and discreet conduct. It would also be necessary to keep him away from Nelanka: while he had every confidence in his daughter-in-law's decorum, Todarko could be guaranteed to flirt with her, if only to antagonise Zanijel. The boy — hardly a boy any more, hard though it was to believe — would need to be kept on a tight leash.

Todarko aside, the evening could only advance his prospects. A mixed party at the house of a man as influential as Aladar was a rare occasion: he had never met Aladar's wife unveiled. It was rare enough to see Dravadan's wife Linnalitha without Hood and Veil. Once he had consolidated these acquaintances he could, in all punctilio, invite them to Tappinetto or even to his summer estate Grandille. With the Emmen alliance in the ascendant, there were bright times ahead for House Vaggio!

He rang the bell to summon the house-slave.

"Luzio", he said when the man appeared. "Kindly fetch Todarko. There are matters I need to discuss with him."

With a half-smile Luzio bowed and set off for Todarko's tower-top chambers.

Todarko was roaming a silver meadow with a being of grace and lightness, at once female and more than female: a creature of fascinating loveliness and sensibility. He sat on a tussock, cooled by a sweet zephyr under a blazing sun. "You really wish to hear my poem?" he asked.

"But of course! The exquisite subtlety of your language, the hints of sublime visions—we dream of them in heaven."

"Well, if you insist—"

Bang bang bang!

Todarko frowned. Was there no respect for his recital? He carried on. "When on a summer's morn I—"

Rat-tat-tat! "Wake up, sir! My master wishes to speak to you!"

With a groan Todarko rolled over in his bed. "Can I not sleep, Luzio? It is yet night."

Luzio pushed the screen back from the window to admit a quantity of light which gave the lie to this statement. "I will tell him you are on your way."

As soon as Luzio had left the room, Todarko slipped from his bed. In truth, he had not slept well. His interview with Ivanka had been unsettling, although it was hard to see any other way he could have responded. Now he would in addition be reproved by his uncle for avoiding last night's soiree.

The Castle of Crostestini, set into the city walls where they met the docks at their farthest north-western extent, had originally been conceived as a defensive fortification to daunt and defy the most determined foe. The boast had never been put to the test, for the Castle's position provided no effective protection for the docks—which in any event were amply defended by the sea-wall across the harbour, which dated from several centuries later—and the city had never, to date, been subjected to a land attack from that direction.

The Masavory were, by temperament, unwilling to allow a potentially valuable asset to remain unexploited. Over time, therefore, the Castle acquired a second and more important function, that of housing important guests from abroad, and—almost as an afterthought—a garrison of the Consiglio who ensured that alien residents did not act to threaten the peace and harmony of Taratanallos.

It was to the Castle of Crostestini that the three Emmen ambassadors were brought on the evening of their arrival. The castle loomed high against the horizon in the long shadows of the setting sun, a massive and imposing building of the same smooth buff stone which the Specchio used to build their houses.

Their ceremonial escort left them at the double-gated entrance where a man of late maturity waited for them in the black robes of the Consiglio; the black battlecat fur which sat at the neck and cuffs hinting that this was no simple functionary.

He bowed as the three ambassadors stood in the courtyard, Oricien shivering in the sudden shade.

"My lords, I bid you welcome to the Castle of Crostestini. I am the Consigli Polijenko." Polijenko accompanied his words with a crisp bow: he might not be of Specchio rank, but here was a man who held his dignity dear.

Oricien gave a bow of mathematically exact equivalence. "I thank you, sir. I am the Lord Ambassador Oricien, and these are my advisors Lord Ribauldequin and Lord Iselin."

"You will no doubt be fatigued after your journey; you will wish, I suspect, both to rest and bathe." Polijenko clicked his fingers and three more junior Consigli appeared. "My colleagues will escort you to your chambers, which are adjacent and command the finest views of the city."

Oricien indicated his thanks once more and the three of them were conducted with a brisk if unsmiling efficiency to a suite of rooms at the top of the north-west tower. His escort—or was he a guard?—said: "Your trunks will be brought forth shortly, my lord. In the interim, perhaps you would care to bathe?"

Oricien realised that he felt grimy from the endless days at sea, with only salt-water in which to wash, and the lather of soap a distant memory. "Thank you," he said with the first warmth he had felt since reaching Taratanallos.

"I will draw you a bath, sir. Perhaps you would care to look around."

Oricien went out on to the balcony of the tower, relishing his first moments of solitude since he had left Emmen. Down in the bay below him, all kind of craft plied the waters, variously loading and unloading their cargoes. Even with dusk beginning to fall, the sense of industry was unceasing. Was this truly a city ready to yield up its independence, whether to Emmen or Gammerling? Iselin seemed to think so, but looking at the vitality spread out below him, Oricien felt less certain.

He walked around the balcony. To the north, a series of roads led out into the forest; he knew that villages and towns which fed on the might of Taratanallos lurked out of sight, farms with their produce for the markets and plentiful labour to support the great machine of the city's economy. To the west, meanwhile, hills stretched up to the far walls, the intervening space packed with red-roofed houses, dense to the south, larger and sparser to the north. This, then, was Taratanallos.

He went back inside the apartments to await his bath. The furnishings inside were solid and serviceable without extravagance. Where the palaces of Emmen were light and airy, all marble and silver, the Castle of Crostestini was altogether more brooding, the walls granite, the metalwork burnished iron. From what he knew of the Specchio, he thought it unlikely that the houses of the Masavory exhibited such asceticism.

"Your bath is ready, sir," said the Consigli. "You will find the cleansarium to your left." He bowed and left the apartment.

The cleansarium was rather more luxurious than the rest of the suite, which Oricien was sure told him something profound about the minds of the men who ruled Taratanallos. A long marble bath was set into the floor, clouds of steam billowing with inviting fingers from the surface. The water roiled slowly at some unseen agitation underneath, and fluffy islands of bubbles circulated. At one end of the bath a spigot of some sort stood, evidently the means by which water was admitted; there had been no buckets that Oricien had seen. The arrangements made his own quarters at Croad seem like a peasant's hut; and if he was honest, there was nothing at the Summer Palace in Emmen to match this. No doubt the water was heated by a dimonetto built into the fabric of the castle: maybe visitors were not so stinted after all.

Swiftly Oricien divested himself of his clothes and slipped under the water up to his neck. Instantly he felt relaxation seeping though his tired muscles, could sense the hot perfumed water loosening the dirt ground into his skin. How much difference could such a little factor make! Now, for the first time, he felt that perhaps his task was not beyond him. He was no longer a travel-stained vagabond; he truly was King Enguerran's Lord Ambassador.

He quickly lost track of time. By depressing the spigot with his toes, he could summon more of the scented hot water, and a pleasant lassitude seeped through his limbs. Eventually he thought he should consider leaving this delightful haven; he could always bathe again tomorrow if he wished to feel truly decadent. He realised that he had not seen a towel; a curious oversight given the attention to detail his hosts had devoted to the art of bathing.

He craned his neck to see if he had missed anything, splashing in startlement when he saw a dark-haired young woman of no more than twenty standing quietly, folded towels in her arms.

"Do not be alarmed, my lord," she said. "I am Vivalda, and I am here to wait upon you."

Oricien checked that the bubbles on the surface of the water concealed all that needed to be concealed. Vivalda caught his gaze and gave a half-smile. "I am here to serve you—however you please. You need feel no embarrassment, my lord."

He sank down slightly deeper in the water. "I am grateful for your solicitude, Damoiselle."

Vivalda curtsied and set the towels down on a bench. She wore a loose white garment which still, somehow, indicated ripeness and amplitude underneath. "I am a slave, my lord," she said. "You need not refer to me as Damoiselle."

Oricien shifted to look into her face. "You are young—and beautiful—to be slave," he said.

"My mother and father are slaves too," she said. "I was born into this condition; I know no different, or better. Come, will you not step from the water and let me dry you?"

"A few moments," said Oricien. "Is this your duty, to wait upon guests at the Castle of Crostestini?"

Vivalda looked demurely at her bare feet. "That would hardly be seemly, my lord," she replied. "Since I am commanded to do as you wish, it would show you little respect were I to be passed from guest to another."

"No, I suppose not," said Oricien. The conversation—and the situation—were strange, but he was almost beginning to enjoy it.

"So what occurs if—for the sake of argument—we assume that certain guests might take advantage of your presence to the maximum extent?"

Once more Vivalda gave her half-smile. "At such a time I am withdrawn from bath-duties and found other employment; generally, since the world likes a pretty face, this is of a relatively congenial nature."

"You do not appear without education, Vivalda. You converse with a foreign lord with intelligence and confidence."

"Thank you, my lord. Those young girls who give promise, at eight, of developing into women of beauty are taken into the Consiglio's lyceum. Here we are schooled in all kinds of accomplishments, that we can please and delight in our maturity."

To Oricien this seemed something of a cold-blooded arrangement, but this was not his city, and not for him to judge. "So you remain on 'bath duties' until such times as one of the city's guests renders you unsuitable for its continuance?"

"You phrase it most delicately, my lord."

"I would not have you think that the men of the Emmenrule are boors, Vivalda."

"You may be assured that I do not, my lord. Do you wish now to step from the bath?"

Oricien felt the languor of the water in his limbs. Vivalda stood above him, her lips slightly parted, and surely ready to gratify any desire he might express. Attractive as the girl was, clean and well-mannered, there was something clinical about the proposition which he could not help but find unappealing. What harm could it do to be towelled down, on the other hand?

He stepped from the water and Vivalda, her gaze discreetly focused on the middle distance, dried him carefully, neither favouring nor sparing any part of his body, before handing him a gown of soft fabric.

"I will be here every day of your stay," she said. "I hope I am not ill-favoured. If you were to wish to release me from bath duties in due course, I should not object, even were I in a position to do so."

Oricien sat on the bench, his gown soft on the back of his legs. "In Emmen perhaps we are old-fashioned," he said. "I would scruple to take advantage of a woman who had not the choice of refusal." As he spoke, it occurred to him that Ribauldequin was no doubt engaged with a bath-slave of his own. Unless his sea-malady was truly prostrating, it was unlikely that he was exercising the same restraint.

Vivalda sat down next to him. "For ten years, my lord, we are prepared for this moment; we hear, of course, of the experiences of those who go before us. Some of them repay all the attention which is spent on our education; others horrify and appal us to our bones. Such are the different appetites clothed in human flesh.

"When we pray to Hissen and Animaxia, as we are taught, we all pray for the same thing: that the man who makes us no longer a bath-slave is truly a man, and not a beast. Sometimes the guest is so captivated that he buys the bath-slave for his own."

Oricien said nothing as he looked into her face.

"My lord, if on your departure from the city I remain untouched, I will be sent to the next guest in these chambers. And he, sir, may be a man of a different stamp altogether."

She stood up and walked to the door. "If you have no further need for me, I will leave you for tonight. Good night, my lord."

Oricien watched the swing of her hips as she left. "Good night, Vivalda," he said softly to the closed door.

Precisely on the Hour of Evening Satiation, the Dignified Aladar's cariolo set down the three ambassadors at Aladar's manse Roblegast. The manse was a structure three storeys high, the red tiles on the roof catching the rays of the setting sun and bathing the Archgate in a rosy glow. Aladar came out from the middle of the three porticoes at the front of the house and warmly clasped Oricien's hands. "Lord Ambassador! I am delighted to entertain on this more informal occasion after our pleasant conversations last night."

Oricien removed his hat and inclined his head. "The honour is mine, Dignity. I know how affairs of state must press upon you."

Aladar made an airy gesture. "And Iselin, I am glad the pressures of your business allow you to join us this evening. Lord Ribauldequin, I trust your sea-malady is now abated."

The ambassadors followed Aladar into the spacious reception hall, their boots ringing on the polished wood. Oricien noted that the hangings draped over the stone walls were even richer than last night: Aladar was keen to display the full wealth of House Tantestro.

Aladar's other guests were already present, and were introduced in a welter of names Oricien had difficulty remembering: Raguslan, Zanijel, Todarko—and the more familiar figure of Dravadan. For the first time he saw ladies freed from the anonymity of Hood and Veil, although once again he could not retain their names. He looked across at Iselin, who appeared to have no such problems. His ready mind was noting down every new acquaintance, stored against the day he might need to conciliate their goodwill for his own advantage.

By the Hour of Noble Pleasures Oricien found himself wishing for a moment's peace. The endless vapidity of the conversation, the succession of well-bred inanities, in no way advanced his mission of securing the submission of Taratanallos. The women, striking as they might be unconfined by Hood and Veil, wielded no influence, and the men, if they were Aladar's intimates, could already be counted among his supporters. Iselin seemed in his element, and the intentness with which Ribauldequin was attending to the conversation of the willowy brunette with the long nose suggested that he was not intolerably bored. Indeed, no-one else seemed to share his ennui, unless it was the tall man with the dark hair and understated clothes who leaned against one of the pillars of the loggia at the rear of the reception hall.

He wandered over to the lounging man. "We have been introduced," he said with a smile, "but I confess I have forgotten your name already. Are you a connection of Aladar's?"

"Only most indirectly," he said. "This is the first—and probably last—time I visit Roblegast. My name is Todarko, and I am the nephew of Raguslan; a man who foolishly believes himself to be Aladar's intimate."

"You appear to show little respect for your uncle."

"I hope you will not be offended when I tell you I find the whole question of the Emmen alliance unutterably tedious. There are many other more agreeable pursuits I might have carried out this evening."

Oricien laughed. "Offended! It is the first honest remark I have heard tonight."

Todarko tilted his head to the side. "You are a curious ambassador, sir. I imagined King Enguerran might have sent a more earnest figure."

"You will find that Lord Iselin is earnest enough for us both," said Oricien.

"Lord Ribauldequin also appears to lack ambassadorial gravity," said Todarko. "I was impressed with the way he knocked back Aladar's best wine, and I left him flirting with my cousin. A man after my own heart, in fact."

Oricien knitted his brows. "Is that so? Ribauldequin, to be frank, suffers from a reputation for dissipation, and I had enjoined him to sober conduct."

"Ah."

"Will you excuse me, sir? I must ensure that he intends no mischief."

He slipped back into the reception room, now noticeably warmer than the freshness of the loggia. In one corner he saw Ribauldequin gesturing in an exaggerated manner before the young lady he had been speaking to earlier—seemingly Todarko's cousin. She was tall, slender, her glossy dark hair tumbling over her shoulders, with an angular face of unconventional attraction.

"Ribauldequin," he said in a conversational tone, "I hope you are not monopolising the ladies' company? There is not enough of it to go round."

Ribauldequin grinned, clapped Oricien on the shoulder. "Allow me to introduce Madam Nelanka, the wife of Zanijel, the son of... I forget."

Nelanka curtsied to Oricien and said in a cool well-modulated voice. "My husband is the Grave Zanijel—his father the Dignified Raguslan is the head of House Vaggio, and a friend of the Dignified Dravadan. You may have met him already."

"I have not had the honour of his attention," said Oricien. "I have spoken with your cousin Todarko, however."

A brief smile flickered across Nelanka's face. "You must not mind him, my lord. He is not one for such events, and sulks for his own amusement."

"I found nothing to take exception to in his conduct. I cannot blame him for wishing to be elsewhere."

"You have a poor opinion of Aladar's hospitality," said Nelanka with a twitch of her wide mouth.

"Ha! She has you, Oricien!" cried Ribauldequin. "A Lord Ambassador must be delighted with everything he sees, and must feign pleasure where he finds none."

"Thank you, Ribauldequin," said Oricien stiffly. "What I meant, madam, was that if Todarko's pursuits and interests lie elsewhere, it is unsurprising if he resents being compelled to attend."

"Whereas you, my lord, can resent nothing, since it is your mission," said Nelanka. "Your friend Lord Ribauldequin is right in that, I think: whatever true feelings you have must subsumed to policy."

"The life of the ambassador is all glory!" Ribauldequin lifted his goblet high. "The endless society of beautiful women—what a shame he may not enjoy their favours!" He gave a shrill, almost girlish, laugh.

"Madam, please excuse Lord Ribauldequin's vulgarity," said Oricien. "He has eaten nothing because of the sea-malady, and wine is a tyrant on an empty stomach."

Nelanka blushed. "It is nothing," she said in a soft voice.

Oricien put an arm around Ribauldequin's shoulder and pulled him aside. "You are disgracing us all," he hissed. "Go and sit down somewhere."

He turned back to Nelanka. "I am told that the gardens of Roblegast are remarkable," he said. "Would it be improper of me to invite you to walk in them awhile?"

CHAPTER NINE

Over the first three years of his tutelage with Farlankas, Malvazan put on four inches, some extra muscle and, most significantly of all, a degree of self-control. The morning of every day was spent at Farlankas' school, and the respect which he had so brashly demanded on the first day of their acquaintance was earned by his skill and dedication. He did not win all his bouts, but his boast of being the best young swordsman in Taratanallos was generally held to be correct—although the quiet and slight Rodizel of House Carmaggio often seemed to have his measure. Dravadan, who remained at Odurazan's school, seemingly failed to make equal progress.

One evening at the beginning of summer, Kropiselko of House Zano hosted a reception at his manse Hanglenook; an event to which invitations were eagerly sought, since House Zano was one of the greatest in the city, wealthy through its monopolies of slaves and jade. Crostadan was pleasantly surprised to receive an invitation: the houses were not normally intimate; and even more to his pleasure, his friend Thrinko of House Zamilio was also invited. Kropiselko's cousin Jadijano was married to Thrinko's brother. Such relationships oiled the wheels of the Specchio, even if on occasion they led to the kind of birth defects better not mentioned.

Malvazan, at eighteen, was of an age where events of this nature had become more appealing. His renown as a swordsman made him a figure of interest and, since the young ladies who were his contemporaries now must walk abroad behind Hood and Veil, such soirees were his only chance to see their faces.

For all his ease of manner, Malvazan had not grown into a convivial young man. He stood, as so often, at the edge of the loggia looking out into the gardens with a goblet of wine in his hand. Inevitably it was Sanouté who came upon him. She gently touched his shoulder.

"Have you been avoiding me, Malvazan?" she said with a soft smile. Her face, as she was all too obviously aware, was not designed to be hidden behind a Veil, and she seemed to relish the freedom of the soiree.

"Of course not," said Malvazan.

"I have not seen you for weeks. I begin to think that I am ill-favoured, although Astrizel clearly believes otherwise."

Malvazan gave a sour smile. "I am busy, Sanoutë; surely you realise that. One does not become a master swordsman through indolence."

She took his arm and led him off the loggia onto the lawns. "You should always have time for your old friends, Malvazan; particularly friends as devoted as me. You know that I am devoted, do you not?"

Malvazan gave a more practised smile. Such devotion was the root of the problem.

"I await the day when our fathers have a conversation," she said in a soft voice.

"They speak all the time," said Malvazan.

"Tush! You know the kind of conversation I mean," she said. "If I am not mistaken, that conversation has not yet occurred."

Malvazan willed his muscles into relaxation. Sanoutë was a fine girl, beautiful if wearing at times. He genuinely liked her: but a betrothal with House Zamilio was not necessarily an advantageous one. There were many unmarried daughters in the Prime Houses who fitted better with his ambitions.

"Such matters are not in our hands, Sanoutë. Come, let us talk of other things."

"How does your swordplay go?" she asked. "You won last week, did you not?"

Malvazan nodded. "It was only a practice tournament. Endanko did not fight and neither did Rodizel; it would have been shaming to lose."

"Your dedication is highly impressive," she said.

Malvazan shrugged. "It is no secret that playing second fiddle to Dravadan galls me," he said. "If I am to make a reputation in my own right, where better than the sword-ring? If I can win the Garland everyone will want to know Malvazan."

"You will still only be a second son," she said.

"A man of talent will always have prospects," he said.

"Including marriage?" she asked, a spot of colour on her cheeks.

"That is not what I meant," said Malvazan levelly.

"The easiest way to advance yourself is to marry into a Prime House," she said, her voice louder.

"People are looking at you, Sanoutë."

"Tell me that is not your plan," she hissed. "Tell me you do not intend to throw me over for some Prime House whore."

"There is no point in talking to you when you are like this," said Malvazan. "Regardless of my inclinations, do you think House Vaggio or Rasteccio would have me simply because I won the Garland?"

Sanoutë pulled her arm away. "I know nothing of House Vaggio's intentions," she said, tears overflowing down her cheeks. "What I had hoped is that your regard for me would be enough for you to avoid such calculations."

She turned and on light feet skittered away across the lawn to the safety of the loggia.

Malvazan stood looking up at the stars. This quarrel with Sanoutë was irritating and unnecessary. Could she not accept matters as they were? He could hardly tell her that he had asked Crostadan not to make a formal betrothal request. For all her prattle about Astrizel, her father would take Malvazan without hesitation; but he was not ready for such a step. Realistically, even if he won the Garland—and there was no reason why he should not—his marriage prospects were not materially advanced. He was still a second son; he would never sit on the Masavory, and his own children would be ever further from the lines of succession. In two generations his descendants would, at best, be living at Folinette. It was difficult to imagine that any Prime House would view him as a desirable match. House Oreste, admittedly, had a surfeit of daughters, but even so… He could not regret his commitment to winning the Garland: he loved the training, felt an exhilaration in the Bezant he found nowhere else; but it was hard to argue that it was significantly advancing his broader goals.

A hand slapped down on his shoulder. "The idea of house receptions," said Glastarko, "is that you mingle with company, not stare up at the stars."

Malvazan bowed. Glastarko, another second son, did not seem burdened with resentments and introspections; his relationship with his elder brother Raguslan always seemed cordial, and Glastarko habitually had a smile on his face.

"I have quarrelled with Sanoutë," he said.

"Oh, women!" laughed Glastarko. "I can assure you they are not worth worrying about. Few things are more vexing than a quarrelsome woman."

"She is displeased that our betrothal is not proceeding more quickly."

"You are too young to concern yourself with betrothals," said Glastarko.

"I am twenty-four, and my betrothal was only last year."

"You are right, of course."

"If she plagues you now, she will be a shrew ever more. Now there—" he pointed to a young woman talking to Raguslan "—there is a woman to admire!"

"Who is that?" Glastarko had indicated a young woman with raven hair hanging artlessly loose.

"You do not know?" asked Glastarko in surprise.

"House Umbinzia does not always move in the same circles as you," said Malvazan.

"You need not be so tetchy. Anyway, that is Monichoë, the daughter of your host. A prize beyond beauty, which almost makes me regret my own betrothal—although do not let Tulerija hear you say that!"

Malvazan could see her face only in profile, and that at a distance; but the grace of her movements, the clear ring of her laugh, sent a jolt through him.

"Aha! You are not indifferent—and why should you be? Come, I will introduce you."

Glastarko strolled over with Malvazan at his side. "Raguslan, you are a wicked dog to monopolise the attention of such a beautiful woman."

Raguslan, only two years older than his brother but with an air of infinitely greater gravity, gave an uncertain smile. "Monichoë has nothing to fear from me: my wife is only on the loggia."

"Stepanija is indulgent, to allow you to fall under the spell of such a captivating sprite."

Monichoë fixed Glastarko with a raised eyebrow. "Glastarko, you are nothing but a bag of mischief." Malvazan had to acknowledge that she was even more alluring close up, her lips rich and red with the wine she had been sipping.

Glastarko bowed. "In beauty lies truth, madam; so I cannot argue with you."

"Who is your friend?" she asked.

"Allow me to introduce Malvazan of House Umbinzia."

Malvazan performed a careful bow.

"Umbinzia?" said Monichoë in a flat tone. "I had not realised my father had invited Crostadan."

"Come now, Monichoë," said Glastarko, "surely we can set aside house rivalries. Malvazan is a very good fellow."

Malvazan said nothing, tightening his mouth as he looked into Monichoë's face, which was undeniably alluring and surrounded by disorderly black curls. She held out her hand to kiss. "Forgive me, good Malvazan," she said. "I meant no offence, although I see you are affronted.

My father is always alert to questions of etiquette and protocol, and he rarely entertains beyond his own circle."

"No offence taken, Damoiselle," said Malvazan stiffly.

"Oh, now I have upset you!" cried Monichoë. "Come, how can I make amends?"

"You have upset me too!" said Glastarko. "I am very clear as to how you may make amends to me, even while Malvazan is making up his mind."

Monichoë smilingly shook her head. "Raguslan, be a good fellow and fetch me another drink," she said. "It seems that Malvazan's cup is empty — perhaps you would like to bring him one too."

Raguslan gave a curt bow and made his way back to the loggia to find a footman.

"You treat him like a puppy," said Glastarko with a grin. "Stepanija will be slashing your gowns if you continue."

"He likes to please me," said Monichoë. "That is the essence of gallantry and breeding, is not? Malvazan, I am sure you agree."

"I hardly know how to respond, Damoiselle. He would have been churlish to refuse your request."

"Monichoë is all too aware of her charms," said Glastarko, "and she has no qualms about using them. I pity the man who becomes her husband."

Malvazan, who was beginning to overlook her slight of House Umbinzia, did not have quite the same sentiments. Monichoë was a creature fascinating beyond any he had yet encountered, with a lightness of manner which made Sanoutë appear almost cloddish in comparison.

"Malvazan is a famous swordsman," said Glastarko. "Farlankas is training him to win the Garland."

Monichoë gave him her full attention. "Malvazan, how fascinating! How old are you?"

"Eighteen, Damoiselle."

"So you fight in two years? Such dedication! I cannot watch the fights in case someone is hurt, but swordsmen are so gallant, are they not?"

"In truth, Damoiselle, there is more drudgery than danger. The swords for the Garland are bated; there is no real danger."

Glastarko drawled: "Malvazan gives away a valuable trade secret. We wish the spectators to believe us in peril every time we fight."

"I am sure every person of sense knows the swords are blunted," said Malvazan.

"Do you say I lack sense?" said Monichoë, licking her lips with a precise pink tongue.

"Damoiselle, I—"

"She is sporting with you," said Glastarko. "It is what she does best."

"Now that you know injuries are rare," said Malvazan, "perhaps you would do me the honour of attending a future competition? I am sure I could only be inspired by your presence."

"Bravo!" cried Glastarko. "That's the way to do it, Malvazan! We will make a gallant of you yet."

"I doubt that my father would permit me to watch a swordfight, even with bated blades," she said. "But I thank you for your kind sentiments."

Glastarko clapped Malvazan on the shoulder. "You are of an age where we might do something with you, Malvazan. Perhaps one night soon we will visit some taverns together, and who knows what might happen. The Hour of Secret Deeds is not so-called for nothing."

"Glastarko, here is your mother," said Monichoë in a level voice.

Malvazan turned to see Raguslan returning, with an auburn-haired woman in the full flush of maturity accompanying them. Her chiselled features were striking but promised little of agreeability.

"Glastarko, wherever I go I find you flirting with someone," she said. "Your father did not spend the winter negotiating your betrothal for this reason."

Glastarko bowed. "Allow me to introduce my mother, Sulinka. This is Malvazan, of House Umbinzia."

Malvazan steeled himself for another slight. Instead Sulinka gave a frosty smile. "Raguslan speaks highly of you. He says you are a most accomplished swordsman."

Malvazan gave an airy wave. "Farlankas is a good master."

"He never did Raguslan much good," said Sulinka. "You should not burden yourself with false modesty. It is a luxury second sons cannot afford."

This so precisely matched Malvazan's opinion that he could not help but smile. "You are correct, of course, madam. I believe I am the best swordsman in my age group, and with Farlankas' guidance I intend to win the Garland."

"Good," said Sulinka. "I despise shilly-shallying. Glastarko, is he as good as he says?"

Glastarko drained his goblet. "I no longer spar with him," he said. "He is already too sharp for me."

Sulinka gave Malvazan a look of appraisal. "I shall go to the market tomorrow and place fifty florins on your victory. You have the look of a capable man. Come, Glastarko, your betrothed will expect to see you this evening."

Malvazan found himself left alone with Monichoë. For all her artlessness, he did not know what to say to her. He sipped his drink in silence.

"You do not weary me with chatter," she said.

"My apologies," he said. "I am no conversationalist."

"I intended no sarcasm," she said. "It is refreshing to enjoy quiet on occasion. You are a very serious young man."

"I do not have a convivial disposition," he said.

"We are the same age, you know," she said. "You seem to carry a greater weight in your soul than I."

"If I may speak candidly?"

"That would be something of a novelty."

"You are the daughter of one of the great houses. You need do nothing in life but be charming and agreeable. The second son of a lesser house—he has to adopt a different approach. He must seize that which he requires: it will not be given to him."

Monichoë was silent a moment, then she nodded. "I hope to meet you again, Malvazan. The young men of my acquaintance are more polished than you, but I think they have less depth. Sulinka is a shrewd judge of character, and you impressed her. She sees you as a man worth watching."

"I hope never to disappoint," said Malvazan.

"You must excuse me now," she said. "There are other young men my father will wish me to flatter. For now, adieu."

CHAPTER TEN

The fencing-master Rodizel maintained a loft occupying the entire top floor of a house on Ropemakers' Lane. The location was not the most august—there were those who would argue it was in the Chale and certainly not the Aspergantia—but it suited Rodizel's budget and, almost as important, was light and roomy enough to provide an ideal fencing gallery.

Todarko had not been to Ropemakers' Lane since he had watched Dravadan butcher Godaijkin. If this was the ultimate aim of swordsmanship, he wanted none of it. Today, however, he had a scheduled lesson with Rodizel, and the requirement to accompany his uncle to Roblegast in the evening had put him in a poor humour. Shortly after the start of the Hour of Afternoon Reflection he made his way up the stairs to the top floor, Bodazar panting in his wake.

Rodizel was lounging on a chaise, polishing a rapier. "Gentlemen! Good afternoon. I was not convinced you would come today. Our last lesson was perhaps sterner than I had intended."

Bodazar wiped his sweating brow with a kerchief. "I will not pretend I found the duel anything other than disgusting in every respect," he said.

Todarko added: "It is not unlikely that I shall have to fight a duel at some point in my life," he said. "If anything, the episode brought home the need for every gentleman to have some proficiency with the blade."

Rodizel nodded and set his blade down on the table. "It is a regrettable necessity that the Specchio must know how to fight—or to duel, at least. What lessons did you draw from your experience of last week?"

Todarko flung himself down on a chair. "Never fight Dravadan," he said with a harsh smile.

"There are worse lessons in life. You will have noticed, though, that Godaijkin had no choice. Dravadan's slanders against his wife had to be rebutted."

"A second lesson, perhaps, is never to marry."

"Also sound advice, for any number of reasons."

"Why," asked Bodazar, "did Dravadan feel the need to kill Godaijkin in the first place?"

Rodizel rose to his feet, bent his knees and stretched his arms above his head. "I know much about Dravadan, and suspect more. In my youth I was well acquainted with both him and his brother," he said. "However, your ten florins buys you a fencing lesson, not girlish gossip."

For the next hour Rodizel put his charges through all kinds of leaps and stretches and, ultimately, some blade-work. At last he called a halt, walked over to a ewer and poured out three wooden beakers of water.

"Good!" he said as they sat down. "Todarko, your feet move much better now, and your execution of Martigen's Move was excellent: I had to adjust my position to parry it. Your style has much of your father about it—a man of great natural gifts."

"You did not appear inconvenienced," said Todarko, wiping a hand across his brow.

Rodizel, who appeared not to be sweating at all, shrugged. "I have been fencing for over thirty years," he said. "Since I have also taught you, it is not hard to predict your moves. The fact remains that against most members of the Specchio—aggrieved husbands, perhaps—you would not be disgraced, and would beat most."

Bodazar still gasped on his chair. "And what encouragement can you offer me, Rodizel?"

Rodizel grimaced. "You are not yet ready for a duel," he said. "You should plan your conduct on this basis. Nonetheless, you are improving. If you worked a little on your fitness, you would not find the drills so draining. When two duellists of equal ability meet, the result is often decided by who tires first."

By the evening, Todarko was in a much better humour. His lesson with Rodizel had soothed away much of his tension. He had to acknowledge that Aladar's manse Roblegast was one of the most appealing in Taratanallos, and the elaborate double loggia was a delightful venue as the sun set before them. He stood on the upper level of the loggia looking at the crowd below.

"I promised you a sonnet, Nelanka," he said, "and I have brought it today."

"My husband will not thank you for it," said Nelanka, brushing a her breeze-blown dark hair from her eyes. In the distance Zanijel stood at his father's shoulder listening to the Emmen lord, Oricien, as he conversed with his host.

"I did not write it for your husband," said Todarko. "I wrote it for you."

Nelanka looked away. "You really are a mooncalf at times, Todarko," she said. "I don't know what you hope to achieve. I am married to your cousin, I have no intention, absolutely none, of…"

Todarko laughed. "I know. That is the entire point. I need not pretend and preen with you. Sometimes a sonnet is just a sonnet."

Nelanka set down her goblet on the balcony. "I don't begin to understand you, Darko—least of all when you affect simplicity. Do you think I don't know that the whole point of the sonnet is to annoy Zanijel?"

Todarko looked into her face. "Do you really believe that, Nel? I am all kinds of things you wouldn't like"—the image of Ivanka came into his mind—"but I am entirely honest when I talk to you. And however fickle you think I am, the one thing I take seriously is poetry. I don't give my sonnets away for spite: it would corrupt them, somehow."

Nelanka put her small hand over his. "It's a beautiful poem, Todarko: thank you. I am churlish to imagine any worse motive."

From behind them came a coarse voice: "What is this! Todarko, one day I will geld you!"

Nelanka sprang away from Todarko. "Zanijel! There was no impropriety. Todarko and I are as brother and sister."

Zanijel, tall and burly, barged over to Todarko. "Brother! He is a parasite on House Vaggio. One day, cousin or brother or whatever you are, I will kill you. When I am head of the house, look to your safety."

Todarko stepped towards him, a whipcord of suppressed tension. "If your lust for my death is so great, Zanijel, kill me know. My rapier is downstairs if you wish to try a pass."

"Another day. For now, there are matters I wish to discuss with my wife. You may leave."

Todarko leaned in, an inch from his cousin's face. "Be assured, Zanijel: if you hurt her, I will kill you. I will cut your throat in the night."

Before Zanijel could respond, Todarko turned on his heel and walked with measured dignity down the stairs.

The bulk of the guests were on the lower loggia; the evening was beginning to chill and groups were unconsciously gathering around the braziers. As Todarko came down the stairs, his uncle beckoned him over to the conversation to which he was attending.

"Have you seen Zanijel?" he asked. "He should be on hand when Lord Oricien is speaking."

Todarko shook his head. "I don't know where he is. Perhaps he is intoxicated."

Raguslan peered at him, evidently pondering a reproof. "Hmmmf. I find that unlikely."

From beside them came an urgent "Shhh! Lord Oricien is speaking!"

Todarko raised an eyebrow. He knew the speaker as well as he wanted, which was not at all: Benada, the wife of the host Aladar. She held her nose so high that it sat horizontally. Todarko considered whether a belch was the most appropriate response: he was on the point of concluding in the affirmative when his eye was caught by a strikingly beautiful woman, her red hair piled high on her head and held in place with a diamond-studded clip, her pale complexion dusted with freckles. She gave Todarko a sympathetic smile at Benada's airs. Todarko rapidly suppressed his belch and smiled back. Who was the woman? He so rarely attended the social gatherings of the Specchio that he was ignorant on the matter. Nonetheless, a person of such beauty and generous temperament would surely repay further acquaintance.

As Aladar and Oricien spoke, the red-haired woman slid away with a quiet grace, perhaps to find a drink. His own goblet, conveniently, was also empty, and he set off towards the liveried footman superintending the wine table.

"Allow me," said Todarko with a bow, and handed her a goblet.

The woman raised an eyebrow. "Aladar keeps slaves to distribute the drinks," she said with a half-smile. "I am honoured and gratified that you should take such a menial duty in hand."

"Consider me your slave, if you choose, madam. I am Todarko, of House Vaggio."

"Ah, the poet!" she cried. "I imagined an older man."

Todarko gulped at his drink. "You are familiar with my poetry?"

The woman gave an airy wave. "Your sonnets are read occasionally at certain afternoon salons," she said. "I confess that yours are better than most."

Todarko could scarcely believe his luck. The woman was beautiful, intelligent, and an admirer of his poetry!

"Let us step aside awhile," he said. "I confess that the political conversation bores me."

Again she raised an eyebrow in what was clearly a characteristic gesture. "I hope you do not mean to malign my husband."

"Husband?"

"I am Linnalitha, the wife of the Dignified Dravadan."

Todarko could feel his shoulders sag. Where was the justice that a remarkable woman, an exemplar of taste and sensitivity, should be cast away on a man like Dravadan?

"Are you quite well, Todarko? You seem a little pale."

"It is the effect of the moon, madam. Poets know that it blanches the complexion."

Linnalitha appeared to be trying not to laugh. "Forgive me, Todarko. In truth your reputation, not just as a poet but as an admirer of the weaker sex, goes before you. I could not resist a little game."

Todarko felt flush creep down his cheeks; even in the moonlight it would be visible. Then he laughed. He could not be angry, especially with such a beautiful woman. He was justly caught in his own trap.

"Touché, madam," he said. "I now understand why ladies are not suffered to fight duels: they would be invincible. Come, let us take a turn around the gardens. I promise I will be all meek humility."

She slipped a hand into the crook of his arm. "Very well," she said. "After all, the politics are as tedious as you suggest. And I truly do like your poems."

Todarko shook his head ruefully. Linnalitha remained, once more, a step ahead of him. He realised with a flash of surprise that he was quite enjoying the experience.

For a house within the city walls, Aladar's gardens were extensive. The ground as it sloped away towards the far boundary was lit with soft lanthorns, and Todarko found it a pleasant experience to walk with Linnalitha. She was not talkative, but he found in her silence a gravity hinting at hidden depths, not the offensive reserve of so many high-born women.

"How have we never met before?" he asked as he helped her through a small gate set into the path. "I would have remembered had I ever seen you."

Linnalitha shrugged. "My husband is a man conscious of his place," she said. "Your uncle has only recently become of use to him. In any event, I know you much better than you know me."

"How so?"

"Consider," she said. "As a woman of breeding I wear the Hood and Veil when I am out on the street. I have seen you around the town, when you would not have recognised me from any other woman of a Specchio family. We see much from behind our veils. Your only chance to have seen my face would have been to be invited to my husband's house; and you are not one for making calls with your uncle."

"No indeed," Todarko replied. "I may be a more attentive nephew in future—particularly if he will be waiting more frequently upon Dravadan."

The moonlight caught a flickering smile on Linnalitha's face. "You cannot resist the silver tongue of flattery," she said. "It does not make you a more charming companion."

"In my experience, few women are averse to flattery."

"I am one," she said. "I prefer honesty and plain speaking."

"What, then, if my honest and plain-spoken opinion was that you were the most beautiful woman of my experience? I would be denying truth to remain silent, but denounced as a rogue for uttering it."

She sat on a wooden bench and gestured for him to join her. "Do you know who my husband is?"

"I have many deficiencies of thought and person," said Todarko, "but senility is not one of them. I seem to recall you told me not ten minutes ago."

"That isn't what I meant," she said, looking into his eyes. "Dravadan is one of the greatest men in the city. Of all the men who favour alliance with Emmen, he is second only to Aladar, and he has qualities Aladar does not. If this embassy of Oricien's bears fruit, there will be no-one mightier than my husband. And the Emmen party is in the ascendant. You do not wish to make an enemy of Dravadan, Todarko. I have known you only a few minutes; already I have a sense of the kind of man you are. My husband will not take kindly to your games."

"Any man would be jealous of such a wife."

She shook her head. "Jealousy does not come into it. He married me for advantage, and he has his advantage. What he will not brook is disrespect. Forgive my candour: your reputation is of one of the most dissipated young men of Taratanallos. Dravadan will not wish our names to be linked."

Todarko stiffened. "You appeared to have no objection to walking in the gardens."

"Do not bridle," she said. "Sometimes I follow my own inclinations. All I am saying is that you are not dallying with Ivanka here."

Todarko did not want to know the extent of Linnalitha's knowledge of this affair: his conduct did not withstand even rudimentary scrutiny, even if her condition were hushed up.

"Perhaps we should return to the loggia, madam. I would not wish to expose you to adverse comment."

"I was raised with three brothers," she said. "Adolescent sulking is not an attractive characteristic."

Todarko acknowledged the justice of the observation with a bow. He smiled. "The night is becoming chill," he said. "We should return in any event."

By the time they reached the loggia the party was repairing indoors, to Aladar's ballroom, lit with a hundred glorious glass globes, each containing an essence of luminance which surpassed understanding. Linnalitha gave his elbow a brief discreet squeeze and slipped away on noiseless feet to find Dravadan. Todarko gave his head a rueful shake: Linnalitha was a woman who would delight and infuriate in equal measure. It was unlikely she was unaware of the fact.

"Where have you been?" asked Nelanka as went over to join her.

"I thought it best to leave you and Zanijel alone for a while. It does not do to upset the husbands of great ladies."

She smiled. "When was I ever a great lady, Darko? Zanijel has gone home with a peevish headache, so your concern is unwarranted."

A bell, clear and high, rang out in the crisp air of the ballroom. Aladar raised a hand to silence the conversation.

"My ladies and gentlemen," he said in the rich confident voice Todarko remembered from the dockside. "I am fortunate tonight to host an informal gathering, modest as it is, to welcome visitors from a far shore to my home. Lord Oricien and his entourage represent a new opportunity for Taratanallos to secure its place during this uncertain pavane between Emmen and Gammerling. In this informal setting, I can be candid in my hope that we may establish a lasting alliance between our realms; and I am gratified beyond measure to announce the endorsement of High Viator Udenko to this programme. We are not all as devout in our adherence to the Way of Harmony as we should be, but we all recognise that Udenko is the spiritual father of our city. Udenko, would you like to say a few words?"

"Just what we require," whispered Todarko to Nelanka. "A sermon to finish the evening." He looked around for Linnalitha, but her face was impassive alongside her husband.

High Viator Udenko was helped from his chair by a black-clad Consiglio, to stand with a precarious erectness. Old as he was, Todarko had to admit that he carried a certain magnetism.

"I bid you greetings," he said. "It is rare—too rare, perhaps—for one of grandees to invite a Viator into his home. It is a loss to the Specchio that so infrequently do they avail ourselves of our counsel on their Way. Be that as it may, I commend the work that Aladar has so nobly carried out over the past years to build our friendships with the Emmenrule. You all know that our own devotional practices in Taratanallos are characterised as heresy by the Consorts in Gammerling. I say it is no heresy to follow the True Way! It is the Consorts who are heretics!"

Aladar leaned and whispered something in Udenko's ear. He appeared to share Todarko's view that a sermon was not required at this point.

Udenko flapped Aladar away. "Be that as it may," he continued, "and everyone here might with profit consider these matters in more detail, it is not my purpose in speaking tonight. Lord Oricien brings with him the assurance that King Enguerran considers that questions of faith should be settled by the individual conscience. In this, he urges the people to Taratanallos to take counsel from their own Viators. Is this not correct, my lord?"

Oricien stepped forward and bowed to the Viator. "It is indeed. King Enguerran has no wish to prescribe the ways in which Hissen and Animaxia may be worshipped."

"With this in mind," said Udenko, "I can give my wholehearted support to Lord Oricien's proposals for a closer bond of amity between the Emmenrule and Taratanallos, the last free city. I lend the voice of the Viatory to the wise counsels of the noble Aladar."

"I thank you," said Aladar.

CHAPTER ELEVEN

Oricien was coming to realise that a large proportion of his embassy was likely to be spent in evening receptions in the manses of the Specchio. He looked around to see Ribauldequin engaged in animated conversation with two young women; Iselin, by contrast, was leaning forward and muttering confidentially to Dravadan. Both, in their own way, seemed in their element. Oricien shook his head in frustration. Not only were the events unutterably tedious, but neither Ribauldequin nor Iselin was materially advancing King Enguerran's interests. Ribauldequin would soon enough end up in a duel with a jealous husband, while Iselin's diplomacy would be better employed on those who were not already his allies.

"You appear pensive amidst such frivolity, my lord."

Oricien turned from the balcony on which he was leaning, looking out on the throng below.

"Madam Nelanka! Am I so transparent?"

Nelanka gave a wan smile. "Those who are keen to avoid the company normally make their way up here," she said. "It is not where I would expect to find the Emmenrule's ambassador."

"There is nothing I can do here, madam," he said, swilling the last of his wine around its goblet. "I assume that every member of the Specchio present already supports the Emmen alliance."

Nelanka paused and nodded. "No doubt. All the more reason, then, to give yourself over to frivolity."

Oricien stood upright. "I am not, for better and worse, a frivolous man. In truth, such occasions bore me."

Nelanka raised her eyebrows in mock surprise. "An invitation to Roblegast is the most desired card in the city. Aladar's favour is highly prized. He would be dismayed to learn your true opinion."

Oricien smiled briskly. "I am sure you will not tell him. And you must have your own reasons for standing here, away from the throng."

Nelanka laughed, a brittle high sound. "It is nothing, a domestic matter only."

"I noticed your husband leave."

Nelanka shrugged. "He quarrelled with Todarko. The situation is not unusual."

"Your family does not seem a model of amity."

"Todarko and Zanijel have never been friends. The Specchio breeds rivalries as a dog breeds fleas."

"I am no stranger to contention," said Oricien with a smile.

Nelanka produced a paper. "Todarko wrote a sonnet for my birthday. My husband was naturally outraged."

Oricien looked sideways at her profile. "Surely the situation is innocent; to argue otherwise would be to question your virtue."

Nelanka turned to look into his face. "You may care to explain that to Zanijel."

"Gladly," said Oricien with more enthusiasm than he had intended.

"Forgive me, my lord. I spoke at random in my vexation. I do not mean to criticise my husband. There are extenuating circumstances."

"How so?" asked Oricien.

"Todarko's reputation is not spotless. There are those who call him a tyrant to the female sex; he is certainly a man who enjoys female company."

"Nonetheless, your husband should not doubt you, unless you have given him cause."

Nelanka flushed. "I am unclear what you are insinuating. I am a good wife, and no-one should think otherwise."

"Madam, I—"

"Your ways may be very different in Emmen, sir, but in Taratanallos a woman's only possession is her reputation."

"I did not mean to suggest—"

"Please excuse me, my lord. I will be expected to circulate among the guests, even if you do not wish to."

Oricien watched her pick her careful way down the stairs. It seemed the women of Taratanallos were as unfathomable and capricious as those of Croad or Emmen.

After a decent interval Oricien made his own way back to the ballroom. It would be necessary to evolve a new strategy with Iselin tomorrow which involved grandees other than Aladar, Dravadan and Raguslan, if only to take the measure of their opponents. For tonight, it seemed there was little better to do than seek out some more of Aladar's admittedly excellent wines.

Todarko too was bored and, like Oricien, finding the wine tray the most satisfactory countermeasure. At that moment came a mighty pounding on the door. "Open up! Open in the name of the Consiglio!"

A footman who skittered over the polished floor and turned the huge key in the lock. Todarko's curiosity was tempered with an undercurrent of alarm. The Consiglio did not appear at the Hour of Secret Deeds at a house like Roblegast without a pressing reason.

The door swung back in a noiseless arc which was a testament to the oiled hinges and the slaves who maintained them. Into the room stepped three men in the black of the Consiglio, their black hats tucked respectfully under their arm.

"My apologies for disturbing you," said the first of them. "I am the Elevant Kesinaro; these are my assistants Mirmijlo and Vislanko. There are matters of importance we must discuss with the Dignified Aladar."

Aladar set his goblet down with a composed grace. "I am he. I take it this business need not be transacted before my guests?"

"This is not a matter where secrecy is possible, sir. The news is already all over the town. By now, you and your guests may be the only ones in ignorance of it."

Aladar gave a curt nod. "If you must speak, then do so quickly."

"Very well," said Kesinaro. "Your cog Humility, faring back from Mettingloom, has been taken by the corsair Ion Issio. The facts are confirmed by the Humility's captain, Ljuboman. The cargo is lost to you."

Distracted by some movement at the periphery of his vision, Todarko turned to see Dravadan, an unreadable expression on his face.

No flicker crossed Aladar's face. "You are right to bring this to my attention," he said. "This matter touches more than me alone. You will be aware that I hold the First Monopoly on silks. Humility was laden with a substantial argosy of the finest Mettingloom tang: there will be no silks in Taratanallos this year."

From around the room came a murmur just at the threshold of audibility. An entire cargo of silks was a vast argosy, an immense packet of wealth in one place: to lose it in one stroke was a disaster.

"My sympathies are with you, sir," said Kesinaro. "The activities of these Garganet corsairs become bolder by the year: no doubt the Masavory will wish consider a punitive course of action."

Aladar's mouth tightened as he said: "The role of the Consiglio is to advise the Masavory, and I thank you for your counsel on this occasion. If you will excuse me a moment, there are matters I wish to adjust in my private chambers. My lords, High Viator; I pray you will not interrupt your revels during my absence."

He turned with a stately gravity and walked from the room with a measured tread.

"That," said Todarko aside to Nelanka, "is how to deal with disaster. You would have thought he had lost a two-florin wager on a cockfight."

"He must be ruined," said Nelanka.

"Inconvenienced, perhaps," said Todarko. "The man who owns Roblegast cannot be ruined."

From beside him came a soft voice. "You might be surprised," said Linnalitha. "A man like Aladar has great wealth, but also great expenses. Many on the Masavory are dependent on indulgent creditors."

"Nelanka, this is Linnalitha," said Todarko. "She is Dravadan's wife, so no doubt she speaks with authority."

Linnalitha seemed to shudder a second as Nelanka said: "We are acquainted. How do you, Linnalitha?"

"Well, I thank you, Nelanka. I hope your husband is not unwell; I saw him leave earlier."

"A passing indisposition," said Nelanka. "He will soon be himself again. Your own husband will not be inconvenienced by tonight's events, I trust?

Dravadan and Aladar have been seen much together. Fortunately I am sure his own credit is exemplary."

Linnalitha's green eyes flashed and a brief flicker animated her face. "My husband would not entrust his wealth to the seas. He is fortunate to enjoy two of the finest First Monopolies in Taratanallos: salt and battlecat pelts have no need to travel by ship. I thank you for your concern."

"I had no idea you two were friends," said Todarko. "I have only made the acquaintance of Linnalitha tonight."

Linnalitha looked down at her feet. Nelanka said: "When the men of the Specchio are taking their pleasures, the ladies must amuse themselves. We have met on occasion at Blagira's salon."

"What a feast of beauty such events must be!" declared Todarko. "Maybe I will don a veil and slip in unnoticed!"

Linnalitha shot him a withering glance. Nelanka shook her head: "This is hardly the time for your idiotic gallantries. Look, something is happening."

Todarko turned to see Kesinaro whispering to the other Consigli. Vislanko walked over to Aladar's wife Benada and spoke short urgent sentences. Immediately the two left the room with Aladar's teenage son. The third Consigli, Mirmijlo, cleared his throat.

"I have grave news," he said. "You will all wish to gather your effects and leave immediately. It grieves me to report that the Dignified Aladar has gone to his chamber and taken poison. He has this night completed his journey along the Way."

From beside Todarko came a piercing scream. "No!" It was Linnalitha.

"Madam, is there anything I can—" said Todarko.

"No! Leave me alone, Todarko!"

He put a hand on her arm to try to calm her. "A seat, a drink perhaps. You must compose yourself."

She let out a bark of laughter, a harsh crude sound to come from a throat of such delicacy. "Compose myself! Animaxia take you all!" Her voice dropped. "I must be with my husband."

She dashed across the room to where Dravadan and Raguslan stood. Raguslan appeared insensible at the news. Todarko saw Linnalitha touch her husband's shoulder, receive a rapid reproof. Linnalitha seemed to say something in response: Dravadan made a decisive sawing gesture.

Todarko considered intervening. This was no way to treat any woman, least of all a wife.

"Take me home, Todarko," said Nelanka from his side. "My own husband is absent, and my father will wish to consider his advantage in the situation. He will not leave now."

"But Linnalitha…"

"She does not need you and she is not your concern. You would be well advised to steer clear of Dravadan's wife." said Nelanka. "I am your cousin and I do need you. Kindly fetch my veil and we will leave immediately."

Todarko bowed. "Of course, Nelanka."

CHAPTER TWELVE

As the summer unfolded so did Malvazan's schemes. He made sound progress with the blade under Farlankas but, perhaps more importantly, fell into the circle of Glastarko and Raguslan who also patronised the school. Invitations to Tappinetto, the manse of House Vaggio, were common, and while the austere Jirno, head of the house, paid him little attention, Sulinka was always solicitous of his comfort. All taken with all, Malvazan felt that his schemes were proceeding solidly, if with no great rapidity. The only matter which unsettled him was Monichoë, who often drifted across his path and more frequently disturbed his dreams. Now that she had turned sixteen, she could not promenade down The Archgate without Hood and Veil, but Malvazan became adept at identifying her by her sensuous walk; when they spoke in the street, the veil could not conceal the depthless pools of her eyes, and if anything he found her even more alluring.

Her behaviour, though, remained maddeningly inconsistent. Sometimes he would visit her father's manse Hanglenook in company with Glastarko or Raguslan and she would be affability itself, or even draw him aside for private conversation; on other days, particularly if young men from other Prime Houses were on hand, she would spare him no attention at all. Malvazan on reflection convinced himself that she nurtured a partiality for him which she would not allow herself to acknowledge because of the obscurity of House Umbinzia. There was little he could do to rectify this: his plans with regard to his own destiny were not modest, and as they came to fruition he would naturally become a more attractive match. His concerns in this regard were that her father Kropiselko, blind to Malvazan's merits, would have betrothed her before his own worth became readily apparent.

One evening Malvazan was taking supper at Tappinetto; he now rarely ate at home if he could avoid it, so insufferable was the scorn of his brother.

"You are out of spirits tonight," said Raguslan. "Is your training going amiss?"

Malvazan gave a wan smile. "Farlankas is no more demanding than usual," he said. "But sometimes I wonder how I will achieve my goals."

Glastarko laughed. "That depends on your goals. Mine are rarely more exalted than a tavern or a wench, and easily enough satisfied."

Sulinka gave him a glance of reproof. "Malvazan has more complex motivations," she said. "In this he should be encouraged. One day Raguslan will be the head of this house, Glastarko, and I shall expect you to support him; and a friend such as Malvazan will not be a trivial gain."

"Raguslan knows he can count upon me," said Glastarko. "But the responsibility will be his alone."

Sulinka looked at Malvazan from under her hooded blue eyes. "Malvazan, you should not be despondent. You are of good birth, and a swordsman always catches the eye. When you win the Garland, you will be a man to reckon with. Are you not often invited to Hanglenook?"

Malvazan set down his fork. "Only in company with your sons, madam."

"Nonsense!" declared Sulinka in a tone which did not invite contradiction. "Kropiselko is not a man to embrace parvenus. You would not be at Hanglenook if he did not want you there. You should have more confidence in your prospects."

Malvazan nodded. In general this was his own view; it was only Monichoë's intolerable flirting with Hristano of House Rasteccio last time he had seen her which had so unsettled him. He set his jaw; there was only way to deal with this.

"Madam, will you excuse me? There is an urgent item of business I have neglected to deal with."

Two long-glasses later, at the Hour of Noble Pleasures, Malvazan stood at the portico of Hanglenook in the outfit of crushed indigo velvet he considered his most presentable: sober, respectable and clearly expensive. Kropiselko's factotum Veltomilo eyed him in surprise. "You are not expected tonight, sir. Damoiselle Monichoë is not at home."

Malvazan gave a brisk nod. "My business is with the Dignified Kropiselko, if he is at liberty."

"Kindly wait a moment while I establish his wishes," said Veltomilo. Some minutes later he returned and wordlessly conducted Malvazan up a flight of stairs to Kropiselko's private study.

Kropiselko, a tall dark-haired man of habitually stern demeanour, looked at Malvazan without any great cordiality, and indicated a seat with a jerk of the head. Malvazan had never been in the room before; the walls were lined with books, with the exception of the one whose window gave out over the bay, tonight to display the moonlight rippling on the waves.

"This is an unexpected pleasure, Malvazan," said Kropiselko in a cool uninflected voice. "Will you take wine?"

Kropiselko appeared to have a cup of his own to hand, and in truth Malvazan's own mouth was somewhat dry.

"I will, thank you, sir," he said, his voice kept cool with an effort. Kropiselko poured him a goblet, passed it over, and sipped from his own.

"There are few things in which I envy House Granguigi ," said Kropiselko. "Nonetheless I have long felt it must be pleasing to enjoy the wine monopoly. Slaves and jade are no doubt more lucrative, but there is something very satisfying about thinking that every tun of wine coming off the ships belongs, in a sense, to oneself. Do you not think so?"

"House Umbinzia is not in the habit of envying House Granguigi, sir. So long as they recognise their place, all is well."

Kropiselko sat back in his seat with a half-smile, placing his goblet on the desk before him. "Place, place—it all comes down to place, does it not? Your father is jealous of Granguigi?"

"I would not speak for him, sir; although I imagine that he would regard jealousy of an inferior as an unworthy emotion."

Kropiselko raised an eyebrow. "It is engraved on the Tablets at Masavory that all houses of the Specchio are equal, is it not?"

"Well, yes—"

"A view I would have expected you to argue with vehemence, seated as you are in the parlour of House Zano."

"Ah—I have not come—argument of any sort is the farthest thing from my mind."

Kropiselko's blue eyes remained fixed on him. "Of course, of course. It is churlish of me to foist my views upon you without inviting you to transact your own business. I take it your purpose in arriving, unannounced, at the Hour of Noble Pleasures, goes beyond the merely social."

Now that the moment was on hand Malvazan was uncertain how to approach it. Reliance on natural facility or glibness seemed now a rash course.

"You have been kind enough to offer me admittance to Hanglenook many times in recent years," he began.

Kropiselko nodded. More was clearly required.

"My respect and admiration for House Zano know no bounds; I am sensible of the honour you have done me, and seek to deserve it."

Kropiselko made an easy gesture. "Such social intercourse is the stuff of the Specchio. I would hate to imagine you consider yourself in my debt for the occasional supper."

"I myself have certain ambitions with regard to my future," said Malvazan in a halting voice. "These go beyond the perpetual life of a second son. You will be aware that many good judges consider I may win the Garland of the Foils next year."

"In this, of course, you have my good wishes. My knowledge of swordcraft is largely theoretical: there is no real assistance I can render you."

"Moni—your daughter—is always kind enough to take an interest—I might even say a keen interest—in my progress."

Kropiselko's blue eyes seemed to grow a shade chillier. "She has always been brought up to demonstrate an interest in the concerns of others. So much is common politeness."

Malvazan took a great gulp of his wine. "I fancy there may be something more in this instance, sir."

"I am, in all candour, indifferent as to the veracity of her interest in your blade-craft."

"It is not wholly irrelevant, sir."

Kropiselko's lips were a slash in his pallid face. "Indeed?"

Malvazan drained off the rest of his goblet.

"Since the context of our present discussion is that I wish to secure your consent to our betrothal."

There was an icy silence which felt to Malvazan several centuries in duration.

"Your betrothal to Monichoë?" said Kropiselko in a level tone.

"Yes, sir."

"Tell me, Malvazan—as a matter of interest—have you secured my daughter's consent before soliciting mine?"

"Ah—no, sir. I judged that such a course would have been imprudent."

"Imprudent? You appear in my study, uninvited, to ask that the hand of my only daughter should be bestowed upon House Umbinzia, and now you think to consider matters of prudence?"

"Do I take it," said Malvazan in as calm a tone as he could muster, "that you withhold your consent?"

Kropiselko rose to his feet. "I am pleased to see that you are as perspicacious as you are prudent. I believe we have nothing further to discuss."

"But—"

"Whatever you wish to say, Malvazan, I would be inclined to reconsider. I already regard you as a knave, a fool and a buffoon: do you wish my opinion of you to sink yet further?"

Head drooping, Malvazan slunk from the study.

"When you have something to offer House Zano, Malvazan, come back then!" called Kropiselko at his back.

Wordlessly Malvazan filed from Hanglenook, down the hill and back to his home, where he went immediately to bed without a word to anyone.

CHAPTER THIRTEEN

A ghastly silence hung over the ballroom at Roblegast at the announcement of Aladar's death. There was nothing Oricien could usefully achieve here; any attempts at advancing his embassy were, for the evening at least, concluded, and his condolences could only be of the pro forma variety given his slight acquaintance with the deceased.

He signalled to Iselin and Ribauldequin and they departed Roblegast with the minimum of ceremony, and passed down the Archgate in a silence punctuated only by the occasional hiccough from Ribauldequin. Above them the moon looked down with the indifference it had shone on a million other human tragedies.

By the time they reached the Castle of Crostestini the news seemed to be all over the city. The Consigli at the portal admitted them to the building with a gravity heightened even beyond their usual mien. It was with some relief that Oricien finally shut the door behind them.

"If you are not too tired, gentlemen," he said, "there is much we might discuss."

Iselin seated himself carefully while Ribauldequin sprawled along a chaise.

"Well, Iselin," said Oricien. "What does this mean for our embassy?"

"Oricien!" cried Ribauldequin. "A man is not yet cold in his death—can we not show him some respect?"

Oricien ran a hand through his hair. "We are here on the business of King Enguerran. Social niceties and finer feelings must of necessity take second place."

"Lord Oricien is right," said Iselin. "Our first thoughts must not be of sympathy, but our own advantage."

Ribauldequin shrugged. "My contribution to your debate is likely to be brief."

Oricien turned his gaze to Iselin. "Can we still carry the Specchio?"

Iselin stroked his beard. "The Emmen alliance rested on Aladar and Dravadan. There are many who counted themselves friends of Aladar who despise Dravadan."

"That is strong language."

"Dravadan is a new man, from an unfashionable house, whose eminence is based on some highly questionable actions and a healthy dose of fear."

Oricien poured himself a glass of wine from the pitcher on the low table at his side. "An ideal associate, I would have thought. It is not necessary that we like him, merely that he is efficient."

"There is no doubt that some of Aladar's supporters will not transfer their votes to Dravadan. Blood carries great weight in Taratanallos, and Dravadan's is not of the clearest."

Ribauldequin uttered a caw of laughter. "So says the candlemaker's grandson!"

"Enough," said Oricien. "Iselin, it seems to me that we have little choice but to support Dravadan. If we show our confidence in him, will that not buttress his standing in the city?"

"My lord, Dravadan is profoundly untrustworthy. I could tell you stories of his past which would chill your blood."

Oricien waved the point away. "I do not conduct my business on rumour and tittle-tattle. Let us make our support for Dravadan as manifest as we can."

"I do not like the man, my lord."

"That is irrelevant. What do we know of his finances?"

"Ha! I would have said that Aladar was safe from ruin."

"So he should have been, the amount we had been bribing him. Am I right in thinking we had paid him 120,000 florins?"

Iselin sucked in his lip. "I believe so, my lord."

"And yet still he was bankrupt."

"Once creditors call in their debts, there is no other way for it."

"What then of Dravadan?"

"I understand he intends to sell his monopoly on battlecat pelts."

"Short of money, then? Surely he would not sell a prestigious monopoly without dire need."

Iselin leaned back in his chair and waved a didactic figure. "All depends on the price he can extract. It may be good business to feel the chink of silver in his vaults."

"Tomorrow we will go to the bank and present our letter of credit," said Oricien. "I am sure that the Dignified Dravadan would not look askance at a princely gift."

Iselin leaned forward. "Are you certain this is wise, my lord? This is a dangerous man, and Aladar is no longer there to check him."

"I see no alternative. In addition, I will put in place the policy you should already have pursued—that of conciliating our enemies. You will arrange for me to visit the leaders of the opposing factions, whoever they may be."

"Sir! Do you question my conduct to date?"

Oricien rose from his seat. "Forgive me, Iselin: it is late, I am tired, and I have not the composure to season my words. Nonetheless, to carry the Specchio we should be reaching an understanding of those who oppose us. If your policies have tended in an opposite direction, you may construe that as a criticism."

Iselin gave a curt bow. "Good night, my lord. We will speak again tomorrow." He turned and left the room.

Oricien sat back down. There was something about Iselin's prickly ambition to which he could not warm. The man was a loyal and devoted servant of the king, low birth or not; and he had knowledge of Taratanallos and contacts in the city which could only be valuable. He would have to set aside his dislike and work constructively with him, now more than ever.

He looked across at Ribauldequin, now softly snoring on the chaise. Here was a man of high birth and great charm; and yet to all intents and purposes he was useless, concerned with nothing more than wenching and drinking. Oricien reached again for the wine pitcher, then thought better and stood up.

Ribauldequin could sleep on the chaise for the night; Oricien opened the door to his bedchamber and composed himself for sleep.

CHAPTER FOURTEEN

Todarko absented himself from breakfast at Tappinetto the next morning; he had appetite neither for food nor the endless analysis of the situation in which Raguslan and Zanijel would be certain to indulge. Instead he slipped down to the kitchens, packed a bag with half a loaf, a flask of water and his writing materials. Leaving discreetly by the back exit he took himself through the narrow streets until he found himself on the northern walls away from all human society.

Normally the view to the west, stretching up into the wooded hills which protected the city from land attack, soothed him and put his mind in that state of receptiveness he needed for his verse. But today, although he had his leather-bound book, he could not achieve the necessary repose. The events of last night were too tumultuous. He had not known Aladar in any significant way; indeed he struggled to remember any conversation they had had. But Aladar had been a great man, one of the most important in Taratanallos. The suddenness and completeness of his fall was surely a lesson, although he was not sure exactly what conclusions to draw. The Viators no doubt would have preached that human ambition was not always the Way of Harmony (and no doubt Aladar had died in Disharmony): for all his superbia, he had been brought as low as the meanest labourer in the Chale.

He realised that even this was not the most profound shock. After all, he already knew that political ambitions and the machinations of the Specchio were arid and unfulfilling—the life of his uncle was sufficient proof of that. The chill came from the fact that it could have been anyone who had fallen so suddenly. Aladar had risen on that last morning with just another day in front of him, with schemes, ambitions, hopes for the future; yet a single knock on his door had brought him to the end of his life. He had faced the reversal with a dignity which Todarko could not but admire. If peril descended on him so quickly, would he be able to show such fortitude? Maybe Aladar had died in Harmony after all.

He packed up his things and made to walk back into the town. As he turned he looked down into the streets. He saw two slender ladies walking along the street, anonymous under their hoods and veils; he wondered what brought them to this part of the city. Who were they? The dress of the female Specchio may have been designed primarily to protect their modesty, but it was also an excellent disguise. Maybe one of them was the lovely lady

Linnalitha. Despite his gloomy mood he smiled. What a glorious creature she had been! Such grace, such liveliness! He wondered if she were happy with Dravadan. Marriages among the Specchio were generally contracted for reasons wider than, and not always including, simple affection. His behaviour at Roblegast last night had not bespoken any strong partiality.

He toyed with the idea of trying to arrange a further meeting with her. Had she not shown some signs of liking for him? Reluctantly he set the idea aside. Linnalitha was a married woman—not that marriage in itself was an insurmountable barrier to dalliance—and her husband was not a wise enemy to contract. Dravadan was a proud man, thin-skinned and unlikely to connive at an amour with his wife. There were plenty of beautiful women inside the Specchio, and indeed outside it, who would be more suitable playfellows. Still, what harm would it do to write her a sonnet?

Todarko had arranged to meet Bodazar in the Northern Star at the Hour of Afternoon Repast. He was a little late, and as he stepped into the gloomy interior, which somehow seemed darker in the day than at night, Bodazar was already sitting in a booth with a half-empty mug.

"Two ales, Florijko, and a jug of mussels if they are good."

Florijko dipped the mugs into the beer barrel. "This is the Northern Star," he said. "The mussels are as they always are. Would you characterise that as good?"

Todarko sighed. "It is certainly adequate," he said. "Put some more vinegar in there too, if you please."

He carried the mugs over to the Bodazar's booth and sat down. A pretty maid scurried over with the mussels. One of the things Todarko had always liked about drinking in the Chale was that the women did not have to wear the Specchio veils. It was rare to see dimples in the better part of town.

Bodazar gave Todarko a curt nod. Evidently the news of Aladar's death had spread.

"Grim news," said Todarko. "Who would have thought to see Aladar fall?"

Bodazar shrugged. "Like Jadinko, he brought it on himself. What kind of man would entrust his fortunes to one ship?"

"A desperate one, I suppose. For a fact Aladar was no fool."

Bodazar had moved onto his second mug. "His conduct was unwise by any standard. Ion Issio is known to be active in the straits, and he has taken three great argosies this past month," said Bodazar. "Who knows, your new friend Dravadan could be next if the Masavory does not take strong action."

"I understand that Dravadan does not entrust his fortunes to the sea. Even Ion Issio will struggle to capture battlecat pelts as they travel down the Dimonetto Road."

Bodazar signalled for more ale. "You are unusually well-informed as to Dravadan's activities."

Todarko smiled. "I was introduced to his wife last night. She had many interesting observations."

Bodazar returned a quick grin. "I see how it is. Not another conquest?"

"Linnalitha is too virtuous a woman to be ensnared in an evening."

"So you have plans?"

"I do not. Dravadan is not a man to antagonise."

"When has a jealous husband ever worried you, Darko?"

"This is no everyday cuckold—and in any event, I have no certainty of Linnalitha's partiality."

Bodazar gave his head a shake. "Always it begins this way. I wager you are in her bed within the month."

Todarko reached into his pouch for a coin to lay down, then dropped it back again.

"Linnalitha is not a lady to demean in that way," he said. "One does not wager on the favours of such a woman."

"It has not stopped you in the past," said Bodazar. "What about Clatida?"

"The situations were not comparable," said Todarko. "Clatida was a woman of a very different sort."

Bodazar set down his mug. "Am I to take it you have a serious regard for Linnalitha?"

"I have only met her once."

Bodazar looked down. "Once can be enough."

"That sounded like the conviction of experience."

A glimmer came into Bodazar's dark eyes. "This is not a topic for today."

"How not?"

"This morning my father has cancelled my betrothal," he said in a fast low voice. "My prospects have been dashed."

"I did not even know you were betrothed, Zar!"

"Strictly speaking, I was not. My father had been contracting an advantageous match, and we hoped to announce it soon. I had met the lady and found her delightful: demure, reserved, with a pleasing wit and every promise of an ardent heart. You know that House Belario is not wealthy: we have long despaired of a good match. But my father's adherence to the

Gammerling party looked to have secured a connection based on political advantage. I am sorry I did not mention it to you; in truth, I thought you would scoff at a match of affections."

Until yesterday, I might have done, thought Todarko. "Who is the unfortunate lady, to have lost her own match?"

"You will not know her. Ivanka, of House Klemenza."

Todarko felt the blood drain from his face. He hoped it was not apparent in the gloom of the tavern.

He shook his head. "I don't think I know her. You say her family are of the Gammerling party?"

"Yes — not in your circle."

"Do you know why — why the match was broken off?"

Bodazar shook his head. "She was sent away. There was talk of a sick aunt at their summer estate, but that's obviously nonsense. For some reason they didn't want the connection after all."

"Do you know if she really cared for you?" asked Todarko.

Bodazar shook his head. "She was always polite and open-hearted. She did not love me, I think, but I could have brought that about in time, for I should have treated her well. But we will never know."

"My commiserations, Bodazar, if you truly liked her. There will be other matches. Come, drink up, I am required at my uncle's."

Even while Bodazar drained his mug, Todarko rose from his seat and made for the door. He had a feeling in his stomach which tasted something like guilt.

No sooner had Todarko arrived back at Tappinetto than his uncle encountered him in the hallway. "Where have you been? We are summoned!"

Todarko removed his jacket. "I do not respond to 'summoning': if somebody wishes my company they must consult my preferences."

Raguslan gave his head a brief shake. "This is Dravadan of whom we speak. When he commands us to his house, we go."

"Dravadan!" cried Todarko, unable to suppress a quick leap in his chest. "Why did you not say so before? Naturally I am delighted to wait upon him."

Raguslan narrowed his eyes and ran his hand across his pate. "You mock me."

"On the contrary, uncle. A man of such distinction honours us with his attention."

Raguslan appeared to sense an undercurrent to Todarko's response but could not pinpoint it. Todarko was in no mood to help him.

"Your acquiescence is helpful," said Raguslan, "since Dravadan specifically requested your presence—Animaxia knows why."

"Your confidence is gratifying," said Todarko, deliberately straining for a sneer.

"Hmmmf. Are you ready? Nelanka will be here in a moment. Zanijel is required at the Masavory and will not be in attendance."

Todarko failed to suppress a smile at the turn events were taking. "Let us go, by all means. Nelanka, where are you?" he called up the stairs.

CHAPTER FIFTEEN

Some ten minutes later the party found itself settled on the evening loggia at Korfez, Dravadan's manse. Their host was detained within the house and Raguslan paced nervously up and down the loggia awaiting the chance to commune on matters of state.

Nelanka handed her veil to a servant and put her hood down. "I know why you are so eager to come here, Darko," she said quietly so as not to alert Raguslan. "You must exercise some decorum."

Todarko merely sipped his langensnap. "When do I ever behave otherwise?"

"When Linnalitha appears, to give a single example," said Nelanka. "Your amorets normally do no real harm, but if you purpose any kind of liaison with her, you court disaster for yourself and us all."

"I 'purpose' nothing of the sort," said Todarko with a forced dignity. "There is nothing amiss in paying compliments, which smooth the irksomeness of everyday discourse."

Nelanka pursed her lips. "Linnalitha is not, in any event, the kind of insipid cherub you normally prefer."

"You appear to have no very high opinion of her."

"In truth, I find her capricious, wilful and manipulative. No doubt her characterisation of me would be equally unflattering."

"Shush! Shush!" quacked Raguslan. "Dravadan is coming! Be on your best attention."

Todarko leaned back with a half-smile. Onto the loggia stepped Dravadan; half a pace behind, in a dress of glorious indigo velvet, was Linnalitha. Todarko looked up, caught her eye for a moment before she turned away to greet Raguslan.

"Welcome to Korfez once more," said Dravadan in a warm tone. "I see Palankijo has served refreshments. I wish your visit to be a pleasant one. Todarko, it is especially agreeable to see you. There comes a time when we must all set aside our youthful follies and attend to the business of state."

Todarko merely inclined his head. If Dravadan wished to patronise him, it did Todarko no real harm. For the first time Todarko inspected the older man: Dravadan was tall, well-built with perhaps the first sign of thickening around the abdomen. His dark hair had a touch of grey at the temples and his face, smooth and gleaming, appeared genial until one looked at the cold grey eyes. This was not an indulgent man, either to his wife or his rivals.

"The company of you all is a great pleasure," said Dravadan. "Nonetheless, on the Masavory we have little time to gratify our inclinations, and I have business to transact with both Raguslan and Todarko. Nelanka, no doubt affairs of state will bore you; I am sure you will enjoy a conversation with Linnalitha while we drone on."

Nelanka gave a frosty smile. "Few women interest me more than Linnalitha," she said. "I am sure she delights in my company as much as I do in hers."

Linnalitha's mouth drooped at one side before she recovered herself. "Dear Nelanka, perhaps you would like to see the flower beds. My husband enjoys the cultivation of blooms as he does the cultivation of connections."

"Yes, thank you, Linnalitha," said Dravadan. "I doubt that Nelanka relishes your metaphors and quibbles. If you are going to show her the blooms, go."

"Yes, husband," said Linnalitha in a quiet voice. "Come, Nelanka."

As they stepped from the loggia onto the lawns, Dravadan said: "Linnalitha is a remarkable woman, intelligent and cultured. Such was her upbringing. I myself find intelligence in a woman a mixed blessing. I am fortunate to have two wives of impeccable connections and lively disposition, but the last thing one wants after a day at the Masavory is a wife poring over one's every act. What say you, Raguslan?"

"My own wife has been dead these many years. I cannot even picture her face clearly," said Raguslan. "I do not recall her being overburdened with accomplishments, but she bore me a fine son. That is the first recommendation of a wife."

Todarko said: "Might it not be true, uncle, that a stupid woman bears stupid sons?"

Raguslan flushed. "I did not describe Stepanija as stupid."

"Naturally not," said Todarko. "I was speaking in general terms; otherwise the stupid son I referred to would have been Zanijel, which is clearly inconceivable."

Raguslan shook his head and glowered. "You must excuse Todarko. He is of a contentious disposition."

Dravadan gave him a smile which reached nearly to the eyes. "You could certainly not be accused of lacking wit, Todarko. I understand you are a poet of some distinction."

Todarko affected a modest shrug and sat back in his chair. "I have a certain natural facility, and I practice a great deal. Some people have been kind enough to commend my verses."

Dravadan nodded. "In all candour, I have never read a verse in my life. I would not know a rhyme from a rhubarb."

Todarko made a gesture to signify that the world comprised all manner of persons.

"Nonetheless," continued Dravadan, "my wife is a great reader and she tells me your verse is excellent."

Todarko was hardly able to stop his eyes from widening. There was no rational reply he could make.

"Dravadan, you should not flatter the boy," said Raguslan. "I do not trouble to encourage him and you need not either."

Dravadan raised a calming hand, rose from his seat to pour more langensnap. "I do not make idle conversation," he said. "These verses of Todarko's go to the heart of our business."

"I am frankly at a loss to understand how," said Raguslan.

Dravadan's raised eyebrow suggested that this was a fact he could readily believe.

"They say, I believe, that art knows no boundaries," said Dravadan, his grey eyes once more on Todarko.

"The sentiment is somewhat florid, sir, but it has a nub of truth."

"In that case art is a most telling medium. I consider myself a powerful man, with allies in every corner of Taratanallos and beyond; but I would not describe my influence as having no boundaries. There are houses in the city where the name of Dravadan is not revered."

"You surprise me, sir."

"It is no secret that I support closer ties with the Emmenrule; indeed, with the unfortunate demise of Aladar, I could be seen as the prime supporter of that view."

Raguslan chimed in. "Indeed you could, Dravadan!"

Dravadan ignored him. "Those houses which support King Ingomer or Duke Lothar do not regard me with approval. I should like to know what occurs in their manses; but ironically, they are the very ones where I cannot gain admittance."

"The life of the grandee must be a frustrating one, sir."

"You may be familiar with the Dignified Bartielko of House Oreste, the leader of the pro-Gammerling party. He is known to receive emissaries from Ingomer."

"I have heard of him," said Todarko.

"His wife, Popisilaija, is a great patron of the arts. She is also a childhood friend of my wife. In my mind I have a scheme whereby Linnalitha introduces the eminent poet Todarko into Popisilaija's salon. From this basis of cordiality you can learn much of Bartielko's doings."

"You wish me to spy upon Bartielko?" said Todarko in a high voice. "I am not convinced my talents lie in that direction. In any event, does your friendship with my uncle not make the stratagem transparent?"

"Ha ha! You will forgive me, Todarko, if I observe that your somewhat brittle relationship with your house is no secret. There are those who have described you as perverse, vindictive and mischievous."

"I can think of worse insults."

"Be that as it may: your character, coupled with Linnalitha's occasionally eccentric nature, will make your introduction into Popisilaija's salon credible. That is, if you wish to help the advancement of your house, and to promote the security of your city through the Emmen alliance."

"Well…"

"You will note," said Dravadan, "that I did not select your nephew Zanijel for this task. It requires a person of daring and discrimination to be a successful intelligencer. If you cannot oblige me, I do not know where I shall turn."

"Todarko!" cried Raguslan. "You cannot deny our friend and ally Dravadan. When the Emmen alliance is sealed he will remember his friends!"

"I shall indeed," said Dravadan with a cold smile. "In my mind I have a register of those who shown me goodwill in the past, that I may reward them in due course. Equally I remember, perhaps even more vividly, those who have obstructed me. In these cases, too, there will be an eventual adjustment."

"If you are judge of character, as you must be, sir," said Todarko, "you will recognise that my temperament does not respond well to threats."

"Todarko!" croaked Raguslan.

Dravadan gave a hearty laugh. "Come, Todarko, there is no threat here, for I am sure you wish to help me. What could be more delightful than to accompany my wife to a most respectable salon, and declaim your verses before the flower of the Specchio, attendant on your every word, their hoods thrown back and their veils away. I gather you are not averse to the female form?"

"Accompany your wife, you say?"

"I mentioned that earlier," said Dravadan. "Of course Linnalitha would introduce you into the salon. You do not find that objectionable, I hope."

Todarko rose and walked to the wall of the loggia to conceal his blush. "No, sir. I am sure I would take every pleasure in your wife's company."

"Excellent! That is settled. You must get to know her a little better. Linnalitha!" he called. "Why do you not escort Todarko around the gardens? He wishes to accompany you to Popisilaija's salon."

"Of course, husband," she called back in a flat voice. "Nelanka and I had finished our conversation."

Nelanka gave a sour expression. "You must excuse me," she said. "I have the headache and must return home."

"Of course," said Dravadan. "Palankijo will find your veil and escort you. I hope you are recovered soon."

Nelanka inclined her head. "Thank you, sir."

"Now then," said Dravadan, "while Linnalitha and Todarko walk the gardens, we must discuss our response to last night's events, Raguslan. There are many plans to make before Lord Oricien addresses the Masavory."

Todarko understood himself to be dismissed, and made his way over the flowerbed where Linnalitha was waiting.

"Good afternoon, madam," he said.

She placed a hand on his forearm. "I hope you are not going to retreat into formality, Todarko. Let us step along to the folly."

"No formality was intended, Linnalitha — if I may refer to you in such a familiar way."

"My friends call me Linna," she said. "I do not see why you should not do the same."

They strolled through an avenue of trees arched over their heads to provide a canopy against the late afternoon sun.

"There is much I would discuss with you, Linna. There are many things I do not know."

Linnalitha gave a weak smile. The dappled sun cast gold highlights in her soft red hair. "Knowledge is not always a good thing," she said. "You would not thank me for sharing mine with you."

"Last night," he said with a trace of hesitation, "when the Consigli said that Aladar was dead…"

"When I screamed…"

"The event was a shock, of course. I myself was stunned, but…"

"You want to ask me why I over-reacted as I did. It had been a long day; I was overwrought."

Todarko did not find the explanation wholly convincing. Linnalitha was nothing if not self-possessed.

She looked away with a half-smile. "You do not believe me."

"I believe," he said, running a hand through his hair, "that you tell me what it is right to tell me. If you have some deeper grief, it is yours to keep if you choose."

As she looked back up into his face he thought to see a hint of tears.

"If you wish, at any point," he continued, "to confide more fully, you can be sure I would not abuse your confidence."

With a visible jerk she stood straighter. "I understand from my husband that we will be working together," she said. "We have been set a task of gathering intelligence. There will be ample time for confidences then."

"I care nothing for your husband, my uncle, or their asinine schemes. I agreed solely for the reason of furthering our acquaintance," he said.

Now she smiled. "I am glad of it," she said. "I cannot say that I regard you as a reliable associate, or a sincere friend, but I enjoy your company."

"I thank you, madam," he said with a grin.

"You are the only man under fifty I ever see," she said. "You must view my partiality in that light."

Todarko swallowed from a suddenly dry mouth. "Linna, I should not say this, and I suspect you will not believe me, but—"

"—If this is any kind of expression of real or simulated feeling, I do not wish to hear it."

"I—"

"First, I am a married woman: married to a highly dangerous man. Second, any sincerely-held emotions you have on the basis of our limited acquaintance can only be of the most superficial kind. And third, if you are sporting with me then your reputation for callousness is well-deserved; in which case I do not wish to know it."

"You make any kind of flattering remark impossible, madam."

"'Flattery' is empty air," she said. "I would never wish to hear it. More frank sentiments, if indeed you possess them, are even more unwelcome."

"I thought you wished us to be friends."

Ahead loomed the folly at the bottom of the gardens, a water-tower disguised with crenellations to look like a small fortress.

"Friendship is a word with many guises," she said. "I enjoy your company. Your friendships with women appear often to have an additional impetus; an impetus I cannot possibly gratify, even were I of a mind to do so."

She sat on the neat wooden bench before the folly; Todarko remained standing looking down into her face.

"You have nothing to fear from me, Linna. I desire only your good."

"Well, then," she said. "There is no more to say on the subject, since any importunities would clearly fall outside this scope."

Todarko shook his head with a grin. "You are perhaps the most frustrating woman alive. I cannot fathom your feelings."

"Since I do not wish you to, that is most satisfactory," she said. "Come, shall we walk back? I am visiting Popisilaija tomorrow: can you be on hand?" She held out her arm for him to take.

"Of course," he said. "I look forward to continuing our friendship."

CHAPTER SIXTEEN

Kropiselko's rejection of Malvazan's schemes with regard to Monichoë, while not wholly unexpected, galled Malvazan into a frenzy of activity: he threw himself into his drills at Farlankas' with redoubled enthusiasm. He kept away not only from Hanglenook but also from Tappinetto from sheerest mortification. He hoped that Kropiselko viewed the proposal as so humiliating to his honour that he would keep it to himself, but such matters had a way of finding a route into common currency. At least his father seemed not to have learned of events; he would have been sure to berate Malvazan for his presumption.

One evening Malvazan took himself down the Archgate towards the docks; he was not inclined for company. With hindsight, his proposal seemed a ludicrous piece of lese majeste; Kropiselko was too concerned with his family's status to consider Malvazan's merits fairly. Nonetheless, he would soon have to resume his social activities: winning the Garland would be no use unless he maintained the contacts to build upon his celebrity. The only person who would provide the uncritical admiration he required was Sanoutë, and he could not bring himself to face her. He winced at the thought that he felt guilty at having slighted her; she, at least, had never doubted him, and he could only view crawling back to her as a humiliation.

From behind him called a soft voice. "Stranger, a moment!"

He turned in the street to see a figure in a dark red dress, her face concealed behind Hood and Veil. He was not deceived: he knew the walk, the bearing, the voice. He swallowed and turned.

"Monichoë," he said in an expressionless voice.

She slid up and stood next to him in the empty street. "I begin to think I have offended you, Malvazan. I have not seen you for weeks and now your address lacks all cordiality."

"I have been busy practising," said Malvazan, falling back on a favourite excuse for any neglected activity.

"Pshah!" said Monichoë. "That has never detained you in the past. You have abandoned all your usual companions; there is no-one to protect me from Glastarko's raillery."

Malvazan's mouth twitched into a smile before he could suppress it. "I cannot imagine anyone needing protection less."

She took his arm and they resumed walking. "You think me a heartless flirt." Her eyes, shining out from behind her Veil, seemed larger than ever in the falling dusk.

"A flirt, perhaps, but not heartless."

He sensed her smiling although he could not see her mouth. They walked in silence for a few paces.

"My father said you asked for my hand," she said in a conversational tone. Malvazan felt a chill sweep over his body, followed immediately by a flush.

"He told you?" he mumbled.

Her eyes met his. "He was too angry to conceal it," she said. "He accused me of—"

"I told him I had not approached you," said Malvazan quickly.

"Good Malvazan! The accusation was more subtle than that. My father said I had inflamed your hopes by my wantonness."

"That was not the case," said Malvazan stiffly. "I made my own decision based on my own feelings."

"I know that," she said. "It is my father who remains to be convinced."

"I am sorry if I have embarrassed you," said Malvazan.

She looked again into his face. "No lady is ever embarrassed to find her hand requested, regardless of the suitor. In this case I confess myself flattered."

Malvazan said nothing.

"Of course, the proposal was entirely misconceived," she said. "There was no way in which my father could have been persuaded to consent."

"You do not speak of your own inclinations," said Malvazan carefully.

"That is deliberate. My own desires will not be considered when my future is arranged," she said.

Malvazan swallowed. "I am interested in your desires, even if your father is not."

She laughed and pulled away. "Malvazan, you must put away any aspirations you have where I am concerned. My father is determined that I will marry as well as possible, and there is no way that can comprise House Umbinzia. I am sorry to give you pain, but it is kindest to speak directly in this matter."

Malvazan sat on a bench and indicated Monichoë to sit next to him. "I am no longer talking of betrothals," he said. "For my own purposes—my pride, if you like—I wonder only what your inclinations would be were you free to follow them."

Monichoë straightened her veil. "You outline a hypothetical situation," she said. "I am resolute in never allowing myself the luxury of considering them."

She stood up and without a backwards glance leaned into the slope and walked back up the Archgate.

The summer Malvazan turned nineteen he reached the final of Juvenilijo, a fencing tournament for those eligible to fight for the Garland next year. His brother Dravadan took part in the Garland itself; his eventual defeat in the quarter-finals if anything exceeded expectations. Malvazan could not regret his failure; if he himself won the Juvenilijo, he knew he would be strong favourite for the Garland itself. His opponent was the slippery Rodizel, the swordsman among his peers who caused him the most problems. Rodizel was quiet and reserved outside of the Bezant, and these qualities characterised his fighting style. Always his opponent seemed on the verge of nicking him, only for the stroke to go fractionally awry.

As another second son, Malvazan might have expected some fellow-feeling with Rodizel, but he was too aware of him as a potential rival to allow himself any cordiality. Rodizel, for his part, regarded Malvazan with a half-smile which just skirted tangible mockery.

One morning before the final Malvazan finished his practice session just before the Hour of Light Repast. Farlankas' school was nearer to Splanatia, the manse of House Zamilio than his own home, and he decided to call in and pay a visit on Sanoutë. Their betrothal still loomed just over the horizon, to Sanoutë's frustration, and while at times her wide-eyed devotion to Malvazan wearied him, today he felt that some adulation would be in order: this morning he had not trained well, and it was galling to be pricked again and again by that one-eyed rogue Farlankas.

Malvazan strolled in through the portico of Splanatia to be met by Sanoutë's father Thrinko. He shook Malvazan's hand and gave him a crafty smile. "You have come to see Sanoutë?" he asked.

Malvazan mopped his brow, still sweating from exertion, with a kerchief. "I have not seen her for a week. I thought to pay my compliments."

Thrinko gave him a heavy stare. "Sanoutë already has a visitor," he said.

"Oh. One of her friends?"

"Why do you not see for yourself? I will bring you to the parlour."

Malvazan followed Thrinko into the room, where to his astonishment he saw Sanoutë in animated conversation with Rodizel. He gave Rodizel a stiff bow, Sanoutë if possible an even stiffer one.

Rodizel came forward and shook his hand. "Malvazan, how do you do? Rumours that you practice all day are clearly exaggerated."

Malvazan squared his shoulders. "I practice enough to win, no more. On occasion some female company soothes and relaxes."

"Exactly my programme!" declared Rodizel, with a smile simmering only just below a laugh. "We shall see next week whose methods are the more effective."

"We shall indeed," said Malvazan with a grim smile.

"Now," said Rodizel, "I see I have outstayed my welcome. Damoiselle, I know that you have a particular understanding with Malvazan; I should not wish to intrude."

Sanouté poured two goblets of wine and handed one to each gentleman. "Please do not depart on that account, good Rodizel," she said. "There is no 'particular understanding'"—she gave Malvazan a pointed side-glance—"and I should be delighted by your continued company."

Rodizel raised his eyebrows. "I had been given to understand that a betrothal existed, or was shortly to be announced. Can it be that so beautiful a lady has no declared suitor?"

Malvazan coloured. "This is hardly a topic for polite conversation."

"Forgive me," said Rodizel with his cool half-smile. "I appear to have blundered into a morass of embarrassment. Sanouté, you really must excuse me: I cannot in good faith stay." He bowed, kissed her hand and turned to leave the room.

As he left he walked past Malvazan who stepped into his path and whispered: "I see your game, Rodizel. Do not imagine I will overlook it."

Rodizel fastidiously stood to the side. "Until next week, sir. I always relish a turn with a snark-blade."

As soon as Rodizel had left the room, Malvazan stepped over to Sanouté. "What was the meaning of that?"

Sanouté glided away to sit on a couch. "Rodizel paid me a call; I entertained him for a few minutes. It is normal social intercourse."

"He is a rival in the Bezant!"

Sanouté looked up with her soft blue eyes. "So?"

"He seeks only to unsettle me—he is not paying you a serious address."

She stood up and walked to the fireplace, her back to Malvazan. "That is not the most flattering assessment. Might he not have been drawn by my own charms?" she said in a voice held level only with an effort.

"Pah!" said Malvazan. "We fight next week—a very important fight—and he looks to annoy and disturb me."

She turned to face him. "And how might this be effected?"

"Do I need to outline every detail? He talks of 'particular understandings' and seeks to insinuate himself between us."

"We have already established that no such understanding exists," said Sanoutë in a quiet fierce tone. "How then can he rupture it?"

He stepped close and put his hands on her forearms. "He is trying to create a jealousy. Do not be fooled by his wiles."

"There is an alternative interpretation," she said. "He might, unlike some, find my company agreeable in itself. This need not be directed at you."

Malvazan gave a soft laugh. "Come, Sanoutë, let us not quarrel. Surely we can have a few moments of cordiality."

She broke free and stepped away. "There is an easy way to resolve the matter," she said with a gleam in her eyes.

"Yes?" Malvazan picked up his goblet.

"If the hypothetical 'understanding' referred to by Rodizel existed in practice, all ambiguity would be gone. I could not in all propriety receive Rodizel, or any other young man, and we would all enjoy complete certainty."

Malvazan slammed his goblet down on the table. "This is intolerable! At every step you seek to fetter me. If our fathers agree a betrothal, then there shall be one. Until that time, all remains as before."

"Leave. Leave now."

"Sanoutë?"

"You assume me to be naïve, gullible, an idiot. I have nothing further to say to you."

Malvazan produced a careful bow. "As you wish, Damoiselle."

He walked from the room with a measured tread. Sanoutë clearly would need cautious handling; while she was by no means his ideal match, if his more ambitious schemes came to naught she might have to suffice. It was certainly not acceptable for Rodizel to pay his addresses: one more reason to ensure he won next week.

Malvazan found himself in a ferocious gloom for the remainder of the week. He had cut a pitiful figure with Monichoë and now he had quarrelled with Sanoutë, who sought to pique him with Rodizel. He had no doubt that he could settle any score with Rodizel in the Bezant, but his judgement in recent weeks was clearly at fault. He had made no real progress in his programme of advancement: while he remained a peerless swordsman,

Kropiselko had laughed in his face when he had proposed a match between their houses, and Sanoutë was losing much of her adulation for him. He was perilously close to becoming a laughing-stock. His brother, when he saw him, invariably jeered at him, and his parents did not understand the drives which animated him. By the time the morning of the Juvenilijo arrived he was keyed up to a jangling pitch of intensity.

He took a run round the city walls before breakfast to release some of his tension. When he returned home he was surprised to find both parents and brother in their best outfits and ready to make their way to the Bezant: to date they had shown almost no interest in his swordcraft; only Dravadan's aspirations had been taken seriously.

"Where are you going?" asked Malvazan.

Flinteska gave him a smothering hug. "We are coming to watch you, of course. The Juvenilijo is a major event!"

Malvazan disengaged himself. "I was always aware of that: that is why I have been training for four years."

"You need not be so prickly," said Crostadan. "We are all proud of you today."

"The lad is nervous," said Flinteska. "He is allowed to growl a little. He would be no swordsman if he was a milksop."

Malvazan forbore from observing that calmness, rather than ferocity, was the fighter's best ally. Dravadan, meanwhile, crowed aloud: "If cantankerousness is all that is required, it is no wonder that Malvazan is so proficient."

Malvazan breathed deeply. Dravadan was no longer worth his scorn; heir or not, he was a young man of trivial accomplishments and petty provocations. Malvazan contented himself with a cool smile, which seemed to rile Dravadan more than overt hostility.

The fight took place at the Hour of Afternoon Reflection, and by the time Malvazan arrived at the Bezant he was surprised to see the arena almost full. There was something about this bout which had captured the Specchio's imagination; the word among the cognoscenti was that this year's crop was the finest for a generation.

As the preliminary fights came to an end, Malvazan looked around the crowd, faces he recognised everywhere. Not just his family, of course, but Glastarko and Raguslan. Under Hood and Veil at this distance he could not tell whether Monichoë was present—or Sanoutë, for that matter. Where did her partisanship lie today? Would she be cheering for him, or Rodizel?

Farlankas was talking to him, and he put the crowd out of mind.

"He is patient," said Farlankas. "Do not let him goad you into a rash stroke. He does not have your reach, or your speed."

"I am patient," said Malvazan. "I can outwait him."

Farlankas rubbed a cream above his eyebrows to prevent the sweat running down into his eyes. "And Malvazan…"

"Yes, sir?"

"I know you do not like Rodizel. You do not have to humiliate him. It is enough that you beat him. Next year, Hissen willing, the pair of you will stand here again in the final of the Garland. Make yourself his master today."

Malvazan nodded, made his way towards the centre of the Bezant where Rodizel already waited. Hissen take Farlankas: he would humiliate Rodizel, and that was an end to it. No-one flirted with Sanouté and expected to laugh in his face. That he cared nothing for Sanouté was not to the point: Rodizel was going to learn a lesson today.

They were introduced to the crowd but Malvazan heard nothing of it. He was in his own restricted, silent world, whose only elements were his own body, the weight of the steel blade, the slippery rasp of the sand under his feet — and of course his opponent, standing startlingly immobile before him.

He caught Rodizel's eye a moment; he might as well have been looking into the face of a snake for all the expression he saw. Rodizel, too, had made his way to his own world, and now those worlds would collide.

"Fight!"

Malvazan heard the call and took two quick steps towards Rodizel, twitched his blade in a feint, or less than a feint. Rodizel did not respond, simply shifted his weight forward to the balls of his feet. A nervous man would have reacted; Rodizel had no nerves today. Malvazan gave a tight grin; he was not in the mood for a facile victory.

Rodizel danced forward, skipped inside Malvazan's defence and thrust forward; Malvazan leaned back from the waist, flicked Rodizel's blade away with a twitch of the wrist. Rodizel moved back, set himself in defence as Malvazan launched a counter-attack, his left-handed angle of attack cramping Rodizel's defence.

Again and again they lunged and parried; it was warm in the early afternoon sun and Malvazan was soon conscious of the sweat sticking his white shirt to his back. If Rodizel had a weakness as a fighter it was passivity; sooner or later he would make a fractional mistake, overcommit himself in a lunge or hold his position too long. Then Malvazan's speed and decisiveness would carry him forward.

Today Rodizel was even more contained than usual; his sallies seemed little more than tests of Malvazan's defences. Malvazan was conscious, without even realising how, that the crowd was becoming restive. It was time to finish it. When Rodizel's next probe came in, Malvazan flipped it to the side, made as if to duck under the blow, and then sprang to his full height and drove down.

Rodizel gave ground but too late; Malvazan was inside his defence. He leaned forward to apply the touch: now I have you! The blunted blade seemed to pass through Rodizel—how could that be? For one wild moment he thought he had skewered his opponent; then Rodizel was sliding aside, under his sword arm. He felt a touch in the ribs.

"Tacto!" called both judges. "Rodizel wins."

Malvazan stood erect, made to protest. How could Rodizel have touched him? There must be a mistake. But the crowd was on its feet, roaring its approval. The result was announced again: "Rodizel wins! He is this year's Champion of the Juvenilijo!"

Rodizel walked over to the judges, handed back his sword. He came and reached out his hand to Malvazan: "Well fought," he said.

After a brief hesitation Malvazan took Rodizel's outstretched hand: it would not do to contract a reputation for ungraciousness. There was nothing he could bring himself to say which would not be either false or inflammatory, so he settled for a brisk nod. Rodizel at least did not seem disposed to gloat. Instead he went to embrace his brother Astrizel, his trainer Odurazan.

Malvazan stood in the centre of the Bezant, outwardly calm, but seething with mortification. In the crowd, if he could bring himself to look, would be Monichoë and her proud father; Sanouté and the other slighted members of House Zamilio; Raguslan and Glastarko who had sparred with him; his family who for once had seemed proud of his achievements. Now they would all be looking at him, their emotions a matter of conjecture, but painted from a narrow palette: disappointment, scorn and worst of all pity.

Farlankas strode towards him and it seemed there was another emotion on display: anger. Malvazan felt a blow to the side of the head.

"Fool!" hissed Farlankas. "Did I not tell you not to commit yourself? At the first opportunity you tried to finish it. Rodizel has only one advantage over you, and that is patience."

"The opening was there," said Malvazan. "I all but had him; it was a lucky blow."

Farlankas scrutinised him for a moment. "I was wrong. He has two advantages over you. Not only is he patient, he is not the slave of his ego. You must learn to subordinate yourself to the moment, or you will be standing here a loser again next year. I take it that is not what you want?"

Malvazan stalked from the Bezant, Farlankas stepping at his side.

"Have you ever trained a Garland winner, Farlankas?"

"You know that I have."

"Sometimes I wonder how. It may be time I found a new master," said Malvazan. "I have much to consider."

Farlankas slowed down and stopped. As Malvazan strode on, Farlankas muttered: "It is not a new master you need; it is a new attitude."

CHAPTER SEVENTEEN

By the time Rodizel was presented with his trophy, Malvazan had walked halfway up the Archgate and climbed the narrow steps up to the city wall. He leaned on the parapet overlooking the sea below as the waves crashed against the wall; sometimes a quirk of breeze carried a hint of spray up onto his face.

How could he have lost? Rodizel was a difficult opponent and had beaten him before. But this was the final of the Juvenilijo, and he had wanted to win so much. Rodizel could not have trained harder than Malvazan; he could not have wanted to win more; he was not a more talented swordsman (even Farlankas admitted it). He could not explain what had happened in the Bezant other than by luck. He was not given to religious sentiment or explanations; defeat was not attributable to Hissen or Animaxia, and it did not help to view it as a step along the Way of Harmony. Was he wrong to dismiss the Way so easily? He had lost to a fighter who was clearly his inferior. Perhaps there was some other agency at work. Could it do any harm to visit the Viatory?

He looked far out to sea, the dominion of the sea-goddess Animaxia. Out at the edge of the bay he saw dolphins disporting themselves around a heavily-laden cog. Was this a sign?

Briskly he shook his head. He was Malvazan; he had no need of the Viators and their counsel! *But my own counsel is not getting me very far. And I am hardly in the mood to go home.* Almost before he realised it, Malvazan was walking back down the Archgate in the direction of the city's grandest Viatory, the Dominikos.

The Dominikos stood a little way from the Ostentatory and the other buildings supporting the slave market: from the sea it was almost invisible, but it was one of the most striking buildings in the city. The walls were a cool white, the perfectly symmetrical dome a soothing terracotta. Like any Viatory, it was nominally open to everyone, and stood nearer the poor Chale district than it did to the Archgate. Nonetheless, any artisan wandering in off the street might find that the Viators were mysteriously absent and not available to give their counsel.

For Malvazan, matters were rather different. A son of the Specchio, he was a conduit to the wealth of the city on which the Viators were dependent to maintain their own affluence. Poverty would be a poor advertisement for the Way of Harmony, and the Viators never flinched from the alms the Specchio made available. When Malvazan stepped into the cool gloom from the glare of the street, therefore, it was only a matter of moments before a young Viator approached him with a deep bow.

"Welcome, friend," said the Viator in a voice softened by the vast interior of the building. "Welcome to this milestone on the Way of Harmony."

Malvazan could not remember when he had last set foot inside a Viatory, let alone the Dominikos. The building was undeniably impressive, simply on a different scale even from the manses of the great houses. The candles guttering in their sconces cast the Viator's face into shadow. Now that he was here, Malvazan was not sure how to begin.

"I am Viator Shalvijo," said the young man. "I am here to help you along the Way, if you will let me."

Malvazan's eyes were becoming accustomed to the interior; the walls were painted with dramatic frescoes: on the left, martial scenes with Hissen at the centre, tall and strong; to the right, the sea-goddess Animaxia, part mermaid, part snake. No doubt there was some symbolism to the representations, but Malvazan had never paid great attention to this element of his lessons.

"I am Malvazan," he said.

Shalvijo nodded. "House Umbinzia."

For once Malvazan did not feel a sub-stratum of judgement.

"You are new to the Viatory, I think," said Shalvijo. Malvazan nodded. "Let us talk awhile," continued the Viator. "I have a cubiculo."

Shalvijo conducted Malvazan up a short flight of stairs and into an alcove overlooking the marbled floor below.

"I can give as much or as little counsel as you require," said Shalvijo. "We each proceed along the Way at our own pace. You may wish to tell me why you are here."

Shalvijo's voice was soothing; it seemed to solicit the listener's confidence. Over the next half hour Malvazan gave vent to the full range of his dissatisfaction: the poor standing of House Umbinzia, the lot of the second son, his ambition to earn respect and consequence; his swordcraft and his plan to win the Garland, brought crashing down by his loss to Rodizel; his suit to Monichoë and his betrayal by Sanouté.

Shalvijo said little, occasionally asking a question without breaking Malvazan's flow. Eventually there was silence.

Shalvijo nodded. "You have brooded much on your condition," he said. "I doubt you have outlined your thoughts this frankly before."

"No."

"And now," said Shalvijo, "you feel a sense of relief, a lightening of the heart, do you not?"

Malvazan realised that this was entirely true. He nodded but said nothing.

"Do you know why that is?"

"No."

"Because you are back on the Way of Harmony. Your life—all of our lives—are shaped towards a particular destiny. That, of course, is Harmony. The Viator helps you along that road. Today, in coming here, is as if you have climbed aboard a strong gallumpher, that will carry you more effectively to your goal."

"I have talked about my goals," said Malvazan. "They are hardly selfless."

Shalvijo leaned back on his bench and smiled. "It is easy to equate Harmony with morality," he said. "The two are only tangentially related. Your destiny may be to spend your life in a blaze of altruism, caring nothing for yourself, only for others; on the other hand, it may be the ennoblement of yourself above all else. One of those may be 'good', the other less so: but both are equally on the Way of Harmony. The Viators can help you find that way. Who knows? For you, that could be the Garland, a brilliant marriage, maybe even the head of House Umbinzia and a seat on the Masavory. And when we achieve Harmony, the afterlife awaits us. To Follow the Way is not some arid dogma: it is an affirmation of your life's meaning!"

Malvazan felt a moment of elation. He had never realised that the Viators would look upon his goals so favourably. But why should they not? He was a man different from the ruck, distinguished by talent, energy, ambition. Why then could his destiny not be a glorious one?

"One can study the Way for a lifetime and not understand all of the details of Hissen and Animaxia," said Shalvijo. "You are not, I suspect, a man who wishes to explore all aspects of our doctrines: fortunately the Viators are on hand."

"I would appreciate of any guidance you can give me," said Malvazan.

"I must consult with my superiors," said Shalvijo. "Others more experienced than I will be better placed to see where your road might lie. Come back tomorrow."

Malvazan inclined his head. "Of course."

"Can you remember a time when you had the lightness of heart like you felt when you had finished your story today?" asked Shalvijo.

Malvazan thought for a moment. "Twice," he said. "The day Farlankas accepted me as a pupil; and when I first saw Monichoë."

Shalvijo nodded portentously. "These moments are sent to us by Hissen and Animaxia. They tell us when we have reached an important post on the Way. You know in your heart, do you not, that both the blade and Monichoë are important to you?"

"Yes—but Monichoë's father rejected me, scorned me."

"The road is not always straight, my friend; and neither does it always lead where it seems. For now, you should consider why those moments were so important to you. We will discuss this again."

Malvazan stood and bowed. He made his way down the stairs, barely feeling the ground under his feet. The gloom of the Dominikos seemed to him to hide a hundred truths and revelations, but the greatest of all was already made clear to him: his great destiny was on the Way of Harmony. He not only could, but should, pursue it with all his might. Harmony was the worthiest goal of existence, and it would bring him the consequence he craved and deserved. Rodizel might have beaten him today, but Rodizel did not have Malvazan's path to Harmony.

Stepping out of the Dominikos into the suddenly-bright afternoon, he broke into a run and dashed towards the Archgate in sheer excitement.

CHAPTER EIGHTEEN

Raguslan was almost childishly excitable as he took dinner with Todarko, Zanijel and Nelanka at Tappinetto that evening.

"It is a great shame you were not present, Zanijel. Dravadan was most condescending, was he not, Todarko?"

"Condescending indeed, uncle."

"He has given Todarko a secret task, and we shall all advance together under Dravadan's patronage."

Zanijel nodded as he spooned his ragout into his loose mouth.

"And there is more," continued Raguslan.

"What could be greater than Dravadan's favour?" asked Todarko.

"He has agreed to sell me a First Monopoly," exclaimed Raguslan. "Imagine, House Vaggio with a First Monopoly! It will make us among the greatest houses in the Specchio."

Zanijel set down his spoon. "This is remarkable news, father! When Nelanka and I have a son he will be heir to this First Monopoly!"

Nelanka said: "I understand that Dravadan holds the monopoly on both salt and battlecat pelts," she said. "Which does he wish to sell?"

"Good girl," said Raguslan with an indulgent beam. "You are always alert. It is the battlecat pelts to which we will be attached. Think of the great trade coming down from Sey for transhipment through Taratanallos; and think of the one and a quarter percent levy flowing into the coffers of House Vaggio. We must change the emblem of the House from the crow to the battlecat!"

"That is foolishness, uncle. House Vaggio has been associated with the crow for four hundred years," said Todarko. "You cannot change it on a whim."

"This is a great event," said Raguslan. "Why should I not change the emblem? It is the greatest moment in our history!"

"Why would Dravadan sell you such a prize?" asked Nelanka. "The monopoly is presumably highly lucrative."

"He wishes to bind our houses more closely," said Raguslan. "It is a mark of his favour. I regret that I do not have a daughter, since he has two grown sons from his first marriage."

Todarko took a sip from his goblet of Garganet wine. "There would be less dramatic ways of showing his regard. I hope that he is not short of ready cash."

"In that case, why would he divest himself of this rich monopoly? Your grasp of trade is superficial, Todarko."

"How much is he asking?"

"The price is still under negotiation," said Raguslan smoothly.

"How much, then, does he ask?"

Raguslan composed his expression. "Two million florins."

"What!" cried Nelanka. "No wonder he wishes to sell."

"I am sure he will settle for rather less."

Todarko said: "I do not fully understand the detail of House Vaggio's finances, but I doubt that we possess even one million florins."

"Naturally not. No man of sense would keep such a sum in his coffers. Nonetheless, I can raise a mortgage against the monopoly's revenues to finance the purchase. It is a long-term investment."

"As long as you do not use my inheritance as security," said Todarko. "Indeed, with your augmented fortunes there is no reason why you cannot pay me the money direct."

"Specchio finances do not work like that," snapped Raguslan. "Your inheritance now forms part of the capital of House Vaggio. The interest on your portion is quite sufficient for your needs. Surely you would not wish to squander the capital?"

"More to the point, uncle, I do not wish you to squander it."

"Come, Todarko," said Zanijel heavily. "This is a wonderful day for House Vaggio. Can you not enter the spirit of the moment?"

"If you can delight in your father speculating with the House's fortune, I wish you joy of it," said Todarko. "I myself do not forget the recent calamities Jadinko and Aladar have brought upon themselves by speculation. I wish no part in it."

"Enough, Todarko," said Raguslan sharply. "The matter is settled."

Todarko raised a napkin to his lips and left the room.

The banking house of Estedino, originally established in Mettingloom, maintained a sizeable building in the Wrill, that part of the city set aside for the business and residence of foreigners. Conveniently for the Emmen ambassadors, it was situated near to the Castle of Crostestini, and the morning after the Dignified Aladar's death, Oricien and Iselin made the short journey; Ribauldequin, meanwhile, had been despatched to procure a condolence gift for Aladar's widow, and a suitable token of esteem for Dravadan.

Oricien and Iselin were ushered in through the wide doorway set into the marble frontage of Estedino's. The floors were covered with smooth rugs and the ambassadors were escorted with noiseless efficiency into the deepest recesses of the building. Here they were met, in a chamber with impossibly lofty ceilings, by Rocazzo, the principal of the house. As they sipped at their tisane, Oricien proffered the letter of credit provided by King Enguerran.

Rocazzo, a man tall and thin, subjected the document to a minute's scrutiny. He looked up and gave a quick chilly smile. "All seems to be in order, my lords. The resources of Estedino are at your disposal."

"Excellent," said Oricien. "You will be aware that King Enguerran wishes to disburse considerable sums in the city. If it were necessary to make large payment in metal, perhaps at short notice, would such a thing be possible?"

Rocazzo smiled his silver-plated smile. "This is a bank, my lord. Such matters are our stock in trade."

"I merely ask," said Oricien, "because we have all learned that matters are often not as they seem. Who would have thought that Aladar stood in such penury, for instance?"

"The situations are rather different," said Rocazzo. "Estedino was his banker, and the extent of his credit was known to us, at least. Regrettably, his ruin was not entirely unpredictable."

Iselin interjected: "Have you, then, suffered loss from Aladar's fall?"

Rocazzo sat back in his chair. "The usual arrangements apply."

Oricien shot Iselin a quick glance. "And these would be?"

"I should not discuss the confidential affairs of Estedino's clients."

"The Dignified Aladar is dead," said Oricien in a flat voice. "The question is moot as to whether he remains a client. King Enguerran, on the other hand, is indubitably alive. The question of your exposure to Aladar's ruin is directly relevant to the confidence His Puissance has in Estedino."

Rocazzo rang a small bell to summon further drinks. "The circumstances are hardly unique," he said. "I lose nothing by explaining them to you. A house which borrows money from Estedino will offer security for repayment of the loan. Invariably this will be the manse, so in this case Roblegast. Estedino will therefore take ownership of Robelegast in full settlement of all outstanding debt."

Iselin furrowed his brow. "So House Tantestro is ruined? With no manse, how can they continue?"

Rocazzo shook his head. "Such an arrangement would suit nobody. Aladar will have an heir; we will sell Roblegast back to him on a mortgage, and all will proceed as before. In twenty or thirty years, Tantestro will once again own Roblegast unfettered."

Oricien scratched his chin. "Why did not Aladar simply sell you Roblegast before his situation became irrecoverable?"

Iselin laughed. "You do not understand the pride of the Specchio, Oricien. Death would be preferable to selling one's own manse—which in any event belongs to the house, and not the individual."

Rocazzo gave a nod of the head. "You are most perceptive, my lord."

Iselin returned a bow of the head. "Perhaps I might broach another matter with you," he said.

"Speak on."

"King Enguerran's credit, although large, is not inexhaustible. His Puissance wishes to incur expense only where it will secure value."

"Understandable enough," said Rocazzo.

"If other grandees were as impecunious as Aladar, it would be most valuable to His Puissance to be aware of it. He would know not to toss silver into a sinking ship, or perhaps where a moment of benevolence would be most appreciated."

Rocazzo smiled and shook his head. "Such a thing is not possible, for three reasons. First I must once again mention issues of confidentiality; second I would observe that not all of the Specchio banks with us; and finally, I must admit that one does not always see a crash coming. Some houses have been adept at hiding their situations."

Oricien cast a sharp glance at Iselin. The question had been crass in its bluntness, and did not reflect well on Iselin's judgement.

"I entirely understand, sir," he said. "Iselin spoke only with the frustration of a man who had advanced 120,000 florins of King Enguerran's money to Aladar, only to see it swallowed up with his death."

Rocazzo cast a puzzled glance at Iselin. "Of course," he said. "I fully understand, although the amount was only 100,000 florins, if that is any consolation."

"I am sure not," said Oricien. "Our records are unequivocal, are they not, Iselin?"

Iselin shifted in his seat and coloured. "Indeed they are. There is surely a mistake of some sort."

Rocazzo once again flashed his sharp smile. "Estedino does not make mistakes of this nature. Aladar was our client, and we facilitated the transaction. I checked only this morning when we closed up Aladar's account."

"Iselin, where is your account book?" said Oricien sharply.

"I—it is not—"

"I saw you put it in your doublet. Come, let us check."

Iselin wordlessly reached into his doublet and pulled out the slim pocketbook. Oricien flipped to the index, looked up Aladar's entry.

"Here," he said, passing the book to Rocazzo. "The entry is unequivocal. 120,000 florins."

"Unequivocal it may be," responded Rocazzo with his mirthless smile. "It is also incorrect. Your accounts are in error. I will not insult your intelligence or Lord Iselin's probity by suggesting the ways in which such an 'error' might have occurred."

Oricien could feel the muscles of his face freezing. "I thank you for your courtesy, sir," he said to Rocazzo. "Iselin, there are matters we must discuss immediately, and in private."

Iselin miserably rose to his feet. "Yes, Lord Ambassador."

Oricien strode back towards the Castle of Crostestini, the paved street ringing with the clangour of his boots. Iselin panted as he struggled to keep up.

"Oricien, I can explain," he gasped.

"That is why we are returning to our apartments," said Oricien. "I hope you do not intend to parade your excuses in the street."

"Oricien—"

"Not another word."

The guards at the Castle of Crostestini took a pace back when they saw the expression on Oricien's face; the two ambassadors stalked across the hallway and up the stairs to their suite of rooms.

"Sit down," snapped Oricien, who made no move to sit himself. He stood looking down at Iselin from his full height. "Now we shall have all the explanation you wish."

Iselin slumped bonelessly in his seat. "What do you wish to know?"

Oricien took two brisk steps forward to crowd into Iselin's legs. "Do not fence with me, Iselin. Where did the 20,000 florins you did not pay Aladar go?"

Iselin composed himself with an effort. "It may be that my record keeping was a touch slapdash…"

Oricien turned and walked away to look from the window. Not looking at Iselin, he said: "On the contrary: your records are meticulous, both in the way they are set out, and in what they conceal. 20,000 florins do not disappear through inattention."

"I—I thought to hold the money as a contingency—one never knows when an emergency disbursement—"

"Do not treat me as a fool, Iselin. I hold a letter of credit with His Puissance's seal. We will not find ourselves short of ready money. Admit, once and for all, that you have retained the sum for your own use."

Oricien could hear Iselin moving behind and turned to face him. Iselin's expression was miserable. "It is common practice," he said with a ghastly bright smile. "Everyone does it. It can be seen as a perquisite of the office."

"I do not do it. I doubt that the King would view the theft of 20,000 florins of his own revenue as a legitimate 'perquisite'."

Iselin said nothing.

"If indeed," said Oricien as a thought occurred to him, "your peculation is capped at 20,000 florins." He saw from Iselin's flush that he had struck a nerve.

"How much, Iselin?" said Oricien through lips that barely moved.

"I cannot—I would need to—"

"For now, an approximation will suffice."

Iselin put his head in his hands. "I will repay everything. I will—"

"How much?"

"Eighty-five thousand, give or take."

Oricien shook his head, stalked across the room. "You are not just a knave; you are a fool. If our embassy is successful, 85,000 florins is as nothing compared to the rewards you would have received."

Iselin stood up. "Surely we can overlook this—in view of my service, and the contribution I can still make."

Oricien walked to the door and opened it. With his hand on the frame, he said: "You will oblige me by quitting the apartments immediately, and securing lodgings elsewhere in the city until you can return home."

"I have no money with me. I cannot pay for—"

"Once you have found rooms, render the account to me—and for your passage home."

"But what will I say to His Puissance?"

"Tell him you stole his money; tell him I sent you home. I do not care what excuse you contrive, since I will be writing an immediate despatch."

"Lord Ambassador—have mercy!"

"You show neither regret nor contrition. Leave me now, before I eject you myself."

As Iselin slunk past him and out of the door, Oricien thought to see tears running into his beard. Oricien slammed the door behind Iselin and flung himself onto the chaise.

He had been in Taratanallos less than two days, and already the embassy was mired in calamity: their main ally in the city dead, one advisor a womanising sot and the other revealed as a peculator and on his way back home. No doubt things could get worse, but it was hard to see how.

At that moment the door burst open. In strode Ribauldequin. "Look what I have bought! Surely Dravadan will be delighted with this fine scabbard."

Oricien looked at the gift Ribauldequin had bought: a solid gold scabbard, encrusted with jewels, and cunningly wrought into the likeness of an erect phallus. A more hideous and tasteless item Oricien had never seen; nor a less appropriate gift for the head of a Tarat house. And this was the man on whose judgement Oricien would now need to rely.

The next few weeks were certainly going to prove interesting.

CHAPTER NINETEEN

Both Todarko and Bodazar were gloomy as they nursed their beer in the Northern Star that night. Bodazar had sunk into a taciturnity that often accompanied his drinking, while Todarko found himself restless and distracted.

"Do you see those three men in the corner?" he asked Bodazar. "I am sure they are staring at us."

"Why would they want to do that?" asked Bodazar with a scowl. "Most people have enough to occupy them without needing to scrutinise others. You are imagining things."

"These are strange times, Bodazar. My uncle is keeping some undesirable company."

"I assume you refer to Dravadan? He is no friend to my house, but he is respectable by any standards. I cannot imagine him associating with men of that stamp. I thought you had a partiality for Dravadan's wife, anyway."

"I did not intend 'undesirable' to refer to Linnalitha," he said. "Quite the contrary. Tomorrow night we visit Popisilaija's salon."

"My father is friends with her husband, Bartielko. Maybe you will join the Gammerling party?"

Todarko stifled a laugh. "Such matters hardly interest me. All are equally foolish."

"So why do you attend the salon? It is something of a political statement."

"You exaggerate: if Dravadan allows his wife to go, it can hardly be an endorsement of King Ingomer."

"Linnalitha is a woman: her opinions carry no weight, by definition. But when a member of the Specchio goes calling, the matter becomes more significant."

"Pah! I am going only because Linnalitha suggests it. She is a remarkable woman, and I should like to know her better."

Bodazar raised an eyebrow. "Dravadan countenances this?"

Todarko realised that he had led himself into a blind alley. He could hardly tell the heir of House Belario that he was spying for their rival Dravadan. Duplicity did not come naturally to him: his career as an intelligencer had not begun auspiciously.

"He is an indulgent husband," said Todarko. "Linnalitha is an admirer of my verse. What harm can come in a respectable salon?"

"You should show care," said Bodazar. "Dravadan is not a man to trifle with. Your best course is to avoid Linnalitha altogether. Your interest in her is merely carnal, and no doubt your urges can be satisfied elsewhere."

He placed his mug on the table with a truculent thump.

"You are naturally jaundiced in affairs of the heart," said Todarko. "If your amour with Ivanka had enjoyed a happier conclusion, you would not be so dismissive. Besides, my relationship with Linnalitha is rather more subtle than you suspect. Indeed, I am minded to compose her a sonnet."

Bodazar shrugged. "You will not be told," he said. "Do not complain to me when you are lying in some ditch with your throat cut."

"I find I have had enough light banter for the evening," said Todarko. "I will return to my verses."

"As you will," said Bodazar. "I have drunk enough, in any event."

As they left the inn, Todarko looked back over his shoulder, to see the three men in the corner leaving their seats in a parody of leisurely movement. He nudged Bodazar. "See?" he said.

"You are an old woman, Todarko."

"Let us be old women who walk at speed."

The Chale at midnight was a dark place. The narrow alleyways and covered passages twisted and turned, doubling back on themselves to create hideaways and concealments. This very quality had made them ideal sites for Todarko's assignations with Ivanka, but now created a warren rich with shadow upon shadow and leering menace around every corner.

They emerged from one sudden switchback to find the three men close on their heels. Before them loomed another three.

One of the men, tall and slighter than the others, said: "Todarko of House Vaggio?"

Todarko swallowed. "I don't think we've been introduced."

A surly bearded character who had been in the inn lisped in an exaggerated falsetto: "I don't think we've been introduced." His cronies laughed.

The thin man said: "We can arrange an introduction. Meet Sir Fist!"

Todarko doubled up at the blow, pitched forward. The second man kicked into his ribcage to send Todarko sprawling onto his back. Two more ruffians set upon Bodazar who had been standing in stunned silence.

Todarko scrambled to his feet; a boot lashed into his face and he felt the skin on his cheek tear. Bodazar slipped aside from his assailant, looked around irresolutely and then made to pull the burly man from Todarko's back.

"Run, Bodazar! Get the Consiglio!" shouted Todarko from the ground. A firm shove smacked his face into the cobbles.

The thin man drew back. "Bodazar? Adromilo, hold him!"

One of the men belabouring Todarko detached himself and pinned Bodazar's arms behind his back. "Don't hurt this one," said the thin man. "It is Todarko who must be chastised."

Todarko lost track of time as two men held him and two hit him in rotation. The thin man stood back, surveying the scene dispassionately. As some unseen threshold was crossed he raised a gloved hand. "Enough," he said. "My instructions were not to kill him."

The men holding Todarko gave him a rough shove and he staggered against the wall. He realised he could not stand unaided and sank to his knees.

"Consider that a gift," said the thin man, a smile flickering just behind his mouth. "From an admirer."

Todarko said nothing. The thin man gave an ironic bow, and then he and his men were gone.

"Can you walk?" asked Bodazar.

Todarko gingerly rose to his feet. He spat blood from his mouth and said: "I think so."

As they limped back though the streets Bodazar said: "You are playing a dangerous game, Todarko."

"Who would want to hurt me? I am a poet!"

"However execrable your verse," said Bodazar, "I think we can discount it as a motive. You should choose your associates with more care. You are moving in elevated circles now."

"You think this was a warning to Dravadan? There would surely be more unambiguous ways. I have only been to Korfez once."

"Exactly," said Bodazar. "If I wished to show that I knew everything that went on in Dravadan's manse, what better way than to assault his newest associate before that association became common knowledge. Are you still drilling with Rodizel?"

"Of course," said Todarko. "I never know when an outraged father or brother might demand satisfaction."

"Then you should start carrying your rapier. These are dark times for us all."

When Todarko returned to Tappinetto he found all the family absent. Dravadan had received an unexpected visit from the Emmen lords and called all his allies around him. Luzio insisted on taking Todarko there in a cariolo and presenting him at Korfez. A party was taking refreshments on the loggia under a starlit sky.

"Todarko!" cried Nelanka. "Whatever has happened to you?"

"I should have thought that was obvious," said Zanijel with a smirk. "Someone has taken exception to Todarko's manner: an event hardly to astound."

Dravadan broke away from his conversation with Lord Ribauldequin. "I will summon my physician immediately," he said. "Did you recognise your assailants?"

Todarko shook his head, and immediately regretted it as a lance of pain shot through his temples. "Six men, three of whom were watching us in the tavern. Two of them I would recognise again, including the leader. They asked for me by name, and they let Bodazar be. This was no casual assault."

"Bodazar?" said Dravadan with a frown. "The House Belario whelp?"

"Just so."

"House Belario are hardly our friends, Todarko."

"Your wife attends Popisilaija's salons. I care nothing for allegiances and neither, it seems, does Linnalitha."

Dravadan's mouth pursed. "Your independence is all part of your value to us, I suppose."

Lord Oricien came over to see them. "Do you believe the attack to have been motivated by some factional dispute?" he said to Todarko.

Zanijel gave a caw of laughter. "More likely the brothers of some lady he has seduced. There is no shortage of men queuing to give Todarko a beating!"

Oricien looked at Zanijel with an expression of appraisal. "It appears more than coincidence that a connection of Dravadan's is assaulted when our embassy is in the city. I do not think our alliance will be concluded without difficulty, Dravadan."

"Taratanallos was ever a fevered place, my lord. The lad has a few bruises, but there is no harm done."

Todarko did not view the event with quite the same detachment. Neither, it seemed, did Lord Oricien. "It starts with a beating, perhaps. That does not mean it ends there. We should all practice caution."

"The person of King Enguerran's ambassador can only be secure, my lord," said Dravadan.

"I prefer to make no assumptions on that score, Dravadan. I look to you to manage the security of the embassy."

Dravadan inclined his head. "Of course, my lord."

Onto the loggia, unnoticed, came Linnalitha. "Todarko! You are hurt!"

"A scratch," winced Todarko. He felt his heart lift at the concern in her voice.

"Has no-one bathed your wounds?" she asked, as Todarko dabbed at his oozing cheek. "Let me."

"Madam," halted Todarko as she approached, looking sideways at Dravadan.

"Enough, wife," snapped her husband. "I have sent for Istevar. You need not demean yourself with such a task."

Linnalitha drew herself erect. "I do not see what is demeaning about giving succour to a guest," she said. "It is meet for House Umbinzia to show hospitality. I thought only to augment your lustre."

"Summoning my own physician, who does not come cheap, is augmentation enough. If you do not wish to play cards with Nelanka, you may retire to bed."

"Yes, husband," said Linnalitha, her face flushed and her green eyes ablaze. "Todarko, I wish you a speedy recovery; I hope you will not be indisposed for your introduction to Popisilaija's salon tomorrow."

Todarko gave a smile that split the newly clotted blood on his lip. "Nothing will keep me away, madam."

CHAPTER TWENTY

It was almost the Hour of Evening Repast when Malvazan stepped back inside Korfez after his defeat by Rodizel.

"Where have you been! We were worried about you!" cried Flinteska.

"Some of us," smirked Dravadan.

"I went for a walk," said Malvazan quietly. "I did not relish listening to your twitterings."

"Let us eat," said Flinteska. "You must be hungry."

Somewhat to his surprise, Malvazan realised he was. They made their way into the refectory chamber, where the factotum Orijaz served them a soup of Paladrian tomatoes richly spiced. As they addressed their food, Crostadan said:

"You have no cause for shame, Malvazan. I know little of the blade, but you fought well today."

Malvazan carefully sipped his soup. "As you say, father, this is not your field. I lost to a man I should have beaten. But I am not downcast."

"I am glad to hear that," said Flinteska. "It is only a bit of sport, after all."

"Wrong!" declared Dravadan. "It is Malvazan's passion, his sole aim in life. Defeat is no trivial matter for him. I fought in the Garland, did my best, and no longer think on the matter: Malvazan does not enjoy this perspective."

There was a moment of silence. Everyone realised the truth—and the cruelty—of Dravadan's assessment.

"On the way home I stopped at the Dominikos and took counsel with the Viators," said Malvazan.

Crostadan paused with his soup halfway to his mouth, before setting his spoon down. "You have never shown any such bent before, Malvazan. Your tutors frequently reported to me your inattention."

Malvazan shrugged. "I prefer to arrive at my own conclusions. Viator Shalvijo spoke much good sense."

"I have never given the Viators much credence," said Crostadan. "In my experience their counsel is based on what is most likely to charm alms from the listener."

"They are bogus hypocrites!" said Dravadan. "Do you not remember that I caught Viator Tsilvao with his robes around his waist and Damoiselle Despijna on his lap? You were as loud in your outrage as anyone else, Malvazan: I seem to remember we both pelted him with dung in the street."

"Viator Tsilvao is long gone," said Malvazan with measured dignity. "He was misguided in his Way. That does not mean that all Viators are wicked, or their counsel corrupt."

Flinteska put her hand on her son's arm. "If Malvazan feels the call of the Viators, who are we to deny him, Crostadan? He has a troubled heart; maybe the Viators can help him."

"Nonsense, woman! The Viators prey on the gullible; I never thought to have their doctrines expounded in Korfez. Malvazan has the dissatisfactions common to every second son, but they do not all fall under the spell of the first Viator who listens to them."

"Crostadan!" snapped Flinteska. "That is no way to talk about our son! He needs your patience and guidance."

"He needs nothing of the sort," said Crostadan sharply. "He needs to understand the way of the world, not the Way of Harmony. He will always be a second son, and the sooner he realises it the better. Indeed, perhaps we have indulged his swordcraft for too long."

Malvazan rose from the table. "I find I am no longer hungry," he said. "My mind is clearer than it has been for many years. I neither require nor desire your good opinion, father."

"Where are you going?"

"Out."

"There is a matter I wish to discuss with you first," said Crostadan. "We will discuss it in my study at the Hour of Evening Satiation. Until that time you will remain at Korfez."

"Yes, father."

Flinteska said: "In that case you might as well eat your dinner. Half a bowl of soup is scarcely sufficient."

"No, thank you, mother. I will undertake some exercises until my father is ready to berate me in private."

By the Hour of Evening Satiation, Malvazan felt calmer. He had gone through a series of punishing sword-drills and sweated out some of his aggression. It was frustrating, but hardly surprising, that his father failed to understand his aspirations: Crostadan was content to be a mediocre head of a mediocre house. He had no ambition to move Umbinzia into the front rank of the Specchio.

Precisely at the appointed hour he knocked on the door of his father's study. He had dressed perhaps more formally than the occasion demanded, his silk shirt richly embroidered with cloth of gold.

"Sit down, Malvazan," said Crostadan, indicating a casual chair next to him. "There are matters requiring our attention."

"I do not wish to discuss the Way of Harmony."

"No more do I," said Crostadan with a harsh smile. He poured them both a goblet of wine. "It is unfortunate we quarrelled at dinner, since we are venturing into a delicate area."

Malvazan's dark eyes were fixed on his father's face. "Since I do not know the topic, you must lead."

"I learned a piece of intelligence which surprised me today; at the Bezant, in fact."

"Oh, yes?"

"This conversation will be much smoother if you adopt at least a pretence of cordiality, Malvazan."

"Speak on, sir."

Crostadan sighed. "I understand that you recently requested a private interview with Kropiselko of House Zano."

Malvazan blinked and looked away. "I understood it to be confidential."

"A marriage proposal concerning House Umbinzia can hardly be confidential to its head."

"Since the betrothal was unacceptable to Kropiselko I did not need to burden you with it."

"That is not how relations between the houses work, Malvazan, as I am sure you know. You made yourself appear a fool, which concerns me to some extent; more importantly, you made me appear one. If you wished to espouse Monichoë, you should have approached me to bear the suit."

Malvazan's hand tightened around his goblet. "You would not have done so."

"Exactly," said Crostadan. "You knew the idea was too hare-brained to be worthy of serious consideration. Kropiselko tells me you had not even discussed the matter with Monichoë herself, and that no understanding exists between you."

"That is correct."

"I am disappointed rather than angry, Malvazan," said Crostadan in a softer tone. "Do not think I am unaware that you outmatch your brother in intelligence, ambition and all the qualities which fit a man to be a head of house."

Malvazan felt his head spinning, perhaps from the wine he had drunk on an empty stomach. "Then why—?"

"Why am I so hard on you?"

"If that is how you think of it."

"Nothing will alter the fact that Dravadan will be the head of House Umbinzia," said Crostadan. "That is the law of the Specchio. You must use your energies in a constructive way. Despite what I said at dinner, swordcraft is a most suitable pastime for you—certainly more suitable than the Way of Harmony. Men whose judgement I respect tell me you have every chance of winning the Garland next year."

Malvazan ran a hand through his hair. This conversation was not developing along expected lines.

"I am a better swordsman than Rodizel, you know."

Crostadan flashed a quick smile. "Best that you lost to him this year, then. But your proficiency has less benign aspects."

"How so?"

"You believe that if you win the Garland you suddenly become a man of importance; the hand of a lady like Damoiselle Monichoë is no longer beyond you."

"Neither should it be. Winning the Garland has made many men."

"It does not appear to impress Kropiselko."

"That is his folly."

Crostadan leaned forward. "It is you who are in folly, Malvazan. You must set it aside. You may win the Garland, you may not. You remain the second son of a house that is not awash with suitors."

"I will not ask why you do not try to improve that status."

Crostadan's eyes flashed. "I am head of the house. I need not explain my policies to you. I am trying to explain why your ambitions, while they reflect credit on you, cannot be satisfied. Restless men, men of energy, often leave the city to find their destiny."

Malvazan said nothing. "I hope you are not among them," said Crostadan softly.

"Is there anything else, father?"

Crostadan gave a wintry smile. "The conversation to date is in the nature of a preamble."

Malvazan felt a small hard knot at the centre of his stomach. "To what?"

"Your misguided desire to unite Houses Umbinzia and Zano has made you unreceptive to more practical business," said Crostadan. "It has been my intention for many years that you are betrothed to Sanoutë of House Zamilio. There has always been amity between you, and I have deferred too long already. Before this nonsense with Monichoë came along you were perfectly happy with the match."

"Thank you for clarifying my feelings, father."

Crostadan rose to his feet. "We have discussed the matter long enough, Malvazan. Our interview is now at an end: tonight I am going to Splanatia to solicit Sanoutë's hand. Be grateful that I, unlike you, have had the courtesy to inform you of my plans in advance."

Malvazan remained in his seat as his father reached for a cloak and left the room. He had known Sanoutë since they were children; he had always liked her, and been comfortable with their likely betrothal. But prospects for advancement for a second son were few; marriage into a Prime House was obviously one of them. If he were united through Sanoutë—a house respectable but if anything inferior to Umbinzia—that avenue became closed to him. His father would certainly not be negotiating to marry Dravadan to a Secondary House.

Crostadan's hint that if he did not like the match, he could seek his fortune outside Taratanallos, had hardly been veiled. It was not a choice which attracted him; if he went to Cloop or Mandry, or even north into the Emmenrule, his pedigree would count for nothing. No doubt with his natural advantages he would prosper wherever he went, but he did not want to make his fortune from nothing like some penniless adventurer. He would not slink from Taratanallos with his tail between his legs like Viator Tsilvao.

The next day Malvazan rose and left the house early; he had no wish to encounter his father over breakfast and certainly did not want to hear the outcome of his conference with Thrinko. It was not yet the Hour of Morning Repast, and Farlankas would not be at the school. He slipped on a loose white shirt, light and baggy pantaloons and a pair of sturdy ankle-boots and ran out on to the Archgate.

The sun was just poking above the top of the city walls, glowing off the underside of the clouds in that shade known as jacinthe, a colour denoting a passion waiting to burst forth. Malvazan set off down the Archgate at a brisk pace, feeling the sweat start from his forehead and glisten on his scalp. By the time he was down at the docks his shirt was damp but he had settled into an easy rhythm. The problems of the day were gone from his mind, overlaid by a surpassing calm as his body responded to his demands.

By the time he turned to run back up the slope through the Chale the sun stood clear in the sky, the early morning mist burned off. Malvazan loved the run uphill, the sensation of leaning into the slope, fighting and overcoming an implacable enemy. Reaching the top, he felt a burning heaviness in his thighs and his breath came only with an effort. What had he been worried about? He was Malvazan, and he could resolve any difficulties put before him.

By the time he reached Korfez once more, the Hour of Morning Repast was past. The chances of encountering Crostadan at breakfast now were remote: his father would wish to be at the Masavory to transact his business of the day at the Hour of Petitions. He made his way up the flights of stairs to his chambers and called on Orijaz to draw him a bath. Here he allowed himself a period of relaxation, soaking the fatigue of the run from his body and allowing his mind to wander, thoughtless, in the steamy void.

Once the water began to cool he stepped from the bath and vigorously towelled himself dry. Any lassitude he might have felt after his exertions was left behind in the tepid water. He had not parted with Farlankas on the best of terms yesterday: now was the time to make amends and to redouble his efforts to win the Garland. He might—or might not—have to espouse Sanoutë, but that only made success in the Bezant that much more important.

CHAPTER TWENTY-ONE

It was close on the Hour of Evening Repast by the time Malvazan trudged back up the hill to Korfez. Farlankas had drilled him not just throughout the morning, as was customary, but most of the afternoon as well. He clearly had not forgotten the high-handed way Malvazan had addressed him yesterday; and Malvazan found it hard to expect him to. Rather than cavil at Farlankas' measures, he threw himself into the exercises with a ferocious energy, drawing a curt nod from Farlankas at the session's end.

Rather than go straight home, Malvazan took himself in the soft late afternoon sun towards the Dominikos. His route took him past a series of waterfront cafés, tables set out in the street packed with chattering and laughing folk. For a moment he felt a pang; such conviviality was alien to him. There was no time to cultivate both acquaintance and accomplishments. He shook his head in irritation: he was Malvazan, and he would not have it any other way. Men who were sitting in the street sipping tisane at the Hour of Afternoon Reflection were unlikely to earn renown at the Hour of Secret Deeds. One had to make choices, and he had long ago made his.

His visit to the Dominikos soothed his disquiet. In addition to the young Viator Shalvijo was the grave and sober Viator Udenko, and together they listened as Malvazan outlined his plans. Viator Udenko provided an analysis of Malvazan's Balance, that ever-changing equipoise between Hissen and Animaxia which influenced mood, mettle and deed. Once more Malvazan went away feeling that he had his own Path to Harmony, and that he could and should follow it without guilt or regret.

His tranquillity was taxed almost immediately he sat down to dinner. Dravadan slouched in his chair, smirking as if at some secret knowledge; Flinteska's eyes were swollen as if she had been crying.

"I am glad you are here, Malvazan." said Crostadan in a firm voice. "It has been an important day for House Umbinzia."

Malvazan looked up warily. House Umbinzia's interests and his own did not always coincide.

"I have managed to secure a highly advantageous betrothal for our house," said Crostadan. Malvazan looked down at his plate, the thin slices of beef lying with unappealing inertness.

"Our heir, Dravadan, is to marry Rullia of House Rasteccio. This is a connection which can only advance us all!"

Another tear rolled from Flinteska eye. "His Dignity Igrinto is so obliging," she sighed. "We are honoured to find ourselves so united."

Malvazan stared around him. It was Dravadan who was betrothed! And to a Prime House. Were his aspirations in a like direction then so vain? Such a connection might make him a more attractive match in Kropiselko's eyes. And while his last conversation with Monichoë had been oblique, it had not seemed to betoken indifference. He gave Dravadan an unfeigned smile.

"Congratulations, brother!"

Dravadan nodded in acknowledgement.

"And," said Crostadan, "our benison does not end there."

Dravadan forked a morsel of beef to his mouth while looking at Malvazan.

"Last night I also went to Splanatia and asked if Thrinko would bestow Sanoutë's hand on Malvazan. I am delighted to say he accepted with alacrity!"

Malvazan gave a weak smile. Dravadan boomed: "And congratulations to you, brother! What a day of delight is this! I shall remember it as long as I live!"

"I sent Orijaz to the market this afternoon," said Crostadan. "The betrothal feast will take place one week hence. Such good news will not keep!"

Malvazan slumped back in his chair in boneless dismay. Whatever his regard for Sanoutë, this was not on the Way of Harmony. He would have to take counsel from the Viators.

Flinteska rose from her chair, kissed first Dravadan, then enfolded Malvazan in her embrace. "I am so happy! Two sons betrothed in a single day. Who will be the first to produce me a grandson?"

"I plan to begin my attempts as soon as feasible," declared Dravadan. "Quite aside from wishing to enjoy my beautiful bride, I have a responsibility to beget the future heirs of our house."

Crostadan gave him a look of reproof. "The generation of heirs, while essential to the furtherance of our house, is hardly a fit topic for the mealtable. Malvazan's restraint is rather more to the point."

Malvazan, whose circumspection arose from nothing more than distaste for the topic, drew no satisfaction from his father's commendation. Surely if they were now married into House Rasteccio, Monichoë was not out of his reach.

"Father, a word in private, if I may?" he said.

"If this is to object to any aspect of my plans for the future of the house, including but not limited to your betrothal, I do not wish to hear it. I am head of the house, and I dispose in our best interests."

Malvazan pursed his lips.

In a softer tone, Crostadan said: "I have arranged a match which is not demeaning to you, Malvazan, and to a young lady both beautiful and agreeable. You can have no reasonable objection to Damoiselle Sanouté; if you will only see that, a marriage of felicity awaits."

Malvazan looked back blankly at his father.

"I will let you into a secret," said Crostadan with a twinkle in his eye. "When my father negotiated my betrothal to your mother, I was not delighted. I felt too young for the responsibilities of marriage, and I hardly knew your mother."

"Crostadan!" cried Flinteska with a heavy red face. "This is not a matter to discuss with our children!"

"Come, my chicken," said Crostadan with a laboured levity. "That was many years ago, and look how well matters have unfolded. This is a tale of joy for Malvazan's profit."

"Well, perhaps," said Flinteska. "If truth be told, you were not necessarily my dream either, for I always admired Spirodan of House Piaccio."

"Hmmph. What a popinjay that lad was," sniffed Crostadan.

"He certainly dressed beautifully," said Flinteska, "and such a wonderful scent about him."

"That is as may be," said Crostadan sharply. "That may explain why he never married, if you take my meaning. His interest in you—and in ladies in general—was no doubt somewhat less than yours in him."

"Just because he took care over his attire does not—"

Malvazan interjected: "In what way is this anecdote intended to reconcile me to my betrothal? If I must marry Sanouté, I will, for she is a pretty girl and good-natured; but I am hardly pleased at the way it is imposed on me."

"I am gratified to find you so compliant," said Crostadan. "You and Dravadan may visit the tailor's tomorrow and order betrothal outfits—charge them to my account."

Dravadan gave a broad grin. "How rarely we do anything together: I look forward to the occasion."

Malvazan mechanically speared the last of his beef into his mouth.

CHAPTER TWENTY-TWO

By the time Istevar had determined that Todarko's injuries, while painful, were confined to cuts and bruises rather than breaks, it was the early hours of the morning. Istevar left a salve with instructions on its application, and Todarko at last took to his bed. His sleep was fitful; whatever position he adopted in the bed chafed one or more of his contusions. In his fretful state his mind raced with speculations on the assault. Who not only wanted to see him injured but was prepared to go to considerable lengths to achieve it? He did not know the thin man, so somebody had recruited a gang of ruffians to set upon him. The beating had been precisely calculated: his enemy had not wanted him dead. The aim had been either punishment for some past misdemeanour, or warning against a future one.

Staring at the ceiling as the dawn began to break outside, he compiled a list of ill-wishers. He had ended amours with a number of women in a way unlikely to secure their goodwill, Ivanka being only the latest—and admittedly most extreme—of them. It was conceivable that her brothers, or others within House Klemenza, had arranged the lesson, but Todarko did not believe it. Her brothers Ivaijlo and Salvazar were proud and contentious men: neither was the type to hide behind hired bravos when there was a score to be settled.

Other petty disputes with members of the Specchio could be discounted. These were generally settled rapier to rapier: such a beating could only bring dishonour on its perpetrator. His most protracted feud was with Hazilan of House Franchino. Todarko had discarded Hazilan's cousin Clatida, but the nub of their rivalry was their poetic ambitions. Todarko had once indiscreetly referred to Hazilan's lovingly crafted villanelle as "marks scratched in the dirt with a stick", and matters had only deteriorated from that point. Todarko could not suppress a snigger: the idea of the unworldly Hazilan setting ruffians upon him was scarcely to be imagined.

If the motive for the assault was not retribution for some previous transgression, then it was hard to look beyond the political scene as the key. He had demonstrated no previous inclination to become involved in the city's political life: although Raguslan was a noisy supporter of the Emmen alliance, Todarko was well-known to be aloof from the debate. Times now were edgy, though: there was an air of uncertainty in the streets, and not just in the Aspergantia. The arrival of Lord Oricien's embassy had made people realise that a choice would soon have to be made. As the Emmenrule and

Gammerling circled each other liked caged battlecats, waiting for an advantageous moment to pounce, Taratanallos would have to take sides—or to hold fast to a neutrality which became harder to maintain by the year. If Lord Oricien went home with his treaty unsigned, the tension would only rise.

It was not, Todarko conceded, a good time to have been drawn into Dravadan's intrigues. Many of the Specchio, including his uncle, were trying to pick the winning side to ensure they were on it, but Todarko did not even have that excuse. He had no desire to rise at Dravadan's right hand: so long as Raguslan did not bankrupt House Vaggio, and with it Todarko's inheritance, he had no real interest in the outcome.

So why had he agreed to Dravadan's schemes? The threats from House Umbinzia if he chose not to comply had been of a pro forma nature: they would not have induced him to act had he not already chosen his course. Which brought him, of course, back to Linnalitha. Captivating, bewitching and surely unhappy under Dravadan's calculating hand, she was almost irresistibly alluring. No, forget the 'almost': she was irresistible. When they had walked to the folly at Korfez—only yesterday!—she had seemed on the point of confiding in him, before moving back out of range again. What a fencer she would make; she was never quite where he thought she was, and his sallies never landed as they should.

He was certain that the attraction was not all on his side. When he had been brought to Korfez last night her concern had been immediate and instinctive, even penetrating Dravadan's self-absorption. There were two things for which he had a natural facility: poetry and seduction, not necessarily in that order. It was clearly not inconceivable that he could bring Linnalitha to his bed, but the advisability of it was harder to weigh. His imagination, not normally stunted, quailed at the prospect of what Dravadan might do were any liaison to come to light. Nelanka, Bodazar and even Linnalitha herself had warned him of the consequences of a miss-step here. The sensible course was to forget Linnalitha completely. She was too beguiling to be safe at arm's length: he would have to break with her altogether. Dravadan would be disappointed, particularly as Todarko could hardly share his true reason; but this was still the course with the least risk.

His eyes were beginning to feel heavy; perhaps sleep was not out of the question. His breath hissing out through clenched teeth in discomfort, he rolled onto his side. As he drifted off into a doze his last thoughts were of Linnalitha's green eyes and the wave of her red hair.

Todarko woke an hour or so later, much refreshed. He summoned Luzio with some hot water and dabbed at his face, wincing as the warmth stung his cuts once more. Gingerly he poked at his face. The cut above his eye was tender and one cheekbone was deeply scored. He decided to defer looking in the glass until later; the sight would not be a cheerful one.

He sent Luzio away to bring some breakfast and settled himself on his balcony, looking out to sea, to polish his verses. He knew from experience that his best work came when he was not trying too hard with it. It was like the strange shapes that swam before his eye after looking into the sun: they could only be perceived if he did not look at them directly. Once he tried to focus on them, they became insubstantial, and whatever meaning they had could not be captured.

This morning he had woken with a couplet in mind. He knew, with an instinct honed over many years, that it was the start of a sonnet:

> *In loving thee thou know'st I am forsworn,*
> *That every word doth almost tell my name.*

As he scratched the words down on the paper he laughed. There was no disguising where this had come from. He might as well have written at the top of the page Sonnet to Madam L. He had said yesterday to Bodazar that he might write her a poem, and so it was coming to pass. So much for putting her aside: his dreaming mind was writing sonnets to her. He tried to look at the words objectively. If the sonnet had any merit it would stand independently of Linnalitha.

Luzio came back with some bread and a jug of light beer. "Raguslan requests your company at the breakfast table, sir."

Todarko shook his head impatiently. "I am indisposed. Thank him for his concern for my well-being—if he expressed any—and say that I hope to be more refreshed later."

"Your indisposition does not appear of the most prostrating nature, sir."

Todarko turned his face to display his wounds to maximum advantage. "Does this look like a face anyone would wish to break their fast opposite?"

"No, sir."

"Excellent. No doubt there is some silver you should be polishing."

"Yes, sir."

Luzio bowed and withdrew from the room. Even before he had closed the door, Todarko had forgotten him, his attention once more on his verse.

Two hours later he had another two lines, to complete the first quatrain. This was not rapid progress, but he was pleased with the result. He had tried and discarded any number of possibilities before settling on the final lines. He turned the paper over and wrote out a fair copy of his progress to date:

> *In loving thee thou know'st I am forsworn,*
> *That every word doth almost tell my name*
> *And place my merit in the eye of scorn.*
> *How sweet and lovely dost thou make the shame!*

Yes, this was not bad at all. It spoke of forbidden feelings long suppressed, but bursting out in all kinds of secret ways, even though their expression could only lead to dismay. And the final line, emphasising how all other considerations were trivial. It was a good morning's work, perhaps the best he had ever done.

And yet he could not share it with anyone. The message was all too pointed. Regardless of his daydreams about Linnalitha, he could not possibly give it to her.

Time enough to worry about that in the future. Now he needed to apply some more of Istevar's salve before contriving an excuse to avoid Popisilaija's salon this afternoon.

Ribauldequin sat on a crisply-upholstered couch in Oricien's apartment.

"Do you really mean to send Iselin back to Emmen?" he asked.

"What choice do I have?" said Oricien. "He has cheated the King, stolen from his purse."

Ribauldequin leaned back in his seat. "I do not like the man; for a candlemaker's grandson he has intolerable airs. So much is known. Nonetheless—"

"You think me rash?" said Oricien with a raised eyebrow.

"I simply wonder whether there is an alternative. Iselin has done much valuable work, much of it tedious in nature which we would not wish to undertake ourselves. He knows the city and its rulers well; he would appear to carry a degree of influence."

"He is a thief and a liar," said Oricien in a flat voice.

Ribauldequin shrugged. "If we only dealt with men we admired, we should all have a smaller circle of acquaintance."

Oricien stroked his chin. "You seriously suggest I should pardon him?"

"Perhaps not quite. If you offered him the chance to atone for his mistakes, no doubt he would display a remarkable zeal. You can still denounce him to the King once we are back in Emmen if you choose."

Oricien gave Ribauldequin a careful scrutiny. He had not previously subjected his character to extensive analysis. His initial impression of a headstrong, impulsive young man was no doubt substantially accurate, but his counsel with regard to Iselin denoted a certain shrewdness. Iselin's counsel would certainly be of use; and after all, 85,000 florins was no huge sum to the King. If it were repaid, it was possible that an arrangement satisfactory to everyone could yet occur.

"Very well," he said. "Ask the Consiglio to find Iselin and you may carry a message to that effect."

There was a soft knock at the door, and Vivalda entered. Tonight she was attired in a clinging gown of darkest blue. "Apologies, my lord: I did not realise you were engaged. I wondered if there was anything you needed."

Ribauldequin raised an appreciative eyebrow. "Rank has its privileges," he said to Oricien with a smirk. "Your bath-slave is a delight—not that I would complain about my own, of course."

Oricien stood up. "Thank you, Ribauldequin: you have many matters to attend to. Vivalda, if you could draw me a bath I would be most grateful. I have had the dirtiest, grimiest, grubbiest day imaginable."

She curtsied with a smile which hinted both at a conspiratorial unity with Oricien and an almost-visible mockery for Ribauldequin. Was she really only eighteen?

"Will you be needing me subsequently, my lord?" She was too accomplished a flirt to pout or preen, but the prospect of retaining her into the later part of the evening was undeniably an appealing one. Who would think the worse of him? The fact remained that her declared willingness to bed with him was synthetic, factitious. The girl was a slave, however cunningly schooled. With a rueful shake of the head, he said: "Not tonight, thank you, Vivalda. There is much on which I need to think."

Her eyes narrowed with what looked like the faintest hint of reproach. "Very well, my lord."

She turned in a graceful movement and went to draw his bath.

CHAPTER TWENTY-THREE

Towards the end of the Hour of Afternoon Reflection, Luzio appeared in Todarko's rooms.

"Madam Linnalitha waits upon you in the reception chamber, sir."

"I have already said I am indisposed," said Todarko.

"She anticipated this contingency, sir, and asked me to give you this." Luzio handed over a single sheet of paper, secured with the wax seal inset with a battlecat, the sigil of House Umbinzia.

After a brief hesitation, Todarko reached out for the paper and broke the seal with a clammy thumb.

> *I am sure you are regretting your decision to accompany me to House Oreste. You are under no obligation to my husband, but I have very much valued our discussions in recent days; I would wish to continue our friendship, if it pleases you.*
>
> *L. of U.*

Todarko read the message twice. It changed nothing; the sensible option was to burn it and reiterate his indisposition. There was something in the tone, however, which barred such a course. Hidden not so far beneath the surface was an appeal, whether Linnalitha had written it deliberately or not. He doubted that she was unaware of the likely effect of her words. She was not making matters any easier.

"I am indisposed," said Todarko with a clenched jaw. "Send my regrets and apologies—no, Hissen take it, I'll tell her myself. I will be down in five minutes."

Luzio bowed and withdrew. If Todarko saw a smirk flash across his face, it was gone too quickly to be certain.

He looked in the glass. One eye was noticeably blackened, but Istevar's salve had taken the worst of the lividity and swelling from his face. His ribs were still sore but he could move relatively freely. He took off his shirt, grimaced at the bruising on his side, before donning fresh linen. He did not look at the apex of health, but neither was he obviously decrepit.

He wiped his boots with his handkerchief, buttoned his favourite black jacket and made to leave the room. On impulse he took a small dagger from his bedside drawer and tucked it inside his pocket. If he were set upon again, he intended to fight back.

The seats in the reception chamber were empty when he entered. Looking around, he saw Linnalitha's slender back towards him as she looked from the window into the gardens to the rear.

"Madam," he said softly.

Linnalitha turned in a movement of cool grace.

"I thought you would not come," she said in a quiet level voice. "Your association with House Umbinzia has not been to your advantage."

"I have only come to say..."

Linnalitha looked down at her feet. "Yes?"

She is nothing to you. You owe her nothing.

"If you are prepared to be seen with me in this unpresentable state, I should be delighted to accompany you to Popisilaija's."

Fool. How many enemies do you want? How many beatings? In which ditch do you want your throat cut?

Linnalitha's eyes danced although her expression did not change.

"The salon begins at the Hour of Cordial Discourse. We may walk, if you are not too sore."

"I would value the exercise."

"Good." She walked towards him. "Will you fasten my veil? My fingers are clumsy today."

Todarko was conscious that his own fingers were not of the most dextrous either. As she stood close he breathed in a scent of soap and lavender. She put her hood up to cover her hair and Todarko clipped both sides of the veil in place. If the purpose of Hooding and Veiling is to make women less tempting, he thought, it is a vain hope. All that could be seen of Linnalitha's head was her glorious green eyes, and they alone could lead a man to ruin: Todarko himself could vouch for that.

"What are you smiling at?" she said.

Todarko shook his head. "A momentary fancy," he said. "I will not embarrass myself by articulating it."

"As you will," she said, a twitch of smile animating her own lips.

Outside in the street the late afternoon sun sparkled on the wavelets breaking against the city walls below them. Fizenar, the manse of House Oreste, was away down the hill and they set off at a leisurely pace. Linnalitha walked close beside him without touching, and she nodded and gave the occasional salute to other veiled women taking the air.

"How do you know who they are?" asked Todarko. "They are behind veils."

"You become used to it," said Linnalitha. "Laraija lists to the left as she walks; Salpana shimmies her hips; only Hokanija would wear that putrid shade of yellow, so reminiscent of dog's vomit."

"And how would your associates recognise you?"

Linnalitha gave a brief laugh. "If I knew, I would change it: I should love to roam the streets incognito."

"You should try the Chale," said Todarko. "I am rarely recognised, and the women do not wear veils at all."

"If they are out on the street unveiled, they are probably prostitutes, or at the very least careless of their virtue."

"The Chale has different standards," said Todarko. "It may be within the walls, but it is a different city. If you find the Specchio stifling, it can be a refreshing place to visit."

"And a dangerous one," she said. "You were not accosted by well-wishers last night."

"That was not Chale business. It emanated, one way or another, from the Aspergantia."

Todarko had never before entered Fizenar. Glasshouse Lane was set at right-angles to the lower slope of the Archgate, not one of the very best locations, but Bartielko was a highly respectable man. His wife Popisilaija was known for her literary salons, and Todarko was ushered out onto the evening loggia with every enthusiasm. As they walked through the reception room, those of Popisilaija's guests who had just arrived were divesting themselves of Hood and Veil—always a moment Todarko enjoyed when visiting a respectable house. He had to acknowledge, though, the women were by and large past the first flush of youth. Some of them, he considered, might with advantage have remained under Hood and Veil, where at least the viewer could exercise a degree of imagination.

"Linnalitha!" cried Popisilaija. "You have brought him!"

She was a short sturdy blonde woman with an air of boundless enthusiasm and energy. Her smile was wide and her cheeks dimpled; Todarko could not help liking her on sight.

"I am honoured, madam," he said. "I thank you for your invitation."

"It is good for Linnalitha to have a new friend," she said. "They can be so very gloomy in the Emmen party, if you'll pardon my frankness."

Todarko had no quibble with frankness; but he had to question the judgement of anyone who thought that a new male friend for Linnalitha could be anything other than a prelude to disaster.

"We do not speak of politics here, of course," she continued. "You will take a slice of cake, I hope, which gives more enduring and substantial satisfaction than any political discourse."

Todarko found this sentiment harder to disagree with. As he bit into the sweet sponge, he noticed with alarm that his old rival Hazilan had taken up station on a seat at the corner of the loggia. Hazilan saw him at the same time and beckoned him with a wave. Todarko responded with a grim nod.

"The ladies have captured you at last," said Hazilan with an expansive gesture. "It is inevitable, I suppose, that all good things become coarsened and corrupted over time. I remember the early days of the salon, when an invitation was a mark of true favour and distinction. Now, I'm afraid, the draff and filth of the literary world can be seen here. I'm sure you agree."

Todarko brought down his eyelids in a dismissive gesture. "Your recent sonnet collection was not your finest work, certainly, but you are too harsh upon yourself. All artists know periods of self-doubt, and for those on the lower plateau of talent, such experiences must be all too frequent."

Hazilan summoned another drink with a wave. "The poets I feel the most pity for are the ones who never have such doubts. I can think of those who imagine themselves creating the most rarefied verses, when in fact they simply pump out a barrage of banality. To have such a gap between their perceptions of themselves, and their true merits, is a cruel irony of life."

"Just so," said Todarko.

"At least you, good Todarko, have the merit of humility. If your verses are not of the first water, at least you have the grace to acknowledge it. I admire you—no, you must hear this, you are too modest—I truly admire you: if I continually produced verse at a pedestrian level, I doubt I would have the persistence to continue. A man who so sincerely believes improvement to be just around the corner deserves the acclaim of all. I consider my talent to be great blessing from Animaxia—I cannot claim the credit for it—but sometimes I regret that my achievements come with so little struggle."

"There is a view," said Todarko, "which is not one I generally endorse, that what is earned without toil is without value. Perhaps there is some truth in the notion that nothing worth having comes without pain." He looked across to where Linnalitha, although talking to Popisilaija, appeared to be listening intently.

"I often hear the position argued," said Hazilan. "Usually it comes from those who have no acquaintance with the muse. I am disappointed, although perhaps not surprised, to hear you articulate it."

Linnalitha came over and touched his arm. "Todarko, I am feeling a little dizzy," she said. "Will you accompany me onto the lawns?"

"Of course, madam."

They took steps down from the loggia to the lawns, which were largely unoccupied. "I hope you are not too indisposed, madam."

Linnalitha gave him a wondering look. "I merely wished to extract you from your foolish dispute with Hazilan. We are here for altogether greater purposes, and we should begin immediately."

Todarko narrowed his eyes. Her remark admitted of more than one meaning. "You refer to—?"

"Our intelligencing, of course. What did you think I meant?"

Todarko pursed his lips. "Nothing."

"Well, then. Let us begin. We may learn something in the remainder of the house."

"You propose to break in to Bartielko's private quarters?"

"You have a better suggestion?"

Todarko stopped and leaned against an ornamental fountain whispering gently in the late afternoon. Tell her, tell her, it burbled. She is waiting for you.

"You truly wish to grub out who knows what facts about Bartielko?"

She gave a quick smile. "The matter is perhaps not as compelling as it appeared earlier."

"Why then are you here?"

She stepped away from the fountain into the shadow of the garden wall, but even in the shade Todarko could see a blush creeping across her cheek. "Why are you?" she said quietly. "You care neither for my husband nor your uncle."

"It was easier to agree than argue."

"That does not accord with what I know of your character," she said. "You do not exert yourself to oblige Raguslan, and you scarcely know my husband."

"I was not going to come at all today," he said.

"I know."

"I do not know why I did."

"Do not expect me to enlighten you, if you cannot tell yourself."

His hand worried at a loose piece of mortar on the fountain.

"I started a new sonnet today. I completed the first quatrain before the Hour of Light Repast," he said, not looking at her.

"This cannot be an usual event for a poet."

"It spoke of love and loss, forbidden feelings which nonetheless cannot be denied. Counsels of good sense weighed against the ardent promptings of something deeper."

"All this in four lines? Your verse is highly economical."

"Perhaps not all of it is on the page yet. There are another ten lines to go. I am unsure whether to continue."

"You do not strike me as a man accustomed to controlling his impulses."

Todarko crumbled the last of the mortar between his fingers. "It can be hard to contain the force of a poem crying to be written. Some impulses do not deserve suppression; the difficulty is in knowing which."

She stepped close and, half a head shorter, looked into his face. "I am no poet, but I think we know, Todarko," she said. "I think we always know."

Todarko felt the blood pounding in his ears. "Yes, we do." He reached out and drew her towards him, kissed her with one long, lingering movement. She responded as if she were an uncoiling spring, then broke away.

"We cannot do this," she said.

"We just did. I have to say I found the experience enjoyable, memorable, and altogether worthy of repetition."

She looked around. "This is hardly a private location. We could be discovered at any point."

"Does that imply that you would have no objections in a more secluded venue?"

She stepped away. "This is not a game, Todarko! Do you think my husband is to be trifled with? Do you think I am?" Her green eyes flared.

"I care nothing for your husband. And I am not trifling with you."

"No doubt you said the same to Clatida. And Ivanka. And who knows which other trollops among the Specchio?"

"Must you refer to Ivanka again? I am striving for discretion, as much to preserve her reputation as mine."

"You are a model of considerate rectitude; but your licentious behaviour is hardly a secret."

"You appeared not to protest before. You cannot kiss me like that and then accuse me of trifling with you!"

She looked into his face for a few moments. "You don't understand."

"I have admitted as much. I look to you for clarification."

Her face burned scarlet. "Here is your clarification. We have spent the past three days circling each other like cats on heat. That in itself is wrong, not to mention unwise. I excuse my conduct with reference to my own feelings, which are unequivocal; I can have no such assurance of your intentions given your history of seduction and desertion."

"Linna, I—"

"There is nothing you can say which will resolve my uncertainties. Men of your stamp will say anything to gain a lady's favours. You could assure me of your undying love and it would mean nothing because of the kind of man you are. In fact, the less you say, the better, since you only condemn yourself with your protestations."

"It was only a kiss!"

She slapped him with surprising force, knocking the scab from his cheekbone.

"It was the prelude, in your mind at least, to something rather more. Now you cannot even admit that. Dravadan is the cruellest man alive: he will sew me up in a sack with scorpions if I ever look that way at another man. And yet the one man I feel like that about is you: a louse, a scabthorn, a loathsome insect! The Viators would have plenty to say about my progress along the Way! Leave me! I cannot endure the sight of you."

"Linna, you are over-reacting." Todarko smoothed down his doublet. "There is much we need to discuss."

"There is nothing we need to discuss. Nothing!"

She turned and fled back towards the house. Even in her flight, Todarko noticed, there was a grace to her every movement.

He ran a hand through his hair. At least he was saved from having to make a decision as to the advisability of any future liaison. A movement in the bushes caught his eye: he stepped briskly over to the shrub but saw no sign of life. Even better! he thought. Now I am fancying unseen watchers too.

CHAPTER TWENTY-FOUR

As Todarko made his way back to the house he saw, to his surprise, that the Emmen ambassador Oricien was being introduced. Popisilaija's salon was notorious for being free of politicking and all such sordid matters. He felt a sense of dissatisfaction both with House Oreste and Lord Oricien for cheapening one of the few occasions in polite society not marred by crude scrambles for petty advantage.

Bartielko himself—not normally on display at literary events—was on hand to welcome Oricien. A tall, florid bulky man with a ruff of white hair, he exuded the aura of a head of house. "My lord, welcome to Fizenar. You honour House Oreste with your presence."

Oricien essayed a modest bow. "The honour is mine, Dignity. I have monopolised the attentions of certain grandees and the very least I can do is to allow them some time for their own pursuits—particularly in the current unfortunate circumstances."

"Of course, of course," murmured Bartielko. "It is no secret that, regrettably, not all members of the Masavory are on cordial terms. It may well be that, however inadvertently, your perceptions of House Oreste have been tainted by the sometimes colourful views of men like Dravadan. I am delighted for the chance to meet you on this friendly footing."

Oricien made a bland response and Bartielko said: "Are you a man for the literary wiffle-waffle, my lord?"

"I take it you are not," said Oricien with a smile. "I myself can take it or leave it. I notice young Todarko of House Vaggio, regarded as something of a poet." He raised a hand in salute, to which Todarko responded with a languid wave.

Bartielko frowned. "The invitations to these events are determined by my esteemed wife. House Vaggio are not among our intimates, but Todarko is less egregious than most of his clan. Come, shall we talk apart?"

He placed a hand in the small of Oricien's back and guided him into a small but well-appointed study, the walls covered with rich hangings. A portrait of a younger, slimmer Bartielko had pride of place above a heavy wooden desk. Bartielko indicated a pair of low chairs and Oricien seated himself. After pouring them both a goblet of wine, Bartielko eased himself into the chair adjacent to Oricien.

For a moment they sipped in unison and silence. Then Oricien said: "This is an excellent vintage, Dignity—and from the Emmenrule, if I am not mistaken."

Bartielko took another pull at his goblet. "You have a discriminating palate," he said. "These grapes are from the slopes to the south of Sey."

"I flatter myself that our wines cannot be bettered, for all the talk of Paladria. I am glad to see that you agree."

Bartielko held up a finger. "I have wines from all over Mondia in my cellars," he said. "I appreciate good things, whatever their provenance."

"Given the well-known association between House Oreste and all things Gammerling, I am pleasantly surprised to see you serving an Emmen wine."

Bartielko crossed his legs. "I am not dogmatic. I take matters as I find them; this approach maximises the zest I gain from life. It is a dynamic philosophy and not, I admit, for everyone. You are wise to take the trouble to make my acquaintance."

Oricien smiled. "Dogmatism is the refuge of small minds; wider perceptions inevitable see wider possibilities."

"It is a pity, my lord, that you represent a power that I can only view as baneful to the health of Taratanallos."

Oricien set his goblet down with a precise movement. "You yourself, I believe, counsel submission to the King of Gammerling rather than the King of Emmen. It may be that my own perceptions lack the breadth of your own, but I do not see any great difference in principle."

"These are hard questions for an outsider to encompass," said Bartielko in a genial tone. "King Ingomer has long been a friend to our city; whereas King Enguerran, undoubtedly a great monarch, is far away. If we knew him better, maybe we would revise our opinions."

"I am sure, Dignity, that His Puissance would like nothing better. It is gratifying that your largeness of spirit extends to such matters."

Bartielko made an airy gesture. "A wise man maintains a wardrobe suitable for all weathers. He may hope for sun, and lay in a store of fine linen shirts; but he is improvident if he does not also have an oilskin against inclement squalls."

Oricien narrowed his eyes. "Just so, Dignity. Might I interpret your flexibility as extending, potentially, to support of one monarch rather than another?"

Bartielko held up both hands. "You go too fast, my lord. I am a man whose word is his bond, who lives or dies by his reputation: in fact, the model of a Masavory grandee. I am seen by many as embodying the

Gammerling alliance. How, then, could I be seen to turn my coat? It is hard to imagine the incentive that could compel such an act."

Oricien thought to catch a nuance in the phrasing and could barely suppress a smile. "We are alone in your study, two men with great affairs of state at our fingertips. As one gentleman to another, and leaving aside all formality, might I ask you what is your price?"

Bartielko winced. "'Price' implies the crudity of coin. It suggests no very great appreciation of my character."

Oricien inclined his head. "It may be that I express myself less delicately than the situation warrants. I am merely seeking to establish if there are any steps that I or my master might take which could persuade you to lend your great influence to our noble cause."

Bartielko leaned back in his chair and looked at Oricien along his aquiline nose. After a pause, he nodded. "One million florins."

Oricien's hand started and he slopped some wine over the rim. "A million!"

"In addition, I would need to be assured of a preferential position within the governance of the city. There are those, inevitably, who would revile me, and in truth I must be recompensed."

Oricien set down his goblet. "There is recompense and recompense," he said. "I doubt that King Enguerran's credit in the city runs to a million florins."

"You need not pay in cash immediately. A promissory note would be sufficient, or even interest on the amount outstanding. At five percent, let us say 50,000 florins a year."

Oricien shook his head. "Much as I value your counsel, and even more your support, you ask for something I cannot offer. I do not have a million florins to commit."

Bartielko shrugged. "I can guarantee the votes of many grandees. A million florins for Taratanallos: I am sure King Enguerran would regard it as a good deal."

Oricien thought of the 100,000 florins Iselin had passed to Aladar. This was the scale of bribe which was more understandable.

"I can offer you a hundred and fifty thousand," said Oricien. "In cash, immediately upon a successful vote. In addition, His Puissance would bestow the title of King's Counsellor."

The title did not exist but this need not impede negotiations, thought Oricien.

Bartielko smiled and shook his head. "My finances are not like Aladar's," he said. "I am not desperate for petty cash. You are asking for a great service, and it is only just that King Enguerran should pay a great price."

Oricien smiled and stood up. "I am grateful for your advice, Dignity. Be assured that I will raise this matter again as circumstances dictate. For now, you will excuse me: I have other calls to pay."

Bartielko shook his hand. "I hope to speak to you again in due course, my lord."

CHAPTER TWENTY-FIVE

Korfez thrummed with activity like a beehive as Crostadan sought to prepare the manse for the forthcoming feast. Malvazan's betrothal on its own would have been an important event, but it was Dravadan's which made it the talk of Taratanallos. It was not every day that the heir to a seat on the Masavory became betrothed, and the addition of a bride from the impeccable House Rasteccio only added to the lustre of the occasion. Crostadan invited the head of the twenty-three other houses—and received twenty-three acceptances, a contingency at once delightful and daunting. Each house would bring not only its head but his spouse and, since this was a betrothal, children as well. Some houses would deploy even more representatives, and while Korfez was a proud and spacious manse, Crostadan could not but hope for good weather so that his guests could make best use of the gardens and loggia. Orijaz was despatched to the marketplace to secure the choicest victuals: calves, deer, poultry, fruits and vegetables from every corner of Mondia. Taratanallos was the greatest market of all and Crostadan was determined that his guests would not be stinted. Flinteska, meanwhile, bustled around the house in a flurry of activity, some of which made a constructive contribution to progress.

Malvazan, meanwhile, accompanied his brother to the tailor Luscijno to be fitted with matching outfits for the occasion. The visit was markedly lacking in cordiality; Dravadan, condescending enough at the best of times, was close to insufferable here. If he had to hear one more time about Rullio's luxuriant red hair, Malvazan felt he would punch his brother, witness or no witness. Sanouté had charms of her own, undoubtedly, but both he and Dravadan knew that the betrothal was unwilling and this lent an uncomfortable edge to their conversation. The brothers had always been rivals, and now it was plain that Dravadan had finally secured the upper hand.

Equally irritating, Malvazan lost two days' practice with Farlankas, so often was he required to be on hand for measurements or to write correspondence. On the evening of the second day he made his way to the Dominikos to take counsel from Viator Shalvijo, who was now confirmed as his personal guide.

"How can I escape this fate?" he asked in exasperation as they sat in the candlelit cubiculo. "Surely my destiny is to marry Monichoë, not Sanouté!"

Shalvijo leaned back and rubbed his chin. "If our Way was so clearly lit, why would we need Viators?" he asked. "Sometimes the obvious path is not the true Way."

"You advised me last time—"

"We felt, did we not, that your path was towards power and consequence?"

"And a great marriage, and—"

"The marriage," continued Shalvijo smoothly, "was a step on the Way: it was not, in itself, the destination."

"Well—"

"In a year's time, things may look very different. House Zano may have failed, and Zamilio prosper. Imagine you are walking along a path in the Forest of Sang Saraille at night. How do you see where you are going?"

"I'd take a lantern."

"Exactly so!" declared Shalvijo as if Malvazan had just uncovered a long-buried truth. "And how far ahead does that light your way?"

Malvazan shrugged. "Fifty yards, I don't know—it depends on the lantern."

Shalvijo beamed, folded his hands over his stomach. "And at the fifty-first yard an angry bindlespith may lie in wait, or a furious leopardillo. Even a Viator, your light along the Way, cannot foresee all outcomes."

Malvazan frowned. "You are advising me to marry Sanouté?"

Shalvijo once more stroked his chin. "Matters are rarely so simple. I counsel neither for nor against. What I am saying is that it need not obstruct your progress. You must make your own decision, but it is not so simple as saying that marrying Monichoë takes you to your goal, and Sanouté does not."

"I am not certain," said Malvazan, "whether you have given me any advice at all. You have certainly not provided unequivocal counsel."

"You are a young man of independent thought," said Shalvijo blandly. "I cannot imagine you would want me to tell you what to do, or follow my instructions if I did."

Malvazan gave a quick hard grin. "You are right, of course."

He got up and stepped out of the Dominikos, leaving behind him the handful of florins he had come to realise was the consideration for which the Viators provided their wisdom.

By the time Malvazan left the Dominikos, night had fallen: it was close upon the Hour of Noble Pleasures. He turned into Redberry Lane to make his way towards the Archgate, a route taking him past the Grand Gallumpher, a tavern frequented by the more louche members of the Specchio. Indeed, Malvazan himself had met Glastarko there on occasion, although it was not an establishment he favoured.

As he strode past the entrance, a heavy wooden door open and a man stumbled into him.

"Watch where you're going!" growled the man in a thick voice.

Malvazan stepped back. "This advice would be better applied to yourself, sir."

The man drew himself up and stared into Malvazan's face. He was maybe an inch shorter, but broad and well-muscled.

"Do you know who you're talking to, boy?"

Malvazan gave the man a cool appraisal. It was a moonless night, and although the modulation of the voice suggested some breeding, he was at a loss to identify him.

"Beyond identifying a lout who should know better," said Malvazan, "I lack precise information."

A heavy hand bunched Malvazan's shirt. "I am Flarijo of House Brenza, and I'll thank you to show some manners."

Malvazan jerked back to break Flarijo's grip. "You stumble into me in your cups, reeking of wine and arrogance, Flarijo of House Brenza, and expect me to bow to you? I am Malvazan of House Umbinzia, and no man's inferior."

Flarijo took another step towards him, reached again for Malvazan's shirt. "I say you are my inferior, boy."

Malvazan knocked the hand aside, pushed at Flarijo who in astonishment fell back in the street. His companions, who had followed him from the tavern, laughed and snorted.

"I think that concludes our business, sir," said Malvazan, and turned to continue down the street. Behind him Flarijo scrabbled on the cobbles, regained his feet, and sprang at Malvazan.

"I think not," he hissed. "No one pushes Flarijo!"

"I just did," said Malvazan. "Is that all?"

Flarijo launched a blow at Malvazan's face; even in his drunkenness, it was a shrewd and well-timed blow, but Malvazan's reflexes, sharp from his swordplay, saw him sway aside in a graceful movement.

"Would you like to settle this the gentleman's way, Flarijo?" said Malvazan in a soft voice. "There is little dignity to brawling in the street."

"Come now!" called one of Flarijo's companions. "Can we not all be friends?"

Malvazan turned to face him. "He struck at me in the street. You may set no value on my honour: I do."

Flarijo gave Malvazan a bleary scrutiny. "You should be careful, boy. Swords have sharp edges."

"I know how to use a sword," said Malvazan. "Few better."

Flarijo's friend said: "This will go too far. Shake hands and we will all go our ways."

"It is already too late," said Malvazan. He had not wanted a fight, but now one loomed he felt a fierce surge of exhilaration. Flarijo might yet back down, but he found himself hoping for the contrary. "Flarijo has a choice: he may apologise, or he may meet me at a place of his choosing."

Flarijo stood tall, looked again at Malvazan. "I have fought duels before," he said. "I am still alive. I give you the chance to withdraw your challenge."

Malvazan returned a level stare. "There will be no withdrawal. Blood or death, the choice is yours."

Flarijo seemed instantly to sober. "How old are you?"

"Nineteen."

"I do not want to kill you," he said. "If you challenge me, my honour requires me to accept. But we fight to blood, not the death."

"Very well," said Malvazan. "The time is the Hour of Secret Deeds tomorrow. Send to Korfez with the location."

"As you wish," said Flarijo stiffly.

Malvazan made a crisp bow and continued his journey towards the Archgate.

Malvazan was in no mood for conversation when he returned home. The house was quiet, and the only illumination was two small torches burning down in the hallway. He took himself immediately to bed, but found sleep elusive.

Staring at the ceiling he ran the events over once more in his mind. He could easily have evaded the duel, at several points. Flarijo had been boorish, but drunkenness excused his conduct to a certain extent: this was not a situation which needed to be settled by the blade. But on some level, he had been spoiling for a fight. He did not know Flarijo's level of skill, but it was unlikely to exceed his own. On the other hand, Malvazan had never fought for real before; the consequences of a mistake were rather more significant—indeed, potentially fatal. It was perhaps no wonder that he could not sleep.

It was not, he realised, fear that was keeping him awake. If anything, the emotion he could identify was excitement. All the years he had practised for the Garland, all the drills, the exercises, the exhaustion. Now he would use the skills he had acquired in the way they were meant to be used. And all the frustrations he felt—about the betrothal, about Dravadan, about losing by a fluke to Rodizel—for a day at least, they would be gone. His whole life, for this one day, would be encapsulated by the duel to come.

With a start, he realised that he would need a second. Habitual duellists no doubt kept a friend primed for such events—although habitual duellists might not have a long life expectancy. Who could he choose? He ran down a mental list. Dravadan? Unthinkable. His list of friends was not extensive. He considered with a snort of amusement asking Rodizel—at least he would understand how to conduct himself at a duel. Still, it would cause larger problems than it solved. Glastarko! He would be the best choice—a swordsman of repute, a fellow alumnus of Farlankas, and with an impeccable pedigree.

Even though it was the middle of the night, he slipped downstairs in his bare feet to light a candle and compose a letter, which he left for Orijaz to convey to Tappinetto first thing in the morning.

By the time Malvazan came down to breakfast, having finally slipped into a fragmentary sleep just before dawn, the letter was gone. Dravadan, it seemed, was still in bed, and his father was already out and about on betrothal business. Only his mother was at the table, quietly sipping her tisane with an expression of quiet satisfaction.

"Good morning, Malvazan! I trust you slept well." She smiled with the particular benevolence of a mother who had seen both her sons betrothed in the same week.

"Tolerably well, thank you," he said, reaching for a slice of bread and some preserves.

"I am visiting Madam Katorinka at Cuspidor tonight," she said. "She wishes to see the young men of the moment, and I have assured her Dravadan and you will be on hand."

Malvazan scowled. "In this you exceeded your certain knowledge," he said. "I cannot speak for Dravadan, but I have another engagement."

"More important than accompanying your mother to a respectable salon? You have always complained you are shown insufficient consequence: this is a period of glory for you."

"My plans cannot be changed," said Malvazan.

"You are determined to hurt me," said Flinteska in a high voice. "Why can you not be agreeable like Dravadan?"

Perhaps because you have arranged a spectacular marriage for him, thought Malvazan.

"Tonight is a matter of honour," said Malvazan. "You must be content with that."

"You are so prickly, Malvazan," said Flinteska, shaking her head with a ghost of a smile. "I cannot imagine how Sanoutë will ever manage you."

CHAPTER TWENTY-SIX

Malvazan sat in the comfortable Reflection Chamber, all soft seats and weathered wood, while he waited for his correspondence. Orijaz brought him in two letters at once. Taking up a knife he deftly broke the seal on the first.

> Sir,
>
> Last night you challenged me to a duel of blood. I remain reluctant to inflict injury on a person of your years for such a trifling address, and if you wish to withdraw your challenge I will never again refer to the matter.
>
> If, however, you remain implacable, you may meet me at Fangardo's Clearing at the Hour of Secret Deeds. My second will be the Grave Putranko, whom you met last night.
>
> This issue of honour will be settled by the Quietus: hostilities will continue until one party is well blooded, disabled, or disarmed; or until, after receiving a wound, and blood being drawn, the aggressor begs pardon.
>
> I will arrange for an apothecary to be on hand in the event of a more serious injury being incurred.
>
> I remain your servant,
> The Grave Flarijo

Malvazan dashed off a quick response expressing his regrets but reiterating that the affront was so marked as to require the shedding of blood. He then opened his second letter.

> My dear Malvazan,
>
> Whatever have you done? There are many reasons one would wish to escape a betrothal, but death by steel seems a somewhat extreme way to go about it!
>
> I am honoured beyond measure that you would select me as your second. Flarijo is a lummox and I can only commend your choice of opponent; while a swordsman of some experience, I doubt that he will seriously discommode you.

I regret that I am unable to act as your second, however. Tulerija was brought to childbed last night, and all etiquette and protocol demands that I remain on hand. I have taken the liberty of discussing the matter with Raguslan—I hope you are not displeased—and I am glad to say he would be delighted to act in my stead.

Please send your response to Tappinetto where my brother waits to attend upon you.
~Your affectionate friend,
Glastarko

Malvazan set down the letter. Tulerija's childbirth was unavoidable, and Glastarko's refusal in the circumstances was no slight. Raguslan, while not the swordsman his brother was, nonetheless could not be seen as a poor choice of second. Indeed, as the heir to House Vaggio, he was an improvement on Glastarko, even if he was a dull dull dog. He would have to do.

So it was that towards the end of the Hour of Noble Pleasures, Malvazan stood in the hallway of Tappinetto awaiting Raguslan's attendance. Soon Raguslan clattered down the stairs, his boots clattering on the worn stone. He saw Malvazan and bowed.

"Well met, sir," he said. "This is an unexpected turn of events."

Malvazan gave a cool smile. "I am not the first and I will not be the last to settle a matter of honour this way."

Raguslan gave a nervous smile. "Where is your sword?"

"I did not think my blunted competition blade would be appropriate," he said. "I do not own a duelling-sword. Do you have one I can borrow?"

Raguslan laughed, a strange high sound. "You would fight a duel with a borrowed sword?"

"It is better than using my bare hands."

Raguslan made his way back upstairs, returning shortly thereafter with two blades. "These are both Glastarko's. Take your pick."

Malvazan took the nearest blade, briefly tested it for weight. "This one will do," he said with a brisk nod. He adjusted the belt and fixed it around his waist.

"You are curiously indifferent," said Raguslan. "This could be a matter of your death."

"I thought my second was supposed to give support and encouragement. Such doomy mutterings scarcely seem to fit the bill."

Raguslan ran a hand through his hair. "I am sorry. I have never stood second before."

"It is the swordsman who wins the fight, not the blade," said Malvazan. "So long as the blade is sharp, I am content."

"Glastarko bloodied Hentispo of Diarvino with that one. You need have no concerns."

Malvazan realised with a start that Raguslan was more nervous than he was. "Be calm," he said. "This is a question of honour; I trust to the rightness of my cause and, more importantly, the speed of my blade. You need do nothing but vouch for fair play."

"Of course," said Raguslan with a strained chuckle. "Glastarko was equally confident as to your prospects."

"In that case, shall we depart?"

Thirty minutes later they reached the end of the well-worn path to Fangardo's Clearing, that break in the woods where matters of honour were so often settled. A scattering of lanterns had been erected around the perimeter and four men were already present: Flarijo, his second Putranko—the man who had tried to talk them out of the duel the day previously—a man in the grey robes of an apothecary, and a fourth figure in black. This was a Consigli, not someone Malvazan had expected to see in the duelling ring.

Flarijo bowed briskly, shook Malvazan's hand. His grip was firm, cool and dry: this was not a man in the grip of terror.

"I regret the events which have brought us here," he said in a crisp voice. "Nonetheless, I am ready to fight."

"As am I," said Malvazan, returning his grip. "Although I had not expected to see a Consigli."

"Do not be alarmed by Jestrizo," said Flarijo. "In the unlikely event of a serious mishap, he is here to witness that all was done within the Quietus Est. It is irregular, but he attends at my request. In view of your youth, I thought it best to avoid any potential misunderstanding."

"I am nineteen."

Flarijo shrugged. "Consider it a formality, if you choose."

Jestrizo stepped forward, a slender dark man of middle years. "You must each disavow malicious intent," he said. "Then you may fight."

"This is a question of honour only," said Flarijo. "I hold no personal animosity towards Malvazan."

"Nor I to you, sir," said Malvazan.

Jestrizo looked into both of their faces. "And can you not be reconciled with soft words?"

Flarijo paused a moment, looked at Malvazan expectantly. Malvazan did not meet his eye.

"My honour is not so cheap," he said.

Jestrizo nodded. "Very well. By the Quietus, fight."

Malvazan took off his cloak, handed it to Raguslan. Flarijo too gave his cloak to his second, and side by side, they walked to the centre of the clearing. Malvazan touched his right hand to the scabbard of his sword, as if to confirm that it was still there. He drew it from the hilt, held it upright before his face, inclined his head. Flarijo did likewise, and they were underway.

Flarijo essayed a tentative stroke in Malvazan's direction; Malvazan eased aside, probed back, to be met by the steel of Flarijo's blade. The ground was uneven underfoot, and Malvazan moved with caution: it would not do to be undone by a tussock.

They circled again, the naked blades making for a more cautious contest than in competition. Malvazan judged Flarijo's swordplay competent, but no more. He lacked the crisp reflexes and the ability to turn parry into instant riposte. Unless he made a crass error, Flarijo would not be able to land a blade on him.

"Come on then!" bawled Flarijo. "I thought you wished to defend your honour!"

He is baiting me, thought Malvazan with a harsh smile. You will have to do better than that.

He skipped in, under and behind Flarijo's defence. Then, with the blooding stroke at his mercy, he flicked his blade aside. Flarijo flinched, staggered back; his incredulity at his escape was obvious.

This is my chance. Today, I can make them respect the name of Malvazan.

With a cold smile, he lunged at the petty-pectis quadrant, rode the parry and then, with Flarijo's ley quadrant open, drove his blade upwards under Flarijo's ribcage. He let out a great cry of triumph as Flarijo staggered back, fell to the ground.

Jestrizo stepped forward. "Blood!" he called.

The duel was over. Jestrizo knelt at Flarijo's side and put two fingers on his wrist. Looking up at Putranko, he shook his head.

"You've killed him!" said Putranko in a voice of quiet astonishment. "You've killed Flarijo."

Malvazan could hear his heart pounding in his chest. His vision felt hazy. But this was what he had wanted.

"It was a duel," he said through gritted teeth. "He slighted my honour."

Jestrizo put an arm around his shoulder and led him aside. "That's enough, lad. You've won; leave it at that."

Putranko said: "It was not even a death duel. How can you have killed him?"

Malvazan said nothing. Jestrizo said: "It is a horrible accident. The contest was within the Quietus: Malvazan drew first blood."

"It was no accident!" said Putranko in a thick voice. "He only needed to nick him. There was no call to thrust the blade so deep."

"Enough, Putranko," said Jestrizo. "It's the lad's first duel; it was the madness of the moment."

"I say it was not," said Putranko, his face pallid in the torchlight.

"You too assail my honour," hissed Malvazan. "Is there no end to it? Perhaps you would care to taste my steel?"

Putranko hand went to his hilt. "This time it might be you who feel the bite of the blade." His face was an inch from Malvazan's.

Jestrizo inserted an arm between them. "Malvazan, that is enough. There will be no more blood shed tonight."

"He accused me of—"

"I heard nothing," said Jestrizo. "You have killed your first man tonight. It is no light matter. I pronounce the duel fair, and in accordance with the Quietus Est. You and Raguslan, go home now. Putranko, stay here with me for a while. If I find that the two of you have fought, I will call it murder."

Malvazan bowed to Jestrizo, Putranko and the apothecary, whose name he had never learned, and now would never need to.

"Come, Raguslan. The hour is late, and you will wish to learn if you are an uncle."

Wordlessly Raguslan handed Malvazan his cloak, and they left the clearing with the eyes of the company on their backs.

CHAPTER TWENTY-SEVEN

After the departure of Linnalitha, Popisilaija's salon had few attractions. Hazilan held court on the loggia, and Todarko lacked any appetite for further debate or posturings. He would have to report to Dravadan on his findings; since these amounted to zero, this would be no very comfortable meeting, even if he managed to avoid Linnalitha. Just before the Hour of Evening Repast he set off to return to Tappinetto for dinner: Nelanka at least might raise his spirits.

He walked up the hill, the city wall at his right, scrutinising the veiled women for characteristics he recognised. Behind him, he heard footsteps and glanced nervously over his shoulder. A man in the all-black garb of the Consiglio raised a hand.

"You are a difficult man to catch, sir," said the man. "I am the Consigli Vislanko."

Todarko stopped and looked into his face. "I recognise you."

Vislanko, a man of wiry muscularity, a bland expression and cold grey eyes, nodded. "I was at Roblegast when Aladar took poison."

"You speak with little respect of a noble citizen."

"The facts are unarguable," said Vislanko. His age was indeterminate, but he spoke with the flat cynicism of an older man.

"I am coming to see that no facts are unarguable. The more one probes, the more questions require answer."

Vislanko gave a cool smile. "I am surprised to find such discrimination," he said. "Your conduct in general does not suggest notable perspicacity."

"I take it that you did not accost me to provide an assessment of my character."

"Indeed not. I find cordiality to be overrated, but I do not seek your enmity. Come, let us climb the wall."

Vislanko led the way as they mounted the steps set into the city wall to look out to sea. Below them, over the waist-high lip of the fortification, was the precipitous plunge to the tide-lashed rocks below.

"One should always take care when transacting confidential business," he said. "You never know who is close by." Todarko thought to see a gleam in his eye. "The slarinto whipping in off the sea swallows our words. What we say remains between us."

"There is nothing I wish to say."

"Do you know the function of the Consiglio?"

"Of course," said Todarko. "You serve the Masavory and the Specchio. No-one would dispute the value of your service."

"You are wrong," said Vislanko in a level voice. "We serve the city of Taratanallos. The city's interests and the Specchio's sometimes, indeed usually, coincide."

"Your point?"

"You are a young man with excellent connections and, it would seem, very little interest in the political life of the city. You are an intimate of Dravadan, yet you gain admittance in the salon of Popisilaija. As such you have perhaps unique information."

"Such as?"

"For the Consiglio to carry out its duties—its wider duties—it is important to have sound intelligence. The Grand Master of the Consiglio is naturally interested in the doings of so eminent a citizen as Dravadan; Dravadan, on the other hand, takes pains to ensure his business does not become public knowledge. You can perhaps see how you might assist the Consiglio."

"Certainly," said Todarko. "Let me summarise my knowledge: Dravadan advocates a closer alliance with the Emmenrule. He entertains the Emmen lords at Korfez."

Vislanko's eyes narrowed. "Do not sport with me, whelp. The Consiglio is all too aware of Dravadan's sympathies. The intelligence required is of a more detailed, everyday nature. Put bluntly, we require a source within Korfez."

"You want me to spy on Dravadan?" Todarko could hardly avoid laughing, although the situation was essentially humourless. There was an irony in being required to spy both on and for Dravadan.

"Yes."

"Do I take it that the Consiglio opposes Dravadan's programmes?"

"Your logic is faulty," said Vislanko. "The Consiglio regards knowledge of this sort as valuable in itself. We never know at which point we might need to check Dravadan's schemes, but the principle applies equally to Bartielko, for example."

"I could spy on him too, if you like," said Todarko with a wild flush of hilarity.

"That will not be necessary," said Vislanko. "The Consiglio maintains other channels of information."

"I thank you for your interest in my affairs, Vislanko. However, I do not consider myself ideally situated for the role of intelligencer. I am sure others would be more apt for your purposes."

Vislanko leaned forward onto the wall, resting on his forearms, and looked out to sea. "You appear to be under the illusion that you have a choice," he said in a level tone.

"I fail to see how you can compel me."

"For a poet you are dismally lacking in imagination," replied Vislanko.

"I hear nothing but bluster."

"A man with your somewhat disorganised private life cannot believe himself immune from persuasion, surely?"

"Say what you wish to say, Vislanko," said Todarko through gritted teeth.

"Even as recently as this afternoon, you have acted imprudently," said Vislanko. "They say that Dravadan is a very dangerous man—a judgement with which I fully concur. I would not like to pique his pride, and I am sure you would not either."

Todarko felt the blood drain from his face. "I am sure I have done nothing to offend Dravadan," he said.

"Then you have nothing to worry about," said Vislanko with a thin smile. "I am sorry to have troubled you. Enjoy your evening: no doubt we shall meet again in due course."

Vislanko turned and walked down the steps without a backward glance, leaving Todarko staring out to the horizon far beyond.

Oricien made his way back from his interview at Fizenar in a pensive mood. He knew at least that Bartielko could be bought; and so, by association, could the Gammerling party. It was conceivable, then, that a bribe of a million florins could secure the success of his embassy. Had Iselin been on hand, he would have been able to explore the extent to which Bartielko really controlled sufficient votes to sway the Specchio, and to what extent he could be trusted. Iselin might also have had useful insights into whether Bartielko could be bought for less than a million florins—although given the way Iselin had destroyed his career for 85,000 florins, this latter point was doubtful.

It was all moot. Ribauldequin's search had yielded nothing: Iselin was nowhere to be found, even if Oricien could bring himself to trust him. Ribauldequin's counsel, for all his charm, was essentially worthless. Only Oricien himself could decide how to proceed. The question of paying Bartielko a million florins was not among his options: Estedino would surely be unwilling to advance so much. It would be best, perhaps, to spend some more time with Dravadan and his allies after all to assess the extent to which they could carry forward his aims. He had a sense of Dravadan's character, unsatisfactory as it was; time now, perhaps, to deepen his acquaintance with House Vaggio.

At the Hour of Cordial Discourse, Oricien presented himself at Tappinetto, where Luzio escorted him into the visitors' parlour.

"I regret to say, my lord, that both the Dignified Raguslan and the Grave Zanijel wait upon Dravadan at Korfez. The Grave Todarko is, I believe, at Fizenar for the hospitality of Madam Popisilaija."

"No matter," said Oricien. "I will return later."

"I will see if Madam Nelanka is on hand, sir."

Oricien shuddered. They had not parted on good terms, and he did not wish another quarrel today.

"Please do not disturb her," he said. "I will have many occasions in the future to visit Tappinetto."

He turned at a rustling of fabrics behind him. Nelanka stood slender and composed in the doorway. "Do not depart on my account, Lord Oricien," she said. "If nothing else, I wish to apologise for my behaviour when we met at Roblegast."

Luzio slipped invisibly from the room and they were alone.

"Forgive me, my lord," she said. "I was in a peevish humour, and took offence at an innocent remark."

Oricien waved the apology away with a shake of his head. "The fault was mine, madam. To refer, however obliquely, to the tenor of your reputation was boorish, especially with a woman of such conspicuous virtue."

Nelanka indicated a seat and they arranged themselves a decorous distance apart.

"Now we have tendered our apologies," she said, "perhaps we can resume a more cordial footing."

"I should be delighted," said Oricien. "Although in truth I think you will find me poor company. Events have not gone smoothly since my arrival, and all I desire is to see Croad again."

"The death of Aladar is a shock to us all, that such a proud and powerful man should topple like a tree in the gales. No doubt his death upsets your embassy too."

Oricien gave her a sharp glance. "It does not make things easier," he said. "He was a man who commanded much influence in the city, and bent it in our favour."

"And you are less confident in Dravadan?"

Oricien was beginning to find her insights uncomfortable. Nelanka laughed.

"I am sorry," she said. "You will not wish to discuss matters of state with a foolish woman."

"It is not your sex which disturbs me," he said. "It is your city. I can hardly take counsel from a Tarat in these circumstances."

She gave him a shrewd look. "Neither of your Emmen advisors appear fully satisfactory. I pity you, for I see a conscientious man. You would do the right thing, the Harmonic thing, would you not—but you cannot see the way?"

Oricien slumped in his chair. He no longer cared if Nelanka had ulterior motives, if she were attempting to manipulate him: she understood and articulated his situation more clearly than anyone else in the city.

"I hope you are not going to recommend the Viators," said Oricien. "Religion has brought nothing but contention in my life. Had it not been for the Viators and their dissension, Croad might never have fallen."

Nelanka looked as if she would ask more. Instead she replied: "I do not know how it goes in the Emmenrule, but in Taratanallos you cannot rely on the Viators for any counsel which is not tinged with their self-interest. Incidentally, that means they are your allies, for they hate and fear the King of Gammerling."

"It seems I can rely on no-one's judgement but my own," he said. "It is not an altogether comforting prospect."

Nelanka sat looking silently at the ground for a moment or two. "You must realise that I have no reason to help you," she said in a soft voice.

"I never asked for it, madam."

"Do not bristle, my lord, for I meant no offence. I do not enjoy seeing a good man in distress, and while I have no reason to lighten your load, I would do what I can to ease your burdens."

Oricien smiled. "The pleasure of conversation with a lady of your grace and charm is succour enough, madam."

"Do not play the courtier with me, my lord. There is enough stifling etiquette in the city without us creating yet more of it."

Oricien gave his head a rueful shake. It was hard to know how to take Nelanka. Was she really as ingenuous as she seemed? Or was she yet another tool of manoeuvring and advantage? No doubt Dravadan and Raguslan would view the thought of Nelanka in his confidence as highly satisfactory. What a cruel city Taratanallos was! No utterance, no feeling, no relationship could be taken at face value; the richest man's wealth was a castle of paper, and honour was a bargaining chip with the value of yesterday's fish — if so much.

"You are distracted, my lord. I hope my company is not so tedious."

Oricien summoned a weak smile. "Nothing could be further from the truth, madam."

A light kindled in Nelanka's eyes. "I see now. You are wondering whether you can trust me. It is a sad day when a visitor to the city must be so suspicious."

A denial sprang to Oricien's lips, where he let it die. Nelanka had given him no reason for distrust, and he would not sink to the standards of the Specchio.

He nodded: "You are right, madam — but the question only has such force for me because you are perhaps the only member of the Specchio who does not excite my instinctive aversion. There, now I have perhaps been too candid."

Nelanka laughed again, a little spring of merriment which seemed so rarely to reach the surface. "I did ask you not to play the courtier," she said. "I cannot complain if you then speak with complete frankness. I now understand you — because you do not see me scheming and plotting, you wonder whether perhaps I am not perhaps the most devious and subtle schemer of all."

Oricien opened his mouth, unsure as to what would come out, but Nelanka interrupted him. "Do not deny it, my lord, for you are a most indifferent liar."

Oricien's mouth drooped. "A quality, no doubt, to make me a most indifferent ambassador also."

Nelanka shook her head, leaned forward and spoke quietly. "Such openness speaks well for you, my lord. The dishonest man may prosper in the short term — but any treaty you negotiated based on lies could not long endure. You should not change, even if you could."

Oricien looked into her eyes for a moment. His instincts told him that here was a woman with a purity of character to equal her shrewdness: a woman to reckon with, and to admire. He realised his gaze might say as much, and looked away.

"It seems the advice I was going to give you will not be needed," she said. "You appear to have established for yourself that my uncle and my husband, and most of all Dravadan, are not men to be trusted lightly. You must deal with them, of course, but do not think to rely on their friendship."

Oricien was about to respond when the door sprung open and Zanijel crashed into the room. "Nelanka! What is—my lord Oricien, forgive me, I did not realise who was here."

Oricien stood and bowed. "Good afternoon, Gravity."

"My father will be with us shortly," Zanijel said. "I am sure he will invite you to stay to dinner, since the Hour of Evening Repast is nearly on us."

"I am honoured by your hospitality, Gravity; but I have been away from business for much of the day, and must write a despatch to His Puissance before the tide turns—so the Castle of Crostestini calls. My compliments to you, and to the Dignified Raguslan." He gave a longer, deeper bow to Nelanka. "And to you, of course, madam."

"I understand," said Zanijel. "I look forward to seeing you again."

As Oricien left the room he saw Zanijel's unfriendly gaze turning to his wife.

CHAPTER TWENTY-EIGHT

Todarko took a dismal dinner at Tappinetto. Raguslan was keen to determine whether he had learned anything valuable at Fizenar, and Todarko's surly evasions did not elevate anybody's mood. At the Hour of Evening Satiation Zanijel left to meet his cronies at the Thrice-Blessed Argosy and Raguslan set off to pay a visit to Dravadan at Korfez. "There are important questions on the purchase of the Monopoly to address. Are you sure you will not accompany me, Todarko?"

Todarko thought of his parting from Linnalitha: he was not eager to renew the acquaintance. On the other hand, it might be better to visit Korfez in company with his uncle; and then there was the question of Vislanko. He gave every appearance of unscrupulousness, and it might be wise to see if he could secure any useful information from Dravadan.

"Very well," he said. "I need to discuss certain questions with Dravadan."

Raguslan beamed. "Excellent! I am gratified by your more responsible behaviour. I suppose I too was a touch wayward in my youth."

They walked up the hill in what Raguslan might have imagined to be companionable silence; Todarko's head was swimming. Popisilaija's salon had been a disaster by any standards: he should not have kissed Linnalitha in the first place; and given that he had done so, the results not been favourable. When he added in the fact that Vislanko, who may or may not have been lurking in the bushes, knew of the whole thing, and intended to use his knowledge—there was no satisfactory construction he could put on events. He still viewed the political machinations around the Emmen alliance as sterile opportunism, but here he was, suborned into spying for more than one side, and with the potential to make a mortal enemy of his patron at any point. It was hard to view events as satisfactory.

Todarko had to acknowledge that Korfez was one of the most desirable residences in Taratanallos. At the very top of the hill, it commanded a view all the way down the Archgate as far as the docks, and looked out over the wall to the sea beyond. Creepers climbed the three storeys of the building to create an impression at once homely and venerable.

Palankijo, a man of middle years with a tall and stately dignity appropriate to his station, met them at the porch and escorted them to the reception room. The night was growing chill and Dravadan had chosen not to use the loggia.

"Raguslan! Todarko! How good to see you," said Dravadan in the treacly voice which Todarko had come to characterise as his 'insincere bonhomie' tone. "I have much to discuss with you both. Palankijo, please arrange langensnap for my guests. Sit, I pray you."

Todarko sat on a seat facing the door; he wanted no-one entering out of his sight. Raguslan threw himself back in his seat, stretched his legs out.

"The Hour of Noble Pleasures is the best of the day," said Dravadan, taking his own seat opposite Todarko. Lanterns cast his face into a sinister shadow against the ochre colouring of the walls. "More useful business is transacted at this time than any other. Raguslan, we must discuss monopolies; Todarko, I will summon Linnalitha and you may converse on literary matters for a while if you choose."

Todarko felt a prickling of sweat at the roots of his hair. He did not know if Linnalitha could bear such a meeting with composure; he certainly feared that his own reactions would betray him.

"I will remain, if I may, sir," said Todarko. "The question of monopolies is of interest to the whole of House Vaggio."

Dravadan shot Raguslan a quick glance, the vector of which Todarko could not read.

"Why not?" said Raguslan. "Todarko's behaviour has impressed me in recent days. He has thrived on his involvement in affairs of state."

"Very well," said Dravadan. "The matter touches you all. To recap for Todarko's benefit: House Umbinzia enjoys two First Monopolies, salt and battlecat pelts. These are of course prestigious and lucrative. House Vaggio has been useful to my ambitions in the past; I hope to make greater use of it in the future. Raguslan is considerably more valuable to me as a man of substance in his own right than as my client."

Raguslan shifted in his seat.

"In days gone by, House Vaggio held its own First Monopolies. Were it to do so once more," Dravadan continued, "I could count on the support of a powerful ally, as well as rewarding a friend. I have therefore agreed, in principle, for Raguslan to consolidate the battlecat monopoly."

"I understood," said Todarko, "that you intended to sell Raguslan the monopoly. You speak as if it were a gift. The two are very different."

Dravadan gave a hollow laugh. "A monopoly worth over two million florins would be a princely gift! Such a monopoly will make the fortune of House Vaggio—it is an investment."

"Why, then, are you selling it?"

Raguslan interjected: "Todarko! This is no way to speak to Dravadan!"

"Either the monopoly is worth the astronomical sum Dravadan quotes, in which case I wonder at his eagerness to relinquish it; or it is worth less, and you are gulled."

"Apologise immediately to Dravadan!" spluttered Raguslan. "You come close to impugning his integrity!"

Dravadan raised a hand although Todarko thought his expression looked strained. "Come Raguslan, the lad negotiates with spirit! We all know that House Vaggio wants the monopoly, and naturally for the minimum amount possible. Let us settle on a sum and dicker no further."

"We do not know, sir, why you wish to sell it," said Todarko, for this seemed to him the central point.

"Enough, lad," said Dravadan. "My motives are my own, and in part reflect my desire to reward a faithful associate—although naturally not at a loss to myself. I might be persuaded to take a million and three-quarters."

Raguslan stroked his chin. "The sum is still considerable."

"As are the revenues. Without wishing to touch upon a delicate area, I assume your credit is sound? I would hate to hear it bruited about the city that your affairs were straitened."

"Unfounded rumours of that nature can ruin a man," said Raguslan with a tight look. "The man who spread them would be no friend; particularly when they are false."

"Excellent!" said Dravadan. "There can then be no obstacle to securing a mortgage on the monopoly revenues."

"A sum in the region of a million florins might be more appropriate," said Raguslan.

"As a joke, perhaps."

Todarko said: "Might I be permitted a clarification?"

Both men turned to look at him. Dravadan gave a stiff nod.

"Are the revenues amenable to verification? I assume you keep accounts?"

"When two heads of house negotiate for monopolies, such an inquiry is usually considered indelicate. The amounts in question are substantial: so much is obvious."

"The term 'substantial' has considerable latitude," said Todarko.

"Over the past five years," said Dravadan briskly, "revenues from the monopoly have averaged one hundred thousand florins per annum. To pay, say, a million and a half florins for ownership of the monopoly looks good business to me."

"If we were to say one and a quarter million," said Raguslan, "I would consider stepping away to talk to Marelko."

Dravadan steepled his hands and leaned back. "The sum is scarcely what I had in mind," he said. "Nonetheless, if it conciliates your goodwill and your enthusiasm for the Emmen alliance, it will have to do. Once we sign a treaty with King Enguerran, all those of his party are made."

Raguslan sprang erect before kneeling to kiss Dravadan's hand: a response Todarko could only view as exaggerated. Dravadan raised Raguslan to his feet and embraced him. "Let this be the seal on the friendship of House Umbinzia and House Vaggio," he said.

Todarko thought to see tears in Raguslan's eyes. For a man who had just agreed to make an investment which would not pay back for over ten years, he seemed unnaturally jubilant.

"There are matters I would discuss with Todarko, if you can spare him," said Dravadan. "You will remember the matters of intelligence we touched upon yesterday."

"Of course, Dravadan," said Raguslan with a bow. "I must in any event go to find Zanijel. He will wish to share our joy!"

At a gesture from Dravadan, Palankijo appeared and escorted Raguslan out.

"Now," said Dravadan, "we may consider our own private business."

"I am at your disposal, sir," said Todarko. It would be best to allow Dravadan to take the lead.

Dravadan rose from his seat to pour more langensnap for them both.

"I confess I have revised my appraisal of you," he said.

Todarko crossed his legs and sat back. "Favourably, I hope."

"You negotiated well on the monopoly. The questions you asked were good ones."

"My uncle is understandably avid to own a monopoly. I was simply eager to ensure he did not acquire it at any cost. If the truth be told, I still feel he may have paid over the odds."

"Fortunate for me, then, that he is head of House Vaggio and not you," said Dravadan. "You have a quickness of perception at odds with your popular reputation. I could make good use of a man such as you."

"I have learned nothing of value of Bartielko's plans."

Dravadan waved the point away. "It is early days. Linnalitha is a frequent visitor to Fizenar: there will be other opportunities."

Todarko tensed.

"Does my wife make you uncomfortable, Todarko?" Dravadan's face had the smooth inexpressiveness of a snake. "I had thought you the great ladies' man."

"Women are easy to deal with if you wish to seduce them," said Todarko. "There is a clear objective, and all force is bent to that goal. Needless to say, this situation does not pertain with Linnalitha." He tried a smile.

"Continue," said Dravadan with a curt nod.

"I am therefore uncertain how to deal with her. Her temper, if you will forgive me, is capricious at times."

Now Dravadan smiled. "She is the flower of House Rasteccio, and came with a most attractive dowry. The support of her father Godijan is a comfort to me. Her personal charm is welcome but scarcely the point. Second marriages are often much less satisfactory. Fortunately I have sons from my first marriage: Dravadaijo is at sea; Stepijo is in Mettingloom learning the ways of trade. The future of House Umbinzia is in safe hands; Linnalitha serves as a glorious ornament to my declining years."

"I am sure these are some way off."

Dravadan slugged back the last of his langensnap. "You are far from the surly stripling your uncle describes."

"Our relationship is not a cordial one. I am his brother's son and he has long resented his duty to give me room at Tappinetto. He would prefer me to be rusticated at Grandille while he favours Zanijel."

Dravadan ran a finger round the rim of his goblet. "Ah, Zanijel. The lad is willing, but essentially pedestrian. When the time comes, I am unsure that he will be a fit head of House Vaggio."

Todarko said nothing.

"The future is never certain," continued Dravadan. "In these difficult times it is hard to see the Way. Tell me, are you a religious man?"

"Not especially," said Todarko.

"You should perhaps give the matter more thought. The Viators are firm in their advocacy of stronger ties with the Emmenrule."

"Only because they fear that the Consorts in Gammerling will rule them heretics."

"Of course. Do you expect them to make their decisions on principle? Udenko is canny. The situation is simple: the people of Taratanallos believe in an afterlife; our Viators give them what they want; the Consorts refer to this belief as 'the Peninsular Heresy'; the Consorts bide in Vasi Vasar; if we become allied to Gammerling then rulings from Vasi Vasar will bind us. Our Viators will be anathematised and—worse—stripped of their benefices.

Therefore they support Enguerran in the knowledge that he will allow us to worship as we please."

"You give a cogent lecture in the ways of the world."

"When the Emmen alliance is sealed, I do not think I flatter myself to suggest I will be the first citizen of Taratanallos. I can expect either to be President of the Masavory or to control election to the post." He gave a satisfied nod.

"I wish you success in your ambition," said Todarko.

"At the point I will be well-placed to advance those who are useful to me. It may be that I consider Zanijel is not the most appropriate heir of House Vaggio when that time comes."

"I doubt you will persuade Raguslan to disinherit his son. Such a thing would be unheard of."

"You would be surprised how persuasive I can be, Todarko. Let us see how matters shape up over the coming months. A loyal ally is a great prize; a capable one is a jewel. Perhaps you understand me?"

"Up to a point, sir."

"Good," said Dravadan. "It does not do to be too explicit when considering affairs which may never come to pass. If you wish to oblige me, present yourself here at the Hour of Petitions tomorrow. Now, if you will excuse me, I wish to devote myself more fully to the Hour of Noble Pleasures."

Todarko understood himself to be dismissed. "I thank you for your hospitality, sir." He bowed and left the room.

As he stepped out into the portico, he heard a brief urgent whisper: "Todarko!"

He turned and looked. From the hallway skipped Linnalitha. "Quickly, in here!" she breathed, opening the door to a vestibule.

"I do not know what you can have to say to me, madam," he said as she closed the door behind them.

"Your behaviour this afternoon was boorish, to say the least," she whispered. "Nonetheless, I overlook it for now."

"I may have recriminations of my own."

"They are irrelevant," said Linnalitha.

"I—"

"You have been in private conference with my husband," she continued. "I do not know what you discussed, and I do not wish to know."

"It was of no great—"

"I said I did not wish to know." In her cheeks were spots of red. Her eyes reflected the chill of the winter ocean. "I will give you one piece of advice. Do not, under any circumstances, trust him. He cares for nothing but his own pride and ambition, tempered to a certain extent by avarice. Any rewards he promises now or in the future are illusory. Whatever you may gain from him is purchased at great price."

"Does this amount to a reconciliation?" asked Todarko. His heart was pounding, but whether from anger or the simple proximity of a feverishly animated Linnalitha he could not say.

"Perhaps you do not enjoy the uncertainty as to another's feelings?" she said with a twitching smile. "Perhaps now you have some conception of how Ivanka felt? Or any woman with whom you have sported?"

"Linna—"

She pulled his head forward and kissed him briefly, then more firmly and longer. "Does that provide greater certainty? Or less?"

Todarko disengaged himself although every inclination told him to respond. "You are—"

She gave another fleeting smile. "Yes, I am, aren't I?" she said. "Go now. We must not be found here."

Todarko stepped out into the street. Even in the cool moonlight, his head was racing, desperate for air. Linnalitha's behaviour went beyond unfathomable to the brink of lunacy. How did she view him? What were his own feelings for her? Add in the fact that her vindictive and dangerous husband now seemed to regard him as a protégé, and events were almost impossible to comprehend. The safest course, by far, would be to leave Taratanallos altogether: maybe Grandille would be appealing at this time of year, although the acerbic company of his grandmother would be less welcome. Even Vislanko's malice might be less potent at a distance. But once away, it could be difficult to return; and—he had to admit—the prospect of leaving Linnalitha so very far behind brought a surprisingly strong pang.

The bell rang for the Hour of Secret Deeds. He shook his head ruefully and made his way back down the hill towards Tappinetto. Perhaps matters would look clearer in the morning.

CHAPTER TWENTY-NINE

"Did you really mean to kill him?" asked Raguslan as they picked their way back along the dark wooded trail.

Malvazan slowed his pace to step over a raised root. "Yes." Although it isn't quite that simple.

"That is not within the Quietus," said Raguslan, his voice sharp. "It was not a mortal duel."

"I was entitled to bloody him. Men sometimes die even in a blood-duel."

Raguslan was silent for a moment. "Could you not be content to blood him? The offence was minor enough."

Malvazan stopped, turned to face Raguslan. His eyes accustomed to the dark, he could see the uneasiness in Raguslan's expression.

"You are the heir to a Prime House, Raguslan. Your presence will always command respect and your opinions demand attention. My situation is less fortunate. The only attention I will receive is that which I force from others. I cannot afford to have my honour slighted. The Grave Flarijo did just that; now he is dead. There is a lesson there for others who seek to mar the lustre of my reputation."

"You have a dark heart, Malvazan," said Raguslan in a voice lacking emphasis.

Malvazan twitched his head. "I do what I must. I Follow the Way."

Raguslan seemed to nod. They walked back to the city, through the Arch Gate and to the portico of Tappinetto without further conversation.

"Will you not come in?" said Raguslan at last. The reluctance in his voice was palpable. "There are still lights in the house."

"I must return Glastarko's sword, if nothing else," said Malvazan. He could not afford to seem cowed or apologetic for the magnitude of the night's events.

"Of course," said Raguslan stiffly. "I am sure you will wish also to take refreshment."

They walked in through the portico, to find the hall more brightly lit than when they had left, even though it was now the middle of the night. Almost immediately Glastarko clattered down the stairs.

"Raguslan! And Malvazan—you are still alive!"

"Yes—" said Raguslan.

"You must both share my joy! I am a father! Tulerija is delivered of a vast baby boy!"

Raguslan embraced him. "You have my congratulations, brother. He will be a playmate for little Zanijel. What friends they will be! I know it."

Malvazan stepped forward and shook Glastarko's hand. "I am happy for you," he said. "This is a great occasion."

"Come, let us adjourn to the parlour," said Glastarko, ushering them into the comfortable gloom of the family's inner sanctum. He poured them both goblets of wine, and one for himself. Malvazan savoured the rich warm soothe; Raguslan drained his in a single gulp. Glastarko laughed and poured him another.

Raguslan approached the second goblet with greater moderation. "Do you have a name for the lad?" he asked.

"Tulerija wants to name him after her father," said Glastarko with a raised eyebrow.

"Frustazar?"

"It is an ugly name, is it not?"

Neither Raguslan nor Malvazan said anything.

"I can deny my wife nothing, but in this case she must learn resignation. I am resolved to name him after our grandfather."

Raguslan smiled. "A good choice. Tulerija will soon be reconciled."

"And what name is that?" asked Malvazan.

Glastarko took a sip from his goblet. "Todarko," he said with a smile.

"I am remiss, Malvazan," said Glastarko. "A man with any manners would have asked after your duel—although clearly you are alive and unhurt."

Malvazan could see Raguslan tense next to him. "I won."

Glastarko grinned and nodded. "That clown Flarijo needed to be taught a lesson. I knew you would win: I congratulate you."

Raguslan said in a quiet voice: "There was a lesson, certainly: but Flarijo will not profit from it."

Glastarko furrowed his brow in puzzlement. "How so?"

Raguslan opened his mouth to respond, but Malvazan was quicker. "He is dead."

"I thought it was a duel of blood only," said Glastarko.

"It was," said Raguslan. "Malvazan spitted him with a single stroke."

Glastarko slapped him on the shoulder. "That is bad luck—and on your first duel, too."

Raguslan laughed harshly. "There was no luck to it. It was deliberate."

Glastarko looked intently at Malvazan.

"Is that true?"

"You do not wish to hear this," said Raguslan. "He will speak in large concepts of his honour, and overlook that he killed a man in cold blood."

Malvazan shot Raguslan a stern look: "I can be trusted to outline my own motivations, I think," said Malvazan. "Duels are a dangerous business. Sometimes people die. I could have died."

Glastarko gave a wry smile. "There are not many men who could put a blade in you, Malvazan. You have a rare gift. I am too happy tonight to condemn you."

"I wish you every joy, Glastarko. Raguslan, I thank you for attending me tonight." He bowed to both, and after a hesitation Raguslan returned the courtesy. "You must now excuse me."

By the time Malvazan returned to Korfez, the house was in darkness. He summoned Orijaz from his bed with a pull on the servants' tassel and went wordlessly up the stairs to his bedchamber.

He awoke late after a surprisingly deep sleep. He had managed easily to put the previous evening's events from his mind; Flarijo now was dead and gone, an outcome he had largely brought upon himself. It was unnecessary to expend further attention on him. Of more moment was Farlankas: his betrothal had prevented him from attending the school on the previous two days, and now he had missed the best part of the morning session. Last night's bout could be viewed as practice of a sort, but Flarijo had been too sorry and unsophisticated an opponent to provide significant development. Rodizel would be altogether more subtle the next time they met.

As he performed his ablutions he wondered whether the news would have reached Korfez yet. His mother would undoubtedly be hysterical, and it was unlikely that his father would view the matter favourably. It would be better if he could slip out without seeing either of them, although this would mean foregoing his breakfast. No doubt Farlankas could be prevailed upon to produce some bread and cheese.

His plans to escape the house unnoticed were not destined to succeed. He was on the way out of the door when he noticed Dravadan coming down the stairs.

"Good morning, brother," he said in a neutral tone.

Dravadan brushed the greeting aside. "Is it true?"

Malvazan did not affect ignorance. "Yes."

There was an expression in Dravadan's eyes which Malvazan did not immediately recognise. Could it be respect?

"Our father is most displeased," said Dravadan. "He does not relish having a butcher for a son."

Malvazan shrugged. "In defending my honour, I defended us all. I am surprised he did not appreciate as much."

Dravadan gave a brief shake of the head. "Our betrothals are tomorrow. A death is hardly the best backdrop to the occasion."

"I doubt that Flarijo would have attended in any event. House Brenza are hardly our intimates."

"You are wilfully misunderstanding me," said Dravadan, confident once more now that he could fall back on truculence.

"I am a man to be reckoned with," said Malvazan. "I have now set about proving it." He set his jaw. "If that has adverse consequences for others, so be it. I doubt anyone will lay hands on me in the street again."

The fleeting expression shot once more across Dravadan's face. Malvazan realised it was not respect. It was fear.

CHAPTER THIRTY

Malvazan awoke on the morning of his betrothal stiff and sore in every muscle. His drills with Farlankas had been so strenuous and protracted that he had not fully recovered. Since his betrothal-day was unlikely to involve extensive swordplay—indeed, any swordplay at all—this should not be an inconvenience. His mother had told him before bed last night that, whatever provocations he might imagine himself subject to, he was to ignore them given the festive nature of the occasion. Malvazan had given a grunting acquiescence: if anyone pulled his nose on the day, he would find a way to pay them off in the future. Flinteska's glorious day would not be spoiled.

Not by a fight, in any event. There was the larger question, which he had largely put out of his mind, of whether he consented to the betrothal. It would be embarrassing for everyone, least of all himself, if he refused to give his oath when asked by the Viator. Nonetheless, his father had not secured his consent before pressing ahead—although his lack of expostulation could have been seen as tacit acceptance—and so he was breaching no faith if he declined the betrothal.

It would hardly be fair to Sanoutë, on the other hand, were he to renounce the betrothal during the ceremony. He did not wish to marry her —so much was clear—but he had some affection for her. The notoriety of being rejected at her own betrothal would live with her forever; there would be a taint on her reputation which no subsequent events could wholly outweigh.

He clenched his fist in frustration. Sanoutë's destiny was no concern of his; he had difficulty enough arranging matters to his own satisfaction, without complicating matters by taking into account the feelings of others. Sanoutë was entirely innocent—although he could not help but remember her flaunting Rodizel in his face—and it would be heartless indeed to throw her over. There would be damage to his own reputation as well, which needed to be taken into account. Perhaps it would be better to go through with the betrothal after all; who was to say that might not be less public ways to repudiate it in due course. He need not worry about a member of House Zamilio calling for a duel—his reputation would see to that.

His reverie was interrupted by Dravadan crashing his door open and blundering into the room. "Mother wants you up immediately! There is no time for you to lie abed."

Dravadan looked flushed; his mood of thrusting good spirits was certainly a rare one. Still, if Malvazan was marrying the beautiful red-haired daughter of one of the Specchio's best houses, he too might allow himself some good humour.

"I am coming," he said, swinging his aching legs out of bed. "I hope you have left me some breakfast."

"Ha!" barked Dravadan. "I am too excited to eat, and as to my bowels, well—"

"—since I do intend to take breakfast, there are no remarks about your evacuations I could possibly wish to hear."

"How can you be so calm? We are to be betrothed today!"

Malvazan splashed some water on his face. "It is a matter of politics, like visiting the Masavory, no more. Our fathers have arranged everything. This is hardly the territory of a love-match."

Dravadan sat down on Malvazan's bed. "I thought that you and Sanoutë —oh, well, she is a nice enough girl. But Rullia—what a pearl, a golden treasure beyond price. It is a love-match indeed."

Malvazan was interested in spite of himself. He turned from his basin to face Dravadan.

"Does Rullia have the same views?"

Dravadan looked away. "We have not fully discussed the matter. Indeed, we have not spoken at all since the betrothal was announced. Still," he said in a brassy voice, "when the strength of my regard becomes apparent, any indifference she may feel will surely melt away."

"No doubt," said Malvazan. The subject had exhausted the little interest it may ever have held.

"Malvazan," said Dravadan in a soft voice, a tone so unlike his usual hectoring that Malvazan turned to look. "We have not always displayed the amity brothers should."

Malvazan considered this a considerable understatement, and chose not to respond.

"Today is an important day for us both. I would not have a shadow between us at such a moment. I appreciate that I have a large destiny, and one that but for an accident of birth would have been yours. Come, let us shake hands and be better friends henceforth."

We will see who has the larger destiny, thought Malvazan, but he held out his hand. Astonishing what a change in attitude could be brought about by killing someone, he thought. Overnight he had become a man to be reckoned with.

"I wish you every joy of Rullia," he said.

Oricien returned to his quarters relishing the prospect of an evening's solitude. Dravadan had engaged his company for the next day, promising an occasion to remember. Since most of the days he had spent in the city thus far had been memorable in ways he could only describe as infamous, the prospect was not necessarily appealing. As if matters were not already complicated enough, he now had to weigh Nelanka's character in his mind: a woman seemingly strong, intelligent and favourably disposed. Was there nothing in Taratanallos he could take at face value?

There was a knock at his door. He realised with a start that Vivalda would no doubt be presenting herself—another complexity he did not need. But on this occasion it was not Vivalda. A Consigli appeared, with Lord Iselin a step behind him.

"My lord," said the Consigli. "Lord Ribauldequin had asked that Lord Iselin be brought to you if he could be located."

"Thank you," said Oricien. "You may go."

The Consigli bowed and left the room, leaving an uncomfortable silence behind him.

"You wished to see me, Lord Ambassador," said Iselin stiffly. "I trust you will be brief, since my vessel sails upon the midnight tide."

"You will need to revise your plans," said Oricien. "You will be remaining in Taratanallos a while longer."

For a moment a flash of hope kindled in Iselin's eyes before it was brought under control. "You intend to pardon me, Lord Ambassador?"

Oricien sat down, pointedly failing to extend an invitation to Iselin. "You have not yet been adjudged," he said. "For now, I intend that you shall remain with the embassy, tendering such advice as required. Once our business is concluded, I shall evaluate your service and determine how to deal with you at that point."

Iselin dropped to one knee in front of Oricien and kissed his hands. "I thank you, Lord Ambassador. I shall not forget this."

"Get up, Iselin," snapped Oricien. "Much depends on your future conduct; it may yet be necessary to lay the matter before His Puissance."

Iselin remained on one knee. "You will not have cause to regret this, my lord. If I were to become Chancellor, you can be sure my policies would tend to the advantage of Croad!"

Oricien strongly doubted this: Iselin having abased himself so completely, Oricien would remain as a reminder of his shame, his mercy a quality to be punished rather than rewarded. But this was a problem to be resolved another day. For now, at least, he had secured the counsel of a useful advisor.

"Excellent," he nodded. "Let us retire to my study: I had a conversation with the Dignified Bartielko today which you may find of interest."

Iselin got to his feet and the two men left the reception room to deliberate at greater length. Oricien shook his head as he followed Iselin out: the candle-maker's grandson remained profoundly untrustworthy, and in many ways it would have been safer to let him return to Emmen. No doubt the reasons would soon have become apparent in Taratanallos, however, and could hardly strengthen his negotiating position. At least this way he kept Iselin where he could see him.

CHAPTER THIRTY-ONE

Taratanallos was set on a rocky outcrop at the foot of a rising expanse of forest which was home both to wild beasts and the summer estates of the Specchio. Todarko appeared at Korfez at the Hour of Petitions to find that a hunting expedition to the west, into the Forest of Sang Saraille, was planned. Dravadan, a bow slung over his back, mounted a giant gallumpher and awaited the others. Todarko was taken away and outfitted with bow, arrow, rapier and flask, and a hunting gallumpher rather better than his own.

By the time he returned from the stables, the entire party was assembled and ready to depart. Dravadan was alongside Lord Oricien, with Lord Ribauldequin nearby. Lord Iselin, it seemed, had pleaded an indisposition and remained at the Castle. Todarko doubted that such costive-looking man was much of a hunter. Raguslan sat gingerly astride his own gallumpher with the air of a man unused to the experience, while Zanijel pranced on his own mount, a mettlesome beast which to Todarko's eyes appeared too narrow in the shoulder to be a first-class hunter.

Hidden under Hood and Veil, sitting side-saddle on their own mounts, were the ladies Dravadan had seen fit to invite. One of them was clearly Nelanka, and Todarko felt a flush of irritation that she had not seen fit to inform him of the event; the other, he surmised, was Linnalitha although the dress, a deep burgundy in shade, was not one he recognised.

A number of retainers completed the party, including the ubiquitous Palankijo. As they made to trot out of the city, a voice called to them: "Wait there! I must accompany you!"

Mounted on a black gallumpher, with a black cloak flapping in his wake, was a Consigli. Todarko saw with a sinking stomach that it was Vislanko. "The Grand Master feels that the ambassadors should have a formal escort. I happened to be at liberty."

If Dravadan was discomposed he did not show it. "You are welcome, fellow. I do not recall your name."

"I am Vislanko, Dignity."

"Well, Vislanko, I am sure you will not intrude yourself on our attention overmuch. Today is an informal event, not a state function."

"An informal event with bows, arrows, and rapiers, sir. I am sure none of us would like to explain to King Enguerran how his ambassadors had come to harm."

Dravadan gave a curt nod to indicate that the conversation was concluded, and spurred his gallumpher forward. The party rode through the Chale with a clatter of hooves to the Peline Gate; artisans had to press against the walls of the narrow lanes to avoid being ridden down.

Once out in the countryside Todarko felt an immediate lightening of spirit. The trees gave off a scent of sweet flower and sap where they stood alongside the trail, and he rode along in silence, apart from the small groups which had formed. Dravadan led the way with the Emmen lords at his side. Raguslan and Zanijel were at the back of the cluster, although largely ignored. Todarko noted with amusement that Nelanka and Linnalitha rode along together without the faintest appearance of cordiality. Next came Todarko himself, and Vislanko rode at the back with Dravadan's retainers.

Oricien felt himself soothed and relaxed by the motion of his gallumpher, a fine strong beast in full maturity called Pippidillo. He had no opportunity to exercise it since his arrival from Emmen and he doubted that the grooms had taken more than ordinary care of it. No doubt both he and Pippidillo would benefit from a day's hunting. He soon managed to disengage himself from Dravadan's conversation and he allowed Nelanka and Linnalitha — both clearly identifiable despite Hood and Veil — to catch up with him.

"Good morning, ladies!" he called in a cheery tone. "Is this not a glorious prospect?"

Linnalitha inclined her head modestly. Nelanka replied: "If you say so, my lord."

Oricien frowned in puzzlement. Her churlish response was hardly in keeping with yesterday's warmth. "Come, madam, surely we can enjoy for a day a break from the cares of state?"

Linnalitha, absolved from the requirement to keep Nelanka company, pressed her heels into her gallumpher's flank and eased ahead.

Nelanka gave her head a brief shake. "You think that today is anything other than high politics, simply because you are out in the fresh air? You are more naïve than I took you for."

"Madam, have I said or done anything to offend you?"

"Forgive me, my lord," she said. "I am out of humour today; I am not fit for human conversation."

Oricien smiled. "I am hardly a man for chitter-chatter," he said. "I will be perfectly content to savour your company in admiring silence."

"As you will," she said, and they rode along quietly together. The Nelanka of yesterday — candid, direct, even vulnerable — was wholly absent,

Oricien reflected ruefully. Perhaps she regretted her openness yesterday. It was a pity, although hardly a surprise, if the stifling formalities of the Specchio had won out over the warmth of normal emotions. Oricien had to acknowledge, though, that it was a relief when ten minutes later Ribauldequin dropped back to overwhelm them both with a string of vacuities.

After an hour's steady ride uphill, Dravadan signalled for a halt at a clearing by the road and the party dismounted, to drink from the water canisters on their belts and eat loaves baked that morning and distributed by Palankijo. As they sat in a broad circle Dravadan declared:

"This is the way to live. How sweet it is to leave behind the cares of state, is that not so, my lords?"

"You have a fair prospect indeed, sir," said Oricien, fastidiously brushing the crumbs from his lap. My home city of Croad is not without its beauty, but it is a crueller, harsher place. One can only envy the inhabitants of Taratanallos, with a situation at once so beautiful and practical."

"Let us enjoy even more beauty," said Dravadan. "Linnalitha, why do you not remove your veil? We are outside the city, among friends: there can be no impropriety. Zanijel, surely you will allow Nelanka to do the same."

"You are generous, husband," said Linnalitha in a level tone, unclipping her veil and throwing back the hood which had confined her lustrous red hair. She looked hot and flushed in the warm spring sunshine. Todarko could not help looking straight at her; he noticed that the Emmen lords were doing the same.

Nelanka did not wait for Zanijel's approval before following Linnalitha's lead. Animated by a measure of bored irritation, her scornful expression was engaging in a disdainful way, thought Todarko.

"My lord," she said to Oricien, "was not your own city destroyed?"

Todarko coughed as he drank from his flask. The remark was accurate but hardly tactful. Nelanka must have been nettled indeed by Linnalitha's hauteur to resort to such spite. Dravadan's eyes narrowed: he appeared not only surprised but offended by the remark.

"You will know, madam," said Oricien in a measured tone, "that Croad was sacked by raiders from Mettingloom. As is the way of bandits, they had not considered any wider strategy, and soon departed the way they had come. The rebuilding of the city is now complete."

"Bandits?" asked Nelanka. "I understood the army to be led by the Crown Prince Brissio."

"As I said," replied Oricien, "bandits. Wearing a crown does not elevate a man's nature."

"Nelanka," said Dravadan in a hearty voice. "I am sure Lord Oricien does not wish to discuss such melancholy events. His city is restored to its former glory, and he is a trusted counsellor of King Enguerran."

"I find tales of thwarted ambition interesting and instructive," said Nelanka. "I am sure there is much we could all learn from Lord Oricien's experiences."

Zanijel, who had been lounging on a blanket, sat upright. "Enough, woman! Who are you to interrogate a king's ambassador?"

"I merely—"

"I will 'merely' whip the skin from your arse if you do not desist! A woman with a tongue is like a plague in the famine. Be told, and stay silent."

Todarko put down his flask and stood erect. "You speak to your wife with scant respect, Zanijel."

"Todarko..." bleated Raguslan. Dravadan looked on with narrowed eyes.

Nelanka looked at her husband with open contempt. "Your boorishness impresses no-one, Zanijel. If Lord Oricien is not offended by my remarks, you can surely have no cause to be."

"I said enough, Nelanka!" roared Zanijel, leaping to his feet.

"Be easy," said Lord Oricien. "The matter is of no consequence."

Zanijel essayed a half-bow to Oricien while glowering at Nelanka. "You are too kind, my lord. However, a disobedient wife is an embarrassment and an affront. Chastisement is in order, and Nelanka, you may be sure it will arrive. I expect to hear no more from you today."

Todarko stepped across the blanket and stood face to face with Zanijel. "I said to you not a week ago that if you harmed Nelanka I would kill you. It was not an idle threat."

"Go back to your poems, boy." He turned away and dragged Nelanka to her feet. "Fasten your veil, woman. You are not fit to be seen or heard."

Before he could think about what he was doing, Todarko grabbed Zanijel's shoulder and spun him around. Zanijel opened his mouth to protest but before he could say anything, Todarko had landed a fist in it. Zanijel staggered back, but did not fall. Todarko followed him and threw another punch into Zanijel's nose, to be met by a splattering of blood and a scream, perhaps from Linnalitha.

"You whoreson cur!" spat Zanijel. He pulled his rapier from its sheath. "Let us settle this now."

Todarko pulled his own rapier. "If you choose."

Vislanko appeared with his own rapier drawn, and put the sword in the space between them. "Now is not the time for this, gentlemen. You need to cool your tempers awhile."

Dravadan's face was ruddy. "You both disgrace your city and House Vaggio," he said. "Raguslan must be dismayed at your conduct—" in fact he simply stared ahead in seeming incomprehension "—and my lords, I can only apologise for such intemperance. I can assure you that both young men will be soundly punished."

Lord Oricien got to his feet. "No apology is necessary, Dravadan: at least not in the case of Todarko. In my city, a woman is a flower to be cherished, not a gallumpher to be beaten. No subject of mine would stand by and see a woman so maltreated by her husband or any man. Todarko, I commend you for your intervention. As for Zanijel, the less said the better."

Todarko looked around the circle to see expressions change as Oricien's words sank in. Raguslan seemed to melt into a puddle on the ground; Zanijel looked around him as he dabbed at his nose, a lone tower buffeted by a storm. Nelanka stared at Todarko with a gaze he could not read, while Linnalitha simply raised her eyebrows. Dravadan, perhaps inevitably, was the first to respond.

"Todarko is one of the finest young men of our city, my lord. As well as a credit to his house and a defender of the weak, he is a poet of considerable renown. I hope you will have a chance to make his acquaintance more fully during your stay."

Lord Oricien bowed to Todarko. "You have my admiration, sir. We will talk more anon."

Dravadan said: "Zanijel's actions shame us all," he said. "I am sure he is formulating his apology even now."

Zanijel haltingly stepped over to Lord Oricien. "For any offence I have caused you, my lord, I give my humblest apologies. I did not wish to bring embarrassment upon you."

Oricien turned his back and strode over to Pippidillo. "Dravadan, shall we press on? We have had no sport yet." Climbing astride his beast, he looked down at the crowd. "Zanijel, your apology should be addressed not to me but to Nelanka. No doubt you will wish to carry on that conversation in private."

He pressed his heels to Pippidillo's flank and set off down the trail.

Zanijel stamped off to his own gallumpher without a glance for the others. Todarko stepped across to Nelanka and helped her to her feet.

Her dark eyes searched his face. "Thank you, Darko," she said quietly. "You need not have done what you did, and I am not sure if you have helped. But you are a true friend and I thank you." She squeezed his arm and walked off to her gallumpher.

He turned to find Linnalitha at his side. "You are gallant, sir," she said.

"I could not stand by to witness such cruelty," he said.

"You have much impressed my husband: I do not know if I have underestimated or overestimated you."

Todarko searched her eyes for a hint of any deeper meaning. Vislanko appeared behind them on noiseless feet. "Do not dally," he said. "The party is moving off now. You will have plenty of time for your confidences in due course."

Linnalitha gave him a wondering look.

"I will explain later," said Todarko as he led her towards her gallumpher.

CHAPTER THIRTY-TWO

The altercation had changed the mood of the party. There was no more ambling along the country track once they had remounted. Palankijo and the other retainers went on ahead, crashing through the woods as they sought to flush out quarry. Oricien's party were all accomplished riders and Todarko struggled to keep up as they plunged deeper into the forest. The sunlight dappled through the treetops, a picturesque sight but one which created patches of dark concealing hazards which could easily bring down a charging gallumpher.

Todarko soon found himself detached from the rest of the group. Somewhere up ahead he could hear the cracks and bellows of hunters in flight. Behind him, but out of sight, were the ladies, certain retainers, and possibly Vislanko and Zanijel. To all intents and purposes they were scattered individuals. The only one whose location he could identify with certainty was Palankijo, whose occasional clarion blasts had so far failed to rouse any game. Sang Saraille was normally well-stocked with beasts of all sorts. Perhaps the presence of such a large and noisy party had driven them all off.

He wondered whether to press on and join the leaders, or drop back to find Linnalitha or Nelanka. This latter contingency would be complicated if Zanijel were with his wife, but given their present relations this seemed a remote possibility. Neither did he relish being caught up in the barbed hauteur that the ladies employed on each other. Best, perhaps, simply to amble along as he was.

From ahead came a call of different timbre from the clarion: pa-da, pa-da, pa-da, pa-da! Quarry was sighted! Palankijo was nearby. Todarko pressed his heels. Here was a chance to impress if he were first on the scene!

He clattered into a clearing to see Palankijo and another retainer looking around. Palankijo pointed, set off behind whatever was smashing its way through the undergrowth. Instantly Lords Oricien and Ribauldequin appeared, Dravadan only a little way behind them. There was no sign of the others, and the four of them set off in pursuit. Todarko had to duck to avoid a low-hanging branch as their prey slipped back into the deeper vegetation.

The woods cleared for a moment and Todarko saw their quarry: a single-horned bindlespith of significant dimension. The rusty gold markings suggested a young male, potentially dangerous and aggressive. Its legs were squat and its massive torso sat close to the ground as it sought to slip away.

"After it!" called Dravadan, which Todarko could not help thinking a foolish remark. Oricien needed no encouragement. He had brought his own gallumpher from the Emmenrule and it was clearly a seasoned hunter. From the strap across his back Oricien drew his crossbow: its twin triggers were already primed.

Behind him Todarko heard a cry of distress from a gallumpher, a curse in a rough human voice. He turned to see Dravadan's gallumpher sprawling on the forest floor, Dravadan lying on his back some feet away. Todarko reined in his own mount; it was against all etiquette to leave a man lying on the ground, even if rescue allowed the quarry to escape. Oricien and Ribauldequin, twenty yards ahead, had not seen the incident; Palankijo was nowhere to be seen.

Todarko dismounted. "Are you hurt, sir?"

"Hissen take that gallumpher!" growled Dravadan. "It tripped on something and I am thrown." He pushed himself upright with a wince. "Nothing is broken." With a grimace he said, "I am sore winded, though."

"Take my gallumpher," said Todarko. Since it was on loan from Dravadan, he hardly had a choice.

Dravadan shook his head. "Follow the ambassadors," he said. "I won't catch them, but you might."

"I'll send Palankijo back," said Todarko, as he leaped back into the saddle.

He came upon Oricien and Ribauldequin at the base of a small hill. At some unseen signal the bindlespith ceased its flight and turned to face them at the top of the incline. It had chosen to fight rather than run. Its golden eyes, with their slitted black pupils, looked down at the three riders. Ribauldequin nodded to Oricien. "Take it now," he said.

Oricien stood in his saddle, took aim and fired a first bolt. There was a whirr, a thud. From the bindlespith came a low growl; the bolt had buried itself in the beast's hide, serving to irritate rather than incapacitate. Oricien adjusted his aim as the bindlespith suddenly rushed down the slope towards him. He fired with the beast fifteen feet away, but the bindlespith's charge unsettled him, and the bolt flew over its head.

Almost simultaneously Ribauldequin fired to head the animal off before it reached Oricien's mount. He too missed, and Oricien's gallumpher swung away in panic. Ribauldequin fired again, missed again as the bindlespith surged forwards. Both ambassadors had shot their bolts; their crossbows would take at least two minutes to reload.

The bindlespith continued to charge Oricien's mount. On all fours it could pass under the gallumpher's legs, but if it reared, its horn could gut the gallumpher or even threaten Oricien. Todarko dropped to the ground and unslung his own crossbow. It was not as elaborate as the ambassadors', holding only a single bolt: if that was squandered, the bindlespith could wreak whatever havoc it chose.

Ribauldequin jumped down from his gallumpher and unsheathed his rapier. Meanwhile Oricien fought to keep control of his gallumpher; just as he brought it around to face their quarry, the bindlespith was upon them. With a surprisingly shrill call of fury, it rose onto its hind legs and lunged at the gallumpher's flank. The gallumpher keened in pain and terror as the bindlespith's horn opened a foot-long gash in its side. Flailing wildly, it pitched Oricien to the ground.

Ribauldequin rushed forward with his rapier drawn; now Todarko dared not fire his own bow, with Ribauldequin in the intervening space and Oricien in dangerously close proximity.

Oricien rolled to the side as the bindlespith dropped to all fours and made to gore him. Ribauldequin skidded onto the scene, slid his rapier in behind the bindlespith's shoulder; the bindlespith shook its flank in irritation and wrenched the rapier from Ribauldequin's hand, to stand ludicrously aloft from its shoulder.

Todarko cursed: Ribauldequin was now unarmed and Oricien immobile on the ground.

"Ribauldequin! Run!" he called. Oricien's only chance was if someone could distract it away. Ribauldequin scampered away in the direction of his gallumpher, but the bright green of his cloak caught the bindlespith's attention. Oricien had the good sense to lie still on the ground, and the bindlespith turned its golden eyes to Ribauldequin.

Todarko swallowed and pursed his lips. He had one shot, and if he missed, or hit somewhere inessential, the bindlespith would surely kill Ribauldequin—and then perhaps Oricien and himself. He allowed himself a second to calibrate the bindlespith's movement, lined up his sight with the great golden eye. With a grunt at the pressure required to release the trigger, he pulled his finger back.

An instant later he saw the red fletch of the bolt protruding from the bindlespith's eye socket—but still the beast charged on. Ribauldequin slipped on damp leaves, sprawled to the ground. The bindlespith continued its maddened charge, seemed to run over the top of Ribauldequin, and then sank to its front knees. With a noise that was half sigh and half sneeze, it toppled sideways to lie motionless on the ground.

Todarko, the only thing in the clearing on his feet, walked over to where the bindlespith lay. Its lips were drawn back to reveal its fangs and the bristles of its muzzle were flecked with red—whether its own, or that of Oricien's gallumpher, Todarko could not tell. Gingerly he pulled Ribauldequin's rapier from its hide. There was no hint of movement; the bindlespith was dead.

He took the rapier over to Ribauldequin, helped him up with other hand, and restored his weapon.

"You were brave to accost the bindlespith with just a blade, my lord."

Ribauldequin gave his head a rueful shake. "If I had been as good a shot as you, sir, I should not have needed my blade at all. You have my thanks; the thing was nearly on me."

"Come," said Todarko, "let us attend to Lord Oricien."

They found him crouching next to his gallumpher, a pallor across his face. "Todarko, well met, sir," he said. "Twice in the hour you have impressed me."

"There was a degree of good fortune, my lord. I could as easily have missed."

"Have you ever been in battle, Todarko?"

"No, my lord. There are few such opportunities in Taratanallos and, in truth, I lack the martial temperament."

Oricien's cool blue eyes seemed elsewhere as he said: "I too 'lack the martial temperament'; but twenty years ago I fought at the Battle of Jehan's Steppe, and I have rarely been off the battlefield since. One thing I learned early is that there are no 'nearlys' and no 'maybes'. You do a deed, or you do not. Your bolt flew true, and you saved one life for certain, perhaps two. You have my gratitude, and you need only name your reward."

Todarko raised an eyebrow. It was hardly right to claim a boon in the circumstances, and in any event he could not think of anything Oricien could give him that he would value.

"I am content with your good opinion, my lord."

Lord Oricien gave a wintry smile. "A courtier as well? We will speak no more of your reward, but perhaps my goodwill will be of help to you one day. Leave me now a moment, friends."

Ribauldequin and Todarko walked back to their own gallumphers. Todarko looked back over his shoulder to see Oricien kneel on the flank of his wounded gallumpher, whisper something in its ear and then, with a single motion, wrench its head towards him and break its neck.

Oricien sat alone in the clearing next to the body of Pippidillo, the sweat running down from his hair into his eyes. He was no stranger to battle and alarm—he had not been boasting to Todarko of his experiences—but the events had been so unexpected as to be startling. A hunting expedition which had started so promisingly had descended into arguments, a brawl and now a dead gallumpher. It was hard to escape the conclusion that nothing was going to go right while he was in Taratanallos. If he were a religious man he would be coming to the conclusion that the city's submission would be an act of Disharmony. Fortunately, however, King Enguerran did not employ him for his conscience. Submission was what was demanded, and submission was what he would deliver.

"My lord!" Dravadan called out to him as he rode into the dappled glade. "Todarko told me what had occurred. I regret the loss of your gallumpher—a truly magnificent beast."

Oricien wearily got to his feet as Dravadan jumped down from his gallumpher. "Did Todarko tell you of his own part in the event?" he asked.

Dravadan raised an eyebrow. "He merely said both your gallumpher and the bindlespith were killed."

"Todarko shot the bindlespith when Ribauldequin and I had discharged our own bolts. The beast would have killed Ribauldequin in a moment more. Todarko showed cool nerve and no little skill."

Dravadan nodded reflectively. "It seems he is modest as well. He is a fine young man, and one whose merits I have underappreciated."

"Zanijel appears to think otherwise."

"Pah! Zanijel! The boy is well-bred, but he lacks judgement." He paused for a moment to assess Oricien's expression. "A woman like Nelanka is wasted on him."

Oricien started. "She seems to me a woman of intelligence and discrimination," he said. "If the Grave Zanijel possess those qualities, he has not chosen to display them. I cannot pretend his conduct today has impressed me."

Dravadan smiled. "But Nelanka cut a rather better figure, did she not?"

"That would not be particularly difficult."

"Your stay in Taratanallos has been somewhat fraught so far," said Dravadan. "You must make sure that you enjoy some relaxation: what is good enough for the Specchio may perhaps be good enough for King

Enguerran's ambassador. I am certain you would relish more of Nelanka's company."

This remark was accompanied by such a strange look that Oricien said: "I am unclear as to your meaning, Dignity."

Dravadan made an easy gesture. "There was no secret meaning, I assure you," he said with a smile. "Tell me, how do you find your bath-slave?"

"Vivalda?" said Oricien in surprise. "She is charming in every way."

"So the life of the ambassador is not all toil and travail, eh?"

"She certainly adds a pleasant decoration to my chambers."

"I am told you have used her most honourably."

"The idea of 'bath-slaves' is not current in the Emmenrule," said Oricien. "I would scruple to take advantage of her."

Dravadan nodded. "Not all are so refined—without naming individuals. You perhaps cavil at taking what is offered only under duress?"

Oricien narrowed his mouth. "In the Emmenrule, such a discussion on the merits of bedding a slave would not be an everyday event."

Dravadan put an arm around his shoulder. "Forgive me, Oricien. Allow me to say that many among us would balk at having a slave, if you will pardon the indelicacy. The charm of pursuing a free woman makes the delights of her eventual yielding all the sweeter, would you not agree?"

"In principle," said Oricien stiffly.

"Come, I mean no offence," he said. "I merely observe that, among the Specchio, affairs of the heart are not unknown. And passions being what they are, sometimes they take root where they should not. A man of the world should look upon such things with equanimity rather than moralism. I am sure you take my meaning."

The only meaning that Oricien could draw from this curiously directed discursion was that Dravadan was encouraging him to conduct—or at least attempt—an amour with Nelanka. Why this should be, he could not guess, and he suspected that Dravadan would take a less broad view if Oricien's gaze turned instead to Linnalitha. The Specchio were an unfathomable group: at once ambitious but servile, rigid but opportunistic.

"I will need another gallumpher if I am to return to the city," he said. "It is a longer walk than I would care to undertake."

Dravadan bowed. "Of course, Lord Ambassador. I will summon one of my men."

The mood of the party was somewhat subdued as they trooped back into Taratanallos just upon the Hour of Cordial Discourse. The booty of a large bindlespith was a fine catch, but the death of Lord Oricien's pure-bred gallumpher, valued at eight thousand florins, detracted from the conviviality of the occasion. One of Dravadan's retainers had given up his own mount, a squint-eyed beast which sat poorly with Lord Oricien's dignity as he entered the city.

Dravadan, by contrast, put on every appearance of raised spirits once they rode through the gates and into the Chale. He had invested much, both in florins and prestige, in a successful day, and he was not to be balked of his triumph now. He decreed a feast at Korfez to roast and consume the bindlespith — Todarko's views on the disposition of his catch were not canvassed — where determined revelry would prevail. The patient Palankijo, who had long acquired a flexible demeanour, was despatched home to make ready for the event while Dravadan escorted his guests on a tour of the city.

Todarko was the celebrity of the hour, having not only killed an aggressive bindlespith but also rescued two of the Emmen ambassadors. Dravadan had long moved beyond any recriminations for Todarko's quarrel with Zanijel, and instead chose to bask in Todarko's reflected glory. Zanijel skulked along at the back of the group, grim-faced with a silent Nelanka at his side; Raguslan had pleaded indisposition and returned to Tappinetto. Todarko himself felt a trifle embarrassed at the attention. He was conscious of having behaved well, both in shooting the bindlespith and even more in punching Zanijel; but the ebullient favour of Dravadan and the more sober approval of Lord Oricien were at best mixed blessings for someone keen to avoid political life.

CHAPTER THIRTY-THREE

For all the commendable qualities of the Specchio—a keen interest in public service, energy, commercial acumen, a grave if sometimes impersonal courtesy—visitors to the city often found a self-regard which could only arouse antipathy. A member of the Specchio—the Dignified Aladar, or the Grave Raguslan, perhaps—if taxed on the matter would no doubt refer to pride in the history of his lineage or the primacy of ensuring a healthy body politic in safeguarding the city's future.

This quality of self-regard was rarely more in evidence than at the time of a betrothal feast. Marriages within the Specchio (in the unlikely event of a liaison taking place outside of this hallowed group, no celebration would occur) were reaffirmations of the health and strength of the city, a promise of more heirs which would carry Taratanallos' prosperity into generations to come. The betrothal of an heir was particularly noteworthy, and a double betrothal, as planned by House Umbinzia, was a great social event. For a house of modest stature, such as Umbinzia, there would be few occasions on which their stock stood so high. Of the twenty-four houses of the Specchio, twenty-three were to be represented. Given that Malvazan had recently killed a member of the twenty-fourth, a full house was not to be contemplated.

An occasion of such grandeur should not be mocked by rain, or even cloud, and Crostadan, despite a sceptical disposition in matters of doctrine, had made a sizeable donation at the Dominikos to ensure that Hissen and Animaxia collaborated to ensure sunshine. Since the week leading up to the event had been uniformly fair, it was difficult to establish whether such intercessions with the gods had been efficacious; but as the day dawned with a rich cerulean sky, few were disposed to investigate further.

Malvazan took a sardonic amusement when he realised that he was more nervous about this event than he had been about a duel which ended a man's life. His outfit, a doublet of rich forest-green velvet, a shirt of soft sage and flared breeches of luxuriant maroon, fitted him perfectly at every point, and showed his slim muscularity to advantage. Not normally given to personal vanity, he could not help admiring himself in the mirror. Dravadan's outfit reversed the colours, maroon and lilac on his top and deep green for the breeches; but Dravadan was both shorter and more squat than his brother, and Malvazan fancied that the overall effect was less impressive.

Flinteska, meanwhile, had reached such a pitch of excitability over her own costume that she had to be led away to a darkened room and salts applied; and even after such expedients the effect was not wholly satisfactory. Crostadan, meanwhile, walked in the gardens, taking in the sea air and supervising the erection of the tables.

As the Hour of Petitions merged into the Hour of Fiscal Scrutiny, the first guests began to arrive. House Vaggio were among the early arrivals, Glastarko grinning at all and sundry, slapping backs wherever he went. His wife Tulerija was absent—the new baby Todarko was at home with a colic—and conceivably this contributed to Glastarko's mood of gayety. Raguslan, as was his wont, presented a more sober impression, and although he was cordial with Malvazan, he inspected him from behind hooded eyes.

Flinteska, meanwhile, became agitated that neither House Rasteccio nor House Zamilio was yet in attendance, meaning that neither of the betrothed ladies were yet to be seen.

"What if they are not coming!" she cried, standing on the loggia as Crostadan welcomed guests. He steered her aside with an arm on her elbow.

"The contingency is remote," he said. "Come, my dear: let us discuss matters inside." He made a bow and excused himself from Sulinka of House Vaggio.

"They may have repudiated the betrothals!" she wailed.

"Both of them? Without telling us? It would be unheard of."

Flinteska looked around and dropped her voice. "After Malvazan killed Flarijo…"

Crostadan brushed his doublet impatiently. "The event was unfortunately timed, but the duel was in no way irregular. No house would break off a betrothal over such a thing."

"Maybe the girls have changed their minds! I was known to suffer occasional vapours in my youth!"

"Your youth?" said Crostadan with a poorly concealed smirk. "Come, madam, you are the most excitable woman alive!"

"You do not know what it is, to be a mother on such a day. Surely I am entitled to a moment of agitation!"

Crostadan made a mollificatory gesture. "There is no cause for alarm, my dear. The ceremony does not begin until the Hour of Light Repast."

"I am sure that Rullia is not coming! She barely knows Dravadan—she will be hiding under her bed!"

Crostadan thought that a lady with the schooled self-possession of Damoiselle Rullia would be unlikely to act in the way Flinteska outlined.

"That is what fathers are for," he said. "You may be certain that Igrinto will ensure Rullia is here on time and well-composed."

Flinteska's concerns were soon to be partially assuaged. Orijaz appeared on the loggia with a bow to Crostadan. "Dignity Thrinko presents his compliments and begs you wait upon him at your convenience."

"And Sanouté?" cried Flinteska. "Surely she is here too!"

The impassivity of Orijaz's expression remained unchanged. "Yes, madam. Dignity Thrinko, Madam Usette, the Grave Lutus and Damoiselle Sanouté are all in attendance."

"Animaxia be praised!" she breathed. "One son at least will be betrothed today."

Crostadan strode back into the house to welcome his new guests standing in the hallway.

"Your Dignity," he said to Thrinko with a bow.

"Ah, Crostadan, my old friend!" said Thrinko, embracing him. His white hair was teased into quiff of unusual dimension which appeared threatened by his proximity to Crostadan.

Madam Usette, a trim blonde woman noticeably younger than her husband, glowed with an energy which threatened an explosion. When she saw Flinteska the two of them burst into tears and hugged. Lutus, Thrinko's heir, looked on in a mixture of embarrassment and disdain. At fourteen, questions of marriage and emotional excess could only excite his vast distaste. Sanouté, meanwhile, was fitted in a gown of rich burgundy, but her normally florid complexion looked drawn and pasty.

Crostadan bowed and kissed her hand. "Welcome, Damoiselle, to House Umbinzia, now and always!"

Sanouté curtsied gently, gave a soft smile. "I thank you, sir," she said in a quiet voice. "I hope you will always find me worthy of your esteem."

Thrinko beamed. "Such modesty. Malvazan is a lucky man!"

"Indeed he is," said Crostadan.

Sanouté spoke in a voice barely audible. "Where is Malvazan, sir? I would see him before the ceremony."

"Why, daughter," said Thrinko, "you know that is not possible. All etiquette would be violated, and surely bad luck brought to all. You will have plenty of time of converse with your betrothed thereafter."

"Yes, father. Might we find a seat? I feel a little dizzy."

Crostadan called out: "Orijaz! Where are you? We have guests who require seating!"

Orijaz scurried away from whatever duties he had been undertaking, motioned for the new arrivals to follow him. Malvazan, who had been watching from a place of concealment on the upstairs landing, felt a pang run through him. Poor Sanouté, he had never seen her so pale or subdued. Could he really reject her in front of all the houses of the Specchio? She had wanted to see him, it seemed. No doubt he could contrive a brief meeting, and Hissen take any bad luck!

He slipped down the stairs, whispered a message to one of the under-servants and made his way to the kitchen garden, a place so lacking in glamour as to be wholly deserted on this most auspicious of days. There he set himself to wait among the cabbages and tomatoes until Sanouté should appear.

A caterpillar caught his eye, munching its way determinedly through a thick leaf. What were the goals of such a creature, he wondered. It was probably absurd to imagine it having goals at all. And yet, a transformation awaited it, far beyond anything it could conceive. It need do nothing to achieve such transcendence: simply keep chewing away at its leaf. With a snort of sardonic amusement he thought of Dravadan, one day to be elevated to the head of the house—the Dignified Dravadan—with a beautiful and well-bred wife, heirs to follow. And like the caterpillar, he had done nothing to merit his elevation, and probably lacked the wit fully to understand it. He pursed his lips, lifted the caterpillar from its leaf: it squirmed, looked around to find meaning for its fate. Malvazan dropped it on the ground and crushed it under his boot. Would that Dravadan could be dealt with so easily.

From behind him came a soft voice. "You wanted to see me?"

Malvazan turned. Sanouté's hair was curled in an elaborate confection, swept back off her face on one side, draping across her eye on the other.

"I was upstairs," he said. "I heard you looking for me, and thought to oblige you."

For a brief second her face twitched into a smile. "You cannot imagine how long I have yearned for this day. But you know that."

He reached out, put a hand on her arm. "Then why are you not happy?"

Her blue eyes were large and moist. "Because you have not yearned for it. You are accepting me because your father told you to."

"Do you think I listen to him any more? I am my own man."

She swept a lock of hair back out of her eye. "They say you killed someone," she said, looking away.

Malvazan shrugged. "You make it sound so sordid. It was a duel, a question of honour. It is regrettable that Flarijo died, but that is the risk of the duel. Quietus Est, as they say."

There was a catch in her voice. "Malvazan, I remember us as children. Once we went on a picnic to Sang Saraille, do you remember? There were fish in the stream, and it seemed we sat and watched them all afternoon."

Malvazan nodded. "I remember," he said.

"That was four years ago, Malvazan, four years. It seems as if it was another lifetime. Now you are talking about killing someone as if it was nothing."

"It is something that men do," he said. "I was a child then; I am a man now."

She turned and walked slowly towards the wall marking the edge of the garden. "When we were children, everyone knew that we would be betrothed. Neither of us seemed to mind."

"No," said Malvazan. "Of course not."

"But we were different people: children. Yet we are bound by those conversations."

Malvazan followed her, put a hand on her shoulder and turned her to face him. "Are you saying you no longer want us to marry?"

Her eyes welled with tears. "Don't you understand anything!" she sobbed. "It is what I want. It what I have always wanted! It is you who have changed, from the dear sweet boy who sat by the stream with me; changed into a man who fights duels, who proposes to Monichoë. I do not know you, Malvazan: you who were my dearest friend!"

"Sanoutë—"

"This is the day set for our betrothal, Malvazan." Her voice dropped to a whisper. "Can you say to me, from your heart, that you would marry me above all other women in the world?"

Malvazan looked into her face. The clear answer to the question was 'no', but the question she should have asked: Will you put aside any reservations you have, and marry me nonetheless, was more difficult to answer. But an answer was needed, and immediately. Cursing himself for his weakness and vacillation, he said: "Yes."

He kissed her on the cheek, turned and walked from the garden with a heavy step, never looking back once at the woman he left behind him.

CHAPTER THIRTY-FOUR

As soon as he stepped back inside the house, Flinteska descended on him. "Where have you been? We were all looking for you!"

"I could hardly have gone far," he said. "I am to be betrothed in an hour."

"And where is Sanoutë?" Flinteska's voice became shriller with each question.

"How should I know? It is bad luck for me to see her before the ceremony. Is Rullia here yet?"

"Yes she is!" exclaimed Flinteska. "And so beautiful she looks! That green so suits her colouring, and it matches her eyes. No mother ever had such glorious daughters come into her house! I am so happy I could cry."

"You appear to be doing so already," said Malvazan. He was almost smiling. Now that he had resolved to marry Sanoutë, he felt a sense of relief: almost of Harmony, in fact. Could it really be that he was doing the right thing? Maybe Sanoutë was what he needed. If he was going to be betrothed, he might as well enjoy the experience.

Stepping outside, he saw that most of the tables were already full. Before him was the party from House Zano: he bowed to the Dignified Kropiselko, received a curt nod in return, and a look in his dark eyes which Malvazan could not read. Monichoë turned to face him, a half-smile on her lips and an appraising expression on her face. Malvazan thought she had never looked more beautiful; but for better or worse, she was in the past: his future lay with Sanoutë.

"Damoiselle," he said, kissing her hand. "I am glad to see you here today."

Kropiselko scowled; Monichoë dimpled and gave a soft curtsey. "I wish you joy of your betrothal," she said, and with a nod Malvazan moved on.

Somewhat to his surprise he saw Viator Shalvijo, seemingly ready to officiate. Shalvijo had not told him he would be on hand.

Dravadan came up behind him, put an arm around his shoulders. "Come, brother. Now is the time!"

Malvazan smiled and nodded. "So it is," he said.

"Let us go and betroth ourselves."

Together they strode down the aisle between the banks of tables to the places laid for them. The table had only four places: two for them, and two already occupied by the veiled figures to whom they were about to commit themselves.

Viator Shalvijo straightened his white robe and rose from his seat.

"The Viator has many pleasurable duties," he said. "But none are at once so profound and so delightful as the pronouncement of a betrothal. Over the next few minutes we will experience, together, one of the greatest steps on the Way of Harmony: the pledging of a young man to a young woman, an undertaking to Follow the Way together, and the conjunction of great houses. If that were not enough, today that pleasure is doubled, for we have two such pledges in view; and three noble houses joined in a pledge of amity. I will not expound at length—for who, in truth, enjoys tedious sermonising when not only great emotion but also superlative victuals await—but lead us instead, on today's short but momentous journey: a path walked by many, but none the less glorious for that."

Shalvijo was as good as his word; the peroration was gratifyingly short. Soon he reached his conclusion. "And so we reach the first of our betrothals. Dravadan, as the senior your betrothal takes precedence. Stand, if you will, Gravity, and speak the words."

Dravadan slowly raised himself from his seat. Next to him sat Rullia, her head concealed by her veil. He took four steps forward, knelt before Igrinto, the head of House Rasteccio.

"Sir, I beg of you, in all humility, the treasure most precious of your house. Will you bestow upon me the hand of your daughter, the fair maid Damoiselle Rullia?"

Igrinto stood, raised Dravadan erect. "I do so bestow. Dravadan, from this day forth, account yourself my son."

From at least two points nearby came sobbing; no doubt the two mothers in question. Viator Shalvijo beamed, reached across to where Rullia sat, and pulled back the veil from her face. A tear rolled down her cheek as Dravadan stepped to across to embrace her, following this with a kiss rather more protracted than demanded by protocol.

There was applause from all the tables across the garden. Shalvijo raised his hands for silence. "In the sight of Hissen and Animaxia, you are as one. By custom and by law, your nuptials shall be celebrated within a year and a day."

Dravadan sat down next to his betrothed, his face all but splitting with the width of his grin. Rullia's raptures appeared more modest, but she was, after all, a young lady known for her exemplary restraint. Malvazan looked across at them with a cool expression. How could he have got to this point?

He scanned the audience, to see Monichoë looking back at him with an emotion he could not read.

"On this most august day," said Shalvijo, "we find ourselves only halfway through our felicity, for another young couple are about to share their joy. The lot of the second son, if I may be permitted a digression, is often a difficult one. Over recent times I have come to know well, and to counsel, Malvazan of House Umbinzia, a young man of spirit and great merit. There are those in life who one knows will overcome accidents of birth, to reach a great destiny regardless of all obstacles. Malvazan, I tell you, Malvazan is such a man."

He paused, looked around the audience. Malvazan could see them, rapt at Shalvijo's words. Next to him he could her Sanoutë's rapid breathing under her veil.

"Malvazan is not a person who repines his lot," continued Shalvijo. "Rather he takes the steps along the Way of Harmony; all are familiar with his skill with the rapier."

A frisson ran across the audience, a chill which Malvazan found curiously exciting. If they did not love him, at least they feared him.

"Will you now, Gravity, arise and speak the words?"

Malvazan cast a rapid side glance at Sanoutë, who remained immobile. He stood up and walked the short distance across the grass to the seat where Thrinko, his prospective father-in-law, sat.

Kneeling, he said the words which every member of the Specchio knew by heart.

"Sir, I beg of you, in all humility, the treasure most precious of your house. Will you bestow upon me the hand of your daughter, the fair maid Damoiselle Sanoutë?"

Thrinko's eyes were moist as he looked down at Malvazan. "I do so bestow. Malvazan, from this day forth, account yourself my son."

He lifted Malvazan to his feet, embraced him. "I welcome you," he whispered into Malvazan's ear. "Be worthy of my daughter."

Malvazan's head was spinning; the event was almost overwhelming. Through the pounding in his ears and the applause in the background, he could barely discern Viator Shalvijo's pronouncement.

"In the sight of Hissen and Animaxia, you are as one. By custom and by law, your nuptials shall be celebrated within a year and a day."

Shalvijo walked to the betrothal table, whisked away Sanoutë's veil to reveal a face blotched and red with weeping. This was hardly a favourable contrast with the impression Rullia had made, thought Malvazan.

Shalvijo gently patted her hand as Malvazan went across to sit with his new betrothed.

Sanouté sprang erect: "No! This cannot be, and it will not be!"

The chatter from guests instantly ceased.

Thrinko strode over to his daughter's table, where Dravadan and Rullia sat open-mouthed. Malvazan did not know whether to sit or stand.

"What nonsense is this!" demanded Thrinko in voice suddenly shrill. "The betrothal is pronounced; I have given my consent."

Sanouté ripped away her veil, threw it to the floor. "Nobody asked my consent! Nobody asked if I wished to spend my life with a man who does not love me and does not want me!"

"Sanouté—" said Malvazan hesitantly. "I said—"

"I asked you if you loved me with all your heart!" Tears were streaming down her face.

"I said yes!" cried Malvazan.

"You said it as if I had offered you a cup of tisane. It is not the way a woman wishes to be addressed by her beloved!"

Shalvijo said: "Damoiselle—gentle lady—such moments are—"

Thrinko overrode Shalvijo's conciliation. "I have no patience with your vapours, Sanouté. You read too much. Life is not arranged around love and deeds of the heart. The Dignified Crostadan asked me for your hand; I was delighted to give it. I do not withdraw my consent now. Viator Shalvijo has pronounced you betrothed, and betrothed you are."

"I will never marry Malvazan!"

Malvazan had sunk into his seat. This could not be happening.

Shalvijo said: "Surely this is a tiff, an attack of bridal nerves? Can we not overlook it and proceed? In a year and a day we will all laugh."

Malvazan looked around the company, saw no-one who appeared to be saving up mirth.

"I am sorry, Viator," said Sanouté. "I cannot marry a man who does not love and respect me. That is how I 'Follow the Way', if you will."

Thrinko leaned forward and slapped Sanouté across the face. "You have embarrassed me, and embarrassed our house, beyond measure. I say you will embrace Malvazan, here and now, and the betrothal feast will proceed."

The blow had instantly staunched Sanouté's tears. Through lips tight with passion, she grated: "I say that I will not, father. You cannot beat me into acquiescence."

"'Father?' You are no longer my daughter, Sanouté."

Crostadan rose from his seat with a dazed expression. "Enough," he said. "Never let it be said that House Umbinzia is so desperate for connections as to coerce a lady. Damoiselle Sanoutë, if you do not wish to marry Malvazan, I am of course disappointed: but I will not hold you to a betrothal so distasteful to you."

Sanoutë once more began to cry. "Sir, I am humbled by your forbearance."

Malvazan said in a quiet voice: "Sanoutë—"

"I cannot talk to you now, Malvazan. Perhaps at some time in the future..."

Malvazan wordlessly shook his head. Here, in his own house, at his own betrothal feast, before every house of the Specchio, he was humiliated in the most grotesque fashion imaginable. He could scarcely believe it was his own voice responding:

"Damoiselle, I would be insensitive to demand an explanation of your obvious disgust: the existence of your repugnance is sufficient reason. I will never trouble you further."

"Father, Viator Shalvijo," he said, bowing to each. "Will you forgive me? I am indisposed."

In the brittle silence Malvazan walked back past the guests' tables and into the house, pausing only to pick up his practice sword before continuing out through the front door and on to the Archgate.

CHAPTER THIRTY-FIVE

Dravadan had excelled himself—or at least Palankijo had done so on his behalf—in readying a feast in the two and a half hours it had taken to view the docks, the Ostentatory and the Masavory. By the Hour of Evening Repast everyone was seated in the Grand Hall of Korfez, a far more formal chamber than any Todarko had yet seen at the manse.

The favour in which Dravadan now held Todarko was reflected in his place at table, seated at the host's left hand (Lord Oricien occupying the place of honour on the right). On Todarko's left was Lord Ribauldequin, whose appetite seemed to have been roused by his recent encounter with the bindlespith. Raguslan was nearby but did not direct his conversation Todarko's way, contenting himself with the occasional side-glance when it seemed his nephew's attention was elsewhere.

Todarko did not, in truth, find the occasion stimulating. Dravadan's high spirits were only increased by the fine Televen wine which flowed with abandon, and to which Todarko readily applied himself. Neither Linnalitha nor Nelanka were within easy conversational distance, and while Nelanka caught his eye several times, Linnalitha seemed if anything to be avoiding his gaze.

A bindlespith, no matter how large and ferocious, does not provide an inexhaustible supply of meat, particularly when split fourteen ways. Todarko's identified his modest portion as haunch, which was undoubtedly more agreeable than the testicles with which Zanijel was forced to content himself. Fortunately Dravadan's larder was well-stocked against the contingency of an impromptu banquet, and few diners had cause to complain or to leave the table hungry. As the wine began to take effect, Todarko found the company less oppressive, even declaiming a salacious ode which called forth demands for an encore. Todarko took even more satisfaction in that the poem was the work of the insufferable Hazilan. Linnalitha raised an eyebrow in his direction, but no-one else would notice the bare-faced plagiarism.

Finally the seventh course reached its conclusion, the pears stewed to a perfect yielding softness and the colyrampis sauce having just the right blend of astringent sweetness. The Hour of Evening Satiation approached and Dravadan clapped his hands for attention. Palankijo appeared, to remove the salvers, and Dravadan rose from his seat to direct his guests to the loggia for informal conversations.

"Todarko, step aside with me, if you will," he said as they walked into the fresh clean air of the garden. "We have much to discuss."

Todarko did not flinch as Dravadan laid an arm around his shoulder. Most men would sell their mothers into slavery to win Dravadan's patronage, but Todarko was not among them. Their relationship was founded on more than one fundamental misconception—that Todarko was interested in his political schemes, that he was not infatuated with Dravadan's wife—and when enlightenment came, it was likely that Dravadan would bear a resentment proportionate to his original misapprehension.

They strolled into a small walled garden with gravel crunching underfoot. "I hold myself a good judge of character, Todarko," said Dravadan. "A man of my ambitions must be able to weigh a man."

"No doubt, sir," said Todarko.

"I am wrong on occasion."

Todarko found the flattery expected of him sticking in his throat and contented himself with a nod.

"I confess I was wrong about you, Todarko. Your uncle Raguslan, a sound and reliable ally, holds your merits cheap, and when we were introduced I had assimilated his views. But you have shown yourself not only sensible of my great designs, but able to advance their realisation. I wondered at your folly when you struck Zanijel—but it seemed you had read the temper of Lord Oricien better than any of us."

"I did not strike Zanijel to impress Oricien; I struck him because he is a buffoon who does not appreciate the jewel to which he is married."

"Indeed, indeed," nodded Dravadan. "That is what made it even more perfect. You acted without calculation, which cannot have been lost on Oricien. He will see in you a man whose character he admires."

"I would have struck Zanijel for abusing Nelanka so, regardless of the circumstances."

"The boy is an imbecile. The woman Nelanka is not as handsome as my own wife, but she is comely enough."

"Her looks are not relevant to Zanijel's treatment of her."

"Perhaps not. I would certainly never strike Linnalitha—to show dissatisfaction with one's wife calls into doubt one's judgement in choosing her in the first place."

"I suspect Linnalitha might strike you back, sir," said Todarko with a grin.

Dravadan pursed his lips. "Very probably she might, although I find the remark over-familiar."

"I meant no offence," said Todarko, sweating slightly in the cool night. "I merely meant that Linnalitha unnerves me a trifle."

Dravadan beamed. "One must be a man indeed to ride such a spirited beast. In that she is a fit mate for one such as myself. Are you quite well, Todarko?"

"A momentary indisposition, sir," said Todarko.

"In any event, you need not associate with her so much in future. Recent events have allied you so firmly with my cause that I doubt Bartielko will welcome you at Popisilaija's salon. You need collect no more intelligence from that source."

"I am grateful."

"I will try to foster your friendship with Oricien. He is due to address the Masavory with his proposals next week; I would surround him with my own men as far as possible. And you are more use to me than Raguslan and Zanijel together."

"Thank you, sir."

"You are yet unmarried, I think?"

"Yes, sir. Raguslan has not seen me as an advantageous match, and failed to include me in his plans."

Dravadan nodded. "It is unfortunate that I have only sons. Nonetheless, I am sure we can secure you a sound match one way or another. Letizana is possible."

Todarko drew back. "I have never seen her without Hood and Veil, but she is nearly forty, and by all accounts corpulent and no beauty."

"Pah! You must set aside such squeamishness where marriage is concerned. She is wealthy and well-connected. Yes, I must look into this."

"Thank you, sir," said Todarko in a quiet voice.

"Now, it seems that Nelanka wishes your company," said Dravadan, indicating the purposefully approaching figure. He bowed to her. "Madam," he said. "I will not impede your family matters."

Nelanka gave a brief nod. "I thank you for your grace and hospitality."

Even in the moonlight, Nelanka's eyes glittered with a fire which raised an apprehension in Todarko's heart. She was clearly in one of her occasional "plain speaking" humours, which usually betokened an imminent harangue.

"Nelanka, a pleasure to see you, sister. We have not had a frank conversation for a while."

Nelanka brushed the point aside. "Do not give me this empty Specchio rhetoric, Darko. Your recent conduct is bizarre and unsatisfactory."

"Except when compared with your husband's."

Nelanka's eyes flashed. "There was no call for that. You are behaving in a ludicrously dangerous and foolish way—and no-one will tell you if I do not, for they all profit from it: Dravadan, Raguslan, Linnalitha. You will bring ruin on yourself."

"You overstate the case, Nel," said Todarko with an easy smile.

"Do you think your new-found intimacy with Dravadan can end in anything other than disaster, particularly the way you are sidling around Linnalitha?"

"The disaster seems to be readying itself for Raguslan and Zanijel. Dravadan has seen them for the bungling oafs they are."

"So you wish to replace them in Dravadan's service? At least Zanijel is honest in his mendacity."

"You compare me unfavourably to your lummox of a husband!" said Todarko through tight lips. "The man who would have beaten you in the woods!"

Nelanka shook her head, either in denial or to clear it.

"You don't understand at all! I know what Zanijel is—no-one better. I don't want you involving yourself in Dravadan's games. You lack the experience and I thought you lacked the desire. It seems I was wrong on the latter point."

"Nel—"

"I have nothing more to say to you, Todarko. If you want to supplant the rest of your family to gain advantage, I don't care. They are nothing to me; but I thought you were. On that, too, perhaps I was wrong."

She turned and walked back towards the loggia.

"Nelanka!" called Todarko.

She turned once more to face him. "And if you are going to become Dravadan's acolyte," she said in a whisper that somehow carried across the still sharp night, "you really ought to think about what you're doing with his wife."

With that she stalked back towards house, leaving Todarko shaking his head in a mixture of bafflement and irritation. If there were thanks for rescuing her from a beating by Zanijel he was at a loss to identify them.

CHAPTER THIRTY-SIX

Oricien had found the banquet predictably tedious. Such occasions of conviviality were tolerable only if one respected and enjoyed the company; a situation far from the truth in this case. Iselin remained 'indisposed' but Dravadan, Raguslan and Zanijel were quite bad enough. Ribauldequin had a very clear idea of what constituted diplomatic hospitality, and as luck would have it, these were precisely the activities he would have chosen to undertake of his own volition: eating, drinking and flirtation. Oricien could not be angry with him; the level of statecraft required was well beyond such an inexperienced young man. Indeed, Oricien reflected, it was probably beyond him as well.

After the meal he was at least able to breathe in the crisp night air, and after a decent period he thought he could legitimately return to the Castle. Who knew, maybe there would even be time for a bath before bed. As he walked back towards the house, he saw Nelanka approaching from another direction. At the same time, Nelanka saw him, coloured and made to change direction.

"Madam!" called Oricien. "I pray that I have not offended you."

Nelanka looked around as if for escape; but the loggia was empty, and the archway to the house out of reach. Seeing herself with no alternative, she gave a brisk curtsy. "Good evening, my lord."

Oricien found himself unreasonably irritated by her new chilly formality.

"Come, madam, walk with me awhile."

"My lord, it is late and—"

Oricien compressed his lips in annoyance. In this city of depravity, calculation and betrayal, was his company really so objectionable? He gave a crisp bow. "Forgive me, madam: I hope you do not think me crass enough to force my presence upon you unwillingly."

He turned to continue his journey to the house. A hand on his arm halted him and he turned to face her.

"Lord Oricien—" she said. Her eyes looked to be full of tears in the moonlight. "Please do not go. I should very much like to walk with you."

She slipped her arm through his and they made their way back out into the garden. "There is much you do not—cannot—understand. In this city, every good thought, every fine intention or feeling, is perverted, turned to the advantage of those who have never felt such things. My behaviour must seem to you most capricious."

Oricien indicated a nearby bench and they sat down. "'Capricious' is a good term," he said. "But I would not presume to suggest that you owe me an explanation."

She looked away into the sky. "Of course I do, my lord."

"Do not distress yourself, madam. If this gives you pain, we will not speak of it."

A sob racked her throat. "This has been such a terrible day," she said in a thick voice. "My husband, this morning—"

"His behaviour was intolerable," said Oricien. "I could not be surprised when Todarko hit him."

For a brief moment she smiled. "Neither could I. But Todarko is in such terrible danger."

"If you will forgive me, madam, I am not certain that your husband is the most daunting enemy—and Todarko has secured his good opinion."

Nelanka turned to look into his eyes. "Oh, Oricien, that is the terror! Todarko does not know what he is dealing with! Dravadan is the most dangerous man in Taratanallos!"

Oricien grimaced. "He is a formidable character, to be sure. But he esteems Todarko—he told me so himself."

Nelanka looked down into her lap. "You will forgive me, my lord," she said, "if there are things I cannot tell you. But if Dravadan knew all that I did, there would be no amity between them: Dravadan would kill him. Todarko has many virtues, but sober judgement is not among them."

Oricien laid a hand on her forearm; Nelanka flinched but did not draw away. "Todarko made a favourable impression on me today; you know that he saved Ribauldequin from the bindlespith, quite aside from the way he protected you. As long as I am in Taratanallos, he will have a friend in me. I hope that will counteract any loss of Dravadan's patronage."

"Thank you, my lord," she said. "I am heartened to hear such words— and from a man of honour, who will keep them true."

"He is very dear to you, is he not?" said Oricien with the faintest edge.

"Yes," said Nelanka. "We are as brother and sister. There is no-one else in that awful household…"

"I do not think your husband would describe his regard as brotherly," said Oricien with a wry smile.

"He merely proves the baseness of his own character," she said with a scornful twist of her mouth.

Oricien said nothing for a moment. He removed his hand from her arm. "Dravadan addressed me today in a way I found offensively familiar," he said. "He insinuated something I found hard to believe—"

"Oricien," she said in a soft voice. "Please go no further. I know the subject of the conversation, since I myself was subjected to it last night. I would not wish to view you as anything other than a man of the highest honour."

Oricien moved slightly apart. "And you need not, madam. I do not know why he felt compelled to manufacture—in any event, his words were wasted. Regardless of my own inclinations, which I would not have regarded as suitable for casual gossip, I knew your own virtue to be impregnable against such insinuations."

Nelanka looked away. "Oh, Oricien, if only you knew! He told me—and my husband looked on—that I must make myself agreeable to you. That you disdained to take your pleasure with a slave-girl, and that if you looked on me in such a way I should encourage you. I was disgusted, sickened to be prostituted by my own husband, who had not the courage to oppose Dravadan."

"Nelanka! No wonder you were so cold today."

She looked up for a moment. "I am sorry," she said, tears choking her voice. "What was worst of all is that I genuinely liked you—and they could see that you liked me. So they thought to corrupt something pure and decent with their schemes. And then I thought you might even have agreed to it..."

Oricien fought down a compulsion—utterly inappropriate in the circumstances—to take her in his arms. "I am not their tool," he said. "Any more than you are. My lady, if you doubt my honour, I will not intrude upon you more—and if you wish, I will inform Dravadan that I find you repulsive."

Nelanka gave a brittle laugh. "I have yet a little vanity, my lord. Now that I know you are not part of the scheme, I can bear your company again. Since we both decline to be pawns, why should we not be friends once more? You can save your 'repulsive' for another day."

Oricien smiled. "Shall we return to the house? I think we have both had a long day."

She stood up and held out her arm. "Would you be kind enough to escort me, my lord?"

Todarko, motivated by an impulse he could neither explain nor justify, made his way down to the folly at the base of Korfez's gardens. The Hour of Noble Pleasures approached, and the sun cast its last rays over the horizon before its temporary exile, leaving a legacy of oranges and purples on the undersides of the scudding clouds.

Sitting on a seat at the base of the folly, looking out over an algae-furred pond, was Linnalitha; for some reason Todarko was not surprised.

"May I join you, madam?" he asked.

Linnalitha looked up from her reverie. "If you promise not to kiss me," she said in a flat voice.

Todarko was unsure how to take the remark. "My sentiments were clearly disgusting to you yesterday," he said. "You may be sure I will not expose myself to humiliation a second time."

Her mouth twitched and she brushed a hair from her eyes. "You and my husband are now such boon companions that I am sure you would not wish to renew your addresses in any event."

"You know better than that, Linna. Dravadan has taken me up because he sees advantages in doing so. He sees me as a route to Oricien's good opinion."

She broke a twig from the overhanging willow. "A more ambitious man would ride the current, to who knows what advancement."

Todarko laughed. "A more ambitious man would not have hit Zanijel in the first place."

Linnalitha tossed the twig into the pond. "No doubt Nelanka was suitably grateful."

"She has only left off reviling me this last five minutes. Like you, she sees me as Dravadan's lapdog."

Linnalitha looked around into the rapidly falling dusk to ensure that they were alone. "I must ask you to swear that you have no interest in Dravadan and his schemes. If you do, I wish you every good fortune, but we cannot be friends."

Todarko crossed his legs. "I understood that we were not friends, regardless of my regard for Dravadan."

"Because of the kiss?"

"Well—"

"You may remember that I subsequently kissed you."

"It was difficult to forget, but I imagined it as a revenge rather than an endearment."

Linnalitha's eyes sparkled for a moment. "You are more perceptive than I give you credit for. That aside, are you Dravadan's man now?"

"No, of course not," said Todarko. "I profoundly distrust and dislike him."

A complex expression skittered across Linnalitha's face. "At least you are not married to him." She stood up and walked to the edge of the pond, her back to Todarko. He strained to hear as she spoke.

"You may have noticed how many of the Specchio have been bankrupted this past year."

Todarko frowned at this seeming non sequitur. "Half a dozen, maybe. It is a bad business, even before Aladar's ruin."

"How many of them are of the Emmen party?"

Todarko ran through the list in his head: Aladar, Jadinko, Lujomir, Svelirno, Patibor. "All of them, to greater or lesser extent."

"Coincidental, is it not?" said Linnalitha in a soft voice.

"Your demeanour invites me to assume not."

She looked over her shoulder with a twitchy smile. "My demeanour. Yes, my demeanour may give matters away. Should Dravadan not be worried that the next Emmen supporter to fall may be himself?"

"I assume his credit is impeccable. He has over a million florins coming from House Vaggio, after all."

Linnalitha gave a brittle laugh. "Yes, and Raguslan has been played for a fool there. The battlecat monopoly is worth at most two hundred thousand florins."

"How can that be?" said Todarko in alarm.

Linnalitha shrugged. "Simple. Ingomer completed the Dimonetto Road two years ago. The pelt factors now transport the goods along the Road, where tolls are modest and the route direct. The trade flowing through Taratanallos is a trickle, the revenues correspondingly reduced. It affects all goods to greater or lesser extent—except maybe slaves—but the pelt trade is particularly affected. Dravadan is delighted to have secured such a favourable price. His political ambitions are not cheap to maintain."

"This is an outrage, and it touches my inheritance. You were right to tell me."

Linnalitha shook her head. "It is a trivial matter. Raguslan has made a bad bargain, and there it must stay, unless you wish to bring me to disaster. His plots are far graver than a spot of sharp practice."

"There is worse?"

"Oh yes, there is worse." She gave a quick bitter smile in the dusk. "My husband need not fear ruin, but not because of his wealth. Because he controls Ion Issio."

"Linna, be reasonable. No one controls Ion Issio! He is a corsair—by definition an independent raider."

"How then does he strike so accurately? How does he know which argosies to plunder and which to leave?"

"I don't—"

"Because Dravadan passes him the manifests. Through an intermediary, of course, but it's still Dravadan at work. Ion Issio gets the guarantee of rich pickings, and my husband sees his political rivals fall. There is none to challenge him as the coming man of the Emmen party now. When the treaty is signed, he has all the wealth and power he could desire."

"This is hardly credible, Linna."

"It is true, nonetheless."

"Oricien would not deal with such a man! I do not know him well, but he is a Knight of the Tarn, an Immaculate."

"I doubt that Oricien much cares about the character of the man he is dealing with," said Linnalitha wearily. "He will be concerned only that someone can deliver the support of the Masavory to King Enguerran. He cannot see Dravadan or Raguslan or any of them as anything but grasping plate-grabbers—but they are the men he needs to deliver his commission. The various factions of the Gammerling party are no better, if that's any consolation."

Todarko ran a hand through his hair. "This is monstrous."

"That is why I required to know if you were one of them. But for all your faults, you are not consumed with ambition," she said with the most relaxed smile she had given.

"Faults?" said Todarko with a raised eyebrow. "In the context, any lapses in judgement I may make scarcely weigh in the scale."

She sat next to him and put a hand on his arm. "Like yesterday?"

"Ah—"

"That was a lapse, you know."

"So I have come to understand," said Todarko with a strained smile.

"Not because of the impulse itself," she said. "In truth it was flattering and only reflected my own desires."

"In that case…" he said, inching closer.

She eased herself towards the farther end of the seat. "Nonetheless it was not only inadvisable, but unrepeatable. The situation is simply too dangerous—for both of us—to take the risk."

Todarko put a finger under her chin and turned her head to face him. "You appear to be implying that were you ruled only by your inclinations, your conduct might be somewhat different."

She jerked her head away. "You know it would be. I surely cannot have dissembled well enough to conceal it. But you are fixing on the inessential. The point I need you to understand, in full and unequivocal measure, is this: whatever feelings might or might not exist between us, they cannot be acted upon. I will never look upon you with anything other than—" her voice caught in a liquid hesitation "—the greatest esteem and affection, but I cannot—we cannot—"

"Linna..." He put his arms around her.

"No, Todarko," she said as she slipped free. "Do not make this any more difficult. I am married to the most evil man in Taratanallos. That is bad enough. Now I meet someone who touches my heart in every imaginable way; that is worse. Please, Todarko, just accept that whatever you might feel for me, whatever I feel for you, we must both forget."

Tears were running down both her cheeks; normally a happenstance which left Todarko either unmoved or irritated. In this case he felt a pounding in his chest, a desire to roar, to set matters to rights: to tell Dravadan that he would henceforth have to put his wife aside and yield her up to a man who would cherish her as she deserved. He realised the absurdity of his fantasy, and sagged back on the seat.

"You recognise what I am saying, do you not?"

Todarko nodded. He could not bring himself to say "yes" outright. "I am grateful for your warnings as to Dravadan's intrigues and character," he said. "It was the only gift you could give me."

"I knew you would understand," she said, applying a handkerchief to her nose.

"There is a gift I can give you, if you will let me," he said.

"Go on."

"The sonnet I was writing—it could only ever have been for you. When it is finished—may I send it to you?"

She looked away, now openly sobbing. "Yes," she said. "Send me your sonnet. When I am an old woman—"

She dashed from the seat in the direction of the house leaving Todarko, for the second day running, staring mutely at her back.

CHAPTER THIRTY-SEVEN

Not for the first time, it was late before Oricien settled down for sleep. His interview with Nelanka had been profoundly unsettling: there was something about her openness, the way it made her vulnerable, which touched his heart. He gave a contemptuous snort at his weakness: such chivalric temper was all very well, but would he be so moved by her plight if her distress was not accompanied by beauty? He had thought himself well beyond such adolescent excess: once he had suggested to his father, a man of grim pragmatism, that he marry a noble lady without a dowry; more recently, a betrothal to one of the most eligible young ladies of the Emmenrule had ended in spectacular humiliation. Affairs of the heart, he had learned the hard way, were not a field in which he excelled. Any sentiments of that sort towards Madam Nelanka, not only married but embroiled in the foulest games of the Specchio, could only end in disaster. Another goblet of wine, he knew, and his thoughts would fix on the melancholy considerations of a man in the prime of life who was yet unmarried and had contrived to see the city he ruled sacked and burned to the ground. He set the goblet down untouched and rang the bell.

"Kindly ask Lords Ribauldequin and Iselin to join me if they are awake so late," he said. Work was usually the solution to such vapours.

Ribauldequin slouched in a few moments later, to be followed by a wary Iselin.

"Lord Ambassador?" said Iselin. "You wished to see us at this hour?"

"I am dissatisfied with our progress," said Oricien. "Now would be suitable moment to take stock." He gave a brief analysis of the situation, touching on the solicitation by Bartielko of the million-florin bribe.

Iselin shook his head. "The scheme is impractical, for several reasons," he said. "Firstly, we do not have a million florins. Secondly, Bartielko could never be considered a trustworthy associate. Thirdly, it would serve only to unsettle Dravadan, who would consider his status usurped—and, incidentally, require a similar bribe himself."

Oricien gave a gloomy shake of the head. "Such was largely my own view," he said.

"I have not been on hand for recent events," said Iselin with a narrowing of his eyes, "for reasons we all understand. You will have noticed, perhaps, my lord, that Dravadan has been at great pains to conciliate your good opinion in recent days?"

Making a whore of your noble ally's wife could reasonably be regarded in that light, thought Oricien. "Just so."

"Why should he do so, when you are already in his camp?"

"Tell us," brayed Ribauldequin. "Your insights astound us all."

Oricien quelled him with a glance. "Continue, good Iselin."

"Dravadan is aware of your conversations with Bartielko. He is concerned that he may lose pre-eminence once the treaty is signed; he is therefore keen to bind you with demonstrations of his regard."

Oricien gave a sour smile. "He has a poor understanding of my tastes, if so." Or an uncannily shrewd one.

"I have arranged further activities for you tomorrow," said Iselin.

"As long as they are not as dramatic as today's."

Iselin shrugged. "First you visit High Viator Udenko," he said. "The Viators are on our side, of course, but he will require guarantees of freedom of worship."

"So much is agreed."

"He will also," said Iselin with a glance at his shoes, "probably request a bribe."

"To do that which is in his own interest?"

"This is Taratanallos," said Iselin in a neutral tone.

Ribauldequin drained his goblet. "I think you will find that avarice is as common in the Emmenrule as Taratanallos, my lord."

Iselin flushed but ignored him. "Later you will visit the Ostentatory, where the slaves are displayed prior to sale."

Oricien raised an eyebrow. "Is this necessary?"

"The Tarats are very proud of the Ostentatory. In addition, the Dignified Bartielko will be in attendance. When I arranged the event, naturally I did not know of the conversations you had already had conducted."

Oricien gave a brisk nod. "It does not matter, Iselin. It may be I can secure his goodwill — or least his neutrality."

"I am glad I am not visiting the Ostentatory," declared Ribauldequin. "Such a place makes my heart quail."

Iselin gave a broad smile. "On the contrary, my lord. Both you and Lord Oricien will be in attendance. It is not appropriate for Oricien to conduct all the visits unaccompanied: it reduces his prestige."

Ribauldequin looked crestfallen. "Surely this is not necessary. I—"

Oricien held up a hand. "Enough. In this instance Iselin's judgement is sound. We shall both go, and make of it what we will."

Ribauldequin inclined his head. "Very well, my lord. If you will excuse me, I will retire to bed."

"Good night," said Oricien.

"Do you require me further, Lord Ambassador?" asked Iselin.

Oricien shook his head, and Iselin followed Ribauldequin to the door. "Lord Iselin!" called Oricien. Iselin turned. "Thank you for your diligence in these matters."

Iselin bowed. "You are welcome, Lord Ambassador."

Oricien watched the door shut with relief. He did not relish the visit to the Ostentatory. He had no particular objection to slavery—although it did not form a major part of Emmen life—but he could not help but think of Vivalda, passed around from one dignitary to another until such time as one of them casually divested her of her innocence. That was the reality of the slave-market.

He rose from his seat and wearily took himself to bed.

CHAPTER THIRTY-EIGHT

Despite not getting to his bed until well into the Hour of Secret Deeds, Todarko awoke early and refreshed the next morning. The sun streamed in through his window and, after ringing the bell to summon Luzio with refreshments, he sat at his desk and opened his folio to continue his sonnet. Bodazar, whom he had not seen since their beating in the Chale, was joining him at the Hour of Light Repast, so he had several hours to work on his verse.

Inspiration did not come rapidly. He could not think about his parting from Linnalitha without a tremor. He still did not know whether she was acutely manipulative or in the grip of an ungovernable passion; it was not out of the question that both views were true. Regardless of her emotional veracity, they had both agreed that their liaison now had nowhere to run. In normal circumstances, he would soon be casting around his acquaintance for another young lady—preferably unmarried—with whom he might enjoy a pleasant and undemanding frolic. Indeed, with his new status as Dravadan's protégé, he might find a larger field on which to draw.

He laid down his quill on the white sheet before him. These were not normal circumstances. Linnalitha was a woman so vibrant, so elemental, so different in degree and kind to any he had previously known, that all other women of his circle were insipid shadows of femininity. The one woman he exempted from his dismissal, Nelanka, did not present any consolation. Their formerly easy and open relationship was entirely of the brother and sister kind—although her behaviour last night had been so extraordinary as to make even that kind of intimacy questionable.

A short while later he looked around to find, to his surprise, that not only had Luzio brought his breakfast, but that he had eaten it. His reverie had been deeper than he realised. Once again he looked from his window. The blue sky and twinkling sea always raised his mood. A couple of cogs plied their way up the bay to disembark whatever cargoes they might carry; closer by, a crow swooped to pick at some unseen carrion on the city wall. The crow, the emblem of House Vaggio—yes, that was what the sonnet needed!

After three abortive attempts he arrived at a second quatrain for the sonnet.

> *Let not my love be called idolatry,*
> *A crow that flies in heaven's sweetest air.*

> *Thy love is better than high birth to me*
> *Past cure I am, now reason is past care.*

The reference to idolatry and heaven gave the depth of the Way's fervour to the whole, even if the Viators would be unlikely to endorse the use to which he had put their imagery. 'Heaven' at least came straight out of the Peninsular Heresy, so he could not be accused of supporting the Consorts. All in all, the quatrain conveyed passionate ardour to one who knew where to look.

Encouraged, he pressed on with his drafting. The third quatrain took little more than an hour:

> *As from my soul which in thy breast doth lie*
> *Like him that travels I return again,*
> *Happy to have thy love, happy to die,*
> *And death once dead, there's no more dying then.*

Did this perhaps err to the melodramatic? Linnalitha would understand the emotion from which it sprang, and the verse had a flexible springiness he was loath to sacrifice. It would have to do. Only the final couplet now, and a few more minutes could see that done.

He heard a noise behind him. "So this is how you spend your time. Fah!"

Even as Todarko cursed Bodazar inwardly for his early arrival, another part of his mind realised that this was not Bodazar. He rose from his seat and faced his visitor.

"It is customary to knock, Zanijel. I do not recall inviting you to my chambers in any event."

His cousin stood in the doorway, blocking both light and exit.

"I have spent the morning at the Masavory," Zanijel said. "I have been toiling for the advancement of House Vaggio. You, it seems, have wasted your time scribbling your pitiful verses."

He snatched up the folio, read a passage at random. "Happy to have thy love, happy to die, and death once dead, there's no more dying then. What nonsense is that?"

Todarko took a step towards him and wrenched the folio back. "It is written to be read by a person of ordinary or better taste and discrimination. I would not expect the meaning to be clear to you."

"There is much talk of death there. I assure you, if you have directed the poem to Nelanka, your own will not be far off."

"The poem argues that death and passion are linked, two sides of the same florin," said Todarko with the beginnings of a smirk.

"If you ever give this poem to my wife, you will be dead upon the morrow." He pushed a meaty hand against Todarko's chest. "You caught me unprepared yesterday. We may resume now, if you choose."

Todarko swatted Zanijel's hand aside. "The poem is neither for nor about Nelanka. If that is the sum of your grievance, you may depart now."

Zanijel's eyes narrowed. "You have another lady in mind? No doubt she is married as well. It will not be long before you receive the reckoning you deserve, Todarko. I had come to chastise you for yesterday's insult. I think perhaps I will defer my vengeance awhile."

"As you will," said Todarko. "Please ensure you notify me when you are exacting your revenge, so that I can arrange to be on hand."

Zanijel's lips curved into an approximation of a smile. "Nonetheless I think I will at least place a deposit on my reckoning now." He moved towards Todarko who was pinned in the corner.

"What is happening here!" came the thin voice of Luzio. "Sirs, desist immediately."

Zanijel sprang back in irritation.

Luzio said: "You have a visitor, Todarko. Bodazar of House Belario is here."

Bodazar stepped into the room. "I hope I have not interrupted anything," he said.

Todarko made an easy gesture. "My cousin objected to my latest verse. His literary criticism took a somewhat direct form."

Bodazar nodded. "I am glad to see him taking the arts seriously. Dilettantism is the curse of so many men of letters."

Zanijel glowered at the pair of them and growled something inaudible. "Come, Luzio," he said. "The matter of my luncheon requires attention."

"I think you have much to tell me," said Bodazar.

"Where to begin?" said Todarko. "You may wish to sit down."

Oricien viewed his visit to the Dominikos with little more enthusiasm than the inspection of slaves at the Ostentatory which was to follow it. He did not look back on his previous encounters with affection; and he well remembered from his childhood the endless sermons—and occasional whippings for inattention or outright mischief—and the frequent difficulties which doctrinal wranglings had caused his father.

Life in Croad had been by no means penurious, but Oricien was taken aback as they were shown into High Viator Udenko's state apartments in company with Dravadan at the Hour of Petitions. Those fittings which were not of silver were of gold, and decorative marble pillars held aloft the high and airy ceiling.

"My lord, please be seated," said Udenko. "And Dravadan, a pleasure to see you again."

For a quarter of an hour they sipped teas and nibbled on wafers. When the bell tolled for the Hour of Fiscal Scrutiny, however, Dravadan eased the conversation onto questions of policy.

"We are grateful you have condescended to take refreshments with us, Your Salience," said Dravadan. "Your time is precious, and no doubt there are many to be instructed in the Way this morning. Nonetheless, I thought you might favour the ambassador with your counsel."

Udenko nodded his white head politely. "In any way I can, Dignity."

"It will not have escaped you that Lord Oricien addresses the Specchio on behalf of King Enguerran next week," he said. "The support of the Viatory in this matter would smooth the Way for us all."

Udenko made a modest gesture. "I am but an old man. I carry little weight in the Specchio."

"Your Salience, no son of House Rasteccio is inconsiderable. There is also the will of the mob to consider. While I am sure we can carry the Specchio, if the man in the Chale opposes the treaty, the potential for unrest remains. But who would oppose a treaty sanctioned by the High Viator?"

Udenko nodded. "Perhaps you are right. My lord, is there anything you can say? The ways of Taratanallos are unchanged for centuries, and matters go well for us. Do we need the influence of a new friend whose customs may not be to our liking?"

Oricien set down his tea. "I am sure you do not, Your Salience: yet that is the danger you court. Because your ways are unchanged for so long, you do not see the perils you court. If Ingomer were content simply to be King of Gammerling, all would be well. But instead, like a man whose rank garden overruns his neighbours', he spreads his ambitions to the north. Ingomer cannot be content with his seat at Vasi Vasar: he must press into Emmen. King Enguerran naturally may not countenance such behaviour."

He paused and once more sipped his tea.

"There is therefore a tension between Gammerling and Emmen, which is not of my master's making, but which he must address if he is to preserve the peace of his realm."

Udenko pursed his lips. "There is much in your analysis which is questionable," he said. "I suspect Ingomer would not recognise the portrait of a rapacious aggressor which you paint."

"Be that as it may," said Oricien in a bland voice, "the friction between Gammerling and Emmen cannot be denied. The result is that Ingomer wishes to consolidate Taratanallos into his realm, an event which would be unacceptable to King Enguerran."

"It is no secret that the Viatory would no more wish us to become part of Ingomer's kingdom than would Enguerran. The Consorts would impose their heretical worship on us the instant such an absorption occurred."

"Then we may count upon your support?" Oricien looked around the chambers. "You have much to lose from the arrival of the Consorts."

Udenko raised a fleshy hand. "You go too fast. The Way stresses the importance of brotherly love—but these precepts are not followed in Ingomer's own family. He may have made Lothar Duke of Aylissia, but there is no amity."

"You seek to preserve your independence by playing off Ingomer against Lothar?"

"The Peninsula is Lothar's territory: only our city and its surrounds are independent."

"I would be a negligent ambassador not to realise this, Your Salience."

"Of course, forgive me," said Udenko in a hearty voice. "At my age even seasoned men appear young. The fact remains that an alliance with Duke Lothar has many attractions; it keeps us out of Ingomer's clutches and, more importantly, the Consorts'."

"Lothar has sworn fealty to his brother the King. At any point he could be forced to yield up Taratanallos."

"He would not do so."

"Do you really believe, Your Salience, that he could defend the city against Ingomer should the King bend his will to its capture?"

Udenko creaked back in his chair. "The advantages of an alliance with Emmen are not overwhelming."

"Consider," said Oricien. "King Enguerran can provide all the military support necessary to guarantee the city's safety: indeed, to preserve such a valuable harbour in the south, he would be foolish not to. He is not, with all due respect, dogmatic or even particularly interested where spiritual matters are concerned: if the people of Taratanallos wish to follow the Peninsular Heresy, King Enguerran would guarantee their freedom to do so."

Udenko knitted his brows. "The term 'Peninsular Heresy' is the language of the Consorts. The religion we practice in this city is the True Way: it is the Consorts who are heretics."

"As you will, Your Salience. I am a simple man who follows the counsels of his own Viators. You need only appreciate the cast-iron guarantee my master gives you."

Udenko nodded. "There is much to ponder, my lord. It may yet be that independence is our best course."

"I would judge it your worst, but it is for you to assess."

"If I might be permitted, my lord," said Dravadan.

Oricien gave a brisk nod.

"The High Viator is a man of legendary probity—" Oricien looked on in wonderment at the straight face with which Dravadan delivered the remark "—who is too mild of temper to raise the prospects of the Viators for fear of being accused of self-interest."

Oricien could feel his jaw sagging at this, sitting as he was in the most opulent parlour he had yet seen in Taratanallos.

"Nonetheless," continued Dravadan, "there might be some means by which the King's goodwill to the Viators in person could be made manifest. This would perhaps assuage any doubts."

"There is much in what you say, Dravadan," said Udenko. "Such arrangements could be misconstrued if they became common gossip, however. Much the best approach would be if any favours or gratuities were channelled through myself, that I might distribute them with the greatest discretion."

The elevation of Oricien's eyebrows was only barely perceptible. "It is not without precedent that proven friends of Emmen are rewarded," he said with a sharp side-glance at Dravadan. "I am sure there are reassurances my master could provide."

A quarter of an hour they left Udenko's apartments, the support of the Viators assured and the High Viator himself in receipt of annual pension of forty thousand florins, to be distributed as he saw fit. This, Oricien supposed, constituted a good morning's work, a conclusion that was not overset by the fact that it was also sordid, grubby and mercenary. Perhaps that was why Lord Iselin found this pavane so congenial.

Outside the Dominikos they were joined by Ribauldequin and Todarko who had been deemed supernumerary to the preceding negotiations.

"If it pleases you, my lord," said Dravadan as they stood under the high midday sun in the main square, "I have arranged your itinerary to include a visit to the slave market before the Hour of Light Repast. It is only a few minutes' walk."

"You are thoughtful, Dravadan."

"The slave markets of Taratanallos are among the wonders of Mondia. No doubt your household is adequately stocked with slaves of the menial sort, but if you were to desire a bed-slave, or indeed a charmingly innocent catamite, I flatter myself that better value can be obtained nowhere else."

"I thank you, Dravadan, although my tastes run in neither of the directions you have outlined. In truth, slaves are rarely used in the Emmenrule: they require constant superintendence against escape or everyday slackness. In my experience affairs go better if free men are paid a small wage. They have no real alternative to their employment, but are less likely to resent their servitude."

"It is a novel perspective, my lord," said Dravadan with a strained smile. Even the most indirect rebuke from Oricien seemed to unsettle him disproportionately.

"Todarko," said Oricien, "you have a reputation for enjoying the company of a fair lady—would you stoop to a bed-slave?"

"I am sure my fame is exaggerated, my lord," said Todarko in a light voice. "But an affair of the heart can only be called so if there is a heart involved. If compulsion is required, the event carries little more satisfaction than can be gained from the hand."

Oricien smiled. "You have the perspectives of an Emmen gentlemen, Todarko. You should travel in due course."

Todarko thought of the steady accumulation of enemies he was amassing. "I think I would enjoy that, my lord."

Dravadan said: "If you do not wish to visit the slave-market, my lord, other entertainments can be arranged."

"King Enguerran will wish to hear my opinions on all aspects of life in the city," said Oricien. "I would be very interested to visit the markets."

"Excellent! Ostentatory Place is just this way."

CHAPTER THIRTY-NINE

The slave-market took up most of Ostentatory Place, a long rectangular expanse abutting the western wall of the city. Two sides of the rectangle were occupied by the long low terraced buildings known as the Ostentatory, where slaves were housed and could be viewed prior to sale. The third side contained the Hall of Assimilation where the new slaves were brought to be processed. The fourth arm of the rectangle was open to allow admission to the central square where, on the final day of every month, the slave auctions took place.

Dravadan briskly led the group containing himself, Lord Oricien, Lord Ribauldequin and Todarko towards the market, outlining its history and the functions of the different buildings to the ambassadors. Oricien felt that the speech was ill-judged; both he and Ribauldequin had made clear their distaste for the proceedings. They were forced to step to the side as a party of new slaves were marched up the street, having been disembarked from the docks. Leading the way was a tall lean man with a cropped black beard and a dashing red cloak. At the back of the group, two begrimed sailors flicked their whips in desultory fashion, but the slaves, mainly women, appeared far too demoralised to escape.

"You see the slaver at the head of the line," said Dravadan. "That is Sandoz, an associate of the corsair Ion Issio."

Oricien raised an eyebrow. "You allow pirates to transact their business in the city when they prey on your shipping?"

"It is the boast of the Masavory that anything can be bought in Taratanallos. The corollary, of course, is that everything can be sold. Slaves fetch a good price, and as long as Ion Issio pays his duties he can sell his wares just as anyone else."

"I have long wondered," said Todarko, "why the Consiglio does not simply arrest Sandoz, and whichever of Ion Issio's lieutenants appear in the city."

He looked over his shoulder to see Vislanko strolling along behind them with every appearance of unconcern. Members of the Consigli were everywhere around, but the sight of a prominent corsair gave them no pause.

"The matter is more complex than it seems," said Dravadan. "If we were to suppress Ion Issio—no straightforward task—another corsair would arise to take his place the next day. We are familiar with Ion Issio's ways, he is no more violent than he needs to be and his exactions have been relatively modest. When we have debated the question in the Masavory the consensus has generally been to allow him a modest degree of latitude."

Todarko thought back to Linnalitha's revelations about Dravadan's relations with Ion Issio. "His depredations have ruined half a dozen houses in the past year, have they not?"

Dravadan narrowed his eyes. "If you will pardon my bluntness, you speak of what you do not know. Your interest in the government of the city, while welcome, is of recent birth. The fact remains that a trader who takes normal precautions is unlikely to suffer worse than inconvenience, even if he has the misfortune to see an argosy taken."

"King Enguerran may take a different view," said Oricien with a frown. "He places great store by the King's Peace, and hangs the man who breaks it. Ion Issio may find his operations severely curtailed in the future."

"No doubt he will take the counsel of the Masavory, my lord, who are rich in the lore of the city."

"His Puissance always listens to the counsel he is offered, Dignity: but he also makes his own decisions. You can be sure he will act for the good of Taratanallos."

Dravadan lapsed into sullen silence. Perhaps Oricien had been too broad. Dravadan had been happy enough to support the Emmen alliance for his own advantage without any real thought as to circumstances once the treaty was signed. It would be as well to keep his thinking on short-term considerations of his own advantage. Would the Masavory really be eager to surrender its sovereignty to a northern overlord as readily as Dravadan believed?

"Perhaps you would like to tour the Ostentatory, my lord. The West Ostentatory houses women and children, the East the adult men."

"No doubt my itinerary is already arranged, Dignity."

Dravadan appeared discomfited. "For the convenience of all, it is well to have considered our plans. This does not mean we cannot alter our programme to suit your convenience."

Oricien shook his head. "Let us proceed as planned."

"The Dignified Bartielko has kindly offered to display his rooms in the Ostentatory. Let us see his current crop of slaves. I believe you are acquainted?" said Dravadan.

Oricien gave a brief nod. "We have conversed briefly," he said casually.

Dravadan looked as if he would say more but in the end contented himself with silence.

Their path was blocked by the new slaves who had been drawn up before the Hall of Assimilation awaiting the necessary tattoos and other formalities. Sandoz gave a loud whistle to his men and they cleared a gap in the slave lines for Dravadan's party to pass. Dravadan's eye caught Sandoz's for a moment and the corsair gave a brief nod.

Two Consigli guarded the door to the Ostentatory with a manner at once relaxed and watchful, but on Dravadan's arrival they stood back to allow the newcomers admittance. As they crossed the threshold into a hall refreshingly cool and dark, with a high ceiling and mullioned windows partly shuttered, Todarko noticed that Vislanko had joined the group. He gave Todarko a nod lacking in cordiality. "Good morning, sir. I am glad to see you in such company."

Todarko could think of no cogent response.

"Perhaps," continued Vislanko in a conversational tone, "we might shortly discuss your recent experiences. I would very much enjoy hearing your insights on current affairs."

Todarko gave a weak smile in response. "I am sure you would find my reflections unremarkable, even banal."

Vislanko smilingly shook his head. "You are too modest. You have the sensibility of a poet and the ear of the greatest men in the city. I cannot imagine I would find your observations anything other than fascinating."

Todarko turned away to see Bartielko and Dravadan conversing. "You do me too much honour," said Bartielko. "I never thought to see a lord of Emmen inspecting my slaves."

Oricien gave a bow. "I am gratified by your condescension, sir."

Bartielko, his yellow-white quiff of hair upstanding, rubbed his hands. "I am nothing if not a businessman, my lord. If you see a slave who catches your fancy, do not be shy. I am sure your credit is impeccable, and we might seal a bargain on the spot."

"The contingency is remote," said Oricien. "Nonetheless I will keep your generous offer in mind."

Bartielko led them up a flight of stairs, into a surprisingly airy and spacious chamber where a dozen or so slaves sat listlessly on padded benches. About eight of the slaves were young women, the remainder children ranging from two to perhaps nine or ten. A man in the livery of Bartielko was showing the slaves to a man Oricien recognised as Hortileijo of House Prugo.

"This one is prime," said Bartielko's man, squeezing the arm of the nearest slave. "She is no more than twenty-two, I'd say, and the lad has no obvious deformities. Since my master is on hand, I'll show my initiative by taking twenty-four thousand for the pair."

"The woman is comely enough, Drasav," said Hortileijo, "but I need no lad. I'll give you eighteen thousand for the woman alone."

"You would sunder mother and child!"

"I need a parlour-woman, not a brat. I'll take the child if I must, but I'll only pay sixteen thousand for the pair."

"The boy will grow into a stout worker. Start training him now and you'll have a manservant for forty years."

"Another mouth to feed! If I want a manservant I'll buy one."

"Please sir!" cried the woman, who had been looking on in slack-jawed apathy. "Do not part me from Felijano!"

Drasav casually back-slapped her across the face. "Know your place! My apologies, Hortileijo."

"She is not yet broken?"

Drasav spread his arms. "There are still a few rough edges."

"I have seen enough. If this is your best, I will return another day."

He turned and stepped from the room.

"Drasav, we will discuss this in due course," said Bartielko. "Your practices are deficient. My lord Oricien, my apologies that you have had to witness this foolishness."

Oricien's mouth was a thin line. "The spectacle has been instructive, if unpleasant. The ways of Taratanallos are somewhat different to my home city of Croad."

"Come," said Bartielko. "There are more rooms to inspect. You may be interested to see the slaves who are not yet on open sale."

Oricien shook his head in bafflement. It should have been apparent that he had no interest in slaves, other than revulsion for the whole business. Since Bartielko was of the party opposed to the Emmenrule, perhaps this was a deliberate policy: Dravadan's judgement in arranging the visit was more questionable. Lord Ribauldequin had not opened his mouth since entering the Ostentatory: Oricien regretted now forcing him to attend, other than to share his dismay.

The second room was larger, and the atmosphere noticeably different. The twenty or so slaves here did not have the listlessness of the outer room. These slaves had not yet been 'broken': they were not reconciled to their new status, and would escape if they could. Some six or seven Consigli paced the room watchfully, swords and their belts and small staves in their hands. As they noticed Vislanko they gave brisk nods of acknowledgement.

"This, my lord, is where we keep the slaves before they are fully trained," said Bartielko. "They are not, therefore, on general sale, although sometimes one will take a gentleman's fancy, in which case a deal can be done. My slaves are all warranted free of pox, visible disease, malnutrition and mental incapacity. No doubt you consider our ways callous, cruel even. Be assured that they are not: if one pays twenty thousand florins for a slave of twenty, it is an investment for forty years. The buyer will wish to have an asset which is happy and healthy for that period, to maximise the value from the purchase price. The welfare of the slaves is paramount!"

Lord Ribauldequin said: "What of those slaves who come to you poxed or lackwitted?"

Bartielko shrugged. "My factors would not buy such goods. The seller will dispose of them as he sees fit. Such questions are not my concern."

A child of two or three toddled over towards Oricien. The Consigli looked on unconcerned; the child's mother called out "Paro! Paro! Must I come and get you?"

She got to her feet, a woman of slight stature, any curves she might possess concealed in her loose smock. "Paro! Come back!"

Oricien smiled and picked the child up. "Here," he said quietly, handing the infant back to its mother. The woman reached out, took Paro and set him gently down to her left. There was a glint in her right hand, her arm swung. Oricien staggered back, seemingly surprised rather than hurt. Lord Ribauldequin let out a cry; amidst the rush Dravadan's mouth gaped like a fish.

The woman lunged at Oricien again, struck out: this time the stiletto in her hand was clear. The blow took Oricien in the chest, knocked him back with a gasp. "Guards!" cried Ribauldequin as he dashed forwards; Vislanko leaped forward with his rapier drawn, the portly Bartielko springing behind him with surprising agility. The woman ducked to the side, rushed once again for Oricien, who rolled aside in a scrambling effort to regain his feet.

All around the room the other slaves were yelling; several threw themselves on the Consigli before they could draw their swords, kicking, scratching, spitting. Oricien's assailant raised her arm for the third time; Ribauldequin stumbled towards her, intercepting the blow. There was a coursing of blood from his throat as he crashed to the floor. As Vislanko and Bartielko tried to wrestle the woman to the ground, Todarko and Dravadan dragged Oricien to the side of the room where he might more easily be succoured.

"My lord! Are you hurt?" gasped Dravadan. Oricien ripped his shirt aside, to reveal a fine-knit mail underneath.

"Hissen be praised!" breathed Dravadan.

Oricien scrambled to his feet. "Look to Ribauldequin!" he called; the Emmen ambassador lay motionless with a pool of blood spreading around his head. Todarko went over to where Ribauldequin lay and lifted his head from the floor. Vislanko seemed to have subdued the assailant; on the point of pinning her arms behind her back, he was pushed aside by Bartielko who plunged his own dagger hilt-deep into the woman's chest.

"You fool!" cried Vislanko, pulling the knife out; it was too late. The woman who would have assassinated Lord Oricien was dead.

There was a moment of utter silence and stillness which Todarko would always remember. The Consigli had the other slaves back under control; Oricien stood looking on in disbelief at the slumped body of Lord Ribauldequin; Vislanko fixed Bartielko with a predatory expression; and the woman who had been the agent lay, almost insubstantial, on the floor.

The silence lasted only a second, although it seemed an eternity. Then the infant Paro, whom the fight had surrounded but not touched, gave a great inarticulate cry and rushed towards the corpse of his mother.

Oricien looked over to where the slaves glowered behind the screen of Consigli. "One of you take the boy," he said. "He should not see his mother so."

"Are you hurt, my lord?" asked Dravadan again.

"I am unharmed," snapped Oricien. "I cannot say the same for Ribauldequin."

Todarko shook his head. "He is dead, my lord."

Vislanko stood erect and wiped the blood on his hands against his breeches. "Sastilar, Radibor: kindly restrain Bartielko."

Bartielko's slave factor Drasav, drawn by the noise, had come up the stairs and entered the room unnoticed. "You cannot arrest my master in his own rooms!"

Vislanko nodded to two more of his men. "Arrest Drasav as well. Take them both back to the Masavory until I arrive. There are many questions to be answered."

"You will regret this," spat Bartielko, his crest of hair now sadly drooping. "You may think your uniform will save you, Vislanko: I assure you it will not."

"Take them," said Vislanko. "You, Dignity, fail to appreciate the gravity of your situation. You will be in no position to enforce your wishes from the gallows."

Before Bartielko could make any rejoinder, the Consigli Sastilar and Radibor had dragged him from the room.

"Dravadan, will you see Lord Oricien to his apartments? I will need to speak to all in due course, but first I must interrogate Bartielko before he composes himself. I will send men to arrange a fitting funeral for Lord Ribauldequin."

"A moment, Vislanko," said Oricien grimly. "This matter must be investigated fully. I do not wish Bartielko hanged simply because he is on hand."

"I understand, my lord. Nonetheless, the outrage occurred in Bartielko's rooms, perpetrated by a slave holding a dagger she could never have smuggled from the Hall of Assimilation. There may be other explanations, but it seems a reasonable hypothesis that the leader of the Gammerling faction sought your death. Your itinerary was common knowledge, and Bartielko was insistent that you see his slaves. Then he kills the woman before she can be questioned."

Oricien gave a brisk nod. "Your theory is not implausible," he said. "Come, Dravadan: there are melancholy arrangements to make."

As Vislanko made to follow them out of the room, Todarko put a hand on his shoulder. "We must speak."

Vislanko turned to face him. "You have information regarding this crime?"

Todarko stepped out on to the landing at the top of the staircase where they would not be overheard. "You have solved the case with commendable briskness."

"The facts are clear. You heard me outline them to Lord Oricien."

"They are open to other interpretations."

"Such as?"

"It is no secret that the Consiglio opposes the Emmen alliance. What better way to retard it than to kill the Emmen ambassador—and to weaken the Gammerling party by imputing their guilt?"

Vislanko gave a bleak laugh. "You are imaginative. Such is the poet's mind, I suppose."

"You do not deny the theory."

Vislanko gave a quick tight grin. "I need not account to you."

"I think any arrangements that we may have had concerning the doings of Dravadan's household are now void."

"Ah," said Vislanko softly. "You think because you have smoked out the Consiglio's scheme that we are now equal?"

"If you wish to think of it in those terms."

Vislanko folded his arms and leaned back against the wall. "I must disabuse you, young sir. Your theory as to this morning's events is risible. Grant, if we must, that the Consiglio views the Emmenrule's interference in Taratanallos's affairs as undesirable. Assassinating Enguerran's ambassador and friend would then be an unwise move, would it not? Rather than slaking the King's desire to rule the town, would it not rather fatten it? The Consiglio plots with skill and discrimination, not the emotional excesses which characterise your own life."

Todarko thrust out his chin. "Nonetheless I might put forward my hypothesis elsewhere, to see what others make of it."

Vislanko sprang forward, caught Todarko's jacket and pushed him back out over the railing above the staircase, held from falling only by Vislanko's hold. "One more corpse would not make much more difference today. You cannot 'put forward your hypothesis' from the grave."

Todarko flailed with his arms to try to regain the railings. He looked wildly over his shoulder to see the drop to the unyielding floor far below. After a pause Vislanko pulled him erect. "I do not need to kill you," he said. "First, your theory is incorrect; second, to whom would you lay your intelligence? To the Consiglio? Foolish if we are the culprits. To your uncle? Or Dravadan? When you know I need only mention the word 'Linnalitha' to make him your mortal enemy?"

Todarko gaped.

"Go back home, boy. Attend to Dravadan's reactions to events. We will converse again in due course."

Looking back into Vislanko's implacable gaze, Todarko knew any hold he might have had over him was purely imaginary.

Vislanko smiled. "If you will excuse me, sir. There are some pregnant questions I must pose elsewhere."

BOOK TWO

EBB TIDE

CHAPTER FORTY

The wealth of Taratanallos—and hence the basis for the lives of measured protocol and carefully graduated luxury of the Specchio—was born out of trade. The twenty-four houses jealously guarded monopolies of tariffed goods among themselves, enriching themselves from customs duties as well as forays into entrepreneurship.

The city's status as the trading centre of the world might be thought to lend the city cosmopolitan air, but nothing could have been further from the truth. Those residents of the city who were not Tarat citizens—traders from other cities; diplomats; artists, actors and other disreputables—lived in a demarcated area of the city known as 'the Wrill'. While not barred from the Aspergantia or the Chale, their presence was not encouraged, and residents of the Wrill took no part in the cultural life of the city.

Outsiders sometimes took this as proof of the intolerable pride of the Specchio, that they should refuse to mingle with those who contributed so much to their coffers. Such a view, playing as it did on the popular perception of the Specchio as effete lordlings, concerned only with their fetes, their duels and their striving for notional advantage over their rivals, naturally gained a widespread currency.

Nonetheless this view was wholly false. While the Specchio occupied themselves in their introspective pastimes, there was a grimly practical reason for the existence of the Wrill: plague. More than any city in Mondia, Taratanallos was a nexus, a meeting point for traders from every city and culture. A disease brought in on a ship from Paladria, say, could run through the population in a month, and once established amongst those with no acquired immunity, would prove almost impossible to eradicate. The Wrill, therefore, served at once as a sink-hole and a quarantine, albeit a liberal one. On those occasions when plague broke loose—fortunately rare—the Consiglio enforced harsh movement restrictions, and those living in the Wrill perforce must wait out the contagion, or leave the city on ships provided for the purpose.

The arrangements were some way short of foolproof. Outbreaks of disease were years, sometimes decades, apart, and the smooth commercial functioning of the city would be impaired if those living within the Wrill were unable to travel. Hence the so-called "soft quarantine" which discouraged foreigners from mingling with the city folk, but did not forbid it.

One winter, at a time when plague had not been seen in the city for half a generation, an outbreak of disease took hold in the Wrill, and through deficient vigilance on the part of the Consiglio, made an incursion not only into the Chale but also the Aspergantia. The countermeasures of quarantine were all the more rigorous for having been neglected in the first place, but by the time the Masavory were able to ring the great bell marking the all-clear, twenty-seven members of the Specchio were dead, including Thrinko, head of House Zamilio and father of Sanouté, and Lustenaijo, who had once been President of the Masavory.

Those who remained were prompted, according to their temperaments, to reflect on the fleeting precariousness of mortality, or to throw themselves into their revels with redoubled seriousness. There is no disaster so severe that it has no beneficiaries, however. The fourteen year-old Lutus, the son of Thrinko, could now style himself 'the Dignified Lutus' and sit on the Masavory as the head of his house; and while his elevation was presumably purchased with some grief, the Viators—who saw attendances rise with a consequent increase in alms—enjoyed the chink of silver while incurring no compensating disadvantages.

As if the depredations of the plague were not enough, by the next summer—the year in which Malvazan was eligible to fight for the Garland—he had killed three men, and before the turn of the winter this was to increase by two more. He had rapidly gained a reputation for a precise sense of his own honour and a willingness to resort to the blade to defend it. Men looked askance at him in the street, and took particular care to avoid giving offence. There were few, if any, swordsmen in the city who would be confident in their ability to best him. Those who had been wont to say that Dravadan had the greater natural talent now kept their opinion to themselves.

This reputation stood Malvazan in good stead in several ways, not all of them anticipated. Few of his rivals for the Garland had fought a duel under Quietus Est, and he advanced with ease through the early rounds against opponents clearly overawed by his pedigree. Only Rodizel appeared unimpressed, and on the occasions they sparred, it was as often Malvazan who came off second-best. Nonetheless, Malvazan enjoyed the wary expressions he encountered as he went about his business. Even down on the dockside, the tavern bravos knew his name and did not tempt him with provocations.

Rather to his surprise, he had also become a figure of some interest to the ladies of the Specchio. A man who had been thrown over at his betrothal feast and killed three men in duels, all before the age of twenty, could not help but have a romantic allure. That Malvazan possessed dark good looks, and a brooding disposition hidden under a veneer or urbanity obviously did no harm either.

Malvazan was flattered by the attention of so many damoiselles, and even on occasion took advantage of the situations which presented themselves. He had always looked on men like Glastarko, however, with a kind of fastidiousness, and by and large chose not dissipate his energies in the pursuit of fleshly pleasures. This restraint, too, only added to his air of mysterious glamour.

One morning, a week before the semi-final of the Garland, Malvazan received a short note from the Dignified Aladar, the head of House Tantestro, inviting him to wait upon him in his office at the Masavory. Tantestro was one of the greatest of all the houses of the Specchio, and Aladar, wily and ambitious despite his relative youth, was an important figure in the city. He had not previously favoured Malvazan with any attention beyond an occasional "good morning".

After the Hour of Light Repast, his training finished for the day, Malvazan washed and made his way to the Masavory. The building cast a shadow of improbable darkness against the high sun, and he felt a chill as he stepped out of the sunlight. A uniformed Consigli escorted him up the stairs to the private offices above.

"Dignity, may I present the Grave Malvazan?"

Aladar looked up from a heavy desk where he was taking a light lunch of bread, olives and a pitcher of wine. He nodded to dismiss the Consigli, waved Malvazan to sit down.

"Welcome, Malvazan," he said. "Have you eaten?"

Aladar was a man in his early thirties, his black hair already streaked with grey at the temples. His voice had a firm timbre, and even his casual pronouncements had an air of authority.

"I have, thank you, Dignity."

"We can dispense with formality, here, I think. Come, we are both young men, are we not?"

Malvazan did not necessarily consider a man over thirty to be young, but felt it would be impolitic to respond thus.

"I am happy to oblige you in any way I can."

Aladar smiled to reveal even white teeth. "Such open-ended guarantees should be given with caution," he said. "I intend nothing more than a simple conversation. Come, you will take some wine, at least?"

He handed Malvazan a goblet and then, as they sipped, he said:

"I have known your father for many years. His views at the Masavory are always expressed with calm good sense. He is perhaps not a worldly man, or an ambitious one, but his devotion to our city cannot be questioned."

Malvazan said nothing. The direction of the conversation was unclear.

"You do not resemble him in all characteristics," continued Aladar. "Certain reports have reached me: it would be fair to say you have acquired something of a reputation."

"I act as I must," said Malvazan. "I take counsel with the Viators as necessary."

"The family of the Specchio is not a large one," said Aladar. "Even when grass-marriages and the like are taken into account, we are few. And at the rate you are going, you will have killed most of them in five years."

Malvazan scanned Aladar's face to sense his underlying mood; but Aladar remained as impassive as a snake.

"On occasion I must defend my honour," said Malvazan. "In such cases mortality is sometimes emphasised."

"I have heard a great deal about your honour," said Aladar smoothly. "Suppose I were to tweak your nose, or pour over you this pitcher of wine? Would your sense of honour lead you to call out the head of a Prime House?"

Malvazan furrowed his brow. "Why would you perform such an act?"

Aladar laughed. "The idea was poorly thought-out. The point remains, that not every offence needs to be settled by the blade. In the best circles, Quietus Est is the last resort, not the first."

"Are you saying that my breeding lacks quality?" bristled Malvazan.

"Peace!" said Aladar. "I am merely suggesting that a man of ambition requires subtlety as well as force. You, I think, are a man of ambition. It is not to your advantage to have a reputation only for thuggery."

Malvazan reflected on the point.

"Nonetheless," said Aladar, "in some circles you are seen as a coming man. Regrettably your birth prevents you from sitting on the Masavory; but you could be valuable to a man who does." He raised an eyebrow. "Is my meaning becoming clear?"

"Up to a point," said Malvazan. "I am unclear how I might be of use, or why I should wish to be."

Aladar nodded, poured Malvazan more wine. "Your reputation, although lacking in finesse, is growing. A man who numbered a renowned swordsman, noted for his ruthlessness, among his associates need not fear footpads, at the very least."

"You are offering me your patronage?"

Aladar winced. "I would not phrase it quite so crudely. I believe I can add a certain refinement, an extra layer, to your mind; you, in turn, carry some influence in salons I do not care to patronise. In that sense, our goals can be said to overlap."

"Refinement?" Malvazan scowled.

"Tell me, Malvazan, how does a city as small as Taratanallos, squeezed on the end of a peninsula on Gammerling's soil, how does it retain its independence, its influence?"

Malvazan sucked in his lip. "I have never considered the matter."

"Exactly," said Aladar. "Yet such things are the essence of the Masavory's business. Some among us favour a close friendship with the King of Gammerling; others wish to play off the Duke of Aylissia, or even the King of the Emmenrule. This is the way of 'politics'."

"The matter is of little interest to me. My advancement will not come through such things."

"Your advancement will require allies, Malvazan. And if you pick one friend, you acquire his enemies. These things must all be weighed. This is a skill I have developed over the years, and one I shall teach you."

"I am not fully clear what you gain from this arrangement," said Malvazan.

Aladar smiled once more. "You must simply take my word that I gain my own advantage. I have enjoyed our conversation."

Malvazan understood himself to be dismissed. He stood and bowed to take his leave.

"And Malvazan," said Aladar as he reached the door. Malvazan looked back over his shoulder.

"Next time you wish to kill someone—please clarify with me whether it is someone we wish to see dead."

CHAPTER FORTY-ONE

Malvazan made a point of taking a stroll down the Archgate to the docks, rapier strapped to his waist, every evening after dinner. Partly this avoided the stultifying conversation of his parents and the solicitude of Dravadan and Rullia, but more importantly it gave him a presence in the city: his easy motion down the road, too composed to be called a swagger, became a part of the city's fabric. There was an unspoken challenge: if you want to fight me, you know where to find me. So far, no-one had sought him out.

On this night, however, things were to go differently. As he walked down the road, a man he did not recognise bowed as they past.

"Gravity Malvazan," he said quietly.

"You have the advantage of me, sir," said Malvazan. His hand dropped to his sword-hilt.

"You will not need your blade; you will see that I am unarmed. Neither is my identity relevant."

"I like to know with whom I speak," said Malvazan. "You carry yourself as a gentleman."

"And so I am. Think of me as a grass-cousin of the Specchio, up from a country estate."

"Of which house?"

The man held wide his arms, smiled. "It does not matter. I merely wish to dispense some advice, which stands or falls on its own merits."

Malvazan took a step closer. The man's tone was cool, polite, but at the same time there was a menace Malvazan could not identify.

"Speak your speech, if that is your intent."

"It is simply this: choose your friends with care."

"I was not accustomed to choosing them at random. If that was the substance of your message, I fear you have wasted your journey."

The man looked into Malvazan's face. "All the time you strut the streets, picking fights you know you can win, you are of no real concern to anyone who matters. Now, it seems, you have found a new friend."

"I am unclear as to your meaning."

"As you will. Let us just say that in keeping company with a certain Dignity, you become rather more interesting. And those who are interesting do not always lead long lives."

"You think to come here, with no weapon, and threaten me in the street? If there is one thing I know, it is how to use a sword."

The man smiled. "If I hold a sword, and you hold a sword, and you kill me, that is a duel. If I do not hold a sword, it is murder." He stepped away from Malvazan, held wide his arms to expose his torso. "Strike away, if you will."

Malvazan curled back his lips to reveal his teeth. "One day, perhaps, we shall both be armed. Then we shall see."

"I doubt that we will meet again, sir. My job here is done. In all humility, I say to you that a wise man does not play a game whose rules he fails to understand." He bowed again and continued walking up the hill.

Malvazan watched him go. He considered going after him, dragging him down an alley to find out what he knew. This was not the way things were done in Aladar's world, though. Indeed, maybe the "grass-cousin" expected it. Let him go for now: no doubt Aladar had ways of learning more if necessary.

He continued his constitutional. At the bottom of the hill two slender ladies in gowns of russet came into view, and he bowed.

"Malvazan!" cried one of them from behind her veil. "Will you not stop to talk to me?"

Malvazan had not recognised her under Hood and Veil. "Damoiselle Monichoë! I beg your pardon."

Monichoë turned to her companion. "Go on home, Lutta. I will join you in due course."

"Damoiselle—"

"Enough, Lutta. I am not in peril from the Grave Malvazan, and my chastity is hardly in danger in the street."

"Very well, Damoiselle." Lutta departed with poor grace.

"It seems months since we have spoken, Malvazan," said Monichoë.

"I spend most of my time at Farlankas' school," he said. "This is not a suitable haunt for one of your birth."

"Fol-de-rol, Malvazan! You have been avoiding me, and we both know it." Even though he could not see her face, he could sense her smiling. "I have missed you," she said in a softer voice.

"I am sure you have been too busy with affairs of your own to be inconvenienced, Damoiselle."

"Why so formal? You once asked my father for my hand!"

Malvazan flushed. "That is the point, is it not? There is little scope for a cordial footing thereafter."

"I never imagined you so oversensitive," she said. "Betrothals are proposed and thrown over every day."

Malvazan flushed yet further. "I am aware of that too."

"Forgive me, I meant no offence."

Malvazan gestured to a heavy stone bench and they sat. "Here is the truth. Your father sent me away with such disdain that I cannot call at Hanglenook without embarrassment to him and myself. In addition, I have come to realise that my advancement may depend on making a suitable marriage; and since you are out of my reach, I can only harm my prospects by being seen to moon over you."

Monichoë's hands were folded in her lap. "How calculating you seem, Malvazan! Can we not converse without it being a matter of betrothals?"

"There are questions of propriety, particularly now you have sent Lutta away."

"Propriety! Fah! I care not a fig for it."

"I am sure your father does," said Malvazan with a half-smile.

"My father has to an extent revised his opinion of you," said Monichoë. "He sees potential in you which he had previously overlooked."

Malvazan caught her dark eye. "Tell me, Monichoë, is your father in any way an intimate of the Dignified Aladar?"

Monichoë raised an eyebrow. "They are generally seen as allies."

"I rather thought they might be," said Malvazan. "Perhaps I will call in due course after all."

Monichoë stood up. "Good! My walk has not been wasted. Come, help me adjust my veil. It is too tight."

Malvazan leaned forward to help her fingers. The veil popped its button to slide down at a crazy angle across her face. Her cheeks were spotted with red, her full lips slightly parted. "Now look what you have done," she whispered.

Malvazan looked away for a moment. He had seen her face any number of times at Hanglenook; but here, in the street, it was as if she was naked before him. And she knew it.

With a steady duellist's hand he reached out, put the veil back across her face and slipped the button through its eye. "That is more respectable," he said.

"Make sure you call upon me," she said. "I will be expecting you."

Over the next few weeks Malvazan paid several visits to Hanglenook. The maid Lutta was present for reasons of propriety, but paid such assiduous attention to her embroidery that she might as well have been invisible. Malvazan viewed the situation with a mixture of puzzlement and fatalism. Monichoë clearly would not be inviting him to Hanglenook without Kropiselko's approval; on the other hand, on those occasions when Kropiselko was present, he evinced no discernible cordiality. Malvazan was at a loss to understand his motivations: a betrothal remained no more attractive to House Zano than it had last year. The only conclusion Malvazan could reach was that, as a protégé of Aladar he was now a person of greater consequence: a consequence which could only increase if he were to win the Garland in the summer.

Crostadan, meanwhile, refrained from arranging a second betrothal for Malvazan. While his son's reputation was so clearly rising, he risked settling for a match below what might be secured in six months' time. Indeed, in retrospect it was a blessing that the arrangement with Sanouté had fallen through. House Zamilio was not of the first water, and with Thrinko dead and succeeded by an inexperienced boy, there seemed little scope for immediate improvement. While a marriage with House Zano was scarcely to be contemplated, the options open to Crostadan were wider than had been the case a year previously.

By the time of the semi-finals of the Garland, interest in the city was running high. There were, by definition, only four potential winners remaining in play, and everyone had their own theories as to the successful candidate. These generally were the result of ignorance, prejudice and caprice; but the bookmakers, who, having a financial stake in the outcome, were compelled to a more rigorous approach, made Malvazan a narrow favourite, slightly ahead of Rodizel, with Valerijo of House Susviero and Penchadar of House Piaccio lagging behind. Malvazan was drawn to fight Valerijo, a swordsman of rapid reflexes and great élan, but with a defensive technique which rarely stood up to sustained examination. While no bout was a foregone conclusion, Malvazan was confident of a relatively straightforward victory.

The other semi-final was if anything even easier to call. Penchadar had been fortunate to survive so far; his quarter-final opponent, Jiladan of House Triscomo, had been contentiously disqualified for Deplorable Conduct when clearly in command of the fight.

If all went to form, therefore, Malvazan would face Rodizel in the final. Before he went to sleep at night, Malvazan on occasion saw Rodizel's face before him. He was a better swordsman than Rodizel in terms of speed, attacking and defensive technique, footwork, and indeed almost every measure. Rodizel had but one advantage, and it was difficult to put it more precisely than this: Rodizel was never quite where you thought he was. A thrust calibrated to take Rodizel petty-pectoris would never quite arrive. Malvazan always felt himself superior, but as often as not the outcome belied him. But time enough to worry about that when Valerijo was out of the way.

Semi-finals day by tradition had a curious air. There were only two main bouts, either of which could be over very rapidly. It was necessary, therefore, to provide additional entertainment to ensure that the large crowd at the Bezant had enough to keep it occupied. Malvazan watched from a vantage in the crowd as a pair of flamboyantly-attired stilt-men fought out a duel fifteen feet above the ground, to gasps of admiration which fell silent when one of the combatants crashed to the ground to lie senseless. Performing animals ran through antic routines, the most accomplished being a troupe of cats in red jackets who marched smartly to a martial theme before launching a choreographed assault upon a hapless dog which bounded howling from the ring.

Malvazan took little notice of such frivolities. This was no time to be diverted from his goals, and in any event it was as important to be seen sitting with the right people. He had acquired a sizeable group of followers, and to one side sat the party from House Vaggio—the Dignified Jirno, Madam Sulinka, plus Raguslan, Glastarko and their spouses. They had brought along their infants, the two-year old Zanijel and one-year-old Todarko, who squabbled perpetually until Zanijel's mother Stepanija smacked him firmly round the head and handed him to his grandmother.

To Malvazan's other side the company was even more illustrious: the Dignified Aladar, now widely recognised as his ally and, only a little further away, the Dignified Kropiselko. There were those who believed that Kropiselko had tacitly acknowledged Malvazan as a suitor for his daughter; but Malvazan knew that should he lose today, Kropiselko's amity, never effusive, would vanish as quickly as it had arrived. Sitting demurely beside Kropiselko, still and silent under Hood and Veil, was Monichoë.

Looking around the crowd, he caught sight of young Lutus, the new head of House Zamilio—and Sanouté's brother. He had not seen Sanouté in the year since their betrothal feast: he heard that she had been packed off to Ciccadillo, their country estate. Indeed, she had not even returned for her father's funeral.

Eventually the buffoonery was out of the way. There were some warm-up bouts, involving youngsters who would in future years compete for the Garland, and then the first two semi-finalists entered together. Rodizel, short and slight with a mat of dust-coloured blond hair, the taller Penchadar at his side. Both were in the traditional attire, loose white shirts and fitted black breeches.

A minute later, it was all over, to the vociferous disdain of the crowd. Penchadar had skipped forward into a lunge, Rodizel had slipped aside and taken Penchadar in the ley quadrant. "Tacto" was called by all three judges, and the bout was over after the first pass.

"Hmph," sniffed Glastarko. "The lad has no concept of showmanship."

"His job is to win," said Malvazan. "What more can you ask?"

"Never think it is just about winning," said Glastarko. "He has irked the crowd—not a wise move for a man who hopes the Garland will make his career. If you give them a little more sport in beating Valerijo, they will cheer for you in the final."

"I have to beat Valerijo first," said Malvazan with a smile.

"And do you doubt it?"

Malvazan laughed. "No. You are right, of course."

"Give us some entertainment, then," said Glastarko. "But now you need to warm up."

Malvazan nodded and got to his feet, walking with a loose-limbed swagger to the competitors' area behind the stand. Rodizel and Penchadar were already there.

"Well fought, Rodizel," said Malvazan curtly. "You did not waste any time."

Rodizel nodded. "I have no appetite for sporting," he said. "The least I could do was to fight Penchadar with full might."

Penchadar ruefully shook his head. "It was not to be," he said. "Rodizel, you are a most accomplished swordsman."

"We will see who is on hand to test my mettle in the final," said Rodizel with a half-smile in Malvazan's direction.

Malvazan went through his range of stretches and drills. Ten minutes later, sweating gently with his pulse ticking along, he stepped out into the Bezant alongside Valerijo. The crowd rose to its feet, cheering and occasionally calling the names of one or other of the combatants. He felt himself slipping into his duelling mind, at once hyper-aware of his surroundings—the granularity of the sand under his feet, the distant call of a thunderbird—yet detached from them. Valerijo next to him was twitching slightly, nervous energy as yet unable to find an outlet. He will come at me quickly. He has not the patience to wait.

"Gentlemen, are you ready?" called the referee, more for the crowd than the combatants. "I am," said Valerijo in a firm voice; Malvazan contented himself with a sharp nod.

"Then walk apart, and you may proceed."

The swordsmen bowed to each other and walked to their marks, some ten feet apart. Valerijo feinted, his tension almost overflowing with his urge to attack. Give them a little sport, Glastarko had said. Against an opponent as aggressive as Valerijo, that should not be too difficult; he simply needed to keep the attacks at bay until such time as he chose to launch the devastating counter.

So it was that they skirted around the Bezant, Valerijo lunging with footstamping flamboyance, Malvazan employing cool and composed footwork to keep him at bay. If this was a duel you would be dead five times over, thought Malvazan. Valerijo seemed to harbour no such doubts, and Malvazan's passivity only seemed to spur him to greater excess. At last he span round, a flying leap displaying his back to Malvazan. As he landed, he used the momentum of his jump to drive him forward. With slightest of movements, Malvazan slipped one way and, as Valerijo followed him, stepped inside and tapped him gran-pectoris. "Tacto" called all three judges. Malvazan was in the final.

The crowd rose and chanted his name. He looked at Glastarko who returned a measured salute. Malvazan shook hands with Valerijo. "Bad luck," he said, although if they had fought all day he would never have breached Malvazan's defence.

He walked back over to his seat in the crowd, clasped hands with Aladar. Kropiselko rose from his seat and came over to the railing separating the crowd from the Bezant. "Well fought, sir. You will dine with us tonight, I hope? The Dignified Aladar will be on hand."

No doubt Crostadan would expect him to eat at home, but his opinions were hardly to the point. Malvazan was a man in demand. And if it was like this after the semi-final, he could scarcely imagine the effect when he won the Garland itself.

"I should be honoured, Dignity."

CHAPTER FORTY-TWO

Hanglenook was, by popular repute, one of the most attractive manses on the Archgate. The soft yellow wash of the walls was overgrown with an artless spray of ivy. What capped its appeal, however, was its exclusivity. There were those among the Specchio who would never assess for themselves the cool grandeur of the marble floors or the airy reception chambers, simply because they would never be invited across the portico.

Malvazan was no stranger to Hanglenook, but it was rare for him to be present on a formal dinner like this evening's. If he had expected to be the guest of honour, however, he was disappointed: he was seated well down the table, away from the Dignified Aladar or his other allies from House Vaggio. Monichoë was also out of conversational distance, although the vivacity of her presence carried the full length of the table. Malvazan hence spent the Hour of Evening Repast conversing in polished inanities with two elderly ladies of House Zano, and a grass-cousin sojourning in the city and outlining his satisfaction with his new surroundings with a gushing enthusiasm which rapidly became wearing.

At the Hour of Evening Satiation, however, the company rose from the table and took the air in Hanglenook's artfully artless gardens. Without any seeming purpose on his part, Malvazan found himself alone with Monichoë. The moon shone full overhead, and he felt a sense of languid mellowness which could only partially be explained by the excellence of Kropiselko's wines.

Monichoë took his arm and they walked towards an ornamental fishpond. "I had never visited the Bezant before," she said. "My father would never allow it. I was not sure what to expect."

"I hope you were not disappointed, or worst of all, bored," replied Malvazan with a smile.

"Rodizel's bout was somewhat anti-climactic," she said. "We had waited all afternoon and he finished it with a single blow."

Malvazan had no wish to defend his rival, but Monichoë's point was essentially misconceived. "It would be more just to blame Penchadar," he said. "It takes two for a compelling duel, and Penchadar's ineptitude spoiled it as a spectacle."

"Your own fight was more exciting," she said, leaning against him a shade. "I thought Valerijo would overwhelm you with his thrusts!"

Malvazan squared his shoulders. "I will let you into a secret," he said. "I could have beaten Valerijo as easily as Rodizel beat Penchadar, had I chosen to do so. Instead I thought to entertain the crowd awhile."

"Fie, Malvazan! You are a shameless liar! You are not a man for frivolity."

Malvazan flushed. "I most certainly do not lie, Damoiselle."

"Tush, you are so prickly! I am just a little surprised if what you say is true."

Malvazan handed her to a bench beside the pond and they sat down. "My ambition to win the Garland is well-known," he said. "I do not desire it for its own sake, regardless of the glory. It is one of my steps on the Way of Harmony. It is not enough that I win; I must charm as well. Today I have won in a way which advances my greater aims."

"Now you need only beat Rodizel," she said.

"Yes," said Malvazan in a neutral tone.

"I am sure you are confident. He cannot match your intensity, which is frankly alarming at times."

Malvazan stared into the pond, saying nothing.

"Malvazan?"

"I do not know whether I will beat him," he said quietly. "There is something about his work—I have never mastered him."

"Can this be the great duellist Malvazan, admitting to doubts?" A faint smile played across her face.

"I thought to share an insight at once important and painful; I did not expect to be met with mockery."

She reached out and took his hand. "Malvazan, forgive me! I am sensible of the honour you do me with your confidence. I have faith in your swordcraft: I am sure you will beat him. You are no Penchadar, after all."

"And he is no Valerijo. There is a quiet mastery to his work, a smoothness to his movement. Do not pin your hopes on me, Monichoë!"

"You are truly serious, are you not?" said Monichoë, looking into his face.

Malvazan shook his shoulders, stood up from the seat. "I should not have said anything. It is the passing doubt of a moment—please forget I have spoken."

"Sit down," she said, taking his hand again. "You have shared confidences with me; the least I can do is share one with you."

Slowly Malvazan sat down.

"Long ago—or so it seems to me—" she said, "you approached my father to ask for my hand."

Malvazan flushed. "I had not forgotten the experience."

"It was a foolish, desperate but endearing thing to do. It could only have ended in the way it did."

"So I now understand," said Malvazan.

"My father has been watching your subsequent development with interest. He notes that you are now the intimate of Aladar, and friends with Raguslan and Glastarko. These are allies to be reckoned with; and so, by association are you."

"The situation has not arisen by accident," said Malvazan. "I am forging my own path."

"My father is considering betrothing us," she said with a tremor in her voice.

"Monichoë!"

"All is not yet decided. There are of course certain—disadvantages—surrounding your birth. But a man who is part of Aladar's affinity, a Garland-winner to boot—such a man would not be a disgraceful match for a Prime House."

"I have not yet won the Garland," said Malvazan. "And you now understand that victory is not guaranteed."

"Then if you wish to marry me," she said, "you must ensure that you do win. What appeals to my father is the faultlessness of your trajectory, the relentlessness of your ascent. He is prepared to gamble a daughter on its continuance. Defeat next month would alter that perception."

"You make it sound very—calculating."

Monichoë gave a high clear laugh. "And you are not, Malvazan! Come, every detail of your rise is planned." Her voice dropped. "Even me."

This time Malvazan took her hand. "No, Monichoë. Never you."

She stood up and smoothed the fabric of her dress, creased from where she had been sitting. "Then you had better make sure you defeat Rodizel, had you not?"

She glided away without a backward glance, leaving Malvazan sitting on the bench. It was only after she was out of sight that he realised he had never asked how she viewed betrothal to him.

CHAPTER FORTY-THREE

Oricien stumbled down the stairs on numb legs, Dravadan at his side. Before his eyes was the image of Ribauldequin, lying on his back with blood oozing from his neck. He had not wanted to come to the Ostentatory at all: Oricien had insisted. And beyond a doubt, Ribauldequin had died trying to protect him. Oricien was culpable in every conceivable way. He stood in the great foyer, casting his gaze around the expanse.

"My lord," said Dravadan, "if there is any assistance I can render, just name it. Allow me at least to send for an undertaker."

Oricien gave him a grim look. "Yes, an undertaker is all we can provide. It is too late for any other assistance."

Dravadan put a hand on his shoulder; only with an effort did Oricien suppress the urge to shake it off. "You must not blame yourself, my lord. Someone has committed a terrible deed, a blow against your mission and all who support it. The Consiglio will soon snuff out the truth."

Oricien turned to face him. "The truth is that Ribauldequin is dead. Other questions are subsidiary."

Dravadan looked away. "Regrettably, my lord, I am unfamiliar with Emmen funerary traditions. Will you wish to transport his body home?"

Oricien stared up at the ceilings, tried to blink away the image of the body on the floor. "An Emmen knight who dies in combat is entitled to the pyre," he said. "In the circumstances I should not wish to deny him the honour. If you can arrange a location for such a ceremony you would have my gratitude."

"Of course, my lord. Is there any other service I can do you?"

Oricien shook his head. "I will return to my chambers: I must immediately prepare a despatch for King Enguerran and Lord Ribauldequin's family. If you can find Lord Iselin, so much the better; I would confer with him immediately."

Dravadan bowed and made his way out of the foyer. A few moments later Oricien followed him out of the building and onto the market square. It was as if nothing had ever happened: men went about their business with a cheerful step, sellers called their wares in loud optimistic voices, and the sun beat down with a disrespectful brightness.

He walked over to the fountain in the square and sat with his back to the water, his forearms along his thighs. Ten minutes ago, twenty at the most, Ribauldequin had been alive, bored, irresponsible and oblivious that his life had run its course. How old had he been? Oricien realised that he did not know—he had never sought his friendship—but he could not have been much more then five and twenty. He had been the heir to some fine estates he would never now inherit. It would be easy to dismiss him as a trifling man, one of superficial tastes who had simply met his destiny too soon; but Oricien could not. Ribauldequin had taken his mortal wound interposing his body between the woman and Oricien. His pastimes might have been whoring, gaming and wine, but at the end he had reached deep into himself to find something greater. And it had cost him his life. Yesterday he had been spared from the bindlespith, seemingly to preserve him for a long life, but his deliverance had lasted less than a day. There was more to the workings of Harmony than he could readily understand.

With an effort he rose from his seat by the fountain and made his way back to the Castle of Crostestini.

Lord Ribauldequin had died far from home, with neither friends nor family to attend him. In the circumstances, there was no merit in delaying the funeral, so at dusk the next evening a small if distinguished group made its way down worn stone steps from the city wall to a beach giving on to clear blue waters. Here a pile of kindling was set up, topped by a bier on which lay what once had been Lord Ribauldequin.

A Viator stood at the base of the pyre, a flaming brand in his hand. He spoke at moderate length, saying nothing to which Oricien could give his attention.

"Would you like to add any oration of your own, my lord?" the Viator concluded. Oricien looked around the group: Dravadan and his wife Linnalitha; Raguslan and Todarko; Zanijel and a stiff-looking Nelanka; and at his side, Lord Iselin. There was nothing he could say that would have meaning for any of these people.

"Lord Ribauldequin's life was its own oration," he said, and took the brand. "Farewell, loyal servant of His Puissance," he said, and touched the brand to the kindling.

With a startling avidity the flames caught hold of the dry wood, and all watched in silence as they licked up towards the bier, crackling and roaring to fill the noiseless space. Oricien looked around at the blank-faced group, the fire casting bizarre and exaggerated shadows on their faces. Lord Ribauldequin in death commanded an attention and respect he had never known in life. Would Oricien be able to say as much?

He felt a touch on his elbow. "My lord, you have my condolences." He turned to see Nelanka, her eyes all the wider for being the only feature visible beneath her veil.

"Thank you, madam. There are few here who feel the horror of what has happened," he said, "you are one of them."

"We cannot speak here and now," she said, her gaze encompassing the intent stares of Dravadan and Zanijel. "If you wish to call upon me, you may be sure I will receive you. It may be that you wish the conversation of one who sees you as a man as well as an ambassador."

He nodded crisply. "I am touched by your attention, madam."

As she walked slowly away into the dusk Todarko approached. "I am sorry, my lord, that Lord Ribauldequin's escape yesterday was of such short duration."

Oricien gave a sad smile. "Your act was none the less worthy for that, Gravity. It was a moment that ennobled him and you."

He shook Todarko by the hand; over his shoulder he saw Dravadan looking at him with an expression he could not read. It occurred to him for the first time that Bartielko had been taken into custody with suspicious facility. Was it impossible that Dravadan had been involved in some way? He shuddered, for he knew that Dravadan was a man who would scruple at no atrocity that advanced his aims.

As the others filed away, he sat on the sand staring into the flames until the moon reached its zenith.

CHAPTER FORTY-FOUR

The atmosphere in Taratanallos was changed by the assassination of Lord Ribauldequin. Although summer was here, there was a chill hanging over the city. When citizens gathered on street corners to discuss the great political questions of the day, they looked over their shoulders before giving voice to any controversial opinion; and whether one supported the Emmen or the Gammerling alliance was a secret to be shared only with the most trusted associates.

Rumour and counter-rumour swept the city. Some said that Bartielko had confessed all, others that he remained mute even under torture. King Enguerran was on his way in person with the Knights of the Tarn at his back; King Ingomer and Duke Lothar were reconciled and even now marched down the Peninsula to secure the city.

Dravadan made a point of riding from Korfez at the top of the Archgate, down past the docks and to the Masavory at least twice a day, to emphasise that he was not giving in to panic. "Now is the time for calm mien and bold strokes," he said. "Within a month the treaty will be signed and tranquillity restored."

The Gammerling party had been thrown into disarray by the imprisonment of Bartielko. Dravadan and Oricien worked deep into the night; there was not a single member of the Masavory, and few among the Specchio, to whom Dravadan had not spoken in a bid to secure their support.

One evening he summoned his lieutenants to Korfez: Raguslan, Zanijel and, now as a matter of course, Todarko. It was the first time Todarko had visited Korfez since his last distressing interview with Linnalitha.

They sat on the loggia alongside Lord Oricien and Lord Iselin. Dravadan called them to attention with a brisk nod. "Now is the time for action," he said. "My lords, you had agreed to be guided by me as to the best time to put your proposals to the Specchio. We are not assured of unanimous support, or even the majority, but events are unlikely to improve. Norielko, as President of the Masavory, has little real power, but he has set a date for Bartielko's trial: it begins two weeks hence. The trial is likely to confuse the situation, whether or not he is guilty. It is not inconceivable that the scope of the enquiry will bring to the surface certain matters we would prefer to remain obscure."

He looked across at Oricien who simply gave a brisk nod.

"The risk of going to the Masavory now, before all the votes are secure, is that we may lose. Nonetheless, I consider that less dangerous than Bartielko's trial upsetting the balance still further, or even calling forth King Ingomer's intervention."

"It seems," said Lord Iselin, stroking his neat red goatee, "that Lord Oricien will need to be at his most persuasive in the chamber."

"He has braved the blade in his zeal for the alliance; he has seen his friend slain before his eyes. Such experiences cannot help but sway the waverers."

"It is good that Ribauldequin did not die in vain," said Oricien in an expressionless voice.

"I did not mean to imply—" said Dravadan.

"Of course not—forgive me," said Oricien. "This embassy has been more demanding than I had expected. Aladar had presented the situation as little more than a formality. His death was a great blow."

"Not that your own efforts are not appreciated, Dravadan," said Iselin with a quiet smile.

"I am sure I have never wavered from my passion to secure the alliance we all crave," said Dravadan, a hint of a flush on his cheek.

Raguslan leaned forward. "Come, gentlemen! Such lack of amity helps none but our enemies."

"Well said, Raguslan!" cried Dravadan. "My lord, I regret that Aladar's naïve optimism misled you. Matters were never as clear-cut as he represented them. The circumstances leading to his tragic demise unfortunately illustrate the deficiencies in his judgement."

Including his choice of friends, thought Todarko.

"I might observe," said Todarko, motivated by a mischievous impulse, "that as soon as you begin to pay a man, he tells you what you want to hear. The only truly reliable ally does not require florins."

Dravadan's faced darkened. Oricien gave a brittle laugh. "You do not say much, Todarko, but what you do is to the point. There is much in your view."

"But—" Dravadan appeared lost for a cogent response.

Lord Iselin made an airy gesture with his goblet. "There is of course no way in which the remark could apply to yourself, Dravadan. Todarko was clearly referring to the unfortunate Aladar."

"Of course," said Dravadan stiffly. "Todarko, I think we may dispense with your services for the remainder of the evening. A young man like yourself has many calls on his time, and the Hour of Noble Pleasures approaches."

Todarko, who had been finding recent events oppressive, was delighted at such an unlooked-for escape. "Thank you, sir. I apologise for any embarrassment my remarks may have caused." An apology cost nothing, now that he was free.

As he made to leave, Oricien said, in a level but penetrating voice: "Todarko! Never apologise for honest counsel, or for speaking your mind."

Todarko bowed. Dravadan's face was set in an expression of clear ill-humour. Oricien's dissatisfaction with him could not be much clearer.

"Before you leave, Todarko," said Dravadan with an approximation of a smile, "ask Palankijo to call down my wife. She is in low spirits these past days and I am sure she would welcome your company."

Todarko was somewhat less certain, but he saw no means of gracefully evading the request. "Of course, sir. I am happy to give succour wherever I can."

Ten minutes later, Todarko was sitting on the smaller Ladies' Loggia at the other side of the house, a cool evening breeze ruffling his hair. Before him sat a fresh bowl of sherbet. The woman he cared for above any other was on her way. It was hard to imagine a more pleasant situation; and Todarko would have given anything to be elsewhere.

Behind him a curtain brushed aside. He turned to look and saw Linnalitha, pale in a deep green dress, with the beginnings of shadows under her eyes, but still unutterably beautiful. The lanterns on the loggia picked up the gold in her hair.

"Madam, I—"

"Why are you here, Todarko?" she said, walking past him to lean on the decorative wall at the edge of the loggia.

"It was not my doing. Your husband thought my company might raise your spirits."

She turned her head to give him an incredulous glance. "You could not have suggested otherwise?"

"In the circumstances, no. If my presence distresses you, I will leave."

She came and sat two seats away from him.

"I do not know what your presence does, Todarko. You are here now, and any damage to my composure is already done."

"How have you kept, madam?"

"You do not wish to know. I cannot sleep, my husband's intrigues will destroy us all, and every day I await a sonnet I was promised. It is a little thing to hope for, but it is all I have."

"I have not been much at my verses, madam. Recent events with the ambassadors…"

"Forgive me, Todarko," she said, leaning forward. "I am selfish to inflict my petty concerns on you when you have been in danger of your life. You were not hurt?"

"I was little more than a witness," he said. "It was horrid to observe, but there was nothing any of us could have done. You are right to reprove me for the sonnet. I will rise early tomorrow and finish it."

She stood up with a brisk movement. "You are under no obligation. I do not look for constancy; how can I when there is nothing for you to be constant to?"

"Linna, you cannot know how I regret the impossibility of any greater intimacy between us. Had you sought constancy, you would have found it."

She sat down again and leaned towards him. "We will never know, Todarko. Perhaps that is for the best."

Todarko said nothing. Linnalitha continued. "Now, more than ever, be careful of my husband. He is playing for high stakes, and he comes to realise that he may not win. If the Masavory rejects the alliance, and Bartielko is acquitted, his position is not safe. The effect on his temper is not—agreeable."

"I had noticed," said Todarko with a half-smile.

"Do not make a joke of this," she said. "Cross him and he will kill you. He will kill you."

Todarko rose and smoothed the creases from his breeches. "I will not cross him, Linna. The sooner I am away from his intrigues, the better."

He bowed and made to leave the loggia.

"Todarko," said Linnalitha softly. "Please be careful. I do not know what I would do if you came to harm."

Todarko could not meet her gaze. "You cannot be more solicitous for my welfare than I am," he said, with an attempt at flippancy he did not feel to be wholly successful. He was glad he had never mentioned Vislanko's scrutiny of their relationship to her.

CHAPTER FORTY-FIVE

The Hour of Secret Deeds came and Todarko was still not in his bed. He sat at the open window of his chamber, a breeze riffling his papers as he looked out at the stars above the sea. Unseen before him lay the first twelve lines of his sonnet. The most recent couplet, in particular, seemed poorly conceived.

Happy to have thy love, happy to die,
And death once dead, there's no more dying then

It was one thing to write about a love surmounting even death when it was a simple poetic conceit. Since he had written the words, however, he had seen what death really meant. Lord Ribauldequin, a brave, decent and honourable man, had bled his life away in the sordid surroundings of the Ostentatory, for no purpose that anyone could define. His sacrifice had not even saved Lord Oricien, whose mail shirt had proved the more effective protection. What would Ribauldequin make of Todarko's poetic fancy that fine and noble feelings, underwritten by a healthy portion of lust, could treat on equal terms with death?

And what of the slave-girl who had killed him? She too was dead, and in circumstances she could not possibly have desired. What could prompt a mother with an infant son to risk her life—and his—to assassinate a man she had never met and could be nothing to her? Someone—Bartielko?—had obviously smuggled the knife in to her. Had he also promised to protect her son? Or had she been so despairing at the thought of a lifetime's servitude that any action was preferable to passivity? Who was she? What had she been before her capture? There were so many questions, and most of them by their nature could never be answered.

He poured himself a goblet of wine from the flask at his elbow. The deaths of Ribauldequin and the unfortunate slave could only be regretted, but it was self-indulgently morbid to dwell on them. If he was that disturbed, he could always ask a Viator to put the deaths in the context of the Way of Harmony. He gave a bitter snort at the thought of High Viator Udenko—a man who showed all the spiritual depth of a bindlespith, concerned with nothing but his alms and his prerogatives. Little useful counsel would come from that source or, he suspected, any of his colleagues. Udenko was the man who would fight to maintain Taratanallos' version of the Way. Who cared whether or not it was the 'Peninsular Heresy'? They were all equally at odds with the business of men's lives.

He gave his head a shake and drained his goblet. What had come over him? First he brooded on the deaths of two strangers, now he condemned the Viators for failing to provide adequate spiritual guidance. This was hardly the wenching and wining at which he was so adept.

It had all started with Linnalitha, he realised. Only a month ago he had cast Ivanka to her fate without a backward glance. Then, because of a fleeting attraction for Dravadan's wife, he allowed himself to become embroiled in Dravadan's intrigues. Once he realised that his feelings for Linnalitha were real, he was ensnared too deeply to escape—and yet, forever sundered from Linnalitha. The situation was disastrous on every level; instead of fretting over Ribauldequin's death, he would be better advised in ensuring he did not join him. A crow that flies in heaven's sweetest air—but not just yet.

He turned his attention once more to the sonnet. Removing the lines about mortality would not bring Ribauldequin back, nor express his feelings for Linnalitha any more powerfully. He knew they would not, could not, be together in any sense he understood—his final interview with Ivanka would certainly never be repeated in this context. So the sonnet had to be everything; there was nothing else.

> *I love not less, though less the show appear*
> *For truth proves thievish for a prize so dear*

That was it exactly. Just because he could not express or act upon his feelings did not make them any less powerful.

He sat down and copied out the scraps of verse scattered across the pages of his portfolio.

> *In loving thee thou know'st I am forsworn,*
> *That every word doth almost tell my name*
> *And place my merit in the eye of scorn.*
> *How sweet and lovely dost thou make the shame!*
>
> *Let not my love be called idolatory,*
> *A crow that flies in heaven's sweetest air.*
> *Thy love is better than high birth to me*
> *Past cure I am, now reason is past care.*

As from my soul which in thy breast doth lie
Like him that travels I return again,
Happy to have thy love, happy to die,
And death once dead, there's no more dying then.

I love not less, though less the show appear
For truth proves thievish for a prize so dear

He leaned back in his chair. It had taken him a month to write, and the Todarko who had finished the poem was not the same man who had started it, but reading through it, he recognised the emotions underlying every line. With a flourish and a wry smile he wrote at the top of the page:

For Madam L—a, of House U—a

He looked around for an envelope: he would send Luzio with a discreet message in the morning. There was no envelope to be found, however. It was late to rouse Luzio from his bed: time enough to deal with the matter tomorrow.

Looking over the sonnet the next morning, he saw an irritating spelling error which had eluded his wine-fuddled mind the previous evening. He rapidly wrote a fair copy and despatched it via Luzio to Korfez. He was not disposed to wait for a reply, and sent another message to Bodazar suggesting that they meet at the Silvermarket at the Hour of Fiscal Scrutiny, still a sandglass away.

He walked down the hill in a better humour than he had enjoyed last night. The sun was bright even at this early hour, with the sea-breeze taking the sultriness from the air. The fine weather had brought out many ladies in Hood and Veil, and he nodded respectfully as he passed: a lady was always worthy of courtesy, even if her identity were concealed.

On this day of the week, the Silvermarket was given over to spices from all corners of Mondia. Todarko inhaled the melange of sweetness and pungency, overlain by a faint whiff from the day's fishing which was being disembarked from the wharf. He handed over a copper minim for a portion of spiced grumpfish and settled down to await the arrival of Bodazar. His friend was rarely an optimistic companion, and he wondered how he would have taken recent events. House Belario was of the Gammerling affinity and could have been touched by Bartielko's fall. Perhaps it would be better to avoid political topics when Bodazar arrived, at least until he had assessed the lie of the land.

So absorbed was he in his thoughts—which by this stage had moved from concerns about House Belario to an indelicate reverie about Linnalitha—that he did not notice as Bodazar came up beside him on the city wall and clapped him on the shoulder.

"How goes it in the world of intrigue?" cried Bodazar in a hearty tone.

Todarko gave a strained smile. "It is scarcely the glamour of popular repute. My experiences at Dravadan's side can be summarised as boredom interspersed with irritation and fear."

"Such is the life of the dashing man of affairs, I suppose. No doubt proximity to the fair Linnalitha provides a certain consolation..."

"Ha! All of the emotions I referred to, with the exception of boredom, apply as much to Madam Linnalitha as the others."

Bodazar smilingly shook his head. "I take you are not making the progress you had hoped for."

"It is not quite so simple," said Todarko.

"I understood you genuinely liked her—beyond the normal ravages of your lusts, I mean."

Todarko frowned. "You have no very high opinion of my previous amours."

"What other interpretation is there? It is ironic that once you fix upon a person with more serious intent, she happens to be married."

"Ironic, as you say."

"You have accepted defeat, I take it. Your recent association cannot leave you in any doubt as to Dravadan's character, or the way in which he might respond to horns."

Todarko threw the remains of his grumpfish to the ground, where it immediately seethed with gulls flapping and screeching.

"It is beneath my dignity to consider Dravadan's opinions in this context. He has a pearl beyond price for a wife, and he hardly looks at her. If I had secured the esteem of Linnalitha I should not consider Dravadan for a moment."

"Your recent acquaintance does not seem to have improved your assessment of his character."

Todarko shrugged. "I had an understanding of the man I was dealing with. The evidence of experience has not caused me to revise my opinion. Nonetheless, Linnalitha does not wish to pursue our intimacy."

Bodazar again clapped him on the shoulder. "Better luck next time. It will do you no harm to suffer a reverse this once!"

"I have written her a sonnet," said Todarko. "I think it a fine piece of work."

"I seem to recall you wrote Nelanka a sonnet."

"The situation was somewhat different."

"Do you hope to change her mind with your verse?"

Todarko looked off to the horizon for a moment. He shook his head. "It is too late for that, and Linnalitha too level-headed. She knows the risk and she will not court it."

Bodazar pushed himself away from the wall. "Come, surely it is not too early for beer. No doubt there are things other than women and verse we can discuss!"

Todarko turned his back to the sea and followed his friend into the crowds of the marketplace.

CHAPTER FORTY-SIX

It would soon be time for Oricien to address the Specchio—a speech on which the success of his embassy would surely hang. One afternoon he excused himself from his engagements and made his way back to his apartments at the Castle of Crostestini. It would be worth spending a few hours considering what he was going to say. Regardless of Dravadan's facile and somewhat desperate optimism, it was clear to him that the Emmen party did not yet command enough votes to seal the alliance. There were some, hard though it was to imagine, who were not swayed by questions of expediency and wished to decide based on the good of the city. These people, by definition, could be convinced by powerful arguments.

The afternoon was still and clear, and Oricien went out on to the circular balcony to set down his thoughts. An hour later he was little further forward; there were those, like Todarko, who it seemed thought better with a quill in their hand, but Oricien found the opposite to be true. The quill weighed like an iron bar, too heavy to be subject to his control. For a moment he thought of commissioning Todarko to write the speech: the young man was intelligent and a strong partisan of their cause. He sighed and shook his head. The speech was his responsibility, and the sooner he buckled down to it, the sooner he would have finished.

He heard a cough from inside the apartment and looked up to see a black-clad Consigli stepping towards him. "My apologies for disturbing you, my lord. Madam Nelanka is here to see you."

Oricien gave a start of surprise, and perhaps more than surprise: he did not inspect his feelings too closely. "Kindly send her in," he said. "Invite her to join me on the balcony."

A moment later Nelanka stood there in a dress of deep maroon, her head largely obscured by Hood and Veil. Oricien indicated a nearby chair and she sat with that still grace Oricien had previously noted in her. "May I pour you a drink, madam?"

Nelanka inclined her head. "In a respectable establishment," she said, "—and what could be more respectable than the Castle of Crostestini?—a gentleman will usually invite a lady to remove her Hood and Veil."

"Of course," said Oricien. "I had not realised an invitation was necessary," he said with a wave of his hand.

Nelanka unclipped her veil with a practised gesture and swept back her hood. "It is considered forward to uncover uninvited," she said. "It is a reputation I am keen to avoid."

Oricien went inside and fetched two goblets and a pitcher of cool white wine. "Might it not be seen as forward for you to call upon me in this way?" he said with a smile.

Nelanka's face clouded for a moment. "This is not a consideration for either Dravadan or my husband. Dravadan is worried—far more than he seems—that things will go awry."

Oricien picked up a sheaf of papers. "My address to the Specchio is not proceeding well," he said. "Dravadan's concerns may be correct."

Nelanka flashed her sharp white teeth. "Losing the vote is the least of Dravadan's worries. He is more worried that you win and cast him aside. He was never more alarmed than when you seemed to be reaching a rapprochement with Bartielko."

Oricien sipped at his goblet, his gaze not leaving her eyes. "And then Bartielko finds himself in prison. A cynical man might regard that as a fortunate outcome for Dravadan."

Nelanka shrugged. "If he planned it, I do not know about it."

Oricien set down his goblet. "I was the target of the attack, not Ribauldequin. My death might well have brought King Enguerran to the gates of Taratanallos."

"You are alive," she said. "I for one am glad." She smiled at him over the rim of her goblet.

"I prefer life to death," said Oricien, then, with a tightening of his mouth, "No doubt poor Ribauldequin would have said the same."

Nelanka seemed to inch in her seat slightly closer. "Were you friends?"

Oricien shook his head reflexively. "Not really. That makes it worse, of course. He died protecting me, and he was not a man I gave half a florin for."

Her deep black eyes looked into his. "You should not blame yourself," she said. "You are far from home, working for your king. Your mission is an honourable one."

Oricien stood up and went to lean on the balcony, looking over the Archgate stretching away up the hill. "I would not have you think me maudlin," he said. "I first fought in battle twenty years ago; I was at my father's side when he was shot from his gallumpher by hill-bandits; I have seen my city taken and sacked, and lived to rebuild it. I have known great woes and great triumphs. You need not concern yourself over my welfare."

She came and leaned on the balcony beside him. "Yet I do, my lord. I think you know that. In truth I care nothing for the success of your mission: for most, life will go on as before regardless of who rules the city. But I would have you return safe to your home."

Oricien pulled his gaze away from the Archgate. "Home is a long way off, madam. If our embassy fails, and I return to Emmen empty-handed... well, King Enguerran is not a magnanimous man. I could not expect to see Croad again, perhaps for years."

She twisted a small jewelled ring around on her finger. "And is that what you truly want? To be back in Croad?"

Oricien smiled crookedly. "It seems such a small desire, does it not, for a man who has been the King's ambassador? But it is my home, the place I was born to rule—and there is still much to be done there, much still to be rebuilt."

Nelanka looked away. "When we were on the hunting expedition, I was thoughtless to speak of it. You know that I was angry, with my husband and Dravadan, but I should never had spoken so freely of the fall of the city. Had I known what it meant to you, I would never have done it. You know that, do you not?"

Oricien gently put a finger on her chin and turned her face towards him. "I know that you would never deliberately cause pain, Nelanka. You are too generous for spite."

He looked into her eyes; if he kissed her, she would not resist, and neither would it advance Dravadan's plans. For a moment he hesitated, then pursed his lips and put his hand back down by his side. He walked over to the door to his apartments and turned to face her.

"Come, there is a breeze rising. Let us go inside," he said.

CHAPTER FORTY-SEVEN

Todarko returned to his chambers, after an afternoon of pleasant conviviality with Bodazar, to find two letters awaiting him. He did not recognise the script on either envelope, although both were clearly female hands. He sat at his desk and opened the first with his paper-knife.

I have read the sheet you enclosed. The sonnet is beautiful beyond measure although I am not sure I understand every aspect of it. I cannot respond in kind or with the fervour your words demand. Be assured that my sentiments are fully as warm as the poem requires. Correspondence of any sort is hazardous, and you will understand that its continuance is impossible.

I love not less, though less the show appear

L.

Todarko set the letter down with a smile and a constriction in his throat. What else had he expected? Had he truly thought his verse so compelling that it would induce Linnalitha to abandon all restraint? This was the best he could have hoped for: he had fulfilled his promise, and now he could, in time, forget her. Taratanallos was full of young ladies, many of them of the most bewitching temperaments.

He took the letter and slipped it into the secret compartment of his cabinet. The sensible course would be to destroy it, but he wanted to read it several times before that. Locking the cabinet, he reached for the second letter.

At the top of the sheet was the crow emblem of House Vaggio. He read on in mounting dismay.

Grandille

Dear Grandson,

I have learned of your recent conduct—do not ask how—with mounting alarm. While I have turned a blind eye to your youthful excesses (you resemble your father more than you can possibly know), your involvement in the political sphere displeases me greatly. It is the duty of all members of the House to advance our fortunes, for the rising tide floats all boats. Imagine, therefore, my dismay when I see you thrusting yourself above the heirs of the House, my son Raguslan and his son Zanijel. This is not the way things are done in House Vaggio!

You will oblige me by waiting upon me at Grandille, at your immediate convenience.

Your affectionate grandmother,

Sulinka.

Todarko gulped and set the letter down. Affectionate! That was not how he remembered her. A summons from Sulinka, the oldest member of the House, was not a thing to be treated lightly. She it was who had commanded Raguslan to take in his nephew on the death of his brother. Although her own husband, Jirno, was many years dead, Sulinka ran the estate at Grandille with a formidable hand. Raguslan rarely, if ever, countermanded her wishes even though, as a dowager, she no longer commanded formal power in House Vaggio.

She retained nonetheless the capacity to cause a great deal of mischief if she were thwarted. Todarko's inheritance, relatively modest as it was, flowed to him through his father Glastarko and so, ultimately, through Sulinka. His grandmother had the nominal right to disinherit him and, despite her advanced years, the energy and the spite to do so. All in all, Sulinka's summons could not be ignored, much as he might wish to. The interview did not promise to be a comfortable one: always formidable, Sulinka had grown more irascible with age; while he had never formally endorsed Nelanka's view of her as "a cantankerous old sow", he fully understood the reasoning behind it. Where the welfare of her favoured grandson Zanijel was concerned, she would stop at nothing. It was both ironic and implausible that he was condemned for excessive political scheming, when he wanted only to be quit of it, but Sulinka had a way of twisting the facts which could make explanation taxing.

He sighed and rang the bell for Luzio. It would be necessary to have the gallumpher ready to leave at first light.

Grandille, the summer estate of House Vaggio, was half a day's ride to the north of the city. It had always been an old persons' place to Todarko, perhaps because Sulinka had ruled in her idiosyncratic way for as long as he could remember. The main house was surrounded by a cluster of buildings, some home to members of the house, others to the retainers and servants who kept it running with unobtrusive efficiency.

There was only one road into the estate, and so it was that Todarko gently impelled his gallumpher through the glade of overhanging trees, cool and tart against the beating sun, as he made his way to the main gate. It was over a year since his last visit; over a year since he had last subjected himself to his grandmother's scrutiny.

The servants on the gate greeted him with deference but little underlying cordiality. Several previous incidents had led to explosions of temper and breakages of the sort which servants tended to remember. Lulijko, the factotum of Grandille, escorted Todarko into the main house. He had been middle-aged for as long as Todarko could remember—never young and now, seemingly, never old either.

"Madam Sulinka will be delighted to see you, sir," Lulijko said with a barely discernible frostiness. "I believe there is much she wishes to discuss with you."

They walked unhurriedly along a crunching gravel path winding across laboriously tended lawns, the scent of watered blooms infiltrating Todarko's nose. "I am sure my grandmother would prefer to raise her business with me directly, rather than through an intermediary, no matter now trusted."

Lulijko gave his head a rueful shake. "You should not be so quick to take offence, Todarko. I have known you since you were a boy, and your temperament is—"

"I have no interest in your assessment of my character, Lulijko. Your role is to conduct me from one part of Grandille to another—and even here your presence is supererogatory, since I am familiar with the estate's layout."

Lulijko returned a bland expression. "As you will, sir."

The factotum hung back to allow Todarko into the dim reception hall, refreshingly cool after the bright sun. "The Hour of Light Repast approaches. Will you wish to dine before waiting upon Madam Sulinka?"

"Luzio furnished me with a staybit for the road," said Todarko politely. "I would be delighted to wait upon Madam Sulinka now, if convenient."

Lulijko bowed. "I will assess her views, sir."

Todarko sat in the hall, leaning his head against a chill marble pillar to dissipate the heat. For the first time, he felt the charm of Grandille—a place not so much torpid as relaxed, a refuge from the bustle of Taratanallos. Perhaps he would visit more frequently, once Sulinka had completed her journey along the Way.

"Madam Sulinka bids you visit her in her chamber," said Lulijko on his return. "She begs you forgive the informality. Animaxia has seen fit to afflict her with certain pains since your last visitation. She rarely descends."

Lulijko led the way up the broad marble staircase. He knocked on a heavy wooden door.

"Enter!" came the sharp voice from within. Todarko followed Lulijko into a high-ceilinged, airy room with a scent of fresh lavender. On a bed of greater width than dictated by practicality lay a woman with abundant snowy-white hair, small black eyes, and nose and chin which vied for prominence in her face. Her yellowish wrinkled skin could not disguise the sharpness of her cheekbones and the fact that, in her youth, she could only have been an extraordinarily beautiful woman.

"Madam, your grandson Todarko."

"I am well aware who is before me, Lulijko," snapped Sulinka. "I may be infirm but, Hissen preserve me, my wits are not addled. I recognise Todarko and I do not need to be told that he is my grandson."

Lulijko, schooled by many long years of practice, maintained a neutral expression.

"You may go, Lulijko. Send up a light confection for our luncheon. Todarko, you will of course join me."

"I have already eaten, grandmother."

"Fah! A lad of your age can no doubt eat again. You would not allow an old woman to eat alone. Lulijko! Luncheon for two!"

"Yes, madam."

Todarko was at least gratified that his memory was reliable. Sulinka was every bit as he remembered her.

"Come here, boy," she said. "My eyes are good enough but you would oblige me by approaching more closely."

"How are you, grandmother?" asked Todarko, perching on the side of her bed.

Sulinka narrowed her eyes. "I am good for another twenty years yet. You need not be scheming to snatch your inheritance."

"My allowance is perfectly satisfactory. I was merely concerned to find you in bed."

"Cah!" With a surprisingly vigorous movement she threw the blankets aside and swung into a sitting position on the side of the bed. "Help me up, boy. We will sit on the balcony. I am not yet wholly decrepit!"

"Indeed not," said Todarko, taking her arm and gently raising her to her feet. Never a large woman, there was almost no weight now as he assisted her onto the balcony and seated her at the small table.

Servants bustled in with plates of meats, small pieces of bread, chopped fruit and a few sweet morsels. Sulinka conveyed these to her mouth with an avidity which belied her slight frame.

"You do not visit your grandmother very frequently, Todarko. I am the mother of House Vaggio."

"My apologies, madam," said Todarko, sipping at a lime cordial. "The press of affairs keeps me in town all too often."

Despite the fact that her mouth was filled with marshmallow, Sulinka let out a cry of scorn: not a sight that Todarko found appealing.

"Press of affairs! I said in my letter how much you remind me of your father. Never more so than now."

"Are you becoming sentimental, grandmother?"

"Pah! Glastarko was an immensely talented boy, far more than Raguslan, but he never showed the slightest application. He always had a glib excuse and a ready avoidance of responsibility. This is the way in which he reminds me of you—this is neither sentimental nor a compliment!"

She began to cough as the marshmallow stuck in her throat. Todarko waited politely for her to continue.

"You have always been a solitary boy, Todarko. You have never really understood what it means to be part of a great house. When your grandfather was alive we were pre-eminent in Taratanallos."

Todarko had never entirely believed this received family wisdom, but chose to keep his scepticism to himself.

"We have always had money aplenty," she continued. "Jirno knew how to play the factions against each other. There were none who could hoodwink House Vaggio."

Todarko smiled and nodded politely. If Sulinka were about to launch into a eulogy for her long-departed husband the only course was to hunker down and wait it out. But Sulinka's eyes crackled and she moved on.

"Unfortunately Raguslan lacks the same aptitudes. He is assiduous in his efforts, but he has an indifferent understanding of money, and even less of politics. His father would have been dismayed to see him trotting at Dravadan's heel. Subservient to House Umbinzia! All is not as it should be."

"I thought you intended to berate me, not my uncle," said Todarko.

Sulinka's mouth contracted to invisibility. A wasp approached her face and rapidly thought better of the adventure.

"I will come to you in due course, Todarko. Have the courtesy to listen while I explain the background."

"Yes, grandmother."

"Raguslan is an earnest trier, without any spark of inspiration. He has nonetheless dragged House Vaggio back to the heart of power. He may not lead, but he has made sure we will be on the winning side. It may demean us to defer to Dravadan, but he is the coming man. Raguslan has played a poor hand relatively well."

"Dravadan is some way short of trustworthy."

Sulinka shot him a penetrating look. "So much is understood. What man in his position would be? What is important is that Raguslan has made himself Dravadan's lieutenant. Zanijel and—to a lesser extent— you can support that."

"That is what I imagined myself to be doing."

"By fighting with Zanijel before the Emmen lords? By ridiculing your uncle's views?"

"I can only ridicule what is inherently ridiculous. Surely by appearing to advantage I do not harm our prospects?"

Sulinka banged her cane on the floor. "What House Vaggio—that is to say, myself—has decided is that Raguslan is the means of our advancement. Through his own hard work and the vigour of his heir, House Vaggio can be lifted back to pre-eminence! You do not help us by making them appear buffoons!"

Todarko said: "What if they are buffoons, grandmother?"

"This is not to be borne!" cried Sulinka. "An artist works with the materials to hand. He does not paint a study in blue when he has only reds on his palette."

"My observations would lead me to believe that Lord Oricien has a low opinion of Zanijel, and little better of Raguslan or even Dravadan. If he esteems me more highly, that is scarcely to my discredit."

Sulinka banged a veined hand upon the table. "You are perhaps the only male member of the family with even a fraction of your grandfather's insight and intelligence—"

"—in that case—"

"—which makes it all the more galling that you have shown no interest in the fate of our great city—and more importantly House Vaggio—until it is far too late. We are now committed to the course we originally laid down: to support Raguslan and Zanijel as they sit at Dravadan's shoulder. The sad truth, for you and perhaps for me, is that you will never be head of House Vaggio. However, Raguslan and Zanijel are both tractable to my wishes, so matters are arranged for the best."

Todarko struggled to follow Sulinka's reasoning. Did she regret her years of mistreatment, of favouritism towards the mediocre and malicious Zanijel?

"What you must understand, Todarko, is that your duty is not to yourself. It is to House Vaggio. I will see us restored to our high seat before I die. And you will not thwart me, through indifference, perversity or spite. Cross me now, and you will not see a florin of your inheritance!"

Todarko was reassured by this return to the Sulinka he knew. No visit to Grandille would be complete without the shadow of disinheritance.

"I will of course comply with your requests, grandmother."

Sulinka gave a sour nod of satisfaction. "Have another marshmallow, boy. You may yet be a credit to your grandfather."

Todarko reached out for one of the sickly sweetmeats.

"And Todarko—"

"Yes, grandmother?"

"If what I hear about your dalliances is even half true, you are far more stupid than I imagined."

"Since I do not know what you have heard, I cannot verify my stupidity."

A crumb fell from Sulinka's lips. "Zanijel is a sensitive boy. He hears much, and he confides in his grandmother."

Todarko gave a polite smile. "He always was a dutiful young man."

Sulinka narrowed her eyes. "I like you least, Todarko, when you adopt that snake's face. Leave me now. An old woman must have her nap. We will speak further at the Hour of Evening Repast."

As Todarko left the room he looked over his shoulder to see Sulinka plucking the last two marshmallows from the plate.

CHAPTER FORTY-EIGHT

Todarko remained at Grandille for the minimum time he judged acceptable to his grandmother, which meant a stay of two nights. Shortly before the Hour of Petitions, on a muggy overcast morning, he saddled up his gallumpher and set off to retrace his journey back to the city. Sulinka had been, if not cordial, then at least able to keep the worst of her acridity under control. Todarko left with the impression that, while he remained far below the exemplar Zanijel in his grandmother's estimation, he was at least no longer a disgrace to House Vaggio.

Sulinka had come to see him off, making her way down to the stables with a speed which made him question the level of affliction she truly suffered. She gave him a birdlike embrace and drew back to look up into his face.

"Your father could have been a great man if he had been spared," she said. "You may yet live to equal him if you will only listen to the advice of the wise."

Todarko knew better than to ask who might best fill the criterion of wisdom.

"I shall do my best to disappoint no-one," he said with a smile.

Sulinka frowned. "I do not care whom you disappoint, as long as it is not me. Now, be off with you: nothing is achieved lurking at Grandille!"

Shortly before the Hour of Light Repast, Todarko rode through the Arch Gate and thence to Tappinetto. "Luzio!" he called as he entered the portico. "Kindly have the gallumpher stabled and send luncheon to my rooms. I have much to attend to."

Todarko's plans included little more than a nap in the cool air of his chamber, but Luzio need not know this. He clattered up the stairs in his riding boots and flung back the door. Before him was a scene of chaos: his bed disarranged, chairs tipped over and papers strewn across every surface. The door to his cabinet hung askew and his portfolio of verse lay, open and face down, on his rattovar rug. Todarko's chambers were not normally models of neatness, but this went well beyond simple slovenliness. Could he have been the victim of robbery at Tappinetto? Such a thing was not possible!

"Luzio!" be bellowed. "Luzio! Come here this instant!"

Luzio grumbled up the stairs bearing a covered tray in each hand. "Luncheon requires a certain amount of time to prepare, sir."

Todarko grabbed Luzio's collar and dragged him into the room. Both trays fell to the floor, adding to the scene of disorder. "What is this?" he snapped.

Luzio stared around. "I—I am sure I do not know, sir."

"Who has been in my chambers?"

"No-one, sir. I did not think to have them cleaned in your absence. I—"

"You clot, Luzio! I am not interested in whether you have skimped on the dusting! Who has had access to despoil my possessions?"

Luzio sagged. "I cannot say, sir. I am sure there has been no unauthorised entry to the buildings: this is Tappinetto!"

Todarko's mouth was a thin line. "Did you ransack my rooms, Luzio?"

"Of course not, sir!"

"Perhaps Raguslan was responsible?"

Luzio started a nervous laugh, choked it off when he saw Todarko's expression.

"The range of potential suspects is small," said Todarko. "Fetch my uncle immediately. I will be in Zanijel's chambers."

"Sir—"

"Your instructions are clear, Luzio. Kindly carry them out."

Without a backward glance Todarko strode from the room, down the stairs into the central hall, and then up the flight which led to the elaborate suite of rooms maintained by Zanijel. Without knocking he crashed open the door, to find Nelanka sewing and looking up at him in astonishment.

"Todarko! It is customary to knock!"

"Where is the dutiful grandson?" snarled Todarko.

Nelanka rose from her seat. "Whatever are you talking about?"

"Bring that worm forth, and we will find out."

"Todarko!"

Another door opened and Zanijel appeared, dabbing crumbs from his lips with a napkin. "Cannot I enjoy my luncheon in peace? Oho, it is Todarko!"

Todarko strode forward and once again smashed him on the nose. Zanijel reeled back, clutched at a curtain for support. It proved inadequate for its new employment, and parted from its pole, swathing the supine Zanijel in a pink nimbus.

"If that is insufficiently direct," said Todarko, "do not enter my chambers without my express permission."

Nelanka sat down. "Who invited you into our chambers, Todarko?"

"I have not—yet—ransacked the room."

"You have destroyed my curtains."

"Perhaps we will repair to my chambers now to see the true meaning of destruction."

Zanijel had by now disentangled himself from the curtain. "How dare you!" he bellowed. "Here, now, I shall kill you!"

He reached down an ornamental rapier from the wall. "This belonged to our grandfather, and will be the agency of your death!"

Nelanka took Zanijel's arm with two hands. "I beg you, husband. Todarko does not know what he doing! There is some misunderstanding."

"Enough!" came a voice from behind them. "Put down the sword, Zanijel." It was Raguslan, accompanied by Luzio. "You will not profane my father's blade with the blood of House Vaggio. But Todarko, you have much to explain."

"Surely Luzio has apprised you of the facts, uncle. My room has been robbed!"

"What is missing?" asked Raguslan.

"I have not checked. In the disorder it would be difficult to be certain."

"And why do you believe your cousin to be the culprit?"

"He has made various remarks outlining his ill-will, and his desire to act upon it."

Raguslan rubbed his chin. "You attract ill-will from many quarters, Todarko. The field of suspects is not materially narrowed."

"How many of them live in Tappinetto?"

"If I may," said Luzio in a hesitant voice. "The catch on your window appears to have been forced. The villain need not reside in Tappinetto."

"Hah!" said Todarko. "Zanijel is surely wily enough to lay a false trail."

There was a silence as all present, including Todarko himself, realised the essential implausibility of the remark.

Raguslan gave a brisk nod. "Todarko, your contention is unsupported by evidence. You will apologise to Zanijel, and we will repair to your room to inventory any losses. This may at least give us a motive for the crime."

Inventory the losses. Suddenly Todarko had an idea of what might be missing. This was not area he wished others to be involved in sifting.

He held up his hands. "I will assess the matter now," he said. "I will work more efficiently alone." He turned and dashed from the room. Raguslan called as he went, "You must not neglect Zanijel's apology!"

In his mind's eye Todarko saw the door to his cabinet hanging open. There was only one thing in his chambers he could not afford to fall into the wrong hands. Be assured that my sentiments are fully as warm as the poem demands. The note from Linnalitha would endanger them both if Dravadan came to possess it.

He sprinted up the stairs, his chest pounding at the exercise. He dived into the room, reached back into the cabinet to expose the secret compartment. It seemed undisturbed. He fumbled with the leather cord around his neck and drew forth the key. His fingers were trembling with anxiety and exertion. With a deep breath he fitted the key into the lock, drew out the drawer.

Lying there was a folded sheet of creamy parchment. Holding his breath, he unfolded it. Before him was Linnalitha's handwriting. He was wrong: this had not been the target of the theft.

Behind was a scraping on the flagstone.

"What have you there, cousin?" said Zanijel.

Todarko scrambled upright and stuffed the note inside his pocket. "Have I not just cautioned you in the most candid fashion not to enter my apartments uninvited?"

"I took the remark as a womanish exaggeration. We are all keen to apprehend the culprit, and need not stand upon ceremony. Perhaps—" his eyes went to Todarko's breast "—there are objects you would not wish to lose."

Todarko stepped forward, chest to chest with his cousin. Zanijel stood half a head taller, two stones heavier. "There is a time, Zanijel, when one of us will kill the other. I would not like to be the man to tell your grandmother what has become of her favourite."

Zanijel gave a dark smile. "How was dear Sulinka? I understand she summoned you."

"Her message was not as pointed as you might believe. She is disappointed with both you and your father; indeed she considers throwing the resources of House Vaggio behind me, as the person who stands best with both Dravadan and Oricien."

Zanijel's face sagged and he took a step back. His mouth twisted as he said: "You lie! Sulinka knows you to be the shame of House Vaggio. She has ordered you to fall into line, and fall into line you shall."

Todarko turned, picked up the open folio from the floor and closed it up. "If you are so certain of her views," he said, "you need have no cause for concern. I envy you your untroubled sleep."

Zanijel's eyes narrowed. "Now," said Todarko, "unless you wish to help me restore order to the room, you may leave."

"When the time comes, cousin—it will not be me who dies." Zanijel turned and stalked from the room.

Todarko mechanically began to clear up the mess on the floor while he tried to think about what had happened. It was inconceivable that this was a random act: somebody had deliberately chosen to ransack his goods, for a motive as yet unclear. There were a number of candidates, and as many potential reasons for the act. Zanijel still remained the likeliest culprit: his animosity was stark and declared, and only last week he had barged into Todarko's rooms. Had he seen something which he sensed an advantage in removing? He also had the readiest access to the rooms: his presence anywhere in Tappinetto would not cause surprise. On the other hand, would he really have had the wit to tamper with the window? It was hard to give him credit for such slyness: whatever his faults, Zanijel was not given to indirection.

His greatest foe, potentially at least, was Dravadan. The enmity would only exist, however, if he knew of Linnalitha's feelings for him, and he had no reason to believe they were common knowledge. He sensed, too, that if Dravadan ever learned of the situation, his response would not be as oblique as ransacking his rooms. The only way in which Dravadan could have come by the information was if Vislanko had passed it on. There was as yet no reason for Vislanko to do so; the secret remained much more powerful if Vislanko could keep it poised above Todarko's head.

Indeed Vislanko was far more likely to have committed the crime himself. Todarko's privileged position within the Emmen party was valuable to the Consiglio, and the more direct pressure they could apply, the happier they would be.

Half an hour later Todarko had finished tidying the room. Nothing appeared to be missing. More attention had been paid to his papers than his valuables—which were untouched—with the culprit having paid his poetry folios particular scrutiny. It was scarcely credible that this was either an over-enthusiastic admirer or indeed a rival—he smiled as the face of Hazilan jumped into his mind—and none of his volumes contained anything of value. The only potentially embarrassing document he possessed, Linnalitha's letter, lay undisturbed in the secret compartment of his cabinet. Whatever the thief had come for, he had left without it.

The only conclusion Todarko could reach was that the incident had been designed as a warning. The intruder had not sought to remove any specific item, but simply to demonstrate to Todarko that he could enter the chamber at will. Such an approach did not fit his extensive knowledge of Zanijel's character: reluctantly he must be removed from the head of the list of suspects. In his place, Todarko was inclined on balance to blame Vislanko. The man was slippery, ruthless and capable. The ability to commit the act clearly lay with him, even if the motive remained obscure.

With that Todarko was forced to be content for the moment. It was likely that the matter would not end here. When his enemy made his move, then Todarko would know him. For now, his only recourse lay in preparation. With that in mind, he picked up his rapier and set off for the establishment of the fencing-master Rodizel on Ropemakers' Lane.

Oricien and Iselin sat on the balcony of Oricien's apartments at a table overlooking the marbled grandeur of the Masavory. In two days' time they would be inside the building, their embassy at its climax.

"I have a despatch from His Puissance," said Oricien, gesturing with an unfolded paper at Iselin. "He sends his compliments, expresses his confidence of a satisfactory conclusion, and reiterates his promises of reward for those who have helped bring about Taratanallos' submission."

Iselin nodded. "Any other sentiments would be surprising at this stage."

"He does not make reference to any of the less promising features of our embassy: the deaths of Aladar and Ribauldequin, certain financial irregularities—" Iselin winced "—and the less than reliable support of Dravadan."

"It may be that His Puissance is not aware of all of these factors."

"I notified him myself of the deaths, and he has settled new estates on Ribauldequin's father."

"And the—financial irregularities?" Iselin did not look directly at Oricien.

"We had agreed that I would say nothing at this stage, and I have not. You may yet earn back my trust."

Iselin crumbled a piece of bread on the plate before him. "I have worked with all diligence," he said. "I would hope that you have no reason to betray me?"

"'Betray'? That is a curious word, when what you are asking is that I conceal your criminal peculation."

Iselin held up a hand. "I did not mean to offend, and I recognise that you have every right to lay the facts before the King. I merely hope that my loyal service, before and during our embassy, has due weight in your mind."

Oricien stood up briskly. "And so it shall, Iselin. If our embassy is successful, I am sure there will be honour and glory enough for the most avid courtier."

Iselin looked up; Oricien, with sun behind him, was an unfathomable dark shadow. "And if we are not successful?"

"Then, Lord Iselin, I suspect we will both have greater matters to ponder."

CHAPTER FORTY-NINE

Malvazan was in the small retiring room at the back of the Bezant, vomiting into a bucket. Holding the bucket in silence was Farlankas, his fencing-master. Malvazan took the bucket and put it on the ground and wiped his mouth with a cloth. From outside came the sound of the crowd cheering at the antics of a pair of clowns; Malvazan grimaced.

"You must think me weak," said Malvazan, spitting out foul-tasting phlegm into the bucket.

"You are anxious," said Farlankas. "It is not the same. We have trained for five years to reach this point: I would be surprised if you were not agitated."

Malvazan sat down and gave a tentative smile. "I have killed men before; I was not like this then."

Farlankas shrugged. "Death is trivial. We all die. It is an unremarkable occurrence. But you only get a single chance to win the Garland. And for you, of course, the Garland offers treasures more important than your life."

Malvazan, his forearms resting on his thighs, looked up. "I did not know you realised that."

"Win today and all your friends, Aladar, Glastarko, Raguslan, will fete you in triumph around the Aspergantia. Kropiselko will let you marry his daughter. All the prizes that life offers will be available to you. I know how much is resting on this for you," said Farlankas with a quiet smile.

"And if I lose it all goes away."

"You will not lose. But if you did—you would find out which of them were your true friends."

Malvazan gave a harsh bark of laughter. "I already know that," he said with a wolfish grin.

Farlankas sat down on the bench next to him. "Have you thought how Rodizel will be feeling now?"

"No—I would not—it does not—"

"You know better than that, Malvazan," said Farlankas. "When you fight a man, you match not just his swordplay but his mind. I do not approve of the way you have been goading men into duels, but when you provoked and killed Flarijo, you manipulated him every bit as much as you outfought him."

"At the very least I have ensured that men take care not to affront me."

"So how do you imagine Rodizel is feeling now?"

Malvazan knitted his brow. Farlankas said: "I will make it easy for you. Like you, he is a second son, belonging to a house less illustrious than yours. He has no powerful friends or patrons and no glorious marriage beckoning. For him, even more than you, what happens today shapes the rest of his life."

"Maybe he too is throwing up in a bucket."

"We cannot rule it out," said Farlankas with a smile. "Come, it is time for the Bezant."

Malvazan rose from his seat. Farlankas said: "I have trained Garland winners before—three, in fact. You are the equal of any of them. Remember that."

Malvazan accepted the encomium with a nod and walked from the retiring room on feet he could barely feel.

At the gate of the Bezant Rodizel stood waiting, for by custom they made their entrance together. He looked slender, cool and composed: if he had been warming up, it did not show. Try as he might, Malvazan could not see the demeanour of a man who had been sick with nerves. As ever, Rodizel looked polished and assured, and no more anxious than if he were taking a day's lessons. This was intolerable! If Malvazan was in such a poor state, how dare Rodizel be so calm? It bordered on the insolent.

"Good afternoon, Malvazan," said Rodizel in a level voice, with a slight bow.

"Rodizel."

"I hope we shall have good sport this afternoon."

Sport? Was Rodizel really so naïve?

"I am sure we shall entertain the crowd richly enough," said Malvazan politely. "The Specchio do not like to be cheated of their pleasures."

"Are you ready?" said Rodizel with a half-smile. "We should not keep them waiting."

He truly is as calm as he looks. He has no fear of defeat of at all.

Malvazan fell into step alongside Rodizel. And why should he? He has beaten me the last three times we have fought.

The crowd rose to its feet as one to acclaim the two young heroes. In ten minutes, one would have his dreams in tatters; the other would be on the road to an eminence that every Dignity in the city would have to acknowledge.

The referee stepped towards them, his rich robe of red flapping behind in the gentle breeze, his feet scuffing softly on the sandy surface. He spoke so quietly that Malvazan and Rodizel had to lean forward to hear him.

"Gentlemen, I recognise that this is the greatest day in your lives to date; for some, the greatest day they ever have. Before you fight, be mindful of the traditions of the Specchio and the Garland." Malvazan fancied that a glance lingered on him an instant longer than necessary. "Consider not just victory and defeat, but the manner of your bearing. The Garland will go with you always, but so does your reputation. Do you understand me?"

"Yes, sir," said Rodizel.

"Malvazan?"

"Of course. I need no lecture."

The referee nodded. "Naturally not, Gravity."

He walked over to the centre of the Bezant, held his arms aloft for silence. "Gentlemen and ladies of the Specchio, before you stand the Grave Malvazan and the Grave Rodizel, about to contend, for your pleasure and their own, to see who is the finest young swordsman of Taratanallos. The winner receives no gold, no silver, no emerald or pearl: a garland made of sixty-four leaves must be his reward. But those sixty-four leaves carry about them an imperishable lustre that no man of sense would swap for any coin or jewel: for what those leaves convey cannot be bought. They denote a prime swordsman, yes, but something nobler even than that. The man who wins the Garland earns the esteem of the whole Specchio, and inherits a glorious tradition stretching back over two hundred years. He becomes a part of something finer than himself. It is a prize, quite literally, beyond price. Gentlemen and ladies, I give you Malvazan and Rodizel!"

The referee stepped aside from them so that they stood in isolation before the roaring crowd. Malvazan felt a roiling in the guts; he hoped he was not about to vomit again, or worse. He shifted a rapid side-glance to Rodizel, who appeared as impassive as a stone.

"Gentlemen—are you ready?"

"Yes."

"Yes."

"Then walk apart, and proceed at your pleasure. Proceed!"

The final of the Garland was underway.

Malvazan's blade made a soft hiss as he drew it from the sheath. Slowly, cautiously, he circled Rodizel at a distance. He caught Rodizel's gaze, the eyes the colour and inexpressiveness of wet slate. Neither seemed keen to make the first move. Rash, impulsive swordsmen did not normally make the final of the Garland.

Eventually Rodizel stepped in closer, essayed a thrust which Malvazan easily parried, enjoying the tension in his arm as he slid the blade aside. Malvazan skipped forward, tried a lunge of his own which Rodizel easily blocked. The crowd were rapt, silent; or perhaps Malvazan had screened them out.

Once again Rodizel stepped forward, suddenly launching into an attack crisp with feints, and Malvazan gave ground. His foot slipped a touch in the sand and Rodizel pounced on the mistake. Malvazan recovered, thrust into the gap left by Rodizel's assault. For an instant it looked as if he would catch Rodizel's side; but by the time his blade arrived, Rodizel was elsewhere, and Malvazan's thrust took the air.

For a period—a minute, five minutes, ten?—each examined the technique and patience of the other with a skill apparent only to the connoisseur. Those among the crowd with less refined sensibilities called out, demanding immediate drama. Malvazan realised that he had shown his best to Rodizel, and come nowhere near breaching his defence. His greatest advantage, left-handedness, was negated because they had fought so often: Rodizel ensured that Malvazan's unconventional lines of attack were never allowed to develop. *Unless he makes a mistake, I cannot touch him.*

Rodizel surged forward again, and Malvazan parried, gave back. He was all but overwhelmed by the speed and precision of the attack, and once more slipped, his right hand dropping to the ground to stop him overbalancing. Only by the width of the blade's edge did he avoid being touched as he scrambled to his feet. *Come on, Malvazan! You cannot let this whelp beat you!*

Once more they stepped apart. Rodizel was breathing heavily but he did not seem on the verge of exhaustion. One more attack like the last and Malvazan would be undone. There was an intentness in Rodizel's eyes which showed he knew it too. The situation had become desperate. He gave a harsh fierce grin in an attempt to daunt his opponent; Rodizel did not respond.

Again Rodizel surged forward. A sudden wild thought came into Malvazan's mind. He let his foot slip on the loose sand again, his right hand in the dirt once more. Rodizel sensed a trick and did not commit himself to the assault, and Malvazan regained his feet. Cautiously he moved forward, his blade out in his left hand, his right arm counterbalancing him. Rodizel shifted his weight to block the thrust and Malvazan pushed forward with his blade, then cast the sand he had picked up with his right hand at Rodizel's eyes. Rodizel blinked, reflexively threw his head to the side, and stumbled away. Malvazan pressed home, jumped inside Rodizel's sword-arm and tapped him on the chest with his blade.

"Tacto!" called the judges. The crowd, so quiet for so long, burst into a hubbub. The referee stepped between them.

"I cannot believe what I have just seen," he said.

"You saw 'tacto'," said Malvazan. "I am the champion."

He held out his hand to Rodizel, who looked at him in disgust. "I need only shake the hand of a gentleman."

The referee looked from one face to the other. "Such a thing has never been seen in a final before," he said. "Rodizel, you would have a case for Deplorable Conduct if you wished to appeal."

Rodizel thrust his blade back into it sheath. "I would not wish to be remembered as the man who won the Garland on a disqualification," he said. "If victory means so much to Malvazan, let him have it."

Squaring his shoulders, he walked from the Bezant. The referee shrugged. "I declare Malvazan Champion of the Garland of the Foils and present him with this laurel." He took the wreath from the purple cushion on which it sat and placed it on Malvazan's head.

"It is customary, at the presentation of the Garland, to make reference to the honour, skill and vigour of the year's champion. In these circumstances, I decline to do so. Malvazan, take your Garland and whatever satisfaction it brings you."

Malvazan set his jaw. Even in his victory—his unarguable and unassailable triumph—his praise was stinted. Was there to be no recognition of his efforts? He saluted the crowd, their boos still ringing in his ears, and walked over to where his associates were sitting. As he arrived at the fence, Glastarko shook his head. "You are not only a knave, Malvazan—which is a not uncommon condition—but a fool with it. Do you think this tainted triumph will carry any weight at all?"

"Can you not be happy for me?" said Malvazan, a hint of self-pity in his voice.

"In the circumstances, Malvazan, I really don't think I can."

Raguslan reached out and shook Malvazan's hand. "I cannot approve of your methods, Malvazan," he said, "but I cannot deny their effectiveness."

Sulinka gave him an icy nod. "You are a very capable, very dangerous young man," she said. "I suspect you will regard that as a compliment."

Malvazan responded with a smile equally cold. "And I suspect, madam, that you intended it as one."

He bowed and walked over to where Kropiselko and his family were sitting. Monichoë was watching him, her eyes peering out from behind her veil with an inscrutable expression. Kropiselko inclined his head with a nod of precisely calculated formality, an expression clearly lacking in cordiality on his face.

"I congratulate you on your victory, Gravity," he said. "I hope it brings you joy."

"That remains to be seen, Dignity."

"I had intended to invite you to Hanglenook for supper tonight, either to savour your victory or condole your defeat. Indeed, there might have been matters of mutual interest for us to discuss. I realise now how graceless and selfish I was," he said. "At such times, families and breeding are what counts, and I am sure you will wish to dine instead at your own house and share your triumph with your own folk."

"I hope there will be other opportunities for me to wait upon you at Hanglenook, Dignity, and to discuss such matters as you see fit."

Kropiselko gave a chilly smile. "In all candour, Malvazan, I am not sure that there will be. Affairs crowd and press upon me, and all is changeable. If you will excuse us." He indicated to his wife and son with a twitch of his head. Monichoë remained in her seat, her eyes resting on Malvazan.

"Damoiselle—" he said.

"Come, daughter," said Kropiselko sharply. "We do not wish to be caught up in the press of the crowd."

"Yes, father." She got up from her seat, and eased her way along to the end of the row. She gave Malvazan one last heavy glance, and then wordlessly followed her father.

Malvazan sat down on the sand, his back leaning against the wall separating the crowd from the arena. Around him, the crowd filed out into the street. His own father had not even acknowledged his victory. At last the Bezant was empty, and he stood up, looking around at the scene of the triumph he had worked so long to achieve, and which now felt so bitter.

But the Bezant was not empty after all. There was the sound of a single round of applause. Malvazan looked around and saw Aladar.

"No doubt you, too, are planning to repudiate me."

"Your conduct is not calculated to increase your popularity in the city," said Aladar. "A man in my position cannot afford to be too closely associated with the sentiments you are likely to attract."

Malvazan looked at him through narrowed eyes.

"A period of retirement on your part is perhaps called for," continued Aladar. "Nonetheless, from my perspective the afternoon has not been unsatisfactory. A man known to be my ally has acquired—or should I say redoubled—a reputation for ruthlessness, sharp practice, duplicity. He has also, or so I should hope, learned something about when subtlety and indirection can be more effective than blatant malfeasance. Am I correct?"

"Yes, but—"

"Keep a soft voice for a while. That is my advice. In a few weeks' time, I shall be happy to renew our acquaintance. In the meanwhile, be assured of my regard, even if I am in no position to display it. The substance of our arrangement remains unaltered."

He rose from his seat and made for the exit. "Good afternoon to you, Malvazan."

Dusk was falling by the time Malvazan made his way home to Korfez. He had sat in the empty Bezant, brooding on the circumstances which seemed always to thwart his advance. He had won the Garland, an achievement which had been a springboard to respect and consequence for many among the Specchio. Yet when Malvazan won, he was reviled and jeered. They would not love him, it seemed; all that remained was that they be made to fear him. Aladar alone recognised that—but Aladar himself had the makings of an unreliable ally. He snorted at a sudden amusement: Aladar was doing nothing that he would not himself, picking his way through the swamps of advancement, trusting his weight to those tussocks which would bear his weight.

"Where have you been, Malvazan?" cried Flinteska as he walked into the dining room. She enfolded him in a smothering embrace.

"I thought to savour my victory awhile," said Malvazan with a sardonic smile.

Crostadan sat at the head of the table. "I find your levity offensive in the circumstances, Malvazan."

Malvazan sat down heavily, nodded to Dravadan and Rullia. "And I find your sour carping offensive, father. I am the first of our house to win the Garland in a century, and this is the welcome I get."

"Malvazan—" said Dravadan in a warning tone.

"No, let me speak," said Malvazan. "I am the only member of House Umbinzia who seeks to raise our station. Now, because I employ unorthodox methods, I am treated as if I carry the plague, and by my own family."

Crostadan straightened the utensils by his plate and spoke in a careful tone. "Tonight I must go to House Carmaggio, and speak in soft tones of apology to my old friend Ostazar. I must beg pardon for the way my son cheated his of the Garland. Can you imagine my humiliation?"

Malvazan shrugged. "If it irks you so much, do not go. Let events speak for themselves."

The colour rose in Crostadan's cheeks. "My duty is clear. You, too, should apologise to Rodizel, in person—or in writing if you are not man enough to do so."

Malvazan stood up, thrust his face into Crostadan's. "What little advantage I have gained from the situation would be dissipated were I to apologise. A gentleman acts as he sees fit, and lives with the consequences. And as to who is a man—how many duels have you fought, father?"

Crostadan stood up. "Sit down, boy. If you think that is the measure of a man, you have much more growing up to do than I thought."

Flinteska said: "Come, can we not be reconciled? Let us take a meal of amity together."

Crostadan walked to the door. "I find that I am no longer hungry. I am taking myself to Ostazar's: you may continue without me."

He shut the door behind him with a firmness which shook the frame. Flinteska said in a bright voice: "Malvazan, there is parsnip soup left—surely you will take a bowl."

Malvazan said nothing and wordlessly accepted the portion his mother had ladled out.

Rullia said: "Malvazan, we have all had a long and draining day. Dravadan and I are taking a picnic up to the cliffs tomorrow, to watch the ships in the bay. We should love it were you to join us, would we not, husband?"

Dravadan hesitated for a moment, then grinned. "Yes, Malvazan, come with us. It will do us all good to get out of the city for a while. I would like to hear all about your victory."

Malvazan considered the day which had unfolded. There was unlikely to be much amusement for him inside the walls for a while. "Very well. When do we leave?"

CHAPTER FIFTY

The mystery of who had ransacked his rooms, which had never featured heavily in anyone else's thoughts, was soon driven from Todarko's mind as well. Dravadan's attention was turned entirely to Lord Oricien's forthcoming address to the Specchio. On the response to this speech would hang not only the fate of Taratanallos, but the influence enjoyed by the various members of the Masavory. Defeat for Oricien would mean political eclipse of uncertain duration for Dravadan and those who overtly supported him—most particularly Dravadan's faithful lapdog House Vaggio.

Dravadan was fretful and snappish in the week leading up to Oricien's address. While he had been promised the votes of more than half the Specchio, Dravadan's intelligence told him the Gammerling party were in the same position: some members of the Specchio were clearly backing both sides. Since this was the only way to ensure finishing with the winners, this approach seemed rational to Todarko, but Dravadan's view was rather different.

Many was the conference held at Korfez, but Linnalitha kept herself well out of sight. Todarko had not knowingly seen her since he had sent her the sonnet; while he thought he recognised her walk under Hood and Veil in the street on occasion, he could not be certain, and felt that too close a scrutiny would be indelicate. He had to accept that Linnalitha remained forever out of reach; Dravadan had promised him an advantageous marriage once the Emmen alliance was sealed so, regardless of his personal liking for Oricien, he was conscious that his success would not be an unmixed blessing.

So it was that one sunny morning, Todarko sat in Dravadan's parlour in his Purpureals, the rich robes worn by the Specchio on grand occasions of state.

"Hurry, Todarko," said Raguslan briskly. "We do not wish to be late!"

"I am finishing my breakfast," said Todarko. "Lord Oricien's oratory may be protracted, and I do not wish to be distracted by hunger pangs."

Dravadan looked over from where Palankijo was giving his Purpureals a final brush. "Now is not the time for your gluttony, Todarko. We must all put our backs to the plough today."

"They will not begin without us," said Todarko. "And a small manchet loaf hardly constitutes gluttony."

"Enough," said Dravadan. "You fail to appreciate the gravity of the day's events."

Todarko ate a last mouthful of bread and stood up from the table. There would be no winning the argument, and if Dravadan wished to transact the most important business of his life on an empty stomach, that was his own affair.

A clear peal of laughter interrupted the event. Linnalitha had entered the room, her plain white dress in contrast to the finery around her. "It looks like a plum tree in here!" she said. "I have never seen so many Purpureals in the room."

Todarko's heart and stomach skittered wildly. He wished he had not had breakfast after all. He looked around, tried to catch her eye before looking away again. Linnalitha was not looking at him; for some reason she was talking to Zanijel, not a pastime Todarko felt would bring her much pleasure. He was not sure whether custom impelled him to approach or not. Before he could decide, he found himself standing next to her. How had he got here?

"Good morning, madam," he said in as level a tone as he could manage.

Linnalitha turned her head away from Zanijel. "Todarko, good morning! I am so pleased you are on hand to support my husband on such an important day."

Todarko thought to see a faint flush beneath her freckles.

"I—I" Some poet I am. I cannot even think what to say beyond "Good morning." "I trust the day finds you well, madam." What a stroke of inspiration that was!

"Very well, thank you, sir."

"Um—the sun is set fair for the day." She cannot take exception to that!

"It so often is, in the summer."

"Yes, indeed, madam." Hmm. "I trust you are well." What a buffoon!

Linnalitha's polite smile slipped into a grin. "You think to catch me out with your questioning! I am very well, just as I was a moment ago."

Todarko felt his tension evaporate. "Forgive me. I am overawed by the weight of the occasion. It is not every day I must chase the moths from my Purpureals."

She leaned forward and said: "I believe your uncle has been less successful where the moths are concerned. You may care to look at his rump later."

"I think not. Most things are grist to the poet's mill, but I draw the line at my uncle's fundament."

They had eased away from Zanijel, but now he stepped forward again. "If you have finished your twitterings, cousin, Dravadan is ready to depart. Lord Oricien's party awaits outside."

Linnalitha touched Todarko's elbow. "I wish you well for the day, Todarko."

Todarko inclined his head. "And I you, my lady. For the day and beyond."

For one last moment their gaze met and held. Her blue-grey eyes swam behind a sheen of moisture. "Adieu," she mouthed as she turned away.

Todarko set his mouth and fell into step with his cousin as they marched out of Korfez into the bright sunshine of the Hour of Petitions.

Outside, insipid among the empurpled Specchio and the harsh black uniforms of the Consiglio, the two Emmen ambassadors sat astride their gallumphers. Lord Oricien wore a white cloak fastened with an amethyst brooch over a light grey silk shirt and brown breeches. For an ambassador the effect was almost flagrantly restrained — the result of long deliberations with Dravadan over how best to woo the Specchio. Lord Iselin's attire was even more sober.

The two ambassadors were surrounded by a guard of the Consiglio. Their role was dual: to honour the visiting dignitaries, but also to prevent a repeat of what had happened at the Ostentatory. Todarko could not know whether Oricien shared his suspicions as to the Consiglio's role in that event, but it was hard to imagine a diplomatic way in which Oricien could have refused the escort on these grounds. *Forgive me, sirs, but I prefer to travel unaccompanied in case you carry out the assassination you are meant to prevent.* No, Oricien had no real choice in the matter. If he had any qualms as he milled within arm's length of his potential murderers, he did not show it. This, no doubt, was one of the skills an ambassador needed to master early in his career.

After only a brief interlude the party formed itself up into the order in which it would proceed to the Masavory. At the front were two mounted Consigli — Todarko noted that Vislanko was nowhere to be seen — and behind them, Oricien and Dravadan. Lord Iselin and Raguslan made up the next rank and then, rather to Todarko's surprise, himself and Zanijel. *Sulinka would be gratified to see House Vaggio so prominent on this auspicious day,* he thought with a wry grin.

The party made a stately progress down the Archgate. Crowds were discouraged from such a respectable area, but the occasional wellwisher called out a message, and on each great house family members stood on the portico. Todarko waved at Nelanka as they passed Tappinetto, to receive a scowl from Zanijel. Zanijel leaned across on his gallumpher and said in a conversational tone: "Soon, cousin, soon."

At the bottom of the Archgate they turned right into the less elevated, although still respectable, Ropemakers' Street. There were the beginnings of a cheering crowd here, and the dark clothes of the Consiglio were more in evidence. The tall narrow buildings with their tiled red roofs blocked out the early morning sun and Todarko, even under his Purpureals, felt a rapid chill. The slarinto swept up off the sea to cause cloaks and robes to flap.

At last they arrived at the Silvermarket, where men and women of all degrees jostled for prominence, deterred from approaching too closely by the warning glances of the Consigli. The sun once more came into view, and Todarko luxuriated in the warmth on his face. The Fountain of Erlando, which worked only sporadically, had been restored to order and the gentle plashing meshed with the hubbub of voices to create an air of expectancy. In front of them, taking up an entire side of the square, stood the Masavory building: a slanted roof held up by the marble pillars which had always reminded Todarko of the fangs of a wild beast. Set into the lintel above the double doorway was a stone graven with the legend:

<blockquote>
THE MASAVORY
OF
TARATANALLOS
The Last Free City
</blockquote>

There were no other members of the Specchio outside the building: clearly they were a touch late; no doubt Dravadan would blame him for lingering overlong at the breakfast table; although by the time Todarko saw Dravadan again, much more important matters would have been resolved, for good or ill. In neither contingency did it seem likely that Todarko's breakfast would be at the forefront of Dravadan's mind.

A flight of some twenty wide shallow steps led up to the entrance to the Masavory. Consigli appeared as if from nowhere and led the gallumphers away once the party had dismounted. Dravadan led Oricien up the steps, the others following in close order behind. Oricien bowed to the graven tablet at the top of the stairs—he had been well coached—and they proceeded from the bright sunlight outside into the cavernous gloom of the Masavory's lobby. Arches led off in several directions: one to the administrative offices of the Consiglio—these took up most of the building—one to the private rooms used by the Masavory themselves, and the final arch led to the Lumenario, the great chamber where the Specchio met to debate the important business of the city. One member of the Masavory, Todarko realised with a grimace, would not be going through that arch: Bartielko would be immured somewhere in the building below the Consiglio's offices. He had paid little attention to the Gammerling party: he did not even know who would be leading them today.

Escorted by the two remaining Consigli, Oricien's party made its way into the Lumenario. Everyone had taken his seat, and the gathering, all in their Purpureals, reminded Todarko of nothing more than a flock of gaudily plumed birds, each chirping alongside his neighbour. By this reckoning, Lord Oricien must have been the cat, for all noise ceased immediately, and the bedizened flock turned to face him with a wary attention.

Todarko mounted the steps to the back of the Lumenario: as one of the younger members of the Specchio, it would have been inappropriately thrusting for him to sit at the front. He looked around for Bodazar but in the cavernous gloom of the chamber he could not pick him out. His vicinity did include Zanijel and—Todarko noticed with a pang of disquiet—Ivanka's brother Ivaijlo, a man by no means clear of suspicion of arranging his beating in the Chale. A few feet away lounged his poetic rival Hazilan, his boots on the back of the seat before him, affecting an air of nonchalant disdain.

From the front of the Lumenario came the rap of a gavel. "First citizens of the Republic, I beg your attention!" called the President, Norielko. Todarko had always thought him the perfect man for the office: tall, slender, with a fine head of immaculate grey hair; impeccably groomed, impeccably spoken, of impeccable family; and an utter nonentity, with neither intelligence nor opinion of his own. He offended no-one, while radiating the grave dignity of the Masavory. If he ever felt any frustration as to the powerlessness of his ceremonial role, he was far too well-bred to show it.

"The Hour of Fiscal Scrutiny is upon us," he continued in a rich voice. "These are strange times in our great city, and I am gratified this morning to welcome a guest from afar: Lord Oricien of Croad, the personal ambassador of King Enguerran of Emmen. He will share his counsel and, if I am not mistaken, put forward proposals designed to secure the peace and prosperity of the city. You will know, sir—" he bowed as he directed his address to Oricien "—that in the city we do not use titles such as lord and lady. Here, we are all citizens, and each contributes according to his fortune and capacity. Nonetheless, my lord, we welcome you to this special session of the Specchio. You have our full attention."

Norielko sat down to a barely perceptible muttering. Seated next to him on the podium was Verbujezar, the Grand Master of the Consiglio, who gave him a nod of approval. By the nuanced etiquette of the Masavory, Norielko's introduction had been a direct denunciation of the lordly ways of the Emmenrule. Todarko could see Dravadan scowling in the front row. It was unlikely that Norielko had formulated an independent or controversial opinion of his own: he had clearly been worked on by the Consiglio.

Oricien rose from his seat and walked with calm grace to the lectern at the front of the Lumenario.

"Gentlemen of the Specchio, President of the Masavory; I thank you for your indulgence in listening to the views of a kingdom far to the north. These are troubled times, and none may think to hide. Today I will give stern counsel, but it is the counsel of one who would be your friend."

Oricien's voice was quiet, unforced, yet in the rapt auditorium every word was as clear and sharp as a diamond. Minimal gestures accompanied his speech; he relied for effect on understatement alone.

"Over the past years, events have taken a turn to the north which you may think do not affect the 'last free city'. Such a view is insular, parochial, misguided. The peninsula on which your city stands belongs to the Duchy of Aylissia, whether you will it or no. Your wonderful natural harbour, the riches of your city, are a jewel to tempt a magpie. None covets it as earnestly, perhaps, as Duke Lothar. He wishes not only the dominion of your great city for himself, but to spite his brother: the King at Vasi Vasar."

"You tell us what we already know!" came a grumbled voice from the middle of the room.

"Silence!" called Verbujezar in a perfunctory tone.

Oricien held up his hand in acknowledgement. "If my words seem a statement of the obvious," he said, "I am pleased. There is much obfuscation, much indirection. It is well that we concentrate on the simple facts before us: they tell us much. My father, Lord Thaume, has been dead these past ten years, but he instilled in me a respect for the straightforward approach. We all agree, it seems, that Duke Lothar casts an envious eye on this great city. He lacks the strength to take it; he lacks also the guile. You feel, perhaps, that you need not fear this ragamuffin lord with his gallumphers and his tournaments and his women and his wine?"

He paused to take the temper of the room. Todarko, schooled in rhetoric, admired his technique.

"You do not, I suspect, view his brother with the same disdain. I will not speak of Ingomer's aggressions towards the Emmenrule, for you will say they are not your quarrel. So they are not, although they show the martial tenor of the man, and his lust for acquisition. He knows—for how could he not—his brother's plans for you. He will wish at all costs to prevent Lothar coming into possession of the city. He will also think of the revenues of the city—revenues largely attributable to yourselves—with which he might arm himself for his assault on the Emmenrule; and he will think of the safe harbour in which he might moor his fleet. He sees all this, and he makes his plan. There are those among you who think an alliance with such a king meet and proper."

"Why should we not?" came a cry from the floor, supported by stamping on the floor from one corner of the room. "How is he worse than Enguerran?"

Oricien nodded and raised a didactic finger. "How indeed is he worse than my master? Here we reach the nub of our debate. I could sit down at this point and hand the floor to the High Viator Udenko if I chose." He nodded at Udenko who smiled and ducked his head in return.

"Every man and woman of Mondia Follows the Way," continued Oricien. "Each does so as he sees fit, with the guidance of the Viators always to hand if required. In Gammerling they are assiduous. None Follows the Way with greater fervour. How could it be otherwise? The Consorts make their home at Vasi Vasar, the fleshly avatars of Hissen and Animaxia. Their word is unchallengeable where Doctrine is concerned. King Ingomer is fortunate that such piety and wisdom reside at his court."

A low muttering ran around the room. Only the nubbin of Gammerling adherents in the corner remained aloof.

"Of course, there are those who choose to Follow a slightly different Way —or perhaps the same Way via a different road: I confess I am a poor theologian. I know that in my own city, Croad, many among my people follow the so-called Wheel, which the Consorts denounce as heresy. King Enguerran is an easy master where conscience is concerned. He believes that faith cannot be compelled, and allows each to choose his own path, so long as they acknowledge his sovereignty. This touches most closely on the folk of Taratanallos. Your beliefs are scarcely as radical as the Wheel: you have your own Viators, and all allow the pre-eminence of their spiritual guidance. Yet the Consorts—the Consorts who sit at Ingomer's side at Vasi Vasar—the Consorts denounce your beliefs. They have a term reserved specifically for your ways: the Peninsular Heresy. Gentlemen, I look around this chamber at your assembled might and wisdom: I see men, honourable men who seek the best for their city. But I do not see heretics. If any man here sees a heretic, kindly point him out to me, that I might be corrected."

There was a pause, which Oricien used to pour water from a carafe. No heretics were identified in the time it took Oricien to drink off his cup, and after a decent interval he continued.

"His Puissance King Enguerran has studied the situation in Taratanallos at length. He has long been the victim of Ingomer's plots and ambitions. The thought of your fair city falling into his hands distresses him not simply as an injustice, but a threat to the peace and security of the Emmenrule. For these reasons he does not wish to sit back and allow this calamity to occur. His proposal is therefore simple and straightforward, for like me he is a simple and straightforward man.

"King Enguerran offers to take the city of Taratanallos under his personal protection. He will guarantee with the full force of Emmen arms that should it suffer attack from Ingomer, Lothar or any other aggressor, he will view it as he would an attack on Emmen territory, and respond with the full force at his command. He guarantees equally full freedom of worship for all within the city. Those traditions to which you currently cleave will remain inviolate, and the final authority on spiritual matters pertaining to Taratanallos will lie with the High Viator."

"And what does he demand in return?" came a raucous voice from the floor.

Oricien permitted himself a smile at the interruption. "His Puissance's terms are light. He requires only a trade duty of one quarter of a percent on the city's monopolies—which the Masavory may make over from its own percentage, or levy an additional impost—and a pro forma acknowledgement by the Specchio of his overlordship of the city. If one must submit to a foreign king, better that it should be one far away to the north, as I am sure you realise. His Puissance has no desire to rule the city in person, simply to prevent it falling into the wrong hands—and we all, I think, know whose hands those are."

There was uproar in the chamber as the substance of Oricien's proposals sank in. "Treason!" "Treason!" "—should have stabbed him when we had the chance—" were among the cries Todarko could make out. As he looked around the chamber, though, he felt they were not spread equally across the room.

Oricien stood silently at the lectern, letting the waves of sound break over him. Eventually a calm of sorts—a feverish sort of calm, waiting to break and dash itself against the walls—fell again.

"Gentlemen," he said, now in a rather louder voice than he had employed heretofore, "I recognise that these proposals go against the way you have become accustomed to view yourselves. How can the last free city submit to any man? I say to you, that now is the time for statesmen, not demagogues. For half a millennium you have stood alone: that time is now gone. If you choose to spurn the offers of friendship before you, your independence will not thereby be preserved. All that will happen is that, rather than honourable marriage, your chastity will fall to rape. King Enguerran implores you to choose your friends, rather than have them choose you. My master's terms are easy, his yoke light. Gentlemen, I thank you for your attention."

He stepped away from the lectern, bowed, and returned to his seat. Dravadan ostentatiously rose to clap him on the back.

Todarko began to applaud, realised he was the only one. Everyone else, transfixed by the stark message—and the implied ultimatum—in Oricien's words, was stunned into silence. Only Todarko, the poet, stood aloof from the message and admired the way in which it had been crafted.

CHAPTER FIFTY-ONE

Norielko rose and silenced the Lumenario with a gesture. "Lord Oricien has been good enough to outline the proposals put forward by His Puissance, King Enguerran. I sense from the tenor of the room that support is not unanimous. Does any of you wish to speak before we proceed to a vote?"

Dravadan rose with a sinuous gesture. "Forgive me, sir, for hogging the floor. I would like briefly to register my commendation for Lord Oricien's address, if I may."

Norielko turned to look at Verbujezar, who gave a faint shrug. "Very well," said Norielko. "I see no reason why not."

Dravadan smoothed his robes and turned to face the body of the hall behind him. "For time long beyond memory," he said, "the city of Taratanallos has known no master. Protected by our walls and the sea, our merchants have ranged the whole of Mondia, building fortunes which enriched the whole city. These have been great days: no city has ever been richer, or mightier.

"It gives me no pleasure, my friends, to say that those days are gone. If the army of King Ingomer came and sat before our walls tomorrow, could we resist it? Maybe for a week, a month, a season; but in the end, the Specchio would be forced to make terms, or see the city sacked. Today we have the chance to make terms before desperation forces them upon us. Our good friend and ally King Enguerran offers us terms that do not humiliate, but rather display the respect in which he holds us. The Masavory and the Specchio will still rule the city, still regulate the monopolies which are our lifeblood. We would know, however, that we have a powerful friend to the north, a friend who guarantees, underwrites and preserves our freedom. The last free city we are, and the last free city we shall remain. There is no more to be said, gentlemen, other than to proceed to an immediate acclamation of these generous and wise proposals."

Dravadan paused and waited for applause, which was not forthcoming. Nonetheless Dravadan gave a modest nod as if acknowledging a rapturous reception, and sat down with a heavy dignity.

Raguslan rose from his own seat a row back. "I would like to add my—"

"No, Raguslan," interrupted Norielko. "Lord Oricien has already set forth his programme and Dravadan has endorsed it. Any further reiteration is redundant. Does anyone wish to articulate a different viewpoint?"

A flush spread up Raguslan's face and across his pate. Another humiliation for House Vaggio and Raguslan, thought Todarko. He looked across at where the Gammerling party were congregated. After some whispering, a short man with scanty black hair arose. Norielko said: "Welcome, Predonko. The Specchio awaits your views with interest."

"Thank you, sir. I am unaccustomed to speaking before this august body," he said in a soft voice which barely carried to Todarko at the back of the hall. "The sentiments I am about to outline would come more naturally from Bartielko, who regrettably is elsewhere in the Masavory, and cannot share his wisdom today."

There was a titter from the Emmen supporters.

"I confess I was intrigued by King Enguerran's choice of ambassador," continued Predonko, his eyes on the floor. "The boon from His Puissance is essentially that he will guarantee the security of our city against any aggressor. Curious, then that he chose Lord Oricien of Croad to deliver the message: a man who less than ten years ago saw his city taken and destroyed by a vagabond raider."

There was a howl of contemptuous laughter from around Predonko, cries of "Shame!" from Dravadan and his neighbours. "When Lord Oricien was menaced by the Dog of the North, not only did he prove unable to save his city, but his King did not lift a finger to save him. And who was that King? Enguerran."

Predonko had shaken off any nerves he might have felt. His delivery could now be characterised as ranting, and his arms sawed the air. "If we wish Taratanallos to suffer the fate of Croad, to be taken by an adventurer like Ion Issio and then destroyed, then let us by all means make homage to King Enguerran! Indeed, let us vote on the matter this minute! I insist!"

His words were nearly drowned out by the clamour in the Lumenario. Once more, though, Predonko declaimed: "I insist! I insist!" He sat down, his arms folded and beaming in triumph.

Dravadan caught Norielko's eye. "If I may..." Norielko nodded.

"Predonko has amused us all with his bumbling caricature of reasoned argument," he said. "I am as jocular as the next man, at the right time—no definition of which could be expanded to include the current moment. We need not rake over ancient history to know that the fall of Croad was a freak event, a lightning raid by a fierce raider which King Enguerran, far away over the mountains, could never have relieved. I need also not point out, that the very raider who so piqued him, the so-called Dog of the North, is now a prisoner in Enguerran's dungeons. His Puissance has a long memory, and few thwart him for long. We may be assured that no-one will besiege Taratanallos by surprise. Predonko wishes an immediate vote: so, sir, do I."

Dravadan sat down. It had been a spirited response, Todarko had to admit. That great knot of Purpureal cloaks in the middle of the room—over half—did not look to have been swayed by Predonko's clever innuendo.

Norielko rose once more. "There seems an appetite to vote on this matter now. I wonder if any others wish to speak before we lay a formal motion."

The door to the Lumenario swung open. Despite the noiselessly oiled hinges, all attention was instantly drawn to it. An unsteady figure limped into the room in torn black breeches, a shirt which had once been white. At his side, cool and composed in black, was Vislanko.

"Forgive me, gentlemen," said the figure in a cracked voice. There was a gasp as Todarko and the rest of the Specchio realised it was Bartielko. "I appear among you on this day improperly attired. The wardrobe of my current quarters is strongly deficient." What might have been a smile played for a second across his lips.

"I am a member of the Specchio, and not only have I been found guilty of no crime, I have not formally been charged with one. I have listened to the debate from outside the Lumenario, and have certain observations of my own I wish to put."

"Very well," said Norielko. "There is no bar to your participation."

"I object most strongly!" called Dravadan.

"Yes," said Norielko. "I am sure you do. Your objection is without merit. Bartielko, please continue."

"Lord Oricien has put forward the views of his master far away to the north. Some among you feel, no doubt, that such a distant overlord can only be a blessing. Am I correct?"

There were nods and murmurs of approval around the room.

Bartielko paused and leaned on Vislanko's arm, to the Consigli's seeming displeasure.

"This view is profoundly misconceived. All agreed that, for better or worse, King Ingomer is a vigorous and decisive man who takes the responsibilities of his office seriously. Can you imagine his response if he learns that Taratanallos, a major port and far to the south of Vasi Vasar, is owned by Enguerran? He will not countenance it: he will turn his whole force to wresting Enguerran's prize away. He cannot, with any regard to the security of the realm, allow Enguerran a base in the south.

"My Lord Oricien, I am sure you would acknowledge that war between Emmen and Gammerling is inevitable. You have painted Ingomer as a rapacious aggressor, intent on devouring all the territory in his grasp. It will not surprise you to know that Ingomer holds a similar view of your master."

Oricien contented himself with a wry smile.

"War, I say, is inevitable. At some point, surely no more than two years hence, the forces of the Emmenrule and Gammerling will face each other: two mighty foes, proud and strong. Many lives will be destroyed, and not just among the soldiers. Can any among you deny this?"

Silence lay across the hall, like a blanket containing a fire raging underneath.

"Gentlemen," said Bartielko. "If we accede to Lord Oricien's proposals and become King Enguerran's subjects, I say to you that the battle we all fear will be fought on the Peninsula of Taratanallos. If you want the two greatest armies in the history of Mondia fighting on our doorstep, over our allegiance, by all means vote in favour of Oricien's proposals."

Dravadan sprang from his seat: "Fol-de-rol! Alarmist nonsense! If war is inevitable, they will fight over us whichever side we choose! Or if we choose no side at all. Do not listen to this treacherous citizen, in rags because of his great crimes! Let us choose with care, and choose the mightier party!"

"Sit down, Dravadan," said Norielko in a heavy voice. "You have spoken to excess today."

"Norielko!" called Predonko. "Kindly allow the sage Dravadan to speak, for there is a question I would ask him."

Norielko allowed him the floor with a brief nod.

"Dravadan," said Predonko. "If, as you say, Enguerran will fight on the Peninsula if we ally ourselves with Ingomer: how will he deploy his troops, when Ingomer then controls the only suitable port? Perhaps he will summon a thaumaturge to convey them via the Unseen Dimensions? For it seems to me that magic is his only option, unless you can clarify my thinking."

"I—Enguerran is not so easily denied," said Dravadan in a faltering voice. "We cannot be deceived by these scoundrels' rhetoric!"

"Perhaps the Specchio may wish to determine who is the scoundrel," said Bartielko in a mild voice.

There was a stamping on the wooden boards, not simply among Bartielko's supporters. Fully three-quarters of the room stood out of their feet, pounding on the floor in time with their chant: "In-go-mer! In-go-mer! In-go-mer!"

Dravadan staggered back to his feet. "I withdraw the motion," he said. "We need take no formal vote today."

Norielko rapped his gavel down on the table. "I declare this special session of the Specchio closed. Lord Oricien, I thank you for the opportunity to debate His Puissance's proposals today. I trust you have sufficient information to report to your master."

Oricien gave a tight-lipped smile. His face bloodless, he said: "I thank you, sir. If my master wishes to put further proposals I will beg once more for the indulgence of this house."

He rose, bowed, and strode from the room, Dravadan at his heel struggling to keep up as the jeers of the Specchio rained down upon him.

CHAPTER FIFTY-TWO

The purple throng jostled to leave the Lumenario, hooting and catcalling in their desire to attend Dravadan's humiliation—for there seemed no other word to describe it. At the back of the hall, Todarko had no very ready exit and contented himself with shuffling behind some of the more elderly members of the Specchio.

He entered the cavernous hallway where those who liked to attend the Masavory armed were collecting their swords from the stewards, Dravadan among them. Dravadan caught sight of him and bellowed: "Todarko! We reconvene at Korfez immediately!"

Todarko winced at the thought of it. The morning had been a disaster by any standards, and tempers would not improve from analysis of the situation in the heat of rage. Oricien gave Todarko a subdued smile.

At the top of the steps, looking out across the plaza, stood Dravadan, Raguslan, Todarko and Zanijel in their Purpureals, the more restrained Oricien and Iselin alongside them. There was a crowd in the square, buzzing for news of the debate. A man standing by the fountain pointed at Dravadan, made a remark to his friend, and flipped his fingers into a derisive gesture. Todarko softly shook his head. It did not take long for the crowd to read the mood, it seemed: Dravadan's reverse was known before it could be voiced.

Todarko felt a pressure on his shoulder. "You may wish to decamp, Gravity." It was Vislanko. "Your present position may very shortly become uncomfortable."

Todarko shook him off. "Your constant threats and innuendo bore me, Vislanko. Either act, or leave me in peace."

Vislanko gave a bland smile. "As you will—although you should thank me for my advice."

Todarko turned away. There was a noise coming from the mob around the fountain—laughter. Fingers were held aloft from the forehead. Some of the men pointed again at Dravadan.

Todarko squinted again the strong sunlight. He felt his stomach tightened and looked around for Vislanko, now nowhere to be seen.

"Who are these insolent wretches?" demanded Dravadan. "Let us see if they are so free with their opinions to my face."

He dashed down the steps, Raguslan flapping in his wake. Todarko followed at a more sedate pace.

From the crowd came a single voice: "Dravadan wears horns!"

Todarko edged along at the back of the group. Whatever was happening here, he did not feel comfortable. He shook his head—what was there to worry about? He had not cuckolded Dravadan, and he was certain no-one else had. The horns could have nothing to do with him.

A young man sitting on the lip of the fountain caught sight of Todarko, called out: "The crow! The crow that flies in heaven's sweetest air!"

Todarko felt the blood drain from his face. While he would normally relish hearing his verse recited in the public square, this was not one of those occasions—not when the verse in question was his sonnet to Linnalitha.

Dravadan shouldered his way towards the fountain. On the railing, Todarko could see a single sheet of paper affixed. He did not need to stand as close as Dravadan to know the text:

For Madam L—a, of House U—a

In loving thee thou know'st I am forsworn,
That every word doth almost tell my name
And place my merit in the eye of scorn.
How sweet and lovely dost thou make the shame!

Let not my love be called idolatory,
A crow that flies in heaven's sweetest air.
Thy love is better than high birth to me
Past cure I am, now reason is past care.

As from my soul which in thy breast doth lie
Like him that travels I return again,
Happy to have thy love, happy to die,
And death once dead, there's no more dying then.

I love not less, though less the show appear
For truth proves thievish for a prize so dear.

The crowd parted to let Dravadan through. Todarko inched forward, for there was one thing he wished to check. He saw the mis-spelled word "idolatory". He had been wrong: something had been stolen from his chambers after all—the first copy of the poem he had written out and sent to Linnalitha. How—? Now was not the time to debate the question. Dravadan might not know the poem's content, but it would not take him long to work it out.

Todarko slipped his cloak from his shoulders, flung it to the ground, slipped back into the gathering crowd. Slowly he eased away, as far away from Dravadan as he could. Everyone had warned him of Dravadan's reaction should he ever suspect inappropriate attentions.

Dravadan reached out, pulled the paper from the railings and compressed it in his hand. "Todarko!" he bellowed.

Todarko tried to remain inconspicuous, but breeches of bright purple worked against this.

"WHERE—IS—TODARKO! Prepare to die! And Linnalitha: I will chop her into messes!"

Todarko turned his back to the crowd and ran from the plaza as fast as his feet would carry him. There could be no concealment, and no brazening the matter out. Flight was the only option.

He left the plaza, dashed along Ropemakers' Street until the point it joined the Archgate. Panting, he looked back over his shoulder to see if there was pursuit. He saw only a single figure: Zanijel, a man eager to please Dravadan and with scores of his own to settle. Where were the others? The sensible course was to duck into the Chale, where none of his likely pursuers would know the winding alleys as well as he. Slowing, he made to duck into Tanners' Street and head back in that direction. Linnalitha! He could not just disappear now. One way or another, he had made the situation—now he would have to resolve it.

With a sigh, he ducked his head and sprinted up the hill for Korfez. Behind him he could hear Zanijel lowing; he did not spare the effort to turn. He felt his legs leadening, his breath coming in ever more laboured gasps. He grimaced: it was unlikely that Zanijel was in any better condition.

He dashed past Tappinetto with scarcely a sideways glance. Korfez was no more than a hundred yards ahead—but a hundred yards uphill. He could feel the sweat trickling down, into his eyes, his ears, down his neck. He risked a look over his shoulder: Zanijel was floundering even further back. Then he saw something which chilled his sweat: at least three men on gallumphers, charging up the hill. That was where the others had been! One of them blew a horn; Palankijo issued forth through the portico.

"Todarko?" he said with a quizzical shake of his head.

"There has been an outrage," panted Todarko. "Let me in immediately! I must see Madam Linnalitha!"

Palankijo drew back. "I will fetch her," said Palankijo.

"There is no time—I will find her myself."

"Is it—Dravadan?"

Todarko shook his head to clear the sweat from his eyes, spraying fine droplets into the air. "Yes, Palankijo—yes it is."

"Up the main stairway, the second door on the left."

"Thank you," gasped Todarko, bounding up the stairs before he had finished. The forthcoming interview was not one he had envisaged, certainly not in this fashion.

As he turned at the top of the stair he skidded on the rattovar rug running down the hallway before finding himself in front of Linnalitha's door.

"Linna! Open up! It's Todarko!"

There were sounds of movement behind the heavy door. "Hurry!" he roared as he banged against the unyielding wood.

The door swung open into the room, and Linnalitha, her hair pinned up and a soft white dress caressing her figure, stood before him.

"What—?"

Todarko stepped inside the room and Linnalitha was forced to jump aside.

"I'm sorry—this is no time for courtesy. We have to leave—now!"

Linnalitha sat down and knitted her brows. "You are most certainly drunk. You should not be here at all, least of all in this bawling humour."

"My sonnet is posted in the plaza. Your husband has read it and understands its import. Do you still wish to debate?"

The blood drained from Linnalitha's face until only her freckles stood out against the white skin. "How—?"

"Now is not the time," said Todarko in a low flat voice. "Dravadan is coming here to kill you—and me, if he finds me."

Linnalitha stood from her seat with a gesture at once languid and stiff, a poignant attempt to recapture a normality now gone for ever. "He will not dare kill me," she said. "I am a woman of family."

From downstairs came the sound of boots on marble, shouts and imprecations.

"Do you wish to test his temper?" snapped Todarko.

Linnalitha looked around the bedchamber Todarko had so longed to see —admittedly in different circumstances. "There is only one way out," she said, nodding at the window. "We can climb down on to the roof of the loggia."

Todarko raised an eyebrow. "Madam, I am sure you are as hardy as any lady, but—"

"I am not an invalid." She dashed for the window and vaulted over the sill.

By the time he reached the window she was standing on the roof of the loggia, no more than ten feet below. "Hurry!" she said in an urgent tone.

Todarko nimbly sprang out of the window and staggered as he landed. "You are heavy on your feet," said Linnalitha with a suppressed grin.

"Where now?" growled Todarko.

"The stables. We can hardly escape on foot."

Todarko said nothing; this had in fact been his plan. He dropped gently to the ground and helped Linnalitha down. "This way," she said, taking his hand.

There was a boy at the entrance to the stables. Todarko blanched. Linnalitha merely smiled and said: "Vaijlato, kindly saddle Bungle and Boodle—Todarko and I will be taking a short ride."

Todarko marvelled at her sangfroid as they stepped inside the gloom of the stables. Linnalitha gave a quick smile. "If my husband is banging about in the hall, he is not here. You can relax."

Relax! It was not the first word which came to mind.

Vaijlato brought over two black and white gallumphers of modest size. "Shall I send to the kitchen for a picnic, madam?"

"Thank-you, but no—we are in somewhat of a hurry."

"Do not forget your Hood and Veil, madam."

"I will collect them on the way out. Todarko, will you help me into the saddle?"

Todarko, his hands shaking, put his hands around her slender waist and picked her up. She seemed to weigh little more than his grandmother Sulinka.

"We may not be back until late," she said to Vaijlato as Todarko vaulted into his own saddle. Boodle—or was it Bungle?—ambled forward at a leisurely pace. Any thoughts he might have had of a breakneck pursuit were hardly consistent with these two garden gallumphers.

"Where are we going?" he asked as they trotted down the gardens.

"There is a gate in the wall by the folly," she said. "The front entrance is perhaps inadvisable."

Todarko's heart was pounding, partly from his exertions and partly from terror at the prospect of being caught by Dravadan, but he could not help but admire Linnalitha's utter coolness. One would have thought this was an everyday occurrence.

Never had the gardens of Korfez seemed so extensive as now. Todarko constantly looked over his shoulder to see if pursuit was coming—but for whatever reason, no-one had thought to come out the back. Soon the crenellations of the folly came into view, and then the gate. Linnalitha leaned forward and opened the gate, and they rode through and out on to the street.

"There," she said. "That was no cause for panic, was it."

Todarko simply shook his head. "Your head is bare—and we must find somewhere to hide. The city will soon be abuzz for us."

"Then we must leave the city. Do you not have an estate?"

"Grandille? I cannot believe that will be much safer."

"It must be safer than the streets of Taratanallos. Shall we go?"

"If you say, madam." Todarko was conscious that he was not providing the dashing and decisive leadership the situation demanded. In its absence, Linnalitha's calm good sense seemed to be at least as satisfactory. He was not sure that Sulinka would be happy to see them in the circumstances, although as house-mother she owed her kinsman a duty of sanctuary. Since he had no better suggestions, he gently dug into Boodle's side and made for the Arch Gate.

As they approached the gate he saw faces turning towards them in surprise. "Here," he said, removing Boodle's saddle-cloth. "Wrap this around your head. You will be less conspicuous."

She grimaced at the cloth which was greasy with repeated contact with the gallumpher's back; but her red hair stood out in the sunlight and she deftly wrapped the cloth over her hair and round the bottom half of her face. The expression in her eyes told Todarko all he needed to know about the smell.

The two Consigli on the gate nodded at the pair and swung the great door wide. Todarko nodded and tossed a coin towards the nearest man. The road stretched away into the distant woods and, as the gate closed once more behind them, Todarko realised they had made the first part of their escape. He did not know what would happen next—but at least they were alive and free.

CHAPTER FIFTY-THREE

Oricien stood still and silent on the steps of the Masavory. At his side Iselin slumped on the steps against the wall. All around him was frantic activity. Dravadan had invited them back to Korfez to consider their next steps, but now he was dashing around the plaza, roaring at the top of his voice for Todarko. Oricien's mind was racing. He had been routed in the Lumenario — the absence of a formal vote did not change that — and now his allies were at open loggerheads, for reasons he did not fully comprehend. Tonight he would have to compose a despatch for King Enguerran and it would be difficult to construct any positive interpretation of events.

He looked down at Iselin. "Do you have any suggestions?"

Iselin shrugged helplessly. "We will need some time for reflection," he said.

"There is no haste to visit Korfez," said Oricien. "Dravadan too will need time for reflection. Come, let us return to the castle and refresh ourselves."

Once they had taken a spare luncheon in Oricien's chambers there was no excuse to defer their duty any longer, and they made their way up the hill to Korfez, where they were immediately conducted into Dravadan's solar. The room was spacious but it seemed far too small to contain Dravadan's furious energy as he paced to and fro, to and fro.

"This is infamous, my lords, infamous!"

"Just so," said Oricien. "But now we must turn our thoughts to how we might remedy the situation."

Dravadan paused and looked at Oricien. "Surely it is obvious? We fetch them back and submit them to the direst punishments imaginable!"

"I am unclear — we must plan how to sway the Specchio."

"Animaxia take the Specchio! This is the least of my worries! We must find that dog Todarko and my whore of a wife and sew them into sacks. This is the most pressing urgency."

"Dignity, I am unclear as to the details of your grievance with Todarko, but should this not wait until we have sealed the alliance?"

Dravadan let out a great roar. "Do you think I can sway the opinion of a single grandee while my wife cavorts with that whoreson poet? I am a laughing-stock, Lord Oricien, a subject of mockery for the whole of the Specchio."

"Perhaps you exagger—"

"My reputation is built upon fear, Lord Oricien. I do not flatter myself I am loved. Men know that Dravadan's enmity is a thing to be avoided at all costs. I am nothing if not respected. Do you think they respect me today, my lord? Do you think the cuckold Dravadan is anything but the butt of gossip this afternoon?"

Iselin held up a hand. "Clearly you are overwrought, Dignity. Lord Oricien and I are not familiar with all the details of the situation."

Once again Dravadan resumed his pacing. "Are you not, my lords? The facts will take less than a minute to recount. I emerged from the Masavory this morning to find a sonnet pinned up in the plaza for all to see: a sonnet declaring Todarko's undying love for my wife Linnalitha. Everyone could see it, and everyone understood it."

Oricien asked: "How did such a sonnet come to be posted in public? Surely neither Todarko nor Linnalitha would have benefited from such an act."

Dravadan stopped once more. "Does it matter? The sonnet was there, and Todarko ran from the scene when he saw it. I returned to Korfez to find the pair of them fled. There can be no doubt as to their guilt."

"Nonetheless," said Oricien, "someone posted it in the plaza, presumably with some end in mind. There is more to this than a simple dalliance."

Dravadan thrust his face into Oricien's. "Simple dalliance, my lord?" he hissed. "The wife of the Dignified Dravadan, trolloping herself around with Todarko, a light and giddy boy whom I had lifted up? I am betrayed by them a hundred times over."

Oricien drew back—Dravadan's countenance was not improved by close proximity—and said: "We cannot allow our efforts to be deflected, Dignity. You and I both need this alliance."

Dravadan drew himself up and seemed to gain a measure of self-control. "Understand this, my lord: until my honour is restored, I am of no use to you as an ally. All my force will be bent in one direction, and that is recapturing and punishing my wife and her lover. If you wish to advance our great alliance, the best you can do is help me."

Oricien thought of all that gone before in his miserable sojourn in the city. Todarko had shown himself headstrong, impetuous—he could well imagine that the affair with Linnalitha was true; he had perhaps saved his life on the day of the bindlespith hunt. And he knew that Nelanka was fond of him too. Dravadan, on the other hand, was corrupt, grasping, unscrupulous. As far as personal inclination went, he had no desire to see Todarko subject to whatever extreme punishment Dravadan intended to mete out. Given his own feelings for Nelanka, it was hypocritical to condemn Todarko for his behaviour with Linnalitha.

"Well, Lord Ambassador? May I count upon your support?"

Oricien looked down at his feet. There really was no choice. "Of course, Dignity." He was the King's ambassador and, whatever his feelings, that overrode all else.

In normal circumstances Todarko would have enjoyed the next few hours. The sun was shining, the woods alive with the gentle noise of insects and birds, and he was riding alongside Linnalitha on a journey to his ancestral home. These were not, however, normal circumstances. At any point they could be overtaken on the road by Dravadan's retainers—although the woods provided ample cover—and at the end of the journey Todarko was uncertain of the welcome he would receive from Sulinka. Those dire concerns fell away to nothing, however, as Linnalitha chattered. She seemed almost unconcerned by their predicament.

"It is inconceivable that anything can be kept secret in Taratanallos," she said as Bungle carried her along the woodland track. "I am not aware of any secrets that have not come to light."

"Naturally not," said Todarko. "The secrets which are never revealed are never known as secrets."

Linnalitha gave a high clear laugh. "I had never thought of it that way. Now I wonder what is buried under the façade of respectability in other houses. Maybe all are as turbulent as House Umbinzia or House Vaggio."

"What is truly galling," said Todarko with a sly sideways glance, "is that I am not even guilty of the crime I am condemned for. I have not cuckolded Dravadan—much as I might have liked to."

Linnalitha stared off into the distance. "Now is not an opportune moment to discuss the matter. If I were disposed to pander to your desires, the point at which my husband is pursuing me to exact vengeance is not the time to do so."

"'If'?"

Linnalitha's mouth flickered in a smile that was gone before it had landed. "You are very easy to tease, Todarko. The fact remains that our future relations are not the most important question for us to resolve today. How to stay ahead of Dravadan is certainly a higher priority."

Todarko gave a glum nod.

"In any event," said Linnalitha in a softer voice, "your sonnet cuckolded Dravadan more effectively than carnality ever could. He was never capable of such sentiments, far less of expressing them. Every man in Taratanallos knows it."

"It is his pride which was piqued more than his heart," said Todarko. "What concerns him is not the loss of your affections, but that he is a public mock."

"That is no very flattering assessment, Todarko. No woman likes to be told that her husband is indifferent to her charms."

"And very charming charms they are. The fact remains that he married House Rasteccio, not Linnalitha."

"There are things I could tell you of his cruelty, his malice, which would freeze your heart," she said. "But it is a cold cruelty. He does not burn with passion: he is a man who calculates at every turn."

"He was hot enough in the plaza. A crowd laughing and making the horns at him will overset the coolest reason."

Linnalitha gave a brief laugh. "I would have liked to be there to see it. I am not sure that reflects well on my character—but I hate him. His downfall would be joyous to see."

"Do not think he is fallen yet. Oricien may yet rise again, and Dravadan with him."

She nodded. "I would never underestimate my husband's capacity—either for recovery, or revenge. I do not worry for myself—he dare not kill me, for all his bluster—but you must never fall into his hands." Clouds scudded across the sun and Todarko felt a moment of chill.

Soon they came upon a clearing where a band of travellers sat grilling meat over a small fire. It was getting late—the Hour of Afternoon Reflection or even of Cordial Discourse, and the travellers invited Todarko and Linnalitha to join them. Todarko on balance would have preferred to press on, but Linnalitha had not eaten since breakfast and was swaying in the saddle.

The travellers were ten or a dozen in number. The place closest by the fire was occupied by a man with grey hair cropped short, evidently the leader. "I am Larkin Dall," said the man with a flourish. "The hospitality of my troupe, poor as it is, awaits your pleasure." He shifted aside to make room for Linnalitha; Todarko was compelled to sit further afield.

"Troupe?" said Todarko. "You are not simple vagabonds?"

Larkin Dall filled two wooden cups with a cloudy liquid. Handing one to each of them, he said: "Vagabonds—yes! Simple—never! We are known as 'Dall's Mummers', and we go where we please with our repertoire. We have just left Taratanallos, and we have played in Aylissia, in Thring, Fadel, Cloop and Mandry—as well as towns and villages too numerous to name. It is a glorious thing to be devoted to the service of Art!"

"No doubt," said Todarko. "You do not appear to live the life of luxury on the proceeds. You travel on foot with only three gallumphers between you."

Larkin Dall picked up his mug and made an expansive gesture. "In truth there is little enough money to be made in Taratanallos at the best of times. Currently, there is some sort of political ferment, and our displays were not well attended."

"Where are you headed now?" asked Linnalitha with a polite smile.

"There are many estates in these woods," replied Larkin Dall. "The grandees of the city maintain establishments out here, and many is the occasion we have gone away with our purses bulging with gold."

"We are familiar with certain of these estates," said Linnalitha.

Larkin Dall scrutinised them a moment. "You are Taratanallos grandees yourselves, are you not?"

"Of a sort," said Todarko. "Although we are presently travelling incognito."

A woman with straggly blonde hair and a receding chin, reclining before the fire, cried: "A tale of secret lovers in dramatic flight through the woods! How romantic!"

Linnalitha shot Todarko a sharp sideways glance.

A squat figure sitting beside her said: "Raswinka, you are incorrigible. Every journey is not a melodramatic adventure!"

"You have no eye for drama, Odo. It is as well you can act, for you would make a most indifferent writer."

Larkin Dall made an understated gesture: Raswinka and Odo fell silent.

"My troupe is not governed with a rigid discipline," he said. "Raswinka realises that it is impolite to erect elaborate structures of speculation around the affairs of strangers. We do not wish to pry into your business, particularly if you are merely enjoying a country picnic. If, however, you are familiar with the estates in these parts, you may wish to supply an introduction. I would be charmed—" he inclined his head towards Linnalitha "—to mount a production of Tarlacchio or Evulsifer at your family estate."

Linnalitha raised an eyebrow. "Neither drama would seem entirely appropriate for the audience you suggest: Tarlacchio in particular would not be welcomed at any house I frequent."

Larkin Dall shrugged. "It is perhaps excessively anti-authoritarian to play before a grandee's household. A tasteful staging of Evulsifer surely cannot offend."

"There are no houses to which I could provide a suitable introduction, in any event. My husband's house is let to a noble tenant, and my father's estate is closed for repairs."

Todarko broke off a chunk of bread from the loaf Raswinka had offered him. "Are you familiar with the estate Grandille? It lies a way along the North Road."

Larkin Dall pondered a moment. "We have played there a couple of times. House Vaggio, no? Run by a sour old crone. It has hardly been worth application in the past."

Linnalitha sniggered. Todarko said: "The old crone is my grandmother."

Larkin Dall made an easy gesture. "No offence meant, good sir."

"None taken," said Todarko. "I have heard her called rather worse, with some justification."

"Do you think she will welcome a performance?"

"Why not?" said Todarko. "I am on my way there, and would welcome diversion. You will get a decent meal, if nothing else."

"I thank you, sir," said Larkin Dall. "Perhaps we will wend our way tomorrow. You have not told me your names."

"I am Todarko, of House Vaggio. My companion is Linnalitha, of House Rasteccio."

"Pleased to meet you, Todarko and Linnalitha. While Raswinka's speculations earlier were a touch feverish, I sense that you are in difficulties of some sort. If Dall's Mummers can help in any way, beyond sharing our supper, we would be glad to do so. You appear, madam, to be familiar with the great plays of Mondia."

"I have seen both Tarlacchio and Evulsifer performed at the Hydranemnon. I am probably less of a connoisseur than Todarko."

Larkin Dall raised his eyebrows. "I did not take you for a theatrical man, sir," he said.

"I am a poet," said Todarko. "On occasion my verses capture the fancy of others." He glanced from under his lashes at Linnalitha.

"You interest me," said Larkin Dall. "If you are in flight—from creditors perhaps, or unsympathetic relatives—I could offer you temporary employment. Todarko, could you write dramatic verse? Our repertoire becomes a little stale. And Madam Linnalitha, you have a face of tragic grandeur. You would certainly be well cast as Azoë, or even Lelanie, were we to play Evulsifer again."

"A moment!" cried Raswinka. "I am accustomed to play Lelanie! Although Linnalitha perhaps has the ethereal air of Azoë."

"I have no desire to join the troupe," said Linnalitha rapidly. "Raswinka, your roles are safe."

Todarko said: "Appealing as the idea is, I do not think that now is an opportune time to join the mummers."

"As you will," said Larkin Dall. "I hope at least that we will see you some evening hence, should we play at Grandille."

Todarko smiled. "I would not suggest playing a comedy," he said. "Grandille is not a frivolous establishment. Present conditions also rule out Tarlacchio: they will not wish to see a tale of mob rule. I can see no objection to Evulsifer if you are ready to play it."

"Evulsifer it is. I wish you both good evening."

CHAPTER FIFTY-FOUR

Evening was falling by the time the gates of Grandille came into view. They had not been overtaken on the road, so it was impossible for the news to have arrived ahead of them. Todarko would have a free hand with Sulinka, for all that was worth.

"I am more apprehensive to meet your grandmother than I was in fleeing Korfez," said Linnalitha.

Todarko considered the matter for a moment. "Sulinka does not wield a sword. She does not rant; she does not threaten. Your physical safety at Grandille should give no cause for alarm. Nonetheless, if I have given you the impression of a woman with strong will and fixed convictions, it is hard to dispute its accuracy."

Linnalitha pondered for a moment. "Do you think she will like me?"

"No."

Linnalitha raised her eyebrows. "Very well, then."

"She cares only for those who advance the fortunes of House Vaggio. It is hard to see how that definition can encompass you."

"She thinks I led her grandson astray?"

Todarko smiled. "She knows I was already astray; and her opinion of me is hardly favourable."

"Can you remind me why you have brought us here?"

"I seem to remember it was your idea," said Todarko in a light voice. "I never imagined a ceremonial reception. The fact remains that Dravadan cannot touch us at Grandille: the estates of the Specchio are inviolate by all custom."

"Good!" said Linnalitha with a smile. "Let us proceed."

Todarko rode up to the gate and pulled on the bell-cord. A man appeared from the guardhouse, his uniform bearing signs of a hastily-interrupted meal.

"We are not expecting visitors," said the guard, shading his eyes against the early evening sun.

"I am not a 'visitor'," said Todarko. "This is the estate of my house."

"Todarko! My apologies, sir. Madam Sulinka did not leave notice that you were arriving."

"Think of it as a doting grandson's surprise. Perhaps you would like to fetch Lulijko."

He gently impelled Bungle through the gates, Linnalitha following him. "Kindly stable the gallumphers," said Todarko. "We will await Lulijko here."

A few minutes later Lulijko scurried down the gravel path towards them. "Sir, this is unexpected, and frankly inconvenient! Why did you not send word of your coming?" He gave Linnalitha an appraising glance. "If you have come to announce your nuptials, there are more formal ways of doing so."

Linnalitha reddened and looked at her feet.

"Nuptials are only indirectly relevant, Lulijko. I have simply brought a guest for a short stay. I fail to see how that can materially inconvenience you."

"Have you eaten?"

"Only in the most cursory fashion."

"Immediately the nuisance begins," said Lulijko peevishly. "The Hour of Evening Repast is all but over and now I must scour the kitchens and cupboards for food!"

"You give a poor impression of the hospitality of Grandille, Lulijko. I am coming to believe that changes must be made."

Lulijko bowed. "Madam Sulinka finds no fault with my regime. I will see what I can scrape together in the kitchens." He signalled to a footman hovering nearby. "Pranadar—please take the guests to Sulinka's retiring room."

Todarko and Linnalitha walked as close as possible without—by some unspoken agreement—touching.

"Grandille is very beautiful," she said. "House Rasteccio has nothing this fine."

"What of Dravadan? Surely House Umbinzia maintains a summer estate?"

"There is Folinette," she said. "It was in any event smaller than Grandille, but Dravadan quietly sold it two years ago, to one of Duke Lothar's lords."

Todarko stopped and looked into her face. "He sold his house estate? To an Aylissian lord? Such news would not sit will with the Emmen party."

Linnalitha shrugged. "He found himself short of cash. It costs a great deal to entertain in Taratanallos the way he does: he is only one angry creditor, one lost argosy, away from ruin. Why else was he so keen to sell the monopoly to your uncle? The sale of Folinette, of course, was highly secret."

"I did not know he sailed so close to the wind."

"Unless he seals the Emmen alliance, House Umbinzia is ruined. As it is, he accepts a pension from Oricien, who could not afford to see such a supporter bankrupted."

"I had no idea," said Todarko in a hushed voice.

"That, of course, is the point," said Linnalitha coolly. "Once there is suspicion against a man's solvency, he is ruined. Therefore he must spend more freely than ever to dispel the suspicion, and so becomes ever more indebted. It is a mudslide from which there is no escape."

As they approached the house, Todarko turned and took her hands. "Linna, there is much we have not yet discussed. Both of our lives have changed today: things can never be as they were. I do not know what our futures hold—but I hope each holds the same."

Linnalitha tucked a hair behind her ear. "It is too soon to make plans, Todarko. If we are staying here indefinitely, there is yet time for us to think. But I am not sorry things have unravelled as they have. If our roads lie together for a while, I will be happy to walk with you."

This seemed to Todarko to leave considerable latitude for interpretation. But he knew Linnalitha enough to realise that he would get no more by pressing. "Shall we meet Sulinka?" he said, following the footman into the entrance hall.

The footman knocked gently on the door and slipped into the room. Todarko could hear the hesitant: "Madam, Todarko sends his compliments and begs to wait upon you."

A shrill exclamation: "Todarko! I did not summon him."

The footman said something inaudible.

"Send him in, for Animaxia's sake! I do not have decades left to live!"

The footman squeezed back out through the door and gave a brusque gesture of the head. Todarko frowned: the demeanour of the servants was some way short of satisfactory.

Linnalitha gave Todarko's hand a quick squeeze, and he led the way into the reception room. The room was on the far side of the house from the setting sun, and the torches were not yet lit. Sulinka sat in a deep chair, the whites of her eyes unnaturally bright against the gloom.

"Todarko?"

"Good afternoon, grandmother."

"I did not expect to see you here. Something must be amiss."

"I enjoyed my last visit to Grandille and thought to repeat it."

Sulinka rapped her cane on the floor. "You came at my express command, and could not wait to be away. Your bearing was not that of a man who wished to return immediately."

"I have brought a guest."

"So I see," said Sulinka with a grim smile. "Who are you, girl? Come here."

Linnalitha moved with a calm grace to stand before Sulinka, who peered into her face with a disarmingly intent scrutiny. "Red hair. Freckles. Long nose. You have the look of a Rasteccio."

Linnalitha gave a wan smile.

"Grandmother, I—"

"Do not tell me you have brought Dravadan's wife here! Not after our conversation on your last visit."

"I am Linnalitha, madam." Her voice was barely audible.

Sulinka raised herself from her chair with a grunt; her head came up to Linnalitha's throat. "You truly are Dravadan's wife?"

"We are no longer married, madam."

Sulinka looked up into her face. "You were married to him the last I heard."

"Marriage requires the consent of both parties. I withdraw mine."

Sulinka made a noise that was part laugh, part croak. "Divorce does not work quite so simply, girl. My grandson has fled Taratanallos with you, which makes him a fool and you a slut."

"Grandmother—"

"You will have your say when I allow it, Todarko. Both of you, sit."

Linnalitha perched precariously on the edge of a chaise; Todarko flung himself with a studied nonchalance into the adjacent seat.

Sulinka sat back down in her chair with a creak which could have emanated from the upholstery or her bones.

"When you were last here, Todarko—little more than a week ago—we discussed how you could advance the fortunes of House Vaggio. No-one has ever accused you of lacking intelligence, and I imagined that my advice needed no further reinforcement. Now, here you are with the wife of the man who should have been our greatest ally on your arm. I cannot imagine a way in which this situation can be reconciled with the instructions I gave you. Do you care to offer an explanation?"

Todarko swallowed. "Dravadan came to the view—an incorrect one, I may add—that an improper relationship existed. He learned of the matter immediately after failing to persuade the Specchio to accept the Emmen alliance, and I judged him unlikely to take a denial seriously."

"The Emmen alliance is dead? This is the basis of House Vaggio's policy!"

"Is this your main concern?"

"Of course! Do you think I care for your foolish dalliances, except where they touch upon House Vaggio? What occurred at the Masavory?"

"Bartielko was dragged up out of the dungeons with a somewhat theatrical flourish. He spoke very eloquently against the alliance, and Dravadan gave a feeble response. He withdrew his motion to avoid a clear defeat."

"And my son? What was his contribution?"

"None, madam. He made a brief intervention and was slapped down."

"Hmm. So the alliance is in ruins?"

"There was no vote," said Todarko. "There may be an opportunity to reintroduce the proposals."

"Neither Dravadan nor Raguslan shows the force or the guile to achieve it. We have backed a spavined gallumpher."

Todarko said nothing. Sulinka's analysis coincided with his own.

"How," continued Sulinka, "did Dravadan reach the conclusion that you were tupping his wife?"

Even in the gloom Todarko could see Linnalitha reddening.

"Linnalitha is your guest, madam. Do not speak to her that way!"

"I am your grandmother. You should not speak to me that way."

"If you showed Linnalitha more respect I would perhaps be more deferential."

Sulinka gave a harsh smile. "My apologies, Madam Linnalitha. I now know the tenor of my grandson's feelings for you, more effectively than if I had asked directly. One of the privileges of being a disagreeable old woman —" she gave Todarko a curt nod "— is that nobody answers back. For Todarko to be baited so tells me all I need to know."

Linnalitha gave a graceful inclination of the head.

"I can tell you that Todarko has serious feelings for you, my girl. On balance, I would not describe that as cause for congratulation."

Linnalitha said nothing. Todarko himself could not think of any response that would have been appropriate.

"I wrote Linnalitha a sonnet, grandmother. Somehow it became public property, and was displayed outside the Masavory. Dravadan was enraged to find it. I chose not to wait to provide an explanation which would surely have been disbelieved."

Sulinka looked from face to face as she appraised the situation.

"My policy of rapprochement with Dravadan has been ruined by your antics."

"I cannot argue it otherwise."

"On the other hand, Dravadan has proved an unsatisfactory ally. Things are as they are, and I must evolve a new policy. What is your expectation in coming here, Todarko?"

"I thought to fall upon the sanctuary of my house. I cannot be touched here."

"Does Dravadan know you are here?"

"We were not followed—but there are only a certain number of courses open to me."

Sulinka rang on a nearby bell with her cane. "You may stay here tonight. Tomorrow we will review the situation afresh. Lulijko will find you chambers for the night."

CHAPTER FIFTY-FIVE

"You have shown me the gardens of Korfez," said Todarko as they stood outside the hallway. "The least I can do is escort you around Grandille."

Linnalitha gave a wan smile. "I am not sure I am in the humour for sightseeing."

"A less elevated reason for a walk is that the servants will not overhear our business outdoors."

She gave him her arm. "In that case, let us walk."

For a few minutes neither of them spoke. Todarko was conscious of the warmth of her small hand as it rested on his forearm. It was hard to comprehend the turn events had taken: only this morning he had been sitting in the parlour of Korfez, taking breakfast as one of Dravadan's intimates. Since that moment, the Emmen alliance had all but collapsed, and Todarko had been forced to flee with Dravadan's wife. As he cared nothing for the Emmen alliance, and everything for Dravadan's wife, it was difficult to view events as unmitigated disaster. There was still scope for significant deterioration—it seemed unlikely that Dravadan would accept the loss of his wife and reputation meekly—but Todarko still found it hard to see events as gravely as they would seem to demand.

"What are you thinking?" asked Linnalitha as they moved out of sight of the house, into a small grove which was home to a hundred flitting bats.

"I am not sure I should tell you. I have taken you away from your place and security; and I cannot find guilt anywhere in my breast."

"Neither should you. You have taken me away from a husband of casual cruelty, callous in every respect and concerned only with his own political advantages."

"Nonetheless we cannot stay at Grandille forever. Sulinka may not, with any regard for etiquette, compel us to leave, but we are essentially imprisoned as long as we choose to stay here. And I would not freely share my cell with Sulinka."

"What can we do?"

"I can think of only one option," he said. "Other than joining the mummers, which we may discount for now. We need to get away from Taratanallos altogether—but that means returning to the city first. The only true way out of Taratanallos is by sea."

"They will be watching the gates—and the docks."

"I have ideas," he said. For most of the day he had been following Linnalitha's lead. While he was glad to find that she was cool-headed and capable, it was demeaning always to be dependent on her stratagems.

"Bring them forth," she said with a smile.

"I will secure us passage on a ship out of the city—perhaps to Paladria, where the weather is warm and the days are long."

"This is the scope of your ideas? How will we get into the city past the watchers? How will we book a passage?"

"I will write to a trusted associate to find us a ship. Getting into the city will be even easier."

"I would be interested to know whom you can trust at this time."

"Other than you?"

"Do not flirt with me. Now is not the time. Who within the city can be of any assistance to us?"

"Nelanka would not betray us—although I am loath to write to Tappinetto unless I must. But Bodazar will do what is needed."

"House Belario opposes the Emmen alliance."

"Bodazar cares as little for such things as I do. Besides, we are hardly bastions of Dravadan's party any more, are we?"

She stopped and looked into his face. "No, we are not."

"We are no party but each other's."

She stepped back and raked him with an appraising eye. "I have to say that for a notorious seducer, you have been most restrained during our acquaintance. I am starting to think that I am ill-favoured, or smell offensive."

Todarko took a step closer. "I can assure you that is not the case. My restraint arises only at your request. You have made it very clear that my addresses were unwelcome."

"You know why that was." There faces were now only inches apart. "The flexible man responds to changing circumstances."

"I would say that circumstances are now definitively and permanently changed."

She parted her lips a fraction. "So too would I."

"This is my response," he said, drawing her into an embrace and kissing her with a fervour that was all the greater for its long deferment.

A while later they walked back up to the house. "Let me escort you to your quarters," Todarko said. They reached the end of a corridor with wooden floors, and hangings on the walls to muffle the echoes of their feet.

"Sulinka has allocated you the Maiden's Chamber," he said. "You may infer as much or as little as you choose; my grandmother rarely acts at random."

Linnalitha ran an embarrassed hand through her hair. "She has already called me a slut."

"As always with Sulinka, it was policy rather than outrage. She cares nothing for your morals, or anyone else's."

"I would not mind if I truly were the wanton she seems to think. But I have been a model of chastity in circumstances where other courses would have been understandable." She looked down at the dark-varnished floorboards.

"We have both had a long day, Linna. You should not be worrying over Sulinka's games now."

"Where do you sleep?"

"I have my own chamber in the other wing."

She opened her door. "I am afraid, Todarko. I do not want to be alone tonight."

Todarko looked into her eyes a moment, nodded. He took her hand, stepped in through the doorway and closed the door behind them.

For various reasons Todarko did not enjoy a restful night's sleep. Nonetheless he was awake and alert early. He thought of slipping back to his own chambers for the sake of propriety, but the sight of Linnalitha sleeping next to him, her arm thrown across his chest, led him to reconsider. It was no-one's business but his own where he spent the night. Many a sun had risen over Taratanallos to find him in another's bed. In this case, perhaps, there was some justification for his behaviour.

He dozed a while longer, to be jerked back to wakefulness by a knock at the door. After a barely decent pause, Lulijko entered.

"Good morning, sir. Madam Sulinka thought to find you here."

Todarko shaded his eyes and scowled at Lulijko. "This is not my room."

"Madam understands best where to look for you. You must rise immediately: your uncle and cousin are here."

Linnalitha stirred next to him.

"I will be down in ten minutes," said Todarko. Lulijko gave a bow, the effect of which was largely undercut by the smirk which accompanied it.

"Raguslan and Zanijel are here," he said to Linnalitha. "You may want to stay upstairs."

"I'm coming with you," she said. "No doubt I will be one of the topics of conversation."

Todarko nodded. If she wanted to be there, so be it.

Fifteen minutes later he led the way down to Sulinka's reception room. Sulinka herself was sitting in a chair by the cold fireplace: Raguslan and Zanijel stood by the window, their backs to the room as they looked out across the lawns.

Todarko bowed. "Good morning, grandmother. You wished to see us?"

Sulinka narrowed her eyes. "Incorrect. None of us really wishes to see you."

Raguslan and Zanijel turned from the window and fixed Todarko with cold stares. Neither of them looked at Linnalitha.

"Your uncle has arrived, proposing to take you back to Taratanallos," said Sulinka.

Todarko invited Linnalitha to sit with a gesture, and then sat next to her on the chaise.

"I cannot imagine that I am popular in the city. I choose to remain here; I hope Linnalitha will also continue to enjoy your hospitality."

"Enough of your yammering!" snapped Raguslan, stepping across the room to stand over him. "I cannot believe what you have done. You must return and account for your actions immediately. Dravadan is enraged beyond measure."

Todarko gave a slow nod. "A degree of irritation is understandable in the circumstances."

Raguslan gave Sulinka a pleading look. "I knew he would be like this, mother. He has no shame, no readiness to make amends."

"Out of deference to Dravadan's pride, I have absented myself from the city. My return will only vex him the more."

"Todarko!" said Sulinka with a harsh smile. "Leave off your foolish quibbles. We must debate this from the perspective of House Vaggio."

Raguslan composed himself with a visible effort and sat down. "Dravadan remains Lord Oricien's ally and confidant. Once Bartielko is tried and convicted, the Gammerling party will fall apart, and the treaty with the Emmenrule will be signed with the minimum of fuss. We must retain Dravadan's good opinion."

"Such has been our policy," said Sulinka.

"And it was working!" cried Zanijel. "Had it not been for Todarko, we would still sit at his right hand today!"

Sulinka raised a hand to silence Zanijel, now leaning against the window frame, arms folded, with glowering menace. "We all understand the past, Zanijel. Now is the time to decide the future. Raguslan, what news do you bring?"

"Dravadan's rage against Todarko—and against you, Madam Linnalitha—is extreme. He wishes to visit a dire, although as yet unspecific, punishment upon Todarko, and to return Madam Linnalitha to Korfez. He is unaware of the whereabouts of either: he suspects you to be lying low in the city. Those more acquainted with Todarko's character instantly understood him to have fled. I propose to take them both back to Taratanallos with me. Todarko, your best course is to throw yourself upon Dravadan's mercy. Magnanimity may become him at this time, and it is possible he will let you live."

"The notion is ludicrous," said Linnalitha in a flat insistent voice.

Sulinka rapped her cane. "Your opinion is not solicited, girl. You are admitted to this house conference as a courtesy only."

"Grandmother," said Todarko. "The course my uncle outlines would lead inevitably to my immediate death. Once I am in Dravadan's power, nothing can save me."

"Unfortunate," said Zanijel from the back of the room.

Sulinka fixed her eyes on Todarko. "Your concern with your own safety, while understandable, is not to the point. We must all think of the good of House Vaggio."

"The good of the house is abstract after my own death."

"You should have thought of that before you took your pleasure with that ginger-headed whore," said Zanijel with a grin. "I hope she was worth it."

Todarko made to rise from his seat. Linnalitha took his arm. "Ignore him. He does not offend me, so you need not avenge my honour."

Sulinka's dark eyes flashed. "If our acquaintance were of a different nature, girl, I would have liked you. You have spirit and sense, a rare enough combination. Dravadan was a fool to neglect you."

Linnalitha smoothed her dress. "I would prefer concrete assistance to praise, however sincerely meant."

Todarko was unsure that this was the best way to deal with Sulinka, but the old woman smiled. "I will assist you to the maximum extent practical," she said. "Although you must be aware that this may not be far."

Linnalitha gave a curt nod.

"May I suggest," said Todarko, "that the time for appeasing Dravadan is past? His conduct during the time I have known him has not been that of a statesman, or even a particularly adept plotter. He has come to the head of the Emmen party through means that are not above suspicion, and then fumbled the chance he has created for himself. Lord Oricien clearly holds him in no personal regard—and neither, indeed, does he esteem either Raguslan or Zanijel. We lose nothing by walking away from the Emmen alliance."

"This is preposterous!" said Raguslan. "We are on the threshold of greatness!"

"The only potential card that House Vaggio has to play is to transfer its allegiance to the Gammerling party. Such a move, at the right time, would destroy Dravadan's faction, expose his flawed judgement—and so earn us the thanks and rewards of King Ingomer."

Sulinka smiled and shook her head ruefully. "What a waste it is that you are ruled by your glands, Todarko. You have insight, imagination, daring. Your analysis is not without merit, although it ignores the damage to our reputation such a turning of the coat would cause. The Gammerling party is not united: Bartielko is imprisoned, the others cannot decide whether to support Duke or King. There is much to ponder here. A few days' reflection will do us no harm. For now, all are guests of Grandille."

"I am not sharing a table with that slut, grandmother," said Zanijel. "Look at her, tossing her hair and flaunting her breasts! She is the agent of this calamity. Whip her back out onto the road and we can conduct a more rational debate."

Linnalitha put a warning hand on Todarko's arm, but this time he was not tempted to respond. Zanijel was a clod if he could not see that Linnalitha had charmed Sulinka: his outburst would only lower him in her eyes.

Sulinka stood from her chair. "The hospitality of Grandille is much lessened if a woman of gentle birth is not spared such remarks under our roof. Apologise this instant, Zanijel!"

"But—" Zanijel shifted his weight from foot to foot. Todarko considered a gloating remark, then reflected that no intervention could make the situation more humiliating than it already was.

"Zanijel!" snapped Raguslan. "Attend to your grandmother's wishes immediately!"

"No apology is necessary," said Linnalitha. "A remark wounds only when the recipient has esteem for the speaker's views. I beg you, Madam Sulinka, do not compel the lad to say what he does not mean."

Sulinka's eyes were fixed on Zanijel; the others might as well not have spoken. "I am waiting, grandson."

Zanijel looked down at the floor. "I am sorry," he mumbled.

Sulinka hobbled over to him, smacked him around the head with her cane. "Is this how you were raised? You reflect infinite discredit upon us all!"

Zanijel stepped back. In a flat voice, he said: "Madam Linnalitha, I apologise for my rash words, which expressed sentiments which should never have been thought nor voiced to a lady."

Todarko thought to sense evasion in the phrasing—more than one interpretation was clearly possible—but Sulinka caught his gaze. It seemed that sufficient humiliation had been endured.

"I accept your apology in the spirit it was tendered," said Linnalitha with a perfectly symmetrical smile. Sulinka's smile was an altogether harsher expression.

Lulijko, almost as if he had been listening outside, sensed a lull in the conversation and slipped deferentially into the room. "Madam, forgive the intrusion. There is a gentleman for Todarko."

A name hung, unspoken, in the air: Dravadan.

Eyes flicked around the room, trying to take the measure of every countenance. Linnalitha gripped Todarko's hand.

Lulijko looked at him. "He goes by the name of Larkin Dall, sir. He wishes to discuss the possibility of a mummers' show at Grandille."

Sulinka looked at Todarko in something approaching astonishment. "You have invited a mummer to Grandille? At this time?"

Zanijel uttered a caw of laughter. "This is not to be believed!"

"We met his troupe on the road. I merely named a house where he might receive a liberal welcome."

"And this was Grandille?" asked Sulinka incredulously.

"I did suggest a comedy might not be a suitable choice."

"Lulijko! Bring in Larkin Dall! The rest of you may leave."

As they filed out of the room, Larkin Dall bowed to Todarko and Linnalitha. "I thank you for your commendation."

CHAPTER FIFTY-SIX

Todarko never learned exactly what Larkin Dall said to Sulinka, but an invitation was conveyed to his room that Evulsifer would be performed in the Grand Hall at the Hour of Noble Pleasures. By unspoken consent, Todarko and Linnalitha spent the day in the gardens, well away from other members of House Vaggio.

"Will Sulinka send us back?" asked Linnalitha as they sat on the banks of a brook flowing inside the farthest wall.

Todarko, lying with his head in her lap, looked up into her face.

"Who knows? I certainly do not. She likes you—rather to my surprise—and she realises that Raguslan and Zanijel are pitiful instruments for her schemes. But she is not in the least sentimental. If she thinks making a present of us to Dravadan will put Vaggio on the winning side, she will do it without qualm."

"Even if she lets us stay here, we will have to move on in the end."

"I have sent a man to Bodazar today. If we return to the city in a week we will be able to find a passage."

Eventually the sun began to sink in the sky: the afternoon was over, and their idyllic day was drawing to a close. Linnalitha stroked Todarko's head. "This may be all the time we ever have together," she said. "Once we leave, we are in the hands of Animaxia."

"Happy to have thy love, happy to die, and death once dead, there's no more dying then," said Todarko with a smile. "We are fortunate to have had the little time we've had. Without my unknown enemy, we might never even have had this."

Linnalitha picked up a pebble, and threw it with a splash into the brook. "It does not seem unreasonable to want a little more," she said. "I had four years of Dravadan, and if things go awry they will not be the last. Did you know, when you wrote the sonnet, that it would come to this? All that talk about death and doom seems a touch prophetic."

Todarko sat up. "When Lord Ribauldequin was killed, I thought the verse self-indulgent, magnifying some trivial emotion. Now I know that the emotion is not trivial, and I have earned the right to liken it to death."

"Do you believe in the Peninsular Heresy?" she asked, leaning her head on his shoulder. "That we go somewhere after we die?"

"We should not call it heresy," said Todarko gently. "It is the belief of our city."

"In many places—everywhere else, in truth—they do not believe as we do. We die, either in Harmony, in Disharmony or in Equilibrium, and that is all there is. I cannot hope but that our Viators are right."

"High Viator Udenko is no very convincing example of spirituality," he said. "No doubt the Consorts are equally worldly. I have never listened to the Viators, and I can have no idea what comes after death. I mistrust anyone who claims special knowledge."

"I only thought—" said Linnalitha in a soft voice.

Todarko ran a finger with barely perceptible lightness along her cheek. "What, my love?"

A tear slipped from her eye onto Todarko's finger. "If something happens to you—or to me—I would at least have the consolation that we might be together once more, in a place we cannot know. If I must live forty years, or fifty, without you, can it be wrong to dream that one day we will know each other again?"

In all the years I have sported with women I have never known this, that such feelings can exist.

"I am sorry," she said, wiping her eyes with the sleeve of her dress. "I am being foolish and sentimental, and I am neither of those things."

Todarko peeled open her clenched fist and kissed the moist fingers. "You should never be sorry for feeling, Linna. Hissen knows, there is little enough of it in Taratanallos. I do not know if heaven is a consolation for those who cannot face the cruelty of the world, but I pray it is not. If there is a place to come where all is perfection, then we will be together—for how could it be perfect otherwise?"

"Sometimes I forget you are a poet, Todarko."

"The matter of heaven cannot be resolved—to my satisfaction at least—until after my death. I am happy to continue in ignorance indefinitely."

"Do not skip away behind your flippancies, Todarko. I want you to understand that, however this ends, it has been worth it. There is nothing Dravadan can take from me that will outweigh what you have given me, if only for a little while."

He closed her eyes and kissed the lids. "We must put this away in our hearts now, Linna. Something this powerful will never be gone, but we must concentrate now on ensuring our safety. All is not yet lost, and Evulsifer is not a play to watch with a melancholy heart."

"No," said Linnalitha with a watery smile and a sniffle. "Let us go and daunt House Vaggio with our unshakeable composure." She jumped to her feet, pulled Todarko to his, and hand in hand they ran towards the house for dinner.

It was an unusual gathering which convened at the Hour of Evening Repast. Todarko was willing to bet that the party would never be assembled again. Sulinka sat, in gloomy majesty, at the head of the table. Her son Raguslan was at her side, his son Zanijel at his. Todarko sat on Sulinka's left, with Linnalitha to his left. Such a group was in itself implausible, particularly given current circumstances. When the additional guests were added — Larkin Dall, Raswinka and Odo — the scene was set for an occasion not to be repeated.

The dining room had a musty smell of long disuse: Sulinka usually entertained in her Grand Hall, which tonight was given over to Evulsifer. From some caprice, Sulinka had not ordered the shutters opened, and the party sat in a candlelit dimness.

"Todarko, Linnalitha," said Sulinka as Lulijko served the first course. "I have resolved that my son will be returning to Taratanallos without you. While we determine our best course, you may remain at Grandille. Raguslan and Zanijel will return to the city tomorrow morning."

Linnalitha inclined her head. "Thank you, madam. There has been intemperate behaviour on our part, but I do not intend to return to my husband, and I am sure Todarko has no desire to present himself as a penitent either."

Sulinka frowned as she sipped her soup, summoned the waiting Lulijko to take it away. "Thank me for nothing, girl. Your future is not yet decided. For now, you may relax at Grandille awhile and think no more of the future. Lulijko! This soup is intolerably salty! Replace it this instant!"

Lulijko bowed and removed the plate.

"The soup is unobjectionable, grandmother," said Todarko. "There is little profit in berating Lulijko."

"Do not contradict me! Zanijel, how do you find the soup?"

"Vastly salty, grandmother. Lulijko, you may remove mine too."

"Remarkable," said Todarko. "I am curious as to how you can evaluate soup you have not yet tasted. You are more talented than you are given credit for."

Raswinka grinned openly. Larkin Dall and Odo ate their soup in silence.

"Well, Raguslan," said Sulinka. "You normally have more than enough to say! How do you judge the soup?"

"I am not partial to soup at the best of times. This certainly has a salty tang. No, Lulijko, do not bother to replace it."

"Perhaps you would like to solicit our guests' views, grandmother," said Todarko.

"That is enough, Todarko," said Linnalitha. "You have made your point adequately."

Larkin Dall set down his spoon. "At the risk of leaving a subject which seems freighted with meanings I do not understand, let me ask how many of you are familiar with tonight's play? Evulsifer is magnificent theatre but it is rarely played these days."

"I saw it as a girl," said Sulinka. "Sadly that was many years ago: King Alazian was on the throne of Emmen, I remember."

"Meaning no disrespect to your calling," said Raguslan, "I have never had a theatrical bent. Tonight will be my first viewing of the play."

"Present company excluded," said Zanijel, "mummers are dilettantes, dandies, and as often as not homosexual. I freely avow my disdain for such behaviour. If you are looking for someone at home in this milieu of garish effeminacy, seek no further than the poet Todarko!"

Larkin Dall made a polite gesture to imply that all shades of opinion existed in the world. "Yes, Todarko, we touched on your literary inclinations. I wished to talk to you in more detail today, but you were not on hand. You, I hope, will be able to appreciate the great spectacle we lay before you: I am sure your knowledge of Evulsifer is unmatched."

Todarko gave a mannered nod. "I would not go so far," he said. "But I have seen the play performed, read it many times and—truth be told—on occasion ransacked it for my own work. I will be fascinated to see what you make of this great text."

Larkin Dall smiled and picked up his goblet. "I rather think you will be, Todarko. I rather think you will."

Linnalitha said: "Raswinka, you will play Lelanie tonight?"

Raswinka narrowed her eyes. "For now, I am the only actress to command the role. Larkin Dall seeks to expand our personnel, and I may have to compete for the role in future."

Larkin Dall set down his goblet. "Raswinka is perhaps melodramatic. The company is short of females with the requisite accomplishment for the leading female roles. As the years go by, what she loses in one dimension, she gains to a certain extent in others. Nonetheless, Dall's Mummers grow no younger. New blood is always to be sought."

"Hmmf," grunted Raswinka. "Lucky for you that at least I learn lines rapidly. We do not normally include at least one of the scenes you insist on playing tonight."

"Fol-de-rol, Raswinka. The bulk of the lines in the scene belong to Prince Evulsifer: that is to say, myself. What is the point of financing a theatrical troupe if I cannot pick the plum parts?"

The meal rarely rose above the level of petty bickering. Even allowing for her normal irascibility, Sulinka was not in good humour. The mummers themselves squabbled incessantly, although Todarko was inclined to think this was their normal behaviour. Linnalitha concentrated on eating her food with grace and delicacy, and Todarko was content to watch the others. Zanijel constantly looked across at him, as if about to launch some verbal sally, but directed his conversation elsewhere. Todarko was not sorry when the Hour of Evening Satiation arrived and the company broke up, allowing Larkin Dall to set up the stage in the Great Hall.

CHAPTER FIFTY-SEVEN

Todarko was surprised at the Hour of Noble Pleasures to find the Great Hall nearly full. Sulinka had allowed the servants not otherwise engaged to attend, and a crowd of twenty or thirty ranged the benches set athwart the hall. The only light in the room was from the lanterns overhanging the stage. Somehow, through artful shadows and hints of cloth, Larkin Dall had contrived to make one end of the hall convince as Asmelond Palace, and when Larkin Dall himself entered there was a suppressed gasp. Gone was the slovenly mountebank leading a raggle-taggle troupe: instead, despite the threadbare robes, here stood a man all could believe was the proud Prince Evulsifer. It was done with nothing more than a tilt of the head and a set of the shoulders. So you really can act, thought Todarko.

"Ladies and gentlemen," cried Larkin Dall, shaking off his princely aura, "tonight we beg your indulgence. Madam Sulinka has bid us welcome to Grandille, and demanded of us the best that Dall's Mummers can offer. We have scoured our repertoire, and tonight we present that famous drama of hate and passion and woe Evulsifer! You will experience poignant realism; you will witness the betrayal of a king, a palace orgy, the death of a traitor in its grisly actuality: a program to edify and instruct the discriminating folk of Grandille. My friends and patrons, I give you Evulsifer!"

Linnalitha leaned against Todarko. "As if we do not have hate and passion and woe enough."

Todarko took her hand. "For tonight, if no other, we can enjoy someone else's woes."

"I am glad, if a touch surprised, that Sulinka has sided with us."

"She sees what clowns the others are. She has no choice. Now, let us watch the play."

The first act passed quickly. Larkin Dall aside, the quality of the performances was indifferent. Larkin Dall himself was at least twenty years too old for the dashing Prince Evulsifer, but at least he acquitted himself without the woodenness of Odo, who played Evulsifer's father despite being notably the younger man. Raswinka's performance as the beguiling Lelanie also left much to be desired: while displaying all the necessary passion required by the role, her histrionic delivery was not an advantage when attempting to convey the alluring sultriness demanded.

In the second act, the intrigues against Evulsifer started to come to fruition. Larkin Dall dashed on the stage and began to declaim a soliloquy:

EVULSIFER: Fortunate am I that Lelanie vouches for my name, else would I be lost tonight. I put my trust in her and know my life is safe. Her love for me can never see me lost.
Exit EVULSIFER. Enter LELANIE.
LELANIE: Tonight send I to Asmelond; tomorrow cometh doom on winged hooves, which will not cease until Evulsifer they find. For when better to betray a man, than when he trusts the most? Tonight he sleeps a sound and gentle sleep, secure that Lelanie will see him safe. Tomorrow comes the howling wind of doom, to pluck the Prince away into his tomb.
Exit LELANIE.

Todarko furrowed his brow. He had not lied to Larkin Dall; his knowledge of the play was excellent. Yet he could not remember this scene. Everyone knew that Lelanie betrayed Evulsifer in the end, but this somewhat crude exposition jarred him. He gave his head a rueful shake: it was wholly consistent with Larkin Dall, playing a part he should have left in his youth, also to think to improve the play. If that was representative of his verse, no wonder he had asked Todarko to join the company. He could certainly do better than that; and for that matter, Linnalitha would not have to display excessive competence to outshine Raswinka. For a glorious moment of reverie he imagined them throwing in their lot with Dall's Mummers. Why not? He shook his head: the idea was inherently ludicrous.

The interval came with Evulsifer's fortunes at a low ebb. He had been drawn into a series of intrigues he did not fully understand, and his passion for an unsuitable woman had given his enemies the chance to destroy him. Todarko snorted and shook his head: he knew exactly what this situation looked like. He also knew that Evulsifer ended the play with his head cut off, a situation Todarko preferred to avoid.

He made broadly that point to Linnalitha as they strolled on the gravel during the brief interlude while Dall's Mummers changed the scenery for the next act.

"This is not a tragic melodrama, Todarko: this is our lives! There is no concordance between them."

"It is hard to avoid the parallels," said Todarko. "Although I hope I am a little more debonair than Larkin Dall."

Linnalitha pursed her lips. In the dying light of the dusk it was difficult to tell if she were trying not to laugh.

"Did you notice that rogue introduced a new scene? He has a high opinion of himself," said Todarko.

"Raswinka mentioned that he had insisted on disinterring some rarely performed scenes."

"Rarely performed! This one was bran-new, and not even good!"

Linnalitha raised an eyebrow. "You have intrigued me now."

"The one where Evulsifer says he is safe because Lelanie has promised him sanctuary, and then Lelanie comes on and says she's done it to keep him quiet, and Barulf's men are on their way to take him."

A bat skittered around Linnalitha's head and she flinched. "That was new?"

"I've never heard of it or seen it played."

Linnalitha was silent in thought a moment. "Todarko…"

He looked at her quizzically.

"Larkin Dall was at great pains to establish that you knew the play in detail. He laid some stress on it."

Todarko shrugged. "Perhaps he did."

"That scene was for you! He wrote it for you!"

"What?"

"Do not trust your safety to someone who has promised you sanctuary — it is a ploy to keep you in place while your enemies come. Is that not the message of the scene?"

"Now it is you who are being melodramatic, Linna! You reproved me for doing exactly that."

Linnalitha shook her head in frustration. "Can't you see that this is entirely different? Larkin Dall wrote that scene for inclusion today, and made Raswinka learn the new lines. Somehow he has learned that Sulinka means to betray us! You sent a message to Bodazar — why could she not have done the same to Dravadan? She has no sentiment, no compassion. You have said so yourself."

Todarko looked up the stars, equally lacking in compassion as they stared back at him from unimaginable distances. Could this be true? Sulinka certainly would not hesitate to betray them if she saw an advantage in it — indeed, would not even see it as betrayal. Raguslan and Zanijel had been suspiciously quiescent at dinner — not like men who had been told that Todarko would be protected. It was not out of the question that Larkin Dall or one of his troupe, conning their soliloquies in some place of concealment, had overheard something they should not.

"We must go now!" said Linnalitha, pulling at Todarko's arm.

"No," said Todarko. "We will be missed if we do not go back for the third act. If you are right, they will be after us in minutes. If we go, we leave in the dead of night."

Linnalitha's pupils were huge in the gloom. "I suppose you are right—but do you believe me?"

"I don't know," said Todarko. "Your theory is certainly plausible. One way or another, we must return to the play, and look as if nothing is amiss."

He offered her his arm, and they strolled back up the gravel path towards the house, for all the world a pair of lovers with no concern but each other. Coming from a different direction they encountered Larkin Dall, carrying a bulging purse, and Sulinka. Larkin Dall gave Todarko a salute.

"I trust you are enjoying the play, Todarko."

"Very much. You invest the Prince with a tragic grandeur; Raswinka brings passion and energy to the role of Lelanie."

Larkin Dall grimaced. "That she does."

"I noticed one of the rare scenes you referred to at dinner."

Larkin Dall met his eyes. "Ah, yes?"

"I am surprised it is not played more often. The soliloquies seem to go beyond simple theatre and speak directly to the audience's heart."

Larkin Dall's lips curved into a wry smile. "I am glad you find it so." He bowed and walked back into the house to change his costume for the third act.

Linnalitha looked across at Todarko, her eyebrows raised in inquiry. Todarko simply nodded.

Sulinka shook her head. "You all speak a different language, with your eternal verities and your tragic grandeur. It means nothing to me. You should never have been in the Specchio, Todarko. You would have been happier—and richer—as a starving poet or a mummer."

"I never gave you credit for such insight, grandmother."

"I was young once, you know. I did not spend my whole life at Grandille. When your grandfather was the finest man in Taratanallos, I learned to read character," she said. "How I regret, Todarko—"

"Yes, grandmother?"

She shook her head vigorously. "The old should never have regrets, boy. Come, the third act will be starting, and I do not wish to miss Evulsifer's downfall."

Todarko had to admit that he did not give Evulsifer's downfall in the third act the attention Larkin Dall's performance deserved. He was sure that the mummer would forgive him. The beheading scene was managed with skill and economy: Todarko could not see how the dummy was introduced although he felt confident that it was not Larkin Dall whose head dropped to the floor with a satisfying thud. Sulinka nodded in evident satisfaction at the bloody denouement, and Todarko caught Zanijel grinning when he thought himself unobserved.

Todarko rapidly excused himself after the play's conclusion. "I am somewhat tired, grandmother. I think perhaps I will lie in and take a late breakfast tomorrow."

Sulinka gave a polite smile. "As you choose, grandson. You are a guest at Grandille and may do as you wish."

CHAPTER FIFTY-EIGHT

Some time after the start of the Hour of Secret Deeds, Todarko and Linnalitha sat astride Boodle and Bungle, ready to begin their journey back to Taratanallos. Rather than leave through the front gate, they rode down the middle of the brook at the back of the estate, both to daunt any dogs who might pursue them, and to avoid being seen leaving via the main entrance.

"We must be alert," whispered Todarko under the moonlight. "There is only one road in and out of the city, and Dravadan's men are likely to be on it at some point."

"There is plenty of cover. We will have time to hide; we will hear them well before we see them."

For the next three hours, then, they rode in an enforced silence under the moon. The air was still, only the faintest of breezes ruffling the treetops, and the journey, in its eerie quiet, seemed nothing more than a dream. Todarko, who had used his facility with language to seduce more often than he could remember, found in this silence an allure, a mood, more powerful than any that could be conjured by words. How much of it was the power of moonlight, how much the effect of silence, and how much was down to the presence of Linnalitha, he could not tell. All he knew was that since he had reached this new level of intimacy with her, he found new facets of the world, new fascinations and new joys, which he had never known existed.

"Todarko!" whispered Linnalitha. "Can you hear something?"

He brought himself back to the mundane. In the distance was undoubtedly the thrum of hooves. Rapidly they rode off the track and peered out from the heavy foliage to see what was coming down the road. They were on the cusp of a bend and could see a cluster of gallumphers coming down the road at some speed. *They are in a hurry to find us.*

As the riders crashed past the glade, any doubts vanished. At the head of the group was a rider bearing the battle-cat standard of House Umbinzia: these were Dravadan's men. And there was Palankijo: Dravadan's dignity would not allow him to rush pell-mell to Grandille, but he had sent his steward.

The party was travelling far too fast to notice the pair hidden in the woods. Once they had passed, Todarko looked across at Linnalitha, her face pale and her breath ragged. Todarko spat on the mossy ground. "That old bitch!"

Linnalitha reached out and touched his leg. "We knew she would do it."

"She is my grandmother, the senior member of House Vaggio. She has sold out her own grandson to another house—no, not even sold out: Dravadan will not have had to pay for the information."

"I am sorry," she said. "Betrayal by family is worst of all."

Todarko shook his head angrily. "She is in her dotage. It is not even the right choice for the advancement of the house. Dravadan cannot win; she has hitched her gallumpher to a losing cause."

"We should go," said Linnalitha. "It will not be long before they realise we are not there. We need to find a hiding place in the city."

Todarko nodded and pressed his heels into Bungle's side.

Now that pursuit had passed them by, there was no longer any need for silence, but still they rode on, their journey punctuated by only the occasional remark. Finally, as dawn was breaking they rode over the crest of the hill to see the city of Taratanallos, the red roofs picked out by the first light of morning. There were no other travellers abroad at such an hour, but the gate would still be guarded. Linnalitha raised her hood, fastened her veil, and they trotted down the road to the entrance.

The Consigli on the gate grunted. "You are about early." Todarko was unclear whether he had been recognised. He had committed no crime, and he wordlessly showed his mirror-token. "Have it your own way," grumbled the Consigli. "Good morning never cost anything."

Todarko nodded a brusque thanks. He was not sure he trusted himself to speak.

Inside the city, a few men scurried about on early morning errands. These would range from the innocent—bread from the ovens distributed to the inns and cafes—to the downright disreputable.

"Where are we going?" asked Linnalitha as they turned towards the Chale.

"I had thought of going back to Tappinetto," he said. "We need to know what is going on with Dravadan, and I must see Nelanka. But it is too dangerous. We will hole up in the Chale awhile: still not safe, but it will do for now. Are you hungry?"

Linnalitha nodded. "I did not realise I was until you asked," she smiled.

"Good. Take off your veil: where we are going it will only make us conspicuous."

The morning had a pleasant freshness, and twenty minutes later, with the Hour of Breaking Fast about to be tolled, they sat at a table outside Colaronko's, a ramshackle but clean cafe which was already busy with those whose employment began early. Todarko ordered teas, some fresh bread and preserves, and also requested paper and a quill. He rapidly set down a brief note and paid over a handful of minims to the boy intended to deliver it.

"Can you read, son?" asked Todarko.

"No, sir," said the wide-eyed lad.

"Excellent," said Todarko. "This is for House Belario. Come back here when it is delivered, and there'll be a florin for you."

The boy scampered off. He would be lucky if he earned a florin a day in the normal course of events. Todarko felt he could be confident of diligence on the errand.

Linnalitha sipped daintily at her tea and nibbled on the bread spread thinly with orange and redder preserve.

"I cannot believe this is happening," she said. "Two days ago we were taking breakfast in the parlour of Korfez. Now we are eating at this odd café in the Chale. It is almost as if we are playing some strange game; but there are men looking for us who mean us no good. Eating breakfast seems almost too normal, if you see what I mean."

"They will not think to look for us in the Chale," said Todarko, reaching for another piece of bread. "Not yet, at any rate. In the meantime, there is no merit to starving ourselves."

The waiter seemed happy to allow them to sit at their table as long as they chose. The sun inched up into the sky in a blaze of orange and purple to promise another warm clear day.

CHAPTER FIFTY-NINE

The morning of Malvazan's picnic with Dravadan and Rullia dawned crisp and bright. Orijaz had made up a picnic basket and would accompany them on a gallumpher until the Hour of Light Repast, and then bring back the remains of the luncheon. Rullia was dressed like a peasant boy in dark brown breeches and a white smock, a cap covering her red curls. She judged the effect so convincing that she dispensed with Hood and Veil, for who would think her anything other than a country lad. Dravadan and Malvazan wore loose garments appropriate for a day's walking, and Malvazan was surprised to realise that, despite a wretched night's sleep, he felt buoyant and energetic.

"We should have done this more often," said Dravadan as they walked through the gate and out onto the cliff path. "I look back at our childhoods and all I remember is us bickering."

That is because you were a smug brat. "Things are different now, are they not?"

Dravadan beamed. "I have Rullia to thank for our accord. She made me realise how fortunate I was—and also that all we have is our family to protect us in this world. When I am head of the house, I shall rely very much on your counsel and discretion."

Malvazan smiled, leaning into the path as it sloped more steeply up the hill. "You know that I have always cared for the advancement of House Umbinzia. I will gladly help you in achieving that."

"I used to think you cared only for advancing yourself. It was Rullia who suggested that if I treated you with the frank courtesy an older brother owes the younger, you would respond with a great heart."

Malvazan looked at Rullia, who had now removed her cap and shaken out the curls. She was undeniably an attractive woman, a typical Rasteccio redhead. Once again his brother had fallen on his feet. It scarcely mattered that she did not appear very intelligent. "I am grateful for your perceptiveness, Damoiselle. If it were not for you, Dravadan and I might have remained estranged forever."

Rullia beamed. "I am so glad that you are friends. When everyone was saying yesterday how badly you had behaved, Dravadan would not hear a word against you. I thought he would call out Astrizel."

"We could not have had that," said Malvazan. "The life of the heir is paramount. Dravadan is a talented swordsman, but there is no sense in taking risks."

"We wanted to tell you something," said Rullia in a bubbling voice. "We have agreed the date for our nuptials – the year and a day is all but up."

"Indeed it is," said Malvazan with a grave bow. "I can scarcely forget the day of your betrothal."

She put a hand on his forearm. "Forgive me, Malvazan. The memory must give you pain."

Malvazan shrugged. "I do not dwell on the past. I fancy that as matters have turned out, Sanouté regrets events more than I; but that is merely conjecture. I am of course delighted that your date is set."

"Our fathers agreed yesterday that the ceremony will be one month from today. It will be announced tomorrow."

"And Malvazan," said Dravadan, "I wish you to be my Companion of Honour."

"I thought Rullia's brother had been asked."

"I am sure Grenko would be happy to carry out the duties," said Dravadan. "But on a day like this, who else would I want but my brother?" He reached out a hand to Malvazan. "Will you do it?"

Malvazan stuck on a smile and took Dravadan's hand. "Of course, brother."

Rullia clapped her hand and let out a squeal. "Oh! How wonderful! It will be the most delightful day."

Dravadan smiled and chucked her cheek. "It will indeed, my love."

They took their lunch on the bluff which jutted out from the peninsula, giving views down over the city and across the bay. Orijaz spread a cloth on the grass and unpacked a cold collation of chicken, salad and potatoes, and a white wine kept cool in a wrapping of tuttleberry leaves. He then rode off on the gallumpher, leaving the three young people to enjoy their meal alone.

Below them the bay teemed with vessels making their way in and out of port, galleys and cogs taking advantage of the good weather to land their cargoes. Dravadan gestured with a chicken-leg. "What a glorious prospect!" he cried. "All of that industry, and a percentage of all the revenues flowing into the Specchio's coffers. That barge there–" he pointed at a long low vessel inching into port "is a salt-tender, the best of all, since House Umbinzia holds the monopoly on salt!"

Rullia nodded. "And what of the House Rasteccio monopolies? Which of those vessels is making my father rich?"

"Hmmm," said Dravadan. "Lead could be transported on any boat. The high cog over to the left, that could be a grain vessel."

Malvazan began to feel drowsy in the early afternoon sun, with a solid lunch filling his belly. He sat up with a start: if he slept now he would be awake again tonight. He stretched and yawned.

"Excuse me, I will take a stroll up the hill," he said. "I am feeling a little languid."

"I will come with you," declared Dravadan. "There is an interesting fane just over the crest. Rullia, will you come with us?"

Rullia raised an eyebrow as she sipped her wine. "Fanes hold little interest for me, and I am still eating my luncheon. Go and see your fane, and I will be here when you return."

"As you wish, sweetling," said Dravadan, bending down to give her a peck on the cheek. "Come, Malvazan, the fane is really most interesting."

Malvazan's opinion of the fane was closer to Rullia's, but he needed the exercise, so he fell into step with Dravadan as he set off up the hill.

"I do believe that affairs are at last coming together," said Dravadan with a satisfied smile. "I am naturally relieved that a date for our nuptials is set; and of course I am delighted to be the brother of the man who won the Garland."

"Even in such circumstances?" said Malvazan.

"Pah! Controversy often surrounds such things. Soon it will all be forgotten, and all anyone will remember is the winner's name. I do not doubt that Kropiselko will soon be suing our father for a betrothal once again."

Malvazan felt that this analysis was so wide of the mark as to verge on the feeble-minded. Not for the first time it occurred to him that Dravadan really would prove a most indifferent head of the house. He looked at him sideways though narrowed eyes.

"What?" asked Dravadan.

"Nothing," said Malvazan. "Are we not at the fane yet?"

"Just a little further."

They came over the brow of the hill, the city below now hidden from their view. At the edge of the cliff was a tumble of stones which might once have been a more imposing structure.

"That is the fane?" asked Malvazan in a mixture of irritation and incredulity.

Dravadan set off in the direction of the stones. "It predates even the worship of Hissen and Animaxia—it may be one of the oldest buildings in Mondia."

Malvazan followed at a more relaxed pace. "Any glories it might once have presented are long faded."

"Let us inspect it more closely. There are inscriptions on it that none can now read." Dravadan clambered up the pile of rocks, only to slip and stumble to the ground.

"Have a care!" cried Malvazan. "We are only feet from the edge of the cliff."

Dravadan gingerly got to his feet with a sheepish grin. "I must have had one too many goblets of the wine at lunch." He looked at the cliff-edge with a shudder. Beside him stood a sheer drop of many hundreds of feet. Below, Malvazan knew, were only sharp-toothed rocks.

He stepped towards his brother. In one moment it could all be over, all the years of bickering, and the condescension which had replaced it. Could it really be so easy? Why had he never thought of it before?

With two more steps he was level with Dravadan, and without further thought he gave him a smart two-handed shove towards the precipice. Dravadan cried and fell back, but managed to twist to the side. "No!" he cried.

Malvazan cursed. Something had held him back at the last minute, prevented him from murdering his brother. This was not the time for weakness!

Dravadan scrambled to his feet, grabbed at Malvazan's shirt. They wrestled, Dravadan striking Malvazan across the face. Malvazan wriggled free, but now Dravadan was enraged and tried to pitch Malvazan over the edge. Malvazan allowed himself to fall, used the momentum of Dravadan's advance to overbalance him, and then twisted to the side. Dravadan was on all fours, teetering on the cliff-edge. For a moment the two men looked at each other. Malvazan realised there was no way out of the situation that did not involve death. He smashed his boot with all his force into Dravadan's thigh and watched as, with a great wordless cry, Dravadan fell out into the void.

Malvazan looked down over the edge, his heart pounding with avidity. Below him, Dravadan fell, turning over and over, his limbs flailing like a windmill in a way which might have been amusing in other circumstances. The wind carried away Dravadan's cries, and Malvazan watched as he plunged down and down until his fall was arrested by the rocks some three hundred feet below.

Malvazan stood in silence looking down into the void. He had not planned this, but one way or another it was done. He was the heir of House Umbinzia.

Behind him he heard a cry. Rullia was running towards him. "Malvazan! I heard something! Where is Dravadan?"

Malvazan realised that he had not thought beyond the moment of the crime at all.

"Rullia!" He ran over to her. "There has been a terrible accident! Dravadan has fallen from the cliff!"

Rullia sank to her knees. "No! No! No!"

"I am sorry," he said, taking her shoulders and lifting her back to her feet. "There was nothing I could do. He was climbing on the fane and he slipped. Before I could catch him he was gone."

She looked into his eyes. "Your face is bleeding," she said.

"I—I tried to catch him—I banged my head on the fane."

Her gaze cast around, like a trapped animal. "We must call the Consiglio!"

"There is nothing for them to say, Damoiselle. Dravadan is away and gone."

"Take me back to Taratanallos now, Malvazan," then, as he reached to take her arm, "no, do not touch me."

They went back down the hill in silence, with Rullia taking the greatest care to ensure that Malvazan walked on the side nearest the drop.

CHAPTER SIXTY

The Presidency of the Masavory was nominally the highest office of state in Taratanallos. By law, the post could only be held for a year at time, however, and could not be re-elected for five years thereafter. These circumstances meant that the Presidency was not in general sought after by the most ambitious men in the city, who preferred to exercise their influence less overtly.

At this time the President of the Masavory was Filozan of House Prugo, the kind of well-bred nonentity for whom the post had been designed. Filozan's optimum day was to rise late, conduct a trifle of ceremonial business over lunch, take a nap in the afternoon before arising for a state dinner in the evening. Events which forced a divergence from this regime were not welcomed, and where possible ignored. It soon became apparent, however, that the death of Dravadan of House Umbinzia in irregular circumstances must overset his regime for the day.

Filozan sat at his desk—a rarely used item—in his state apartments on the top floor of the Masavory, a petulant expression on his florid face. Before him stood Landozar, the Grand Master of the Consiglio.

"It is clear, Most Dignified," said Landozar, "that there must be a full investigation."

"Is that really necessary?" asked Filozan with a drooping underlip. "It is tragic that an accident should rob us of a fine young man, to be sure, but Crostadan has another heir, does he not? The future of the house is not in question?"

Landozar, evidently concluding that Filozan would not invite him to sit, took a chair on his own initiative. "That is the problem, Most Dignified. You will be aware that the Grave Malvazan, who only days ago won the Garland amidst some controversy, has already acquired a somewhat dubious reputation."

"Youthful high spirits, no more, surely?"

Landozar stroked the neat black goatee he had been cultivating. "May I speak freely about a member of the Specchio, Most Dignified?"

Filozan's eyes seemed to sink back into his head. "Must I sit through again the contents of your secret files and dossiers, your surveillances and informants?"

Landozar did not allow a wince to cross his impassive features. "You characterise the work of the Consiglio in a way which might pain a more sensitive man, Most Dignified. In this case, however, I speak only from common knowledge. The Grave Malvazan is twenty years old, has already killed four men in duels, cheated to win the Garland and made his frustration with second son status all too clear. Now his elder brother has died in a freakish accident to which Malvazan was the only witness. These are surely circumstances which you must recognise warrant further examination."

Filozan sucked in his lip. "This is most inconvenient, and indeed embarrassing, Landozar."

"This is regrettable, but true, Most Dignified."

"Very well. We shall go to Korfez immediately."

Landozar had taken over a small room on the first floor, overlooking the gardens, for his investigations. His interview with Crostadan yielded no insights — Dravadan had been "a fine boy" with great promise, Malvazan his "beloved brother" and Flinteska had been incoherent with grief throughout. Rullia alternated between icy reserve and, at times, naked terror. All in all, he had learned nothing of value; but he had still to speak to the only witness.

"Please, sit down, Gravity," he said as Malvazan entered the room. He appeared to have washed and changed his clothes since the incident, unlike Rullia who had presented herself in her pathetically inappropriate peasant's costume.

"I need no invitation to sit in my own house, sir," said Malvazan.

Landozar acknowledged the point with a wave. "Allow me to express my condolences, Gravity. Such a shocking event is not to be thought on."

Malvazan crossed his legs. "I thank you. It is hard to believe that a picnic could end in such horror."

"I regret the need to pick over the circumstances again, Gravity. You will appreciate that, as the only witness to the tragedy, your recollections are most valuable."

"Am I to assume, sir, that I am suspected of some complicity in the event?"

"You leap very rapidly to that conclusion, Gravity. There are some men, I am sure, to whom the notion would never occur."

Malvazan crossed his legs again. "Do not play with me, Landozar. The Grand Master of the Consiglio does not interrogate men of birth in their own manses on a whim."

Landozar gave a thoughtful nod. "You are clearly a man of the world, despite your years, Gravity. Why do you not tell me what happened, and then we can put matters to rest."

"There is very little to tell," said Malvazan. "Dravadan wished to show me a fane on the hill. He climbed high on the fane to inspect an inscription. He had drunk wine at lunch, and he overbalanced. I tried to grab him as he fell, but I was too late. He tumbled over the cliff, with consequences we all know."

"You are very calm in your account. Your mother, who was not even present, is incapable of consecutive thought."

"My family's loss is immeasurable, but no demeanour of mine will change the facts: Dravadan lies dead at the bottom of the cliff. I pride myself on keeping my emotions under control."

Landozar raised an eyebrow. "You surprise me. How many duels have you fought? Three? That would argue for a contentious disposition."

"You will forgive me, sir, for observing your birth. You are outside of the Specchio, and must know little of duels. I fought to protect my honour; this is not a question of emotion or anger, but pride."

"I notice a mark on your cheek," said Landozar. "A cut. How did you come by it?"

"I tried to grab at Dravadan as he fell. I scraped against a rock as I did so."

"Is there anyone who can verify any aspect of your story?"

"I am a gentleman. My word is its own 'verification'."

Landozar leaned back in his chair. "As you have already observed, Gravity, I am not a gentleman. I may therefore doubt your word without incurring the risk of a duel."

"I am puzzled as to why you wish to flaunt your low breeding."

"Let me outline a hypothesis, Gravity."

"If you must."

"I can imagine a situation in which you lured your brother away from his betrothed, out of sight of all other eyes. You might then have approached the fane, and pitched Dravadan over the cliff. Perhaps he had an inkling at the last moment of your intentions, and struggled—hence the injury to your face. He would not have stood a chance, of course, against a man as practised in combat as yourself. A scuffle, a shove—and you are the heir of House Umbinzia."

Malvazan looked back at him with cold eyes. "You mean to provoke me into repentance and confession?"

"I merely outline a hypothesis, Gravity."

"I note and reject it. Rullia will already have testified that the visit to the fane was Dravadan's idea, in any event."

"By your own admission you have already killed three men."

"These were duels. There is no culpability in Quietus Est."

"In each case you fought a man you knew you could beat."

Malvazan smiled. "There are very few men not in that category. If this is the sum of your accusation, your evidence might at best be described as 'circumstantial.'"

"Your responses—and particularly your tone—do not assuage my suspicions, Gravity."

Malvazan rose from his seat. "Since you continue to speak of 'suspicion', sir, may I take it that you recognise you have no evidence at all? In that case I will take my leave of you." He turned and walked to the door.

Landozar called out softly: "Malvazan."

Malvazan turned. Landozar said: "We both know what happened on the cliff today."

"And we both know that you cannot prove it, sir. Good evening to you."

The next morning Filozan and Landozar returned to Korfez to seek an interview with Crostadan. In the reception hall sat the head of the house, Malvazan and Rullia. Flinteska had sent her apologies; she was overwrought and the apothecary had prescribed her a draught.

"Dignity, you will understand that we have had to investigate the circumstances of this tragedy," said Filozan.

"Naturally," replied Crostadan. "I am grateful that you have brought matters to a swift conclusion. While a shadow of suspicion hangs over my remaining son—" he cast a swift glance at Malvazan "—the position of House Umbinzia remains irregular."

"Grand Master Landozar has conducted his enquiries with despatch, for which we all give thanks. Our conclusion is that the death of your son was a terrible accident, a freak event for which condolences and not blame are appropriate. Is that not so, Landozar?"

Landozar's eyes lingered on Malvazan for a second. "It is indeed, Most Dignified."

Malvazan smiled quietly.

Crostadan nodded. "I thank you both. Malvazan is my heir, without a stain on his character. Indeed, he has intimated to me, as a sign of the warmth with which he remembers his brother, that he should adopt his name."

Malvazan inclined his head. "Just so, sir. From this moment forth, in tribute to my beloved brother, I shall be known as Dravadan, that the memory of his name might live on. On that sad day when I put on my father's robe, he will be remembered."

Filozan nodded. "A noble gesture, Gravity. I trust that after suitable mourning, House Umbinzia will return to play a full part in the Specchio."

"We will of course undergo a period of retirement," said Crostadan. "After that point, I hope once again to reaffirm our alliance with House Rasteccio."

Rullia stirred. "Sir—"

"It is perhaps premature to consider these matters," said Crostadan, "and if my wife were present I would not discuss it. Nonetheless, in due course, I see no reason why Rullia, who has been such a delight to us, should not once again become betrothed to my heir."

Rullia screamed, an inarticulate sound too large for the room. "No! Murderer! Murderer!"

Malvazan raised an eyebrow. "Forgive me, father: I have too much experience of an unwilling betrothed to risk another. Rullia's impression of my character is—" he looked around the room "—clearly unfavourable. In any event, I have other plans."

When you have something to offer House Zano, Malvazan, come back then! Well, thought, Malvazan: winner of the Garland, heir of House Umbinzia, ally of Aladar. I think I have something to offer now.

And Malvazan made his excuses, left the room, and went upstairs to consider his expanded destiny. It was surely not too early to visit Hanglenook and pay his compliments to Monichoë.

CHAPTER SIXTY-ONE

While Todarko and Linnalitha made plans in the Chale, Oricien too was taking an uneasy breakfast on his balcony. This morning he overlooked the still waters to the east, and beyond the indistinct coast of Aylissia. He would have preferred to eat alone, but Iselin sat at his side.

"As I said yesterday—" Iselin spoke through a mouthful of bread, and Oricien could not help but be reminded of his low origins "—all is not lost. Once Bartielko is brought to trial and convicted, the Gammerling party will be in disarray. We can then put our proposals to the Masavory once again."

"Bartielko may not be guilty," said Oricien.

"That is by the by. He will surely be convicted, and hanged."

Oricien set down his bread. "You are curiously indifferent to the identity of the man who planned Ribauldequin's death—and mine."

Iselin sipped from a mug of small beer. "You must realise that this is a peripheral question, my lord. What is important is that we secure the city's submission. I need not remind you that, for both of our sakes, this outcome is paramount."

Oricien looked at him with cold grey eyes. "No, you need not remind me, Iselin. It does not prevent me from wanting to see justice for a brave man who died for King Enguerran."

"'Justice'? The concept is almost infinitely elastic. Its pursuit here is a luxury we cannot afford."

Oricien looked at him with distaste, an emotion magnified by the fact that he knew Iselin was right. "Dravadan is perhaps a more immediate concern, in any event," he said. "We are dependent on his support and his influence; you have seen his behaviour this past day. He is not just untrustworthy, which was always understood; he is unstable."

Iselin stroked his beard. "Neither of us is married. It cannot be pleasant to be cuckolded."

"Dravadan does not strike me as an uxorious man."

"It is his pride which is hurt. He cannot accept loss of face. I would not like to be in Todarko's shoes when he is caught."

Oricien gave his head a rueful shake. "Poor Todarko. I cannot help but like the lad."

"He is no lad—he is an adult who knew the risks he was taking. Do not waste your sympathy on him."

Oricien gave a sardonic smile. "I have assured Dravadan he will have my support in bringing him to bay. The sooner Dravadan has settled his scores, the sooner he will be focused on delivering us the votes of the Specchio."

There was a cold light in Iselin's eyes. "Exactly so, Lord Ambassador."

On the balcony Vivalda appeared in a soft white cotton dress. "Lord Oricien, Madam Nelanka is here. She begs pardon for disturbing you at breakfast but asks if she might see you."

Oricien dabbed his lips with a napkin and brushed the crumbs from his lap. "Of course."

"Alone, my lord," she said with a heavy glance at Iselin.

"Iselin, naturally you have business to be getting on with?"

Iselin stood and made a tight bow. "Indeed, Lord Ambassador." He stalked from the balcony on stiff legs.

"Thank you, Vivalda. You may bring Madam Nelanka in."

"My lord—?"

"Yes?"

"It does not matter." She turned and slipped away on noiseless feet.

Nelanka looked as if she had not slept at all. "I am sorry to disturb you, my lord. You must think me forward."

He indicated the breakfast platter with a wave. "You are hungry?"

She shook her head. Her eyes were moist pools. "I am so worried about Todarko," she said.

"He has not been found?"

"He was hiding at Grandille; it seems he escaped before my husband's men could capture him. I do not know where he has gone."

Oricien leaned back. "In a sense, that is encouraging. If you do not know, will anyone else?"

A single tear rolled from each eye. "Dravadan will catch him and kill him. It is all that bitch Linnalitha's fault."

Oricien strongly doubted that Todarko could so easily be acquitted of responsibility, but merely took her hand. "Surely there are laws in Taratanallos? Dravadan cannot simply do as he pleases."

She gently pulled her hand away and looked into his eyes. "There are few who will check Dravadan; and any man he calls to a duel is dead, for he is the most peerless swordsman."

Oricien was unclear what comfort he could give. It was hard to view Todarko as anything other than doomed, not an insight he felt Nelanka would welcome.

"I cannot stand it here," she hissed in a low passionate voice. "My husband crows at the thought of Dravadan killing Todarko: he has asked to be Dravadan's second if they fight."

"I would not speak ill of your husband, madam."

A fierce harsh smile came to her lips. "Then you must be silent on the subject, for there is nothing else to say of him. I am resolved to leave him." Her eyes, which had been fixed on the linen tablecloth, flashed up to meet Oricien's. "I will leave Taratanallos altogether."

"You have wealth, consequence here. Where would you go?"

A fleeting look of pain flashed across her eyes. "I thought you understood, Oricien. You care nothing for consequence, or so you told me."

Oricien sighed. "I am not a young woman friendless in a foreign city. There are times when it is better to be pragmatic." *I sound like Iselin.*

"I hoped not to be friendless," she said in a soft voice. "In the cities of the Emmenrule, in ancient Glount or even in Croad, I thought there might be those who would show me some tenderness."

She stopped and looked into Oricien's eyes. There was no mistaking what she meant. "Was I wrong to hope for that?"

Oricien sighed and closed his eyes. This did not make the situation any more straightforward; but he could scarcely leave her to her fate.

"No, Nelanka," he said. "You were not wrong. In Croad, at least, you will always find a welcome."

She stood and walked round the table, put her arms around Oricien's neck and sobbed without restraint. After a while she looked up. "You will help me protect Todarko, will you not, Oricien?"

Oricien put his hand on her cheek, ran his thumb along the bone. "As far as I can, Nelanka, as far as I can."

CHAPTER SIXTY-TWO

As Todarko and Linnalitha were finishing breakfast, Bodazar appeared at the cafe. He clapped Todarko on the shoulder and flopped down into the seat beside him.

"I never thought to see you again," he grinned.

"I had my own doubts," replied Todarko.

"You have not made any new friends," said Bodazar.

Linnalitha said: "I would have thought we were popular with your affinity, sir. My husband's woes can only help the Gammerling party."

Bodazar gave his head a rueful shake, signalled for tea. "I keep myself well out of the intrigues," he said. "As Todarko used, very wisely, to do. Nonetheless, I see them all thrashing around like fish dumped on the dockside. With Bartielko in jail, no-one knows who is in charge; the ones who are left argue whether they are better supporting Ingomer or his brother. The best thing Dravadan can do is leave them alone; in a week they will have made their cause ridiculous."

Linnalitha ran a finger around the rim of her cup. "Dravadan is leaving them alone, I imagine. He has other matters to attend to."

"You know your own husband best, I am sure, madam. He is enraged at events, and he has spies all over the city. You are not safe here, and the ships are watched. In the Chale, you may evade capture a while longer, but soon enough he will find you."

"We are not staying," said Todarko. "Do you have the departure schedule?"

Bodazar brought forth a folded paper from his jacket and smoothed it out on the table before them. "These are the sailings today and tomorrow, as notified to the Consiglio."

Todarko ran a finger down the list. "We can rule out the galleys: they rarely take passengers. How many cogs today? Three? Another two tomorrow."

Bodazar smiled. "You do not seem concerned as to your destination."

"It is of secondary interest," he said.

"I do not like the cold," said Linnalitha. "Mettingloom is too far north. Can we not take passage south?"

"Lost Horizons fares to Thring and then Aylissia," said Bodazar. "It sails at the Hour of Evening Satiation."

"Too close," said Todarko. "Dravadan could track us to Thring easily enough."

"Very well, then. If you want to go today, it's Mettingloom on the Queen Jessique, or Paladria on the Dryad."

"Paladria it is," said Todarko.

"You do not wish to wait until tomorrow?"

"And give Dravadan another day to find us? Can you go and book us two passages, Bodazar?"

Bodazar nodded. "Allow me to finish my tea. There is ample time. The Dryad sails at the Hour of Afternoon Reflection. You need simply arrive at the gangplank: I will have secured your booking."

Todarko rose from his seat and shook Bodazar's hand. "Thank you, my friend. I know this course is not without risk for you."

Bodazar shrugged, ran a hand through his curls. "Your own risk is somewhat greater," he said. "I do what I can."

He bowed again and walked off into the stream of pedestrians passing the cafe. Todarko sat down and poured himself more tea.

As the bells rang for the Hour of Petitions, Todarko and Linnalitha left the café behind. Todarko bought some bread and cheese for their lunch; Linnalitha meanwhile affixed her Hood and Veil. More elaborate disguise was neither practical nor advisable. This would have to do. Cautiously they made their way from the Chale, past the Aspergantia to stand at the back of the docks, where workers and merchants milled before them. Overhead the gulls swooped and cried, and Todarko looked around. There were Consigli in evidence, although seemingly no more than usual. His nerves were heightened to a pitch of alertness, but he saw nothing to evoke alarm. Moored at the docks, probably no more than fifty yards away, sat the Dryad, their ticket to safety.

"It does not look particularly seaworthy," she said. If the vessel had ever been painted, it was long in the past.

"I would be more worried if it was sparkling clean," said Todarko. "If it has lasted long enough to look like that, it must be of sound construction. We need not fear sinking."

Linnalitha's eyes behind her veil looked dubious. "Maybe. Look at the Consiglio around. Surely they will spot us!"

"Keep walking," he said; the Dryad was only a few moments walk away. "We have done nothing wrong, and the Consiglio have no reason to help Dravadan."

She held on to his arm. "Nonetheless... look how many people are around. Any of them could recognise us!"

"Of course it is busy," said Todarko. "This is the biggest port of Mondia."

Linnalitha nodded uncertainly.

"All we need to do," he said, "is walk across to the gangplank. In ten minutes we will be in our cabin and out of reach."

Todarko felt it difficult to sound authoritative. His heart was pounding so loudly he could barely hear himself speak. But Linnalitha nodded. She seemed to be convinced. They picked up their pace and stepped out towards the Dryad.

Behind them came a call: "Madam! A moment if you will!"

Linnalitha stiffened beside him; Todarko felt his own palms grow clammy. He turned to see a suntanned man of late maturity. He did not seem someone bent on their destruction. Todarko gave Linnalitha a pointed look: keep calm and all will be well..

"I am a trifle lost," said the man. He reached forward with a piece of paper. "Could you kindly direct me to Slavetakers' Lane."

Linnalitha's voice smiled even if her mouth could not be seen. "Of course, sir. Turn to your right, walk up the hill—"

Subsequently Todarko remembered the map more clearly than anything. The man dropped it, and it spiralled to the ground with an eccentric flutter. Less distinct to him was the man falling forward, his arms around Linnalitha, bearing her to the ground.

"No!" she screamed. "Help!"

Todarko sprang to life, threw himself on the man. Two other men leaped towards him, pushed him off balance. As the first man pinned Linnalitha's arms behind her back, Todarko squirmed free of the men attacking him to gain his feet, his pulse racing and a roar of fierce triumph in his throat. Now he was a match for anyone!

One of Todarko's assailants ran over to Linnalitha, dragged her erect and helped the other man to his feet. The two of them held Linnalitha immobile, began to drag her towards a waiting cariolo. Todarko punched at the third man, sent him crashing to the paving, where his head rang with a satisfying clang.

"Todarko! Run!" cried Linnalitha.

Todarko had no intention of running. He kicked at the nearest man, who skipped out of the way, still holding Linnalitha. As Todarko adjusted his position to face him, he saw another group of six or seven men running across the docks. Was this help? One of them reached out a knife from his belt, threw it, blade over hilt, blade over hilt, through the air towards him. Probably not help, then.

"Take him alive, you fool!" shouted one of his companions: he saw it was Dravadan's steward Palankijo. "Dravadan won't thank you for a corpse!"

"Run, Todarko! It's your only hope! They will kill you!" cried Linnalitha.

Todarko looked around in desperation. His stomach felt like water. He could not fight seven men single-handed. But how could he leave Linnalitha to her fate?

"Run! Run, my love!"

He looked into her eyes for a final moment, less than a second, but the longest second of his life. He knew that he had no choice; and he saw no reproach in Linna's eyes.

With a gesture part apology and part farewell, he took to his heels and ran for the Dryad.

Meanwhile, two Consigli, attracted by the commotion made their way towards the scene. "Over there! Over there!" cried Todarko. "They are kidnapping Linnalitha."

Three of the men continued their pursuit of Todarko, and one of the Consigli put his fingers to his mouth and summoned his colleagues with a whistle. "Now, let us sort this out rationally," he said.

"It is too late!" shouted Todarko. "They have taken Linnalitha."

And indeed it was too late, for the cariolo was making its way towards the base of the hill which marked the Archgate. Linnalitha was back in Dravadan's hands.

Todarko stared irresolutely at the cariolo as it eased away. He set off to chase after it, then realised the futility of pursuit: if he had wanted to go to Korfez, he might as well as let Dravadan's men save him the walk up the hill.

"Todarko, a moment!" called Palankijo with a grim smile. "My master would like to talk to you." The three men remaining on the dockside walked towards him. From a nearby doorway came a man in black: Vislanko.

"You will have to wait your turn," he said to Palankijo. "The Consiglio has a number of questions it would like to raise with the Grave Todarko."

Todarko raised an eyebrow and turned to Vislanko. "It is Palankijo you should be detaining! He has kidnapped Madam Linnalitha."

Vislanko said in a mild tone: "The lady cannot be kidnapped by her own household: in a strict legal sense, she is already Dravadan's property. Now, if you are wise, Gravity, you will return with us to the Masavory."

"I am under arrest while Palankijo is not?"

"Would you rather accompany Palankijo to Korfez?"

"Naturally not, but—"

"In that case, let us simply take an informal stroll. Good afternoon to you, Palankijo."

Palankijo said nothing as Todarko walked with Vislanko and the other Consigli towards the Masavory building.

CHAPTER SIXTY-THREE

"What do you want with me?" said Todarko as they walked through the entrance into the cool hall of the Masavory. "You should be turning your attention to protecting Linnalitha."

"She will come to no immediate harm," said Vislanko. "Dravadan will know there were witnesses. She may suffer a period of confinement but she is in no danger. To be frank, it is you whom Dravadan wishes to punish: both death and pain feature in his plans."

Vislanko ushered them down a narrow steep set of stairs and into a windowless room lit by candles. The air had a dank metallic taste.

"Let us talk awhile, Gravity."

"Am I under arrest?" asked Todarko, sitting on a hard wooden bench.

"Do you want to be? I have sufficient evidence to hold you for criminal congress, even if Dravadan has neglected to make a formal complaint."

"Is this necessary?"

Vislanko shrugged and leaned back in his seat, one side of his face hidden in shadow. "I have no desire to arrest you, but I do not intend that you should leave, if only for your own protection. If you remain voluntarily, I need not arrest you."

Todarko ran a hand through his hair. It seemed he had no choice. "There is much here I do not understand."

"Naturally," said Vislanko. "You are by nature most unobservant, and you take little interest in the life of the city, for a man of your birth."

"Did you kidnap me simply for the pleasure of insulting me?"

Vislanko stared at him from smoky grey eyes. "Your character might have been improved by greater frankness at an earlier age, but I suspect it is too late now. You are as you are."

Todarko frowned. "I am unclear what you hope to achieve. You have blackmailed me into spying on Dravadan for you, a scheme which clearly has now come to an end. I doubt that you are motivated by concern for my welfare."

Vislanko gave a bleak smile. "Sentimentality is not a vice I can afford. Your use to the Consiglio is not yet over; as such I do not wish you to fall into Dravadan's hands."

"I thought the Consiglio was devoted to the wellbeing of the city. You are somewhat cavalier in discharging your duties: you have misused me and I suspect you are not well-disposed towards Dravadan."

Vislanko's eyes kindled. "You mistake the welfare of Taratanallos with the welfare of the Specchio. They do not always coincide. Consider, for instance, the corsair Ion Issio: by any standards, a nuisance. For the likes of Aladar, he was clearly far worse. Nonetheless—" his tone hardened "—the activities of Aladar himself were to the detriment of Taratanallos. By extension, his downfall was to the city's good. Ion Issio has therefore worked to the Consiglio's goals."

"Not deliberately."

"Even better. Ion Issio is motivated purely by avarice. Avarice is one of the easiest impulses to understand and control."

"You tolerate, or even approve, of Ion Issio's conduct?"

Vislanko shrugged. "He is a necessary evil. He responds to certain stimuli in a predictable way. In that sense he can be seen as a tool of public policy."

"It was suggested to me," said Todarko after a pause, "that the destruction of Aladar and certain of his associates was brought about by information Dravadan passed to Ion Issio."

Vislanko brushed a speck of fluff from his black breeches. "So much is common knowledge—at least among the Consiglio. Ion Issio is not particular about the sources of information he cultivates."

"But—"

"Yes?"

"You knew—and you did nothing?"

Vislanko gave a bleak smile. "There was very little which could be proved. And more importantly, the men that Dravadan destroyed were dangerous parasites on the body of the city. They advocated a treasonous submission to the Emmenrule, the ruin of the last free city!"

"So too does Dravadan. He now leads the Emmen party."

"Just so. And now he is the only man of influence left—with all due apologies to your distinguished uncle Raguslan. Dravadan has implemented our policies most effectively, without the Consiglio needing to involve itself."

Todarko half stood. "This is monstrous—that the Consiglio should connive in one Dignity destroying others."

"Sit down," said Vislanko in a level tone. "I will explain something that is rarely made explicit, although it should be obvious. The Consiglio, as I have said, exists to protect the welfare of the city. It is a matter beyond argument that submission of any sort—either to the Emmenrule or Gammerling—is detrimental to that welfare. We therefore act to impose a balance between competing factions. At one stage, the Gammerling party was in the ascendant: we took steps to reduce its influence. Now the Emmen party rises, and again we act. The affairs of the Specchio, set against this, are trivial."

Todarko sat back in his chair, puffed out his cheeks.

"Our policies do not please you?" said Vislanko in a quiet voice.

"They come as something of a shock. I am of the Specchio, and accustomed to think that we rule the city, as we have done for centuries past. To find the Consiglio, little better than our servants—if you will forgive me—pulling our strings like puppets is both unwelcome and unbelievable."

Vislanko permitted himself an approach to a grin. "Believe or not, as you choose: it does not alter the facts. If you can think of a member of the Specchio who exercises more power than Grand Master Verbujezar, by all means tell me, so that I can arrange for him to meet with an accident."

Todarko stared back at Vislanko. He was not sure how much of this to believe.

"I have been more direct with you than I would be with any other member of the Specchio," said Vislanko, "if only because your influence is so minuscule. While I am feeling so expansive, is there anything else you would like to know?"

Todarko was conscious of his mouth gaping like a fish's.

Vislanko took silence as his cue to carry on. "I take it that our conversation has not increased your esteem for Dravadan?"

Todarko narrowed his eyes. "If anything, he is worse than you."

Vislanko gave a brief rusty laugh. "Perhaps he is, as well. You may have heard rumours as to how he came to be head of House Umbinzia: I can assure you they are understated. You have no reason to be well-disposed towards him, of course. It is hard to look kindly on a man you have cuckolded."

"Just a m—"

Vislanko held up a hand and Todarko fell silent. "Your relations with Dravadan's wife can be saved for another day. For now: may I take your hostility to Dravadan as read?"

Todarko nodded.

"Good. Because you are going to kill him."

CHAPTER SIXTY-FOUR

Todarko sagged in his chair. His legs sprawled in front of him, gangling and seemingly outside of his control.

"You want me to kill Dravadan?"

Vislanko smiled his frosty smile. "You want to kill Dravadan; in fact, you need to kill him. I am merely drawing this to your attention."

"Uh—"

"Dravadan will kill you when he finds you. My suggestion—clearly a reasonable one—is that you kill him first. What could be simpler?"

"I—I have never killed anyone."

"Your range of experiences is thereby augmented. It may even enrich your verse to carry out such a dynamic escapade."

"Ah—"

"Shall we sit awhile until you regain your composure? You are showing all the intellectual prowess of a bindlespith."

Todarko leaned forward, his forearms running along his thighs and his head in his hands. He sat up and looked into Vislanko's face. "I cannot do this."

Vislanko gave his head a rueful shake. "I am not giving you a choice. The Consiglio needs Dravadan dead: Taratanallos needs Dravadan dead. You will do it."

"Why—why do you not simply do it yourself?"

Vislanko uncrossed and re-crossed his legs. "The Consiglio does not wish to make a martyr; neither does it wish to become overtly involved in political debate. This must appear a domestic matter, a young man afraid for his life acting out of panic. Dravadan will be dead; the Emmenrule party will be at an end."

"I would go to the block for such an act; I would prefer to die without blood on my hands."

Vislanko smiled. "Excellent! You are beginning to approach the practicalities! You will not be punished: Dravadan will die in a duel. Such deaths are not a crime."

Todarko gave a high laugh. "I am a most indifferent swordsman."

"It does not matter. There are means of evening—more than evening—the contest. I guarantee that when you face Dravadan with a blade, you will be able to kill him."

"Will Dravadan consent to face me in a duel?"

"If you doubt it, you underestimate how much he objects to you tupping his wife."

Todarko flushed. "But—"

"We will discuss your instructions more fully in due course. For now, you are a guest of the Consiglio."

"I need some fresh air. I cannot rot in here until you plan to let me loose on Dravadan."

Vislanko nodded. "Very well—although for my protection and your own, an escort will be advisable. I will attend to it."

Ten minutes later, Todarko stood outside the Masavory, having taken a back exit he had never known existed. He was accompanied by three Consigli, their black livery partly covered by the heavy armour on their chests. Swords hung at their sides. Even if Dravadan's men came across them, the Consigli were equipped for business.

"You need not hem around me quite so closely," said Todarko. "The effect is as if we were still in the Masavory."

The closest of the Consigli gave an apologetic smile. "We act only for your protection, Gravity. One would need to be a clod indeed not to have heard you have made some powerful enemies."

"What is your name?" asked Todarko.

"I am Thraldazar, Gravity."

"Well, Thraldazar, we are in broad daylight and the docks are all but deserted here. If suspicious characters arise we can all huddle together like virgins when the corsairs land."

Thraldazar laughed. "Very well, Gravity. Lisko, Margijn, give the man some space."

Lisko grumbled. "It's bad enough that we should have to wear armour on a hot afternoon like today—now he's giving us orders as well."

"Enough," said Thraldazar. "The Grave Todarko has difficulties enough, and I am sure none of us would wish to exchange places with him."

Todarko led the group on a leisurely tour of the dockside before making his way over towards the Wrill Gate.

"Gravity, I think this is inadvisable," said Thraldazar. "We cannot protect you effectively in the Wrill."

Todarko stopped and turned to him. "Perhaps you would rather we walked up the hill to the Aspergantia. We could wave at Dravadan as we walked past Korfez. Or maybe you will allow me into the Chale instead."

Spots of colour came into Thraldazar's cheeks. "Vislanko's instructions were that your perambulations should be confined to the docks. That way, if you choose to—"

"—to escape? I thought I was not under arrest?"

"Patience, Gravity. These arrangements are solely for your protection."

So that I can be kept safe to kill Dravadan? You are all heart, Vislanko.

"You could not be persuaded to turn your back for a second, good Thraldazar?"

Thraldazar smiled. "My fear of Vislanko far outweighs my fear of you and my avarice combined. You need not think I can be suborned."

Todarko rubbed his chin. "You are refreshingly honest, sir."

"Are we not finished yet?" grumbled Lisko. "These armour plates chafe abominably, and it takes ten minutes to unfasten the buckles."

Todarko raised an eyebrow and wandered towards the dockside wall. Below the sea plashed gently against the stone.

"Lisko, this patrol is not arranged for your convenience," snapped Thraldazar. "If you have complaints, raise them with Vislanko later." He turned to Todarko. "Gravity, do not walk too close to the edge!"

Todarko paused and looked around him. It was late afternoon and the dock was almost empty; high tide had taken the last of the ships from the port an hour ago. There was no-one within a hundred yards other than his escorts.

Before Thraldazar or the others could react, he dashed to the wall and dived into the sea headfirst, closing his eyes and breathing out against the shattering impact of the water. He resurfaced, gasping, a moment later.

"You fool!" shouted Thraldazar. "You have nowhere to go! Come on, out now!"

"Come and get me!" called Todarko, taking a deep breath and plunging under the surface. He opened his eyes, saw the sky above him and the shapes of the Consigli shimmering before him. In their heavy armour plates, they could not jump in after him. With powerful kicks he carried on under the surface. When he came up for air, Lisko had rushed off to look for a boat, while Thraldazar and Margijn tracked him along the docks, waiting to intercept him when he emerged.

His head was still above the water when he heard their cries of outrage. They had reached the high walls which marked the boundary of the Wrill: designed to keep foreigners in at times of plague, it now very effectively kept Thraldazar and Margijn out. The walls did not extend into the water, and Todarko simply swam past the boundary. Soon Thraldazar's roars were out of earshot, and Todarko swam over to a set of steps leading up to the street. Dripping wet, he clambered up onto the pavement.

For now, at least, he had eluded Vislanko and his schemes. It would not take the Consiglio long to organise a search of the Wrill, but it was a sizeable area, densely packed. They would not necessarily find him quickly. He had a head start and this time he did not intend to waste it.

He knew the Wrill well—many of the city's best taverns were run by foreigners—and it was only the work of a few minutes to find a laundry house and abstract some clothes from the soiled linen basket. None of it seemed too dirty, and if the breeches were a little loose in the rear, at least they were dry.

He took his purse from his wet trousers and made his way to a tavern where he was not known. As he nursed a mug of dark beer—from Emmen, he noticed with a sour smirk—he considered his options, which were not extensive. He could see from the rear window of the tavern the Castle of Crostestini where he knew the Emmen ambassadors were in residence. Lord Oricien had shown himself well-disposed towards him, and indeed had even pronounced himself in Todarko's debt. It was tempting simply to present himself at the Castle and throw himself on Oricien's mercy: the danger of this approach, other than outright refusal, was that no doubt the Lord Ambassador commanded a Consiglio guard. Regretfully he set the scheme aside.

There was always Bodazar, who had secured his passage on the Dryad. It was not Bodazar's fault that they had been spotted on the docks by Dravadan's men. Nonetheless, the failure of the plan might mean that Bodazar was now watched. Bodazar, too, would not now be the means of his escape.

He swilled the dregs of the beer round the bottom of the mug. There were only two people he trusted without reservation: Linnalitha was in Dravadan's custody, and unable to offer any assistance; which left Nelanka. He could be certain that she would not betray him, even if he was unclear what practical help she could offer.

Gloomily he signalled for another mug of beer, which could only stimulate his thinking. What if Nelanka... of course! She had been much in Oricien's company; there was a clear cordiality between them.

"Boy!" he called out. "Kindly bring quill, ink and paper on the instant!"

CHAPTER SIXTY-FIVE

By the time Nelanka, hidden under a cloak and loose hood which obscured her face, arrived at the tavern it was nearly the Hour of Secret Deeds. As Todarko had to acknowledge, this was not inappropriate.

"Darko!" she said softly with a catch in her voice. "I have been so worried about you!"

Todarko essayed a nonchalant smile. "The worries have been entirely justified," he said. "Dravadan and the Consiglio are searching for me with equal vigour."

"You can include your own family in the list," she said. "Both Zanijel and your uncle are avid to be the one who brings you before Dravadan."

"I do not have time to tell you all that has happened," he said. "I need you to get a message to Lord Oricien. Do you think he will help me? And Linnalitha?"

Nelanka put down her hood and looked around the inn. No-one seemed to be attending to their business. "Can you not forget Linnalitha?" she asked. "It is your passion for her that has brought you to this."

Todarko grimaced. "The damage is done. I gain nothing by foreswearing her now. I did not seek this situation; but now I must make the best of it."

"How have we come to this, Darko?"

Todarko smiled, a brief jagged ray of light in the gloom of the tavern. "I cannot regret what has happened, Nel. All my life I have sported with the affections of ladies better than I; none knows it better than you. Now I find that my feelings for Linna are entirely real. If it ends in disaster, so be it." He shrugged. "Have you never felt a passion so extreme it oversets all caution?"

Nelanka flushed scarlet, her cheeks shining in the muddy light. Todarko thought of what could only be a miserable union with Zanijel; no doubt she never had felt the racing emotions he had experienced with Linnalitha.

"I'm sorry, Nel. That was an indelicate question. I merely thought to—"

"It doesn't matter, Todarko. I understand the point you are making. What do you want me to do?"

"I need at the very least for passage out of Taratanallos to be arranged, I do not care where. If Oricien is somehow able to arrange for that to include Linnalitha, so much the better. If not, I would look to him to ensure her safety while she remains immured at Korfez. I am sure the King of Emmen would not wish to be allied to a wife-murderer; no doubt Lord Oricien can impress this upon Dravadan."

Nelanka looked at him coolly down her nose. "For a man hiding in a tavern in lousy clothes, you take a most peremptory tone. Lord Oricien may not take kindly to such an attitude."

Todarko took her hand. "I look to you to sweeten the message in your own way, Nel. Lord Oricien pronounced himself in my debt; I now seek a relatively modest repayment of the favour, in ways which surely will not outrage his conscience. Do I ask so much?"

Nelanka sighed. "No, Todarko. What you ask is only reasonable. I will speak to him, and he will send you word. Are you staying here?"

Todarko looked around him. "The Consiglio has little weight in the Wrill. I am as safe here as anywhere. But the more rapid the assistance, the more comfortable I will be."

Nelanka nodded and pulled up her hood. "Be careful, Todarko. I do not have so many friends in Taratanallos that I can afford to lose one. I can spare you to exile, but not to…"

He took her hand in both of his. "Courage, Nel. This is all part of the adventures of scapegrace Todarko. One day we will both hoot at this." He smiled with a confidence he did not feel in the least. Nelanka's uncertain laugh from the back of her hood suggested that she did not either.

In the Castle of Crostestini, Oricien was struggling to compose a despatch to King Enguerran, when Nelanka was announced. He had, with some effort, avoided thinking about her too deeply since their last interview. His position in Taratanallos, already difficult, was complicated even further by their relationship. It was clear that if he agreed to take her back to Emmen with him, she would accede; and the prospect of returning without her caused a pang in his stomach.

On the other hand, she was the wife of one of his allies, and while they had been happy enough to prostitute her to ensure his goodwill, he doubted that their accommodation would extend to him leaving the city with her. There was a legend somewhere in the dim and distant past about a man who had eloped with his host's wife, to the eventual dismay of all concerned. He did not want to be the flashpoint of a similar tale.

More subtly, there was Nelanka's insistence that he assist Todarko in evading Dravadan's vengeance. He had every sympathy for Todarko—given his own position with Nelanka it would be hypocritical otherwise—and he liked the young man. Moreover, he did owe him a debt for the affair with the bindlespith. His own inclination, regardless of Nelanka's wishes, was to do whatever he could to save Todarko from what could only be a grim fate at Dravadan's hands. His private views were not paramount in this case, however. He had been hoping that a stratagem would present itself which would preserve Todarko's life, secure the city's submission and allow him, literally, to sail into the sunset with Nelanka. So far, no such scheme had come to mind.

And now, here was Nelanka; it was unlikely that her visit would simplify matters in any way.

He tidied away his papers and stood up to receive her. Nelanka dashed into the room, her face unveiled and her hood thrown back. "My lord! I have seen him! I have seen Todarko!"

She flung herself into his arms with such force that he was nearly knocked over.

"Slow down!" he said. "Where, and in what circumstances?"

"A tavern in the Wrill," she gasped. "And he begs you to help him!"

Oricien disengaged himself and walked to look out of the window. "And what form would this assistance take?" he said in a tight voice.

She dashed over to his side. "Oricien! You promised you would protect him! Do not hedge now, I beg you."

I promised nothing.

"I can only deliver what is possible to deliver," he said. "The service he requires might be for the moon to fall and crush Dravadan—assistance which would clearly prove beyond my resources."

"He wants only passage out of the city, for himself and Madam Linnalitha. If you cannot free Linnalitha, he asks only that you make clear King Enguerran would not tolerate her coming to harm."

Oricien stared off into the distance. The request was not, in the circumstances, unreasonable. It did not require anyone else to be killed, and if it could be done in secret, might even be feasible.

"Surely you can do this much, Oricien."

Oricien rubbed his chin. "It is not impossible."

"It will all come to light in the end, of course. Nothing on the docks stays secret for long; but once Todarko is on board ship, that will not matter! He will be free!"

Ah, but it does matter, Nelanka. It matters terribly, for it would cost my treaty. There is no way that I can save Todarko and the Emmen alliance both.

He sighed. It was time to decide. There would be no gift from Animaxia: he had to choose for himself. "Very well, Nelanka. I will find a ship for him tomorrow. Have him meet me on the beach where we lit Ribauldequin's funeral pyre: I will have him rowed to his craft."

She kissed him full on the lips and pressed her body against him. "Oricien, you are a true knight," she said.

He gave a crooked smile. "Do not thank me until it is over, Nelanka. There is yet much that can go wrong."

"I trust you, Oricien: I have trusted you from the moment I met you."

Oricien looked away out of the window so that she would not see the tears in his eyes. "Nelanka," he said softly. "Tomorrow—the matter will not be without risk. I pray you, do not come to the beach. I would not have you in danger."

She squeezed his hand. "Can I not say goodbye to my friend?"

Oricien shook his head in a harsh sharp movement. "It is better that you do not," he said. "The fewer folk who are on hand, the better."

CHAPTER SIXTY-SIX

Todarko spent a miserable day in the tavern hunched in his room awaiting the Hour of Secret Deeds. Nelanka had brought him a change of clothes, a purse of money, and an undertaking that Oricien would arrange his passage out of the city. He was too apathetic even to ask where he was going, for he knew that Linnalitha would not be coming with him. The best he could hope was that he would be able to send for her later. But there was no triumph in this miserable skulking escape. Even his sword remained at Tappinetto; but his duelling days were no doubt behind him.

Just before the Hour of Secret Deeds he stepped out of the tavern without a backward glance. Even so late at night the streets were not empty, but no-one gave him a second look. He was just another bravo turning out of the tavern to stagger home to his bed.

There was a half-moon in the sky, a scud of cloud flitting across it in a snapping easterly wind: a good wind on which to leave Taratanallos, the city of his birth, his fortune, forever. He could summon no regret for that: the only people he would miss, even fleetingly, were Linnalitha, Nelanka and Bodazar. They were shallow roots for twenty-five years of life.

The two Consigli on the gate of the Wrill were inattentive and did not even notice as Todarko slipped out under into the main city, his cloak swirling behind him in the breeze. He walked on quiet feet across the docks into the Aspergantia and the base of the Archgate. Now would not be a good time to stumble across one of Dravadan's retainers, but luck was on his side. He let himself out of the wall-gate onto the steep worn steps leading down to the wide expanse of beach where only three weeks earlier he had stood for Lord Ribauldequin's funeral. In the muddy moonlight no-one was visible. As he walked down the steps he realised his heart was pounding: somehow his indifference had become something earthier while his attention was elsewhere.

He reached the bottom of the steps to stand on the uneven sand. Breakers rolled in from the sea, their gentle plashing the only sound he could hear. There was no sign of Oricien, or any boat to take him to safety. Was he early?

"Lord Oricien?" he called hesitantly. He was not sure what he would do if the ambassador was not here.

"Here," came a soft voice. Todarko turned to see Oricien standing tall and straight before him: he had been concealed behind one of the high dunes.

Todarko gave a brief bow. "My lord," he said. "I am grateful—"

Oricien held up a hand. "Do not be. I am sorry, Todarko."

"My lord?"

"I will not magnify my betrayal with excuses."

"Betr—"

From over the dune stepped three figures holding flaming torches high above their heads. "Todarko!" hissed Dravadan. "How I have yearned for this day! I will carve your liver from your breathing body!" At his side stood his steward Palankijo, an impassive expression on his face, and Zanijel, with an expression of triumph so avid that in other circumstances it would have been comical.

Todarko could feel the blood draining from his face, a loosening of his bowels which he controlled only with an effort.

"You dog!" he snapped at Oricien. "Why—when you had promised me a boon?"

Oricien shrugged. "I am King Enguerran's representative," he said. "I must act in accordance with his wishes, and save his treaty."

"Enough talk," said Dravadan in a brash voice. "I have waited long for requital, and now we shall have it."

"I swore to kill you, Todarko," breathed Zanijel. "It looks like I shall not have the pleasure after all."

"Remember our agreement, Dignity," said Oricien.

Dravadan scowled. "You mean to enforce it, then."

"I do. You may have your vengeance, much as it pains me. But it must be proportionate. I do not wish to see you arraigned for murder: if you kill him, let it be via honourable duel."

"Todarko has no honour."

Oricien shot Todarko a brief glance. "Then let him regain it, even if it means his death. Vislanko, are you there?"

From the shadows stepped Vislanko, barely visible against the night in his back uniform. Thraldazar was at his side. He bowed. "Gentlemen, the grievance between you is well understood, and it is hard to see how it can be ended without blood. In the circumstances, I am on hand to see that due process is followed."

Dravadan turned to Oricien. "You have brought the Consiglio?"

Oricien shrugged. "No-one's interest is served by casual murder—even yours. The Consiglio will ensure there are no awkward questions tomorrow, regardless of the outcome."

"If that is how it must be," said Dravadan. "Let us fight under Quietus Est, to the death."

Vislanko gave a half-smile. "I take it an apology from Todarko will not suffice? I am sure he heartily repents his behaviour."

Dravadan raised an eyebrow. "You think an offence of this public and humiliating nature can be offset with a smirking word or two? Blood it is."

"Blood," hissed Zanijel.

Vislanko nodded. "Very well. It is your right."

Todarko could barely speak through his dry mouth. "I have no sword."

Dravadan smiled. "I had Palankijo bring two. Palankijo, fetch the swords, and the others."

Vislanko drew Todarko aside. "You should not have tried to escape," he said. "You have greatly prejudiced my plans."

Todarko paused for a moment. "Your plans are the least of my concerns, Vislanko."

"All can yet be recovered," he said. "You will kill Dravadan now, in accordance with our agreement: all will be well."

Todarko gave him a look of mute astonishment. "Dravadan is the greatest duellist in the city. He is implacable." The image of Godaijkin, blinded and butchered on his knees by Dravadan only a month ago, leapt up before his eyes, and bile rose in his throat. "I—I cannot survive."

"I have taken—certain measures," said Vislanko. "When you were a boy, did you not read the stories about enchanted swords, whose possessors could not come to harm?"

"They were tales—"

"I have provided something similar," he said. "Simply draw blood, and all will be well. It is the best I can do."

"You are a thaumaturge?"

Vislanko gave a harsh laugh. "If you wish to think so," he said. "You may find that Dravadan does not fight as well as we all expect tonight."

From behind them came a cry. "Todarko!"

Todarko turned. "Linna!"

He ran towards her, took her in his arms. "How are you—why are you—?"

Dravadan spoke through gritted teeth. "However touching this reunion may be," he said, "I brought her to see you die."

"I came for the same purpose," said a cloaked and hooded figure beside Palankijo. He drew back the cowl to reveal his face.

"Bodazar?" cried Todarko.

"I did not want to miss the fruition of my revenge," Bodazar said.

"Revenge? How have I ever harmed you, Bodazar?"

Even in the dark Todarko could see his eyes flash. "You thought I did not know about you and Ivanka? I loved her, Todarko, and I was going to marry her. Now her character is ruined; my father will never have her. In the circumstances, posting one piece of paper in the marketplace seems a modest response."

"It was you—"

Bodazar bowed. "You took my future," he said. "Now I am taking yours. I found that arranging a beating for you was not nearly enough."

"That was you too?" said Todarko in a flat voice.

Vislanko shook his head ruefully. "Bodazar could have enjoyed a productive career in the Consiglio," he said. "He has a head for intrigue."

"This is monstrous!" cried Todarko, anger now driving out fear. "You have done all this, for the most trivial of offences. Rather complain of your father, who could easily have winked at this."

Bodazar nodded. "Yes, trivial. Trivial enough that I shall be satisfied with your death, and hold no further grudge."

Dravadan shifted impatiently. "Come, let us be done. I do not wish to be up all night. Palankijo, hand me a cup of wine to fortify me. Zanijel, it seems that Todarko does not have a second, so you are stood down for the nonce. You need only observe."

Zanijel grinned but said nothing as Palankijo unslung a wineskin from his shoulder and passed it to Dravadan who drank deeply. He tossed a rapier to Todarko.

Todarko felt as if the whole situation were happening to someone else. He did not feel afraid; instead he felt a wild exultation. If he were to die, so be it. "I too will drink," he said. "Palankijo, pass me the wine."

Palankijo looked down his nose. "The wine belongs to the Dignified Dravadan. Where you are going, you will not experience thirst."

Vislanko said: "The time for wine is past. It is late: let us conclude this sorry business."

CHAPTER SIXTY-SEVEN

Todarko looked around him. The small group of spectators were grouped in a loose circle: Vislanko and Thraldazar motionless and expressionless; Bodazar peering with an unconcealed avidity; Oricien, a study in stiffness and misery; Palankijo cool and alert behind his master; Zanijel leaning forward as if he wished to thrust his own sword into Todarko; and Linnalitha, softly weeping as she stood apart. He sprang across and kissed her, his sword loose in his hand.

"You told me once," he said, "that however this ends, it has been worth it."

She buried her head in his shoulder. "Linna," he whispered. "You were right. You were right. This is Harmony."

She looked up into his eyes. "I love you," she said. "Now go and kill my husband," she said with an attempt at a smile.

Todarko disengaged himself and bowed. "At your command, madam."

Todarko and Dravadan looked at each other, their blades drawn, the audience forgotten. Whatever Dravadan was thinking, it was subordinated to his tense alertness, his focus on the blade in his hand.

This man has killed eighteen people under Quietus. How many more have died through his agency? Todarko fought down the thought, stepped forward and feinted. Dravadan did not respond; he had seen through the move.

Todarko thought back to his lessons with Rodizel. *When you are fighting a left-hander, let him make the first move so that you can gauge his angle of attack.* He backed away: surely Dravadan would commit himself in his impatience.

But Dravadan merely circled, a flicker of a smile on his face. "Come on, boy. Die like a man." Todarko said nothing, kept his blade high.

Almost before he could react, Dravadan was on him: Todarko jerked back out of the way, with not even time to parry. He staggered, dropped to one knee before springing up again. He had not even seen the thrust until the last second. If Vislanko really had given him an enchanted sword, it did not seem a very effective one.

Dravadan surged forward again. There was a scream—it could only be Linnalitha—and Todarko flicked up his blade to parry. *I nearly saw that one. If he could survive another couple of lunges, he might begin to read*

Dravadan—but it was looking unlikely. Dravadan had nearly had him twice, and he had not yet launched a meaningful attack of his own.

Todarko feinted, pushed forward tentatively; Dravadan pushed the blade away with an economical gesture and followed up with another attack. Todarko moved to block, only to find it was a feint. Desperately he twisted to avoid the blade reaching for his side but he was too slow. He felt a flash of pain in his side and stumbled. There was a caw of laughter—Zanijel?—and another scream: "No!"

Todarko pressed his hand to his side and looked down. His hand came away streaked with red but it was only a nick.

Dravadan had moved back out of range, balanced on the balls of his feet, watchful as he assessed the extent of Todarko's injury. Todarko looked around the circle at a sea of impassive faces: only Vislanko, who seemed to be smiling broadly, showed any animation. He nodded as Todarko caught his eye.

Once more Dravadan danced on to the attack. This time it was not a feint, but Todarko, jerked into alertness by his wound, parried with ease and even stepped forward into a riposte. Dravadan evaded the charge with a precise movement but Todarko noticed a sheen of sweat on his brow. Surely he couldn't be tiring: Dravadan was not a young man but he was fit and strong.

Heartened nonetheless, Todarko thrust again. Dravadan flicked his blade aside with a grunt, stumbled and recovered his balance before Todarko could profit. In the torchlight Dravadan's face had taken on a greyish pallor, and his movements had lost their earlier crisp assurance. His expression creased into a frown and he looked around him. Todarko skipped in; Dravadan's fugue could not last and this was his chance to finish the fight.

With a lumbering movement Dravadan stepped aside; Todarko committed himself to the killing stroke but Dravadan slid away at the last moment. Todarko, overstretching, slipped forward onto the sand to lie on his front. Dravadan gave a great howl of triumph and snaked his arm towards Todarko, who rolled frantically aside.

He looked up to see Dravadan standing over him, blade poised. He wanted to shut his eyes but he could not. Then Dravadan staggered and slipped sideways, his right hand in the sand. He cried out as Todarko sprang erect; his hand clutched at the sand, and he made to throw at Todarko. But Todarko was too fast. He jumped at Dravadan and thrust the blade into his chest. Dravadan gasped, tried to roll aside. Todarko knew he could not let him back up. With another ugly thrust he forced the blade into

Dravadan's throat; it emerged from the back of his neck to pinion to him to the sand.

A hideous gurgle in the throat, a bubbling of blood where the sword stood out from the throat, and Dravadan was dead. His own sword fell from his left hand, and as Todarko stood over him he saw the sand in the right hand trickling between Dravadan's lifeless fingers.

Todarko had beaten the invincible Dravadan. He had killed him, and survived. Linnalitha dashed from the edge of the circle, flung herself into his arms. "Oh, Todarko! You have done it; you have saved us!"

From the others there was a moment of stunned silence. Oricien sank to the ground, his head in his hands. Bodazar, standing behind Todarko, gave a great inarticulate cry. He sprang forward, a dagger in his hand. "Am I always to be thwarted!"

Todarko, Linnalitha's arms around him, could not move to defend himself even though he saw from the corner of his eye Bodazar leaping towards him. He was a dead man: there was nothing he could do.

Suddenly Bodazar crumpled sideways to the ground as Oricien sprang at him. Bodazar struggled, turned his dagger towards Oricien, who was too quick. He buried his own knife hilt deep in Bodazar's chest. Once more there was silence, more profound this time than after Dravadan's death. Zanijel reached to draw his own blade, but found Vislanko's hand on his arm.

"Enough, Gravity," said Vislanko. "We have had enough death tonight. If I were you I should go back to Tappinetto now, and forget you were ever here."

Zanijel shook off Vislanko's hand and made his way back up the beach towards the walls, pausing only to spit in Todarko's direction. "This is not finished," he said.

Eventually Oricien got to his feet. "Everything is ruined," he said. "My honour, the Emmen alliance—all thrown away over the favours of a woman. Todarko, I have repaid my debt. But it is too late—for both of us."

Todarko reached out to shake hands with Oricien while trying to calm the trembling. "You saved my life, my lord. I cannot forget you betrayed me to Dravadan, but let us go our ways in peace. We have helped each other and we have hurt each other; if nothing else, we are both wiser men."

Oricien pursed his lips. "You are more generous to me than I deserve, Gravity. My time here is done."

Vislanko stepped forwards. "You mean to return to Emmen, Lord Ambassador?"

"There is nothing for me here: the leaders of the Emmen party are dead, and I cannot carry the Masavory without them. I have failed; I cannot be quit of Taratanallos soon enough."

Vislanko smiled politely. "I wish you a safe journey, my lord."

Oricien turned and walked slowly back up the beach, the wind swirling his cloak behind him.

Todarko watched Oricien recede into the distance until he was lost in the night. *You were too honourable for this city, my lord. I forgive you your betrayal.* He put his arms around Linnalitha and looked at the two still forms on the sand.

"This has all ended most conveniently for you, Vislanko. You wished to see Dravadan dead and lo! he is dead. There is no Emmen party, and the leader of the Gammerling party is in gaol for a crime he did not commit. You are a fortunate man."

Vislanko raised his eyebrows. "Good fortune is usually earned, Gravity. In your case, however, you have succeeded far beyond your deserts."

"You are ungrateful. I killed the man you wanted dead, through my own courage and enterprise."

"Up to a point," said Vislanko. "Thraldazar, kindly take the steward Palankijo into custody. You will also want to examine Todarko's sword and the winesack. I would not be surprised to find poison in both cases."

"You provided them!" bellowed Palankijo. "You treacherous dog, Vislanko!"

Vislanko smiled a bland smile. "You would do well not repeat such allegations, sir. No-one would believe them, and if they were made too loudly — well, the dungeons beneath the Masavory have seen accidents in the past."

Palankijo stared open-mouthed as Thraldazar bound his wrists.

"You set all this up," breathed Todarko. "You have played us all for fools."

Vislanko shook his head. "You overestimate me, Gravity. It was necessary to check the Emmen party, certainly, and you could never have beaten Dravadan without some assistance — but I never intended anything quite so dramatic. If you had not tried to escape, you could simply have slit Dravadan's throat in an alley. And, if it interests you, I did not frame Bartielko. As far as my men can tell, he truly is guilty — although I should perhaps have mentioned to Lord Oricien that Lord Iselin was party to the plot. The Consiglio would never have wanted to assassinate the Lord Ambassador—far better for us that he returns home in disgrace."

Todarko sat down on the sand and folded his arms around his knees. "And Bodazar—the sonnet?"

"He had plenty of malice, and plenty of cunning. But he was not very intelligent. It was easy enough to steer him into Dravadan's way. And the rest, of course, you know."

Todarko narrowed his eyes. "You are despicable; perhaps the greatest rogue in Taratanallos."

Vislanko gave a broad smile. "It may interest you to know that I did not find you the most satisfactory of associates either," he said. "My conscience is clear—or would be if I had one. My charge is to defend the good of Taratanallos. Today the last free city remains just that."

"But—"

Vislanko held up a hand. "You need not thank me."

Linnalitha spoke for the first time. "You have told us a great deal," she said. "A dangerously great deal."

Todarko scrambled to his feet.

Vislanko laughed. "You have a keener nose for danger than Todarko, madam; but you need have no fear. Violent death among the Specchio is problematic to explain, and I have two already tonight. I do not wish to add to the tally."

Todarko said: "You are not a man to leave loose threads."

Vislanko reached into his doublet and Todarko tensed; but he emerged with a purse which he tossed to Linnalitha. Then he put two fingers in his mouth and whistled.

"There is nothing for you here—either of you. Take ship to Thring and we are all happy. You see the Grave Zanijel walking back to his home. Several times he has promised to kill you. In your position I would not be eager to give him the chance."

"I—I don't—" said Todarko.

"Don't make me regret this, Gravity. Here is your passage." He inclined his head to the tall bearded man who had come at Vislanko's whistle. "Two for Thring," he said.

Todarko said: "You are Sandoz – Ion Issio's associate."

Sandoz grinned and shook his head. "As you said, Vislanko: an innocent."

Vislanko said: "You will know Sandoz better as Ion Issio—although naturally he does not use that name in the city."

"You know this?" said Todarko with a slack jaw. "And you let him walk the streets of Taratanallos."

"He is a tool like any other," said Vislanko with a sour smile. "Like you, like Bodazar, like Palankijo. A man in my position cannot be too nice."

Todarko turned to Ion Issio. "Shall we go, sir? I feel safer with a corsair like you than I do with a man like Vislanko."

Ion Issio's white teeth shone into the darkness as he grinned. "Maybe you are not such a fool as I thought, Gravity."

Vislanko turned and beckoned Thraldazar with his head. With the captive Palankijo between them they made their way back up the beach, towards the gate in the wall and the last free city of Mondia.

CHAPTER SIXTY-EIGHT

Oricien rose the next morning to find a despatch with seal of King Enguerran brought to his chambers. Wearily he slit the wax.

The Summer Palace
Emmen
From His Puissant Majesty,
Enguerran, King of the Emmenrule

Lord Ambassador,

I have received grave and most disturbing tidings from Lord Iselin as to your conduct. He has sent me proofs of peccancy in regards to your administration of my finances. It is clear from the evidence that at least 20,000 florins have been abstracted from my account in the city under your signature.

You will oblige me by returning immediately to Emmen to make reckoning for your behaviour at which point I will fix your punishment; I am not inclined towards mercy.

I am disappointed beyond measure to have been betrayed by a man I trusted; I give thanks for loyal servants such as Lord Iselin.
Enguerran, of Emmen

Oricien sat on his bed and sighed. Judging by the date, Iselin must have written to Enguerran the instant his fraud was discovered, muddying the waters by accusing Oricien instead. No doubt Iselin had concocted the most convincing of evidence. The matter would be resolved on his return, but it was one more blow against his reputation at court. His chances of an early return to Croad were ever more remote.

While he finished his packing he sent for Lord Iselin, only to find that he had quit his chambers and taken a silent passage out of the city: no doubt he had been alert for the King's letter.

His embassy to Taratanallos had been a disaster in every conceivable way. Corpses were strewn in his wake, all hopes of alliance destroyed, and Nelanka had not responded to his final letter. Now that she knew he had betrayed Todarko, she could not bear to look on him. There was only one tiny piece of good he could achieve. He rang the bell to send for Vivalda.

Shortly after, she entered the room with a curtsy.

"Vivalda, I leave the city today," he said.

He thought to see a flicker in her eye of something like reproach.

"I am sorry that I was not able to remedy your situation in the time I was here," he said. "You carried out your duties with efficiency and a pleasant demeanour."

She cast her eyes down at her feet. "You need not apologise, my lord. One way or another I am sure my servitude will end soon."

He picked up a slip of paper from the table. "It seems that Lord Iselin will not be needing his passage home," he said. "He has made other arrangements."

Vivalda said nothing.

"Go down to the docks, to the Emmen packet," he said. "Hand the purser this chit. It is as good for your passage as anyone else's."

"But, sir, I am a slave..." Moisture welled up in her eyes.

"Do you wish to visit Emmen, or not?"

"Of course—"

"Then go," said Oricien. "And Vivalda—"

"My lord?"

"Do not thank me. I have done little enough to earn anyone's gratitude."

Vivalda stepped over to Oricien and kissed his hand.

"I will see you on the ship, my lord."

Oricien finished his packing in silence and looked around his chambers at the Castle of Crostestini for the last time. Whatever awaited him at court —and Iselin was likely to ensure it was nothing good—it could not be worse than this city, which guarded its privileges and its freedoms with such guile and malice, and then squandered them on petty rivalries.

There was a knock at the door. "Come in."

He turned to see Nelanka, her eyes wary behind her veil. Oricien indicated a seat. "I thought you would not come, madam" he said.

Nelanka unfastened her veil. "You extended me an invitation, my lord," she said.

"To return to Emmen with me? It still stands," he said. "I thought, in the circumstances..."

A tear rolled down her cheek. "You are the only man I have ever loved, Oricien."

Oricien bit the inside of his lip. "And I you, Nelanka." He dared not hope.

"The only other person I care for in Taratanallos is Todarko," she said. "He is the brother I never had."

"I am sorry for—"

She looked down. "Let me finish, please, Oricien. You betrayed Todarko to Dravadan: you have never explained why, and you owe me no explanation. You put your embassy for the king above whatever duty you may have felt to Todarko."

Oricien looked into her face. "Yes. It was as simple as that. It was not an easy choice."

She took his hand. "When you betrayed Todarko, you betrayed me, Oricien. I had asked you to protect him, and you let me believe you would. However noble your motives, you betrayed me."

Oricien ran a hand across his eyes. "I cannot deny it, my lady. I had to make a choice, and I made it."

Tears were streaming down her face. "Oh, Oricien, you do not make this easy. A lesser man would point out that it was all for nothing, that you failed anyway, to engage my sympathy. A lesser man would point out that you saved him from Bodazar, to befuddle the fact that your falseness put him there in the first place."

Oricien shrugged. "You are as aware of those facts as I am. I would not insult you by belabouring them. I am not certain that makes me a better man."

She sprang up from her seat. "If you were less, if you tried to evade or excuse, I would know I was right to stay here! But you are so upright, so honourable, that you would betray the woman you say you love and then, when it all turns to disaster, you do not even complain!"

"I do not know what to say to you, Nelanka. I acted as I saw fit, and others must judge as they can. If you would return to Emmen, to Croad, with me then I would have a treasure I did not deserve; but I would not reject it for that reason."

She came over to him and took his hands in hers. "I cannot, Oricien. I can admire a man who puts his principles before his heart; but I cannot give myself to him. I did not want you to go without saying goodbye. But it has to be goodbye. Can you see that?"

Oricien stood up and kissed her. "Yes, my lady." For a moment he held her, felt her heart racing against his body. "I will never forget you. Never."

Nelanka stepped away and looked into his grey eyes. "Goodbye, my lord."

And as she turned and walked to the door Oricien compressed his lips against the words he knew would have called her back. The door closed behind him and he rang the bell to summon the porters to take his luggage to the ship.

EPILOGUE
Thring
One year later

"My lords and ladies!" cried Larkin Dall. "I thank you for your attention to our humble performance tonight of the great comedy The Lost Loves of Langobardi. You have been as attentive and enthusiastic an audience as we could wish. The good Odo will be among you with the hat for any small gratuities you may wish to bestow upon the players."

In Lord Attemar's hall the audience applauded politely. Larkin Dall continued. "May I present to you our company – the aforementioned Odo, who played Scamp with such vigour; the fair Raswinka, who rendered Lady Pfiferkin with such passion—and of course, the lovely Linnalitha who I am sure you will all agree gave such a rousing performance as Lady Happenstance. I of course played Prince Tarlacchio, and let us not forget Todarko, who as well as playing the Fool and Sly Knoll, also wrote the marvellous verse of the play. Thank you, one and all!"

The company linked hands and bowed as the curtain fell. "Quickly, Odo," hissed Larkin Dall. "I know their sort—they'll be out of the hall before the hat if you're not careful." As Odo scampered off Larkin Dall reached into his doublet for a letter. "Todarko, this came from Taratanallos—I thought it best to give it to you after the performance."

Todarko pulled Linnalitha aside and, under the guttering stage lanterns, he slit the seal.

Grandille

Dear Grandson,

You have proved most difficult to locate, but I have instructions of a most pressing nature which brook no further delay. I regret to inform you that your cousin Zanijel is dead of a fever. As of this moment, you are heir presumptive to House Vaggio. You have shown good judgement in absenting yourself from Taratanallos in the year since Dravadan's death, but all scandals pass, and it is now imperative that you return to the city. You may, if you wish, bring Madam Linnalitha, since although her name is not untainted, she is nonetheless a widow of good birth and, on my limited acquaintance, also a woman of good sense.

You may now leave aside the buffoons with whom you currently consort and take ship for Taratanallos instantly. On arrival you will report to Grandille where I will issue further instructions. House Vaggio will soon be restored to the head of affairs once more!

Your affectionate grandmother

Sulinka

Todarko wordlessly passed the letter to Linnalitha. She read it over in a couple of glances. "Our fortune is made," she said. "No more playing for pennies. We are rich."

Todarko grinned. "And we have the benefit of Sulinka's wisdom. Our time has come."

"She is a magnanimous woman, to overlook the fact that she sold us out to Dravadan last time we were at Grandille."

"You are a hard woman, Linna. Don't you want to be rich, and once more one of the greatest folk of Taratanallos?"

"No."

Todarko laughed. "Neither do I. Let us play for pennies a while longer."

He took her hand. "Come on," he said. "I want to tighten your soliloquy in Act Three and we will need to rehearse it for tomorrow."

He screwed up Sulinka's letter and thrust the ball into the lantern where it took light, soon to be a thing of ashes.

THE END